GORDON

FORCE

Swansea Libraries
WITHDRAWN

HarperCollins*Publishers*
77–85 Fulham Palace Road,
Hammersmith, London W6 8JB

www.harpercollins.co.uk

1

First published in Great Britain by
HarperCollins*Publishers* 2004

ISBN-13: 9780007786312
ISBN-10: 000778631X

Set in Meridien by Palimpsest Book Production Limited,
Polmont, Stirlingshire

Printed and bound in Great Britain by
Bookmarque Ltd, Croydon, Surrey

*For intelligence analysts
who sort truth from lies.*

Prologue

The old bull elephant stamped.

The matriarch let the stripped acacia branch drop at her feet and turned her head a little. The bull stamped again, snorted. She took a step toward him and then looked down at her calf, unsure. He stamped again.

All through their band, heads came up.

The old bull's ears shot forward, full display, and he stamped, louder, and trumpeted. There was a noise now, a noise they all knew, and the alien metal smell. *Too close*, the old bull was saying. She turned away, her calf at her side, and began to move along the nearly dry watercourse, away from the noise. She was the matriarch, and the others followed her lead. She moved quickly, easily, fitting her bulk between trees or just knocking older wood down. She wanted to get into deeper cover first, while the bull did his job.

Braaat. A noise like a tree being torn out of the ground right beside her. She whirled and her calf was gone. She started to go back. She could smell her own fear and that of her sisters all around her. Her calf was kneeling at the base of a tree, slumping down slowly, and she knew he was done. She keened a little, and *Braaat* sounded again. Something punched her in the head and stung her ear and she bellowed her pain. One of her sisters stumbled, fell, didn't rise. The ripping noises were all around her, everywhere, and she

1

watched another, younger bull go down heavily, his feet thrashing and tearing at the dry earth even as he gave his death cry. All their shrieks tore the air, audible for miles, the message clear to other elephants. *Panic and death*.

Angry and afraid, she whirled her bulk back and forth, looking for her assailants, looking for the predator killing her family. She hated with a wild hate, and called, standing over her dead calf, until the *braaat* finished her, too.

He was a big, confident white man with a sneering smile. His black soldiers feared him. He walked through the carnage, his 'boys' already cutting the ivory and in two cases taking the hides. Younger men were cutting the tails for bracelets. He shook his head at the two dead calves.

'That's a waste of ammunition,' he said to a young black man, his own South African accent plain. 'No reason to shoot 'em. Nothing on 'em worth taking back.' He made 'back' sound like 'beck.' The boy nodded, his eyes still wide from shooting the elephants. The South African thought that killing elephants was an excellent way to train his men. He walked back to the big truck that they had come in to lay their ambush hours before, took a long drink of water to wash the red dust from his throat, and reached for the cell phone on the seat.

Sixty miles down the coast of Kenya, in the small city of Malindi, a man also reached for his cell phone. He was dark with sun but not African – Mediterranean, rather, perhaps Maltese or even Spanish. His English was accented but clear, slightly Americanized. He was

2

a small man, not quite middle-aged, muscular. He was sitting in the well of a thirty-foot power boat in the Malindi marina, sipping Byrrh and looking at a handsome black woman in a thong.

'Uh,' he said into the phone.

'This is Cousin Eddie.'

He knew the voice and the South African accent. A prick, but a necessary prick, was his view. 'Uh,' he said again. The topless woman was lying on the deck of the next boat over. Her nipples pointed skyward like little antiaircraft guns, he thought. He'd had experience of antiaircraft guns.

'We got eleven nice pianos.' 'Pianos' were elephants (because piano keys used to be made from elephant ivory).

'Send them down. Everything okay? The kids, they're okay?' The 'kids' were fifty adult mercenaries, mostly Rwandan Hutus.

'Kids are fine. They're playing every day.'

'Ready for the celebration?'

'Can't wait! Everything going nicely.'

'I sent you three new kids with toy boats.'

'Yeah, got here last night. Very eager.'

The man in Malindi thought that for what he was paying, they should have been very eager indeed, but he didn't say anything about that. Instead, he said that the kids should be kept busy with their toy boats, and he didn't want anything to go wrong at the celebration, was that perfectly clear? The South African at the other end said that was perfectly clear, in the voice that men use to show that they don't take shit from anybody, to which the man in Malindi responded by grunting and shutting down his cell phone and watching the topless woman grease herself with lotion. Then he turned the phone back on and put in a call that went by way of a pass-through in Indonesia to a number in Sicily.

Carmine Santangelo-Fugosi was the son of a small-time smuggler who had been born in a mountain village and who now lived in an eighteenth-century palace that had been built by the family that had once ruled this part of Sicily. The head of the family had been called 'Count;' that had lasted almost until Carmine's father had been a young man. Now Carmine lived there, and people showed him even more reverence than they had shown the counts, and they called him *Don*.

He was tall for a Sicilian, slightly stooped, fifty, a solidly built man with thick features and a head of graying hair that he left long because he was trying to hide pattern baldness. He wore a collarless white shirt and pleated trousers and felt slippers, and from time to time he spat on the floor of his own terrace, big gobs, to show he was a peasant and came from peasants.

'This is very nice,' a small Lebanese man said in French from the shade of an umbrella, ignoring the spit. The umbrella was fixed in a cast-iron table with a glass top and rather too much filigree work in the legs – more of Carmine's peasant taste – and matched by the chairs around it. The Lebanese wore sunglasses and a weary-looking cotton suit the color of muddy water. With him at the table was an almost pretty man who translated the French into Italian for Carmine Santangelo-Fugosi.

Carmine looked around at his terrace, his eighteenth-century palazzo, his flowers and his French doors and

4

his tiled floors. Of course it was *nice*. Carmine was a fucking billionaire – what did he expect? 'I don't want any shit from Hizbollah,' Carmine said.

The Lebanese made a gesture that indicated that shit was something that Hizbollah would never in a million years give him. He said in French that none of this would ever get back to Hizbollah and that if it ever did, he, the Lebanese, swore on his mother's grave – he was a Christian – that he would kill himself.

Carmine looked at him as the translation came and said, 'Tell him that if Hizbollah finds out, he'll wish he'd killed himself today.'

Then Carmine's cell phone went off and he turned away, the phone at his ear, and walked to the edge of his terrace, where a balustrade separated him from the twenty-meter drop to the town below. Down there were a street, a café, roofs, and then the port and the Mediterranean, sparkling away to Africa.

'And?' he said into the phone when the man in Malindi had finished his report. Carmine kept his voice low and his back turned to the table, which, because the terrace was so big, was too far away for anybody to have heard him, anyway. Plus the Lebanese wasn't supposed to understand Italian, but Carmine never trusted things like that. People lied about themselves all the time. He leaned on the balustrade and carried on his side of the conversation in grunts and mono-syllables, turning slowly to look around the terrace. Two other men were there, one at each doorway, arms folded, impassive, both the children of his father's relatives. Both armed.

'So,' he said. He covered the phone with his other hand so he could look at the Lebanese while he talked. The Lebanese was getting a lot of money to do the job,

5

but could he do it? Carmine wondered if he should get rid of the man and start over. No, there wasn't time. 'I don't care about that,' he said into the phone when the other man started to give him details. 'All I want is your assurance that everything will be ready for the celebration. Your *absolute* assurance.' When he heard the reply, he grunted and switched off, but the grunt was a positive one. He trusted the man in Malindi.

He spat. He couldn't spit like that without a certain run-up, a certain amount of sound not unlike retching. He went back to the table and waved a hand at one of the other men, who came over and poured him more coffee and then backed away.

Carmine took a biscotto in his right hand and, holding it between his thumb and third finger, used it to lecture the Lebanese. 'I want the only face on this to be Muslim, you follow me?' Carmine came from a village where they had still now and then been visited by puppeteers who did plays from the romances about Saracens and Christian knights; his sense of Islam was based in that half-sophisticated, half-ignorant past. 'That's what the world is to see. That's what Jean-Marc is for.' He gestured with the cookie at the handsome translator, who was actually a freelance television journalist and who smiled at them as if he was on camera. 'You deliver Mombasa,' Carmine said to the Lebanese. He dipped the biscotto, sucked the now-soaked end. 'No mistakes. You don't get a second chance. Eh?'

'Of course, of course –' The Lebanese was afraid of him and showed it – never a bad idea with Carmine, who liked fear in the people around him. The Lebanese tapped the glass top of the table. 'I have everything arranged –' He stopped. The translator was shaking his head at him.

6

Carmine hawked and spat and waved his left hand. 'Don't tell me details. Tell Carlo or somebody. Get out.' He looked toward a door. 'Carlo!'

The Lebanese was hustled out, his right hand halfway up to give a parting handshake, his mouth still open. He would be back in his Christian village in Lebanon by midnight. It might seem he would have nothing to fear there from somebody living in Sicily. But he knew better.

Carmine sat at the table with the translator, wiping his mouth with a cloth napkin. 'What do you think?' he said.

'I think I don't understand what is going on, *Don*,' he murmured.

'You don't need to understand!' Carmine's head was down like a bull's. 'You do what I pay you to do – you talk nice, look pretty on the camera, you keep saying what I tell you. You don't hear nothing, you don't know nothing, you weren't here today, and you didn't meet this no-balls Lebanese! Yes?'

'Yes, yes – of course – *Don*.'

Carmine sat back. He fingered a cigarette out of a pack on the table without looking. 'You want to keep a secret, you chop it into pieces and you give each guy a piece. They look at it, they say, "I don't know what I got here." That's how it stays a secret.'

He lit the cigarette and turned and looked across the terrace at the sea, his legs spread, his forearms on his knees and his hands joined, smoke blowing from the side of his mouth. The sea was empty but he seemed to see something there, because he said, 'The US Navy, that's what I worry about. Fucking US Navy.'

Day One

16 August 1999

1

Jomo Kenyatta International Airport, Nairobi, Kenya.

Laura had tarted herself up so that she was quite a distraction, he thought, watching her approach the passport-control slot with her hidden contraband. She walked with a bouncy stride that wasn't really her own, chest up and out, her rear also very much on view in tight yellow shorts that barely reached her hips. Her navel rode calmly in all this motion, its ring with the diamond chip winking. Laura had made herself, in fact, *all* distractions, and every male eye in the shed-like arrival area was on some part of her. The fact that she didn't have a really pretty face was irrelevant.

Alan Craik grinned despite himself. She was enjoying it! He, on the other hand, was nervous, for her as much as for himself, and he tensed as she sashayed to the passport-control booth and started to chat with a security officer. More balls than he had, he thought. He had only to move a 9mm pistol through; she had something far more dangerous.

He flexed his fingers to relax them, felt the odd sensation in his left hand where two fingers were missing. Or, rather, were red stumps. He forced himself to look at them, felt disbelief, slight disgust. *My hand.* The fingers had been blown off by a bullet seven weeks before. There had been talk of his leaving the Navy.

He balled the hand into a fist and forced himself to concentrate. *Back to work.*

Alan laid his US passport, a twenty-dollar bill sticking from its top, in front of the black man at passport control. The man, too, had been looking at Laura, and Alan grinned.

'*Maridadi*,' Alan said. *Pretty.*

The man's eyes flicked over Alan's shoulder again to Laura, fifty feet away, and he growled *Whore* in Swahili, which Alan wasn't supposed to understand. He stamped the passport and waved Alan through. The twenty had disappeared.

Alan took three steps, clearing passport control, and looked for her. For a moment he lost her, then saw the bright yellow of her buns swinging up the stairs to the balcony above. He guessed that she had seen the sign up there for a ladies' room, used that excuse to bypass customs temporarily. Up there, however, farther along the balcony, was a uniformed Kenyan soldier with an automatic weapon, strategically located between the stairs and the exit at the far end that led directly to the terminal. He was there to turn back anybody who tried to get out that way.

The yellow shorts flashed and the door to the ladies' room closed. Alan turned and walked out.

He waited for her in the terminal hall. His pulse had leveled off again, and the sweat that had threatened to leak down his sides had stopped. His part was over: he had moved the weapon and fifty cartridges through the airport's security. Now, if Laura didn't get arrested for moving drugs –

A wooden dhow moved south along the Kenyan coast, nearing Mombasa. It was going slowly under motor power, its sail useless in the humid breeze that blew from the shore. The men aboard could smell the land beyond, an odor slightly spicy, smoky, earthy, overlaid with the moist decay of the mangrove swamps where Africa met the ocean.

A dark man sat at the foot of the mast, waiting for the first sight of the city. Just now, he could see only blue-green haze where the land lay, and here and there a darker mass where a point thrust out. He had binoculars hung around his neck, but he did not use them. He was in fact seeing far more clearly with an inner eye, which looked beyond the haze, beyond Africa even, into his future.

In four hours, he would be in paradise.

He believed this more completely than he believed that he was sitting on a ship on an ocean on a ball rolling through space. He believed with both passion and simplicity; he believed utterly. He had no fear of the destruction of his physical self that would send him there. They had assured him that he would feel nothing: a flash, a pressure, and he would wake in paradise.

Another man approached him. He had a bag of tools in one hand and, in the other, a black plastic case that held a detonator. 'Time,' the man said.

The dark man shook his head. 'Not yet.' He returned to his contemplation of paradise.

'Hey, man,' he heard her voice say behind him.

'My God, you made it!'

'Piece of cake!' She shrugged. Grinned. Held up a hand so that he could see that the fingers were trembling. 'Little reaction after the fact.' Laughed. Her distractions bounced, and Alan Craik, loyal husband,

13

father, moral man, pursed his lips and thought that it was going to be a long three days – and three nights – before she went on to other duties.

'How'd you get by the guy with the gun?'

'Walked.' She moved a little closer. 'Want to see how I walked?' She wasn't wearing a bra, he knew – she had told him earlier – and her silk T-shirt was definitely a little small.

'I think we ought to do our report.'

'You're a great partner, Craik. I tell you, man, I sure lucked out with you!' She sighed. Laura Sweigert was a Naval Criminal Investigative Service special agent, good at her work, tough, but she had a reputation for liking what she called 'contact sports' when the workday was over. 'I just scored big, man – you think I want to write some fucking report?' He remembered a news report about a female tennis star who, after a big win, said she just wanted to get laid.

A *long* three nights.

He was saved by a voice, calling his name. Behind them and to their right was the exit lane from immigration, lined on both sides by a crowd of greeters – family, hustlers, tourist reps, women in saris, men with hand-lettered signs that said 'Adamson' and 'Client of Simba, Ltd.' The voice calling 'Mister Craik! Mister Craik!' came from there, and Alan searched the two crowds, feeling Laura's hand on his bare arm. He thought he recognized the voice and searched for a face, a white face in the mostly black crowd, and then he saw a Navy ball cap and knew he had the right man, and he waved.

'Craw! Hey, Craw!'

Master Chief Martin Craw had been one of the people who had got him through being an ensign. Craw

14

had taught him the back end of the S-3. Craw had shown him how to massage old tapes and older computers and pull up targets from electronic mush. Craw had given him an example of what a Navy man should be.

Now Martin Craw came toward them, a little grin on his face as he took in both Alan and Laura, hand outstretched.

'Laura, I want you to meet the best master chief in the US Navy. Martin, this is Laura Sweigert, who just brought a kilo of white powder through Kenyatta arrivals.'

'Ma'am.' Craw was in his early forties but seemed an ancient to Alan because of his great, quiet authority. His grin, however, and his quick appraisal of Laura, were not an old man's. 'How'd you do that?'

Laura rocked back a little and smiled at him. 'I think it was the T-shirt.'

Craw reddened only a little. 'Kinda dangerous.' He didn't make clear whether he meant the T-shirt or the white powder. Craw was from Maine.

She made a sound that pooh-poohed the idea. 'Hell's bells, Craik brought through a goddamned gun!'

'Not so loud –'

'And bullets!'

'Laura, hey –'

She held up her hands. 'Okay, okay.' Her fingernails, like her toenails, were painted a glittery red. Her lipstick was pink, her eyeshadow violet, her hair a mousy brown that you ignored because it was gelled to look as if she'd just got very, very wet. 'Entirely legit,' she said. 'We're testing airport security for NCIS.'

'I figured.' Craw grinned. He jerked his head at Alan. 'He's always legit.'

Laura made a face. 'So I'm discovering.' She put a hand through Craw's arm. 'What are your plans for the next couple of days, sailor?' Alan, caused abruptly to see Craw through her eyes, realized that the senior chief was a damned good-looking man.

Craw saw Alan's look, blushed. 'I'm goin' to be working for Mister Craik.'

Alan bent and picked up his helmet bag, which held the H&K. 'You want to bring me up to date, Chief? Like, um, what you're doing here?' He had last seen Craw on board the USS *Thomas Jefferson* a week ago, when he had had to fly back to CONUS to be deposed for a national-security case.

With Laura leaning against him, Craw explained that he had flown into Mombasa the evening before from the CV to set up the US hangar there as their home base while they shore-deployed. 'Orders from the CAG.' He raised his free hand, which held a black attaché case.

'Yeah, I know, I got 'em, too. But I didn't expect to be met at Nairobi.'

'Thought I could brief you flying back to Mombasa. The admiral's goin' to inspect us tomorrow.' Again, he gestured with the attaché case. 'Got some paper-work –'

'What the hell, we just got here!'

'Well, he's makin' a shore visit, so it's some ship today, us tomorrow.'

That changed the price of fish. What he and Laura had just done – moving illicit items through airport security for the Naval Criminal Investigative Service – was a peripheral responsibility, a test of local condi-tions that would become part of a report. He had treated it as a game; however, with this return to the realities

16

of his detachment, the pleasures of the game faded and the serious trivia of Navy life took over.

They began moving away from the arrivals area. 'What's our space like down there?'

'Kinda filthy. One of the old air-force hangars at Mombasa airport. Not been used for a while – dust, gear missing – been a lotta thievin', I'd guess. I put everybody to cleanin' up, but the place is big – room for a couple P-3s in there and to spare, if you had to.'

They were walking toward the Air Kenya desk now to start the flight to Mombasa. 'How many personnel?'

'Aircrew for one plane plus seventeen – other plane comin' in a few days.'

'Staying where?'

'Nyali International.' American military, like government people, got put up in the big international hotels on the beach because they were supposed to be more secure than hotels in Mombasa itself. 'But I told 'em, you boys just plan to be in this hangar nonstop till the admiral's blown through, then I'll get you some rack time. They're all good boys.'

They were, Alan thought; they were all good boys now, although when he and Craw had first encountered them some months before, they had been pretty bad boys. Detachment 424 was a one-shot unit put together to test-drive a 3-D radar-imaging system called MARI, and it had been almost run into extinction by its acting officer-in-charge before Alan and Craw and a few others had been able to shape it up. Now deployed with the *Jefferson* in the Indian Ocean, it had been ordered to fly off to Mombasa for two weeks as an advance party for a visit by the entire battle group.

'Give me a rundown.'

*   *   *

The men on the dhow smelled Mombasa before they saw it – a dustier air, car exhaust, garbage, people. The dark man raised his binoculars but couldn't penetrate the haze; Mombasa is a low city, anyway, most of its seafront masked by trees, and the dhow was still well out, although in the shipping lane so as to seem as much a part of normal traffic as it could. Other dhows and rusty merchant ships had passed them going the other way; once, a sparkling-white Kenyan Coast Guard ship had approached and the men had tensed, but it had passed without hailing.

The dark man gestured toward the deeper haze of Mombasa. 'We go on past the city. Kilindini Harbor is beyond. Tell Simoum that he and the crew can take to the boat once he has sailed us into Kilindini.'

The other man – paler, nervous – squatted in front of him, holding out the tools as if they were an offering. 'Haji, I am ashamed – I am losing my, my – I want to go with them.'

The dark man shook his head. His face was severe, but his voice was kind. 'Pray. You will be with me in paradise. God is great.'

The other man began to weep.

They talked business, then a few personal things, then a little scuttlebutt, Laura laughing with them. When they got to talking about individuals in the det, Craw laughed – a loud, staccato sound, like a series of backfires – and said, 'You know what Mister Soleck did now?'

Alan prepared himself. LTJG Soleck was their idiot savant, their divine fool. He had once managed to miss their departure from CONUS and then spend three days catching up with them because, as he had said

18

quite frankly, there had been a bookstore he had had to visit.

'What's Soleck?' Laura said.

'My cross,' Alan groaned. 'A good kid, but a royal screwup – when he isn't being brilliant.'

'He's a doozer,' Craw said.

'So what'd he do?' Alan had a vision of a wrecked aircraft.

'He was trolling for fish from the stern of the carrier.'

'The *fantail?*'

'No, sir, the CIWS mount.' Craw pronounced it 'cee-wiz' – the cee-wiz mount. 'Somebody saw him and told me and I didn't believe it, so I went down and there he was, with a gawd-dam spinnin' rod, just standin' there like he was bass fishin'. And the CV makin' better'n twenty knots!'

'Well –' He looked at Laura. 'Soleck is a little, mm, eccentric. He didn't do anything really, um, stupid, did he?' He had a terrible thought. 'He didn't fall overboard, did he?'

'No, sir. *But he caught a fish!* A gawd-dam big fish! Which he carried by hand all the way to the galley so's they could cook it for his dinner.' Craw's smile became small, almost evil. 'And not just *his* dinner.'

'Oh, no.'

'Yes, sir.'

'He didn't.'

'Yes, sir. Direct to the flag deck, courtesy of LTJG Soleck and Detachment 424.'

Laura guffawed. They were having a beer now in a crowded bar near the departure lounge. She leaned back to laugh, and conversation in the bar died.

'Was it – edible?'

'It was gawd-dam delicious! Some big red fish I never

19

saw before, spines on it like a cactus, but it cut like steak and tasted like tuna. Admiral said it was the best fish he ever ate!'

Alan let out a sigh of relief. 'That's okay, then.'

'Well, no. Next day, twenty guys was fishin' there, and the day after, forty, so the ship's captain put it out of bounds and sent a memo specially to Mister Soleck, telling him to stop having good ideas.'

Alan sighed. 'I suppose I got a copy.'

'Yes, sir. Ship's captain would like a word with you when you're back aboard.'

Alan nodded. *Right*. One week away in Washington, back one hour, and he was going to be up to his ass in Mickey Mouse. *Welcome to the US Navy*. He flexed his hands and glanced down to where the fingers should have been. *Welcome to the US Navy*.

Then they were moving down the ramp toward the aircraft that would take them to Mombasa. 'Don't worry,' Craw said softly. 'Everything'll be fine.'

'Right.'

'We'll make things shipshape for the admiral, then we got two weeks on the beach to relax.'

'Right.'

Alan didn't tell Craw that he had a set of orders that would keep them busy for longer than two weeks, or that his orders had a secret addendum that gave him the responsibility for assessing the consequences if the United States and the UN went back into Somalia. He was returning not only to assess Mombasa as a port of call, but to gather information for a war.

The dhow anchored in Kilindini Road. Ten minutes after she swung to rest on her anchor cable, a boat put over, and six men motored away for the distant shore.

On the dhow, the dark man was standing by the landward side, peering through his binoculars. A distant gray vessel was barely visible in the haze at dockside, but he studied it for some minutes, then turned to the only two men left on the dhow with him.

'Now,' he said. 'Bring the detonator.'

Over the Indian Ocean.

LTjg Evan Soleck was worried.

The S-3 in whose right-hand seat he rode was mostly older than he was, but that wasn't what worried him. They were flying at twenty-three thousand feet, two hundred miles from the carrier, and the gauge for the starboard fuel tank wasn't registering, but that wasn't what worried him. The man in the left-hand seat was a lieutenant-commander and hated his guts, but that didn't worry him, either.

What worried Soleck was that in three days he was going to make lieutenant, and he didn't know what he was going to do about a wetting-down party. It was tradition that you gave a party for your shipmates for a promotion, and you wet down the new bars with the most drinkable stuff available. *Not* giving a party wasn't an option. Soleck had heard a story about a new jg in a squadron – nobody ever said what squadron it was, but everybody swore it was true – who had refused to give a party, and his CO had sent him away every weekend for months – courier duty, bullshit trips, hand-carried messages – until he broke and gave a party at last, *and nobody went*. Soleck couldn't imagine that degree of isolation. You'd be frozen right out of a squadron. A pariah. He'd kill himself.

So he had to give a party. But it had to be just right. Really *phat*. Something they'd tell stories about long after he'd been ordered someplace else. So that when he was, let's say, an old guy – a commander, a squadron CO, even – the nuggets would stare at him and nudge each other and say, 'The Old Man's the one that gave a party so cool that –' That what? There was the problem.

'You take it?' the man beside him said.

Soleck snapped out of it. 'Yes, sir!'

LCDR Paul Stevens was a difficult man. He didn't like Soleck, the jg knew, because Soleck hero-worshipped Alan Craik, their CO, and Stevens and Craik didn't get along. What Soleck didn't understand was that Stevens never would have liked him anyway, because Soleck was an optimist and a doer and a happy guy, and Stevens went through life with his own personal cloud raining on him all the time. Now he scowled at the much younger man and sneered, 'You awake?'

'Yes, sir.'

Stevens grunted. They had both been put up for the Air Medal for flying into a war zone seven weeks ago to pull out Craik and an NCIS agent and a spy they'd captured, and they'd flown back out with two Chinese aircraft pissing missiles at them and had lived to tell about it – but was Stevens happy? No. He'd done brilliantly, evading missiles with the slow, fat S-3, hoarding fuel long past the gauges' limit, getting two wounded men back to the CV in time to get the blood they needed. But was he happy? No. All he'd said was, 'That trip gets me O-5 and a medal, and I'm goddamned if I ever do anything that stupid again.' The talk before had been that Stevens would get passed over for commander and would have to leave the Navy, but now he'd made O-5 *and* got a medal, and he remained

22

as sour as a ripe lemon, a weight on the entire detachment.

'I need to take a piss,' he was saying. 'Keep it level on 270 if you can manage it – you're already three goddam points off.'

Soleck started to object, then shut up. 'Anything you say, sir.'

'Yeah, I bet.'

Stevens headed for the tunnel. Alone in the front end, Soleck brought the S-3 back on course and ran through the things he might have said. He knew what Stevens's beef was: when Craik had taken over the det several months ago, Stevens had been acting CO and things had been a shambles. Craik had whipped them into a first-class outfit; then, with Craik home on convalescent leave after the wild ride out of Pakistan, Stevens had been made acting CO again, and the CAG had been right on his ass the whole time to keep him up to the mark. The CAG was Craik's personal friend, Captain Rafehausen. 'His asshole buddy,' Stevens had sneered. *Yeah, well, I admire both of them a hell of a lot more than I admire you, Stevens*, Soleck said inside his head. *You don't even have a friend! Mister Craik gave you the chance that got you the medal and your fucking O-5, and you're not even grateful! The trouble with you, Stevens, is that you're –*

He was what? Soleck was too young, too inexperienced to know that there are people incapable of happiness. He thought that Stevens was lazy, but he also wondered if Stevens was actually afraid of failure: better not to try than to fail.

Which brought him back to the wetting-down party: would he have to invite Stevens?

He slid into a reverie about a private banquet room

23

somewhere, maybe champagne – champagne, really? did aviators even like champagne? – well, booze, certainly. And women. He didn't know what kind of women or how he'd get them, but they'd remember a party with women, wouldn't they? And a theme. Something Navy – maybe a few musicians playing Navy stuff –

'Jeez, you're on course.' Stevens dropped back into the left-hand seat. 'You get any reading on that gas gauge?'

'No, sir.'

They were flying in tandem with the det's other S-3, running MARI scans on surface ships in the Aden-India sea lane. Slowly, they were building a library of computer-stored images, and someday, when a classification system was evolved, you'd be able to bring an unknown contact up on MARI, and the computer would scan the data banks and give you an ID. Great stuff, but this part of it was really tedious.

'Sir –' Soleck began.

Stevens ducked his bullish head as if prepared for a blow. 'Yeah?'

Soleck swallowed. 'Sir, what did you do for a wetting-down party when you made lieutenant? If you don't mind me asking.'

Stevens stared at him. He hunched his shoulders, shook himself deeper into the seat and put his hands on the con. 'I got it.' Stevens looked away from him then, checking the gauges, doing a quick visual check out the windows. He was the best pilot in the det, maybe the best on the carrier, you had to give him that. *Why was he such a prick?*

'I bought everybody a beer at the O Club. That's what everybody does.' He started to say something else and then thought better of it, but his tone had been kinder than Soleck had ever heard. Soleck wanted to say something more but could think of nothing. The moment passed, and when Stevens next looked at him, it was the old, sour face he turned. 'Forty minutes to turnback. Call Preacher and tell them section's forty from RTF, right tank uncertain, but estimate fuel okay to touch down.'

'Yes, sir.'

Soleck decided then that he'd have to ask Mister Craik. He wouldn't see him for some days – the word was they'd fly off to Mombasa within the week – and then, when they were more or less alone sometime, he'd just ask him. The way he'd asked Stevens. Craik would know. He'd know if women or music or goddam fireworks were in order. Or if he should just buy everybody a beer and let it go.

But what would be memorable about *that*?

USS *Franklin D. Roosevelt*, Inbound Channel, Straits of Gibraltar.

'You know Al Craik?' asked a lieutenant-commander in a rumpled flight suit. He wore an old leather flight jacket against the forty-knot wind that blew through the Straits of Gibraltar. He was short, compact, and thin-faced, and the pocket of his flight jacket, embroidered in the blue and gold of VS-53, said 'Narc.'

'Never met him. But I went through AOCS with his wife. Rose Siciliano, then. Man, she's a tough chick. Great pilot, too.' He grinned at the memory and turned to look up at Narc as he descended the ladder from the O–3 level to the hangar deck. He, too, wore a flight suit and a jacket, only his was embroidered with the black and white of chopper squadron HS-9. It said

'Skipper Van Sluyt.' They were both officers in the same air wing: CAG 14, six days away from transiting the Suez Canal to relieve the USS *Thomas Jefferson* off Africa.

Narc nodded. 'She's at NASA, going to fly the shuttle.'

'No shit? Well, good work if you like that sort of thing.' Skipper Van Sluyt started down the ladder again.

Narc followed him down, surprised. 'What, the publicity?' Narc *did* like that sort of thing. He had an Air Medal of which he was very proud.

'Yeah, Narc. That and the ever-present corporate –' Van Sluyt had turned his head, perhaps wondering if his anti-NASA speech was going to have the right effect on Narc the Navy Yuppie, when the carrier hit the crosscurrent at the entrance to the Mediterranean. Ninety-five thousand tons of carrier are not easily moved, but the constant flow of water between the Mediterranean and the Atlantic creates something like a wall. The great ship gave a lurch, and Skipper Van Sluyt's feet jerked out from under him. He fell down the rest of the ladder, his tailbone breaking on the second to last step and his collarbone at the bottom. As he said later to his wife, 'That's what you get for bad-mouthing NASA.'

Mombasa.

From the landward walls of Fort Jesus, he could see the Muslim neighborhoods of Old Town laid out at his feet like a map, although the streets were tiny and twisted like a collection of old rubber bands. The fort served to draw the tourists, and nearest to it were prosperous shops owned by Kikuyu or Hindus with money; plastic Masai spears and plastic Masai beads woven in China grabbed at the attention of German and American tourists, and sad-looking tall men with heavy spears and a trace of Masai in their veins guarded the shops. Farther off toward the dhow port were the real shops of the Muslim residents, tiny shops with deeply embrasured doors and windows capable of resisting a siege. The smell of cardamom and curry carried even to the top of the wall. And to the north, he could see the slow rise of the ground into the natural amphitheater of the park in front of the old colonial offices.

The man atop the walls squatted in the coral ruins of a tiny sentry kiosk on the landward side and carefully unwrapped the burlap package under his arm. Seventy feet above the streets of Old Town, he exposed the receiver of an AK-74 and inserted a clip.

Alan Craik loved Africa. He'd seen the bad parts – Rwanda, Zaire, Somalia. He'd seen the parts in Tanzania and South Africa that looked like wildlife shows on the Discovery Channel. But this is where his love of Africa had had its birth, at the top of this narrow Mombasa street that ran down from the shiny oddness of a Hard Rock Café to a fifteenth-century mosque and the Old Town of Mombasa. He smiled broadly, boyishly, looking at the coral walls of Fort Jesus, where he had first tried his halting Swahili, and at the glint of the water in the dhow harbor beyond. It wasn't like coming home, but it was like returning to a beloved vacation spot. He didn't even realize he had started walking down toward Old Town until Martin Craw's hand grasped his arm.

'Whoa, there, Commander. We got less than an hour before we're due at the det.'

Alan smiled back at him. *I'm in Africa!* was what he wanted to say, but he swallowed it. Then he thought, *Screw the command image.*

'You're the one who said we should leave them alone until they got the place straightened up, Martin. That's why I'm still lugging this ball and chain.' He indicated the heavy helmet bag in his maimed left hand, the two green loop handles wrapped around his wrist to keep the pressure off the stumps of his fingers. 'I thought dropping Laura at the *Harker* would take longer.' USNS *Jonathan Harker* was a ship supplying the battle group, in port for three days. Laura had drawn the duty of checking with the captain and crew on their experience of Mombasa as a liberty port – plus, as she had found when they had pulled up at the dock, the BG's flag was making a tour of the ship, and she'd got roped into his party. She hadn't been a happy force-protection investigator.

Craw smiled as if he wished it had taken longer and looked at his watch again. 'If I let you loose in an African city, you'll be out till all hours.'

'Martin, you look to me like a man who needs a beer.'

'Beer? And air-conditioning? That's a *big* yes.'

'We'll have one, repeat, one beer here, and then I get to cruise Old Town for thirty minutes.'

'Yes, sir!' Craw's reply was deliberate overenthusiasm; he was a man capable of quiet sarcasm, often so deep it was difficult to detect. He paused on the crowded sidewalk to ogle a local woman in blended Western and African clothes. Alan hustled him inside.

The interior of the Hard Rock was cool, pleasant, and entirely American; only physique and face shape made the crowd different from a bunch of American blacks in an American city. Most of them were speaking English. The Hard Rock franchise was genuine, unlike that in Bahrain; it had been hit hard by the

Nairobi embassy bombing, but was still a bastion of burgers, milkshakes, and beer – and a magnet for sailors. One wall had plaques from ships of the US, British, and Canadian navies, and one from an Australian destroyer.

They sat at a table and ordered beers: Alan a White Cap, because it was Kenyan, Craw a Rolling Rock, because he was delighted to find it. Alan watched the city bustle by the huge picture window. He could see the park in front of the old British Colonial Office away to the left, surrounded by monolithic bank buildings – still a spiritual center of the town, although the real economic center had moved up Moi Avenue since he was last here. He was growing nostalgic for a town he had barely visited. 'I know a great restaurant here, really world class, called the Tamarind Dhow,' he said, still bursting with the notion of being in Mombasa. 'Want to grab some food there after we visit the det? It's on me.'

Craw smiled slowly, not raising his eyes from the menu of the Hard Rock. 'I sort o' have some plans, tonight, skipper, if you don't mind. Rain check?' he drawled, and then looked up with a sudden laugh.

'Master Chief, do you have a *date*?'

'That would be "need to know," sir.' He smiled again. He seemed happy about it. 'Do you really need to know?'

'Nope.' Alan thought of saying *Don't hurt yourself*, but he let it pass. 'But if you're going to sit here and drool over your good fortune, I'm going to shop.' Craw smiled again. Alan couldn't remember seeing him smile so often, at least since he had reached command rank. Craw waved him away. 'It's only Mombasa, skipper; I can find you. I'll catch you in ten minutes. If I don't

29

see you in Old Town, I'll catch you around Fort Jesus. Leave the helmet bag.' He reached out for it. 'I'll watch it.'

'I'm signed for it.' Alan wrapped the handles around his wrist again. He waved, tossed an American ten-dollar bill on the table, and headed out into the street, checking his watch. Time to see if the same old silver-smith was still in business.

The interior of the shop was dark and cool, a profound contrast with the white-hot street outside. Three young boys were working in the back, two of them drawing wire by pulling a core through ever-smaller holes in a steel plate. He had seen the same craft demonstrated at Colonial Williamsburg, but these boys did it better. They were doing it for real. The third boy was polishing silver with ashes and a lot of elbow grease. Alan smiled and called a greeting as he entered; later, he couldn't remember what language he had used, but he would remember the slight tension in their body language as they turned to him. He knew the shop was off the beaten track, but couldn't imagine they were *against* tourists.

A fine old sword stood in a niche behind the counter; that caught his eye as he ignored cases of bangles and earrings. Rose never fancied such stuff. He couldn't remember the last time he had seen her in any earrings except military studs. But just under his hands, as he leaned on the counter, there was a heavy chain of solid links, almost like big beads; it was crisp and very well made. He smiled; it was usually so difficult to find anything for Rose.

'May I see the heavy silver necklace?'

'Oh, yes.' One of the young men sprang down from

the bunk-like bench where he was working and opened the case. Alan couldn't pin down what was out of place, except that the young man should have been talking a great deal more.

The necklace was just as handsome close-up as in the case. He caught the young man's eye. *'Bei gani?'* he asked. He showed a US twenty-dollar bill. When here many years before, he had learned that it was easier to buy everything with US dollars. Cheaper, too.

The boy held up his hand and spoke rapidly without smiling. He went too fast. Alan thought he heard something like *'Mia moja na thelathini na sita,'* which would have been a hundred and something. More than a hundred. That seemed unlikely; silver wasn't that expensive.

'Ghali sana. Pudunza bei kidogo, rafik'.'

The young man on the other side of the counter kept looking past him into the street, and Alan wanted to turn around, except that the other young men were just as interesting. They seemed to be listening for something, utterly still. *Not getting much work done.*

The boy at the counter muttered something about his father. Perhaps serious bargaining had to be done by an adult, although in most of Africa all three of the shop boys would be thought men. In Somalia they would have been fighting for years. One of them even looked Somali. Not impossible.

'Lini?' Alan couldn't remember how to ask something as complex as when the father would be in. It might not even be polite.

'Kesho!' Did he really mean tomorrow? The young man at the counter waved his hand as if eager for Alan to go. He *was* eager. Then, swiftly, his expression changed and he retreated to his work area, his face blank, as a

31

new, older man came in through a beaded curtain to the side of the counter. He was looking at the three boys in puzzlement, but he smiled as he looked at Alan. 'My son. I do not know why he torments me this way. You are interested in the necklace? I made it myself.'

'It is very good.'

'It is, isn't it? Too good, I think. Tourists want a cheap memento of Africa, not a good piece of silver.' Alan liked him instantly; he had the directness that Alan associated with craftsmen. *Men too busy for bullshit*. The young men were listening; no wire was being drawn, no silver polished.

'What price did my son quote you?'

'*Tafadhali, mzee*. I did not really understand him. My Swahili is never as good as I think it is. Not nearly as good as your English, for instance.'

The older man polished the chain idly, unfazed by flattery. 'Hmm. Yes. It is. One hundred twenty dollars.'

'I could perhaps go as far as eighty dollars.' Alan wanted it more now than when he had first looked at it. He also wanted an excuse to prolong the meeting. The older man was interesting, a type; and the young men were clearly on edge – waiting for something, something that a foreigner, an *mzungu*, was not part of.

The *mzee* looked at him, one eyebrow raised. Alan settled on to a bench by the counter with a sigh, as if ready for a long siege.

'Perhaps if we had some tea?' The *mzee* was happy to dicker; indeed, would have been sorry if the business had been concluded directly.

The plan to meet Craw was somewhere around the edge of Alan's consciousness, but Craw wouldn't worry and Alan knew where to find him. The tourist part of

Old Town wasn't more than a couple of streets, really. And tea, sweet cardamom tea, drunk in this medieval shop, would make Alan's day. The det wasn't going anywhere without him, either.

The older man turned to the boys and said something in Arabic, a language Alan didn't speak but easily recognized. Arabic was the language of education in Old Town Mombasa, the language of the Koran. Alan's attention sharpened. Nobody answered the *mzee*, and Alan was surprised, but it was of a piece; they were waiting for something. Finally, the one who had first come to the counter dropped his eyes and darted out of the main door. He returned with a small tray, rattled off some Arabic as he entered. Alan was reaching for a cup when the older man caught his eye and motioned with his hand. He looked very serious.

'My son says there is a bad crowd in the street. Perhaps you should go now.'

Alan looked out the shop doorway, wondering how long the boy had been waiting for this 'bad crowd.' Then he could hear, in the distance toward Fort Jesus, a sound like waves on a beach.

The street in front of the little shop was empty.

Bad crowd?

Alan took his little cup of tea and drank it off, holding the other man's eye. Now he was more than a customer; he was a guest.

'How bad is it, *mzee*?'

'I have no idea.' The *mzee* was calm, attentive, dignified. 'It might be better, after all, if you stayed here; these things soon pass.' He picked up the necklace, studied it, said in the low voice of a man speaking to one who he thinks is sympathetic, 'You understand: we are Muslims, and the government is not our friend.'

33

'I appreciate your hospitality.' Alan could hear the beach noise louder now, as if waves were breaking higher. It was a crowd, all right. But it didn't sound angry.

'But I should go. I have a friend looking for me by Fort Jesus.'

'Please go carefully.'

'I'll be back for the necklace,' Alan said. The noise was growing louder still, and the young men were restless.

'*Inshallah*,' the older man said with a bow.

The old man had had no idea there was trouble in the street. But the young ones had expected it.

'*Allahu Akbar*,' Alan said and hoisted the helmet bag through the door. *God is great.*

The crowd was thicker at the end of the street; men and women mixed, so not immediately dangerous. Still, the non-Muslim Kikuyu shops that pretended to be part of Old Town seemed to be closed, their half-Masai guards glowering from the height advantage of their steps. The street he entered from the back street with the silver shop was narrow at the best of times; now it was claustrophobic, with at least a thousand men and women jammed along its length. Alan began to shoulder his way along it, looking for Craw, for any white face, but there was none. He got as far as the gap between two ancient houses and he turned into it and pushed along through a smell of urine until he reached the next street, which was almost as full. He shoved himself toward Fort Jesus, navigating by the minarets of two mosques.

Men were pulling prepared signs about a jailed leader and economic conditions out of their houses.

Some were in English, but all were labeled with the green sigil of the Islamic Party of Kenya – the IPK. Women were pulling the black *abyas* over their street clothes. He was acutely conscious of his color and of the fact that he was in the dressing room of a major demonstration – Old Town Mombasa was emptying into the streets that led up past Fort Jesus and into the center of town.

Despite his unease, he kept pushing his way along, apologizing – *sameheni, pole, sameheni, pole.* Twice, men bumped him hard or elbowed him; not enough to do damage, but enough to remind him to keep moving. His missing fingers itched and he felt trapped. If it hadn't been for Craw, he would have gone around the other end, through the back alleys below the dhow port; he could walk that way and come out high up on Kenyatta Avenue. But if he did that, he'd be leaving Craw wandering Old Town in a riot.

He could see the corner and the peach flank of Fort Jesus rising beyond it, and then he caught sight of a white face and bushy eyebrows, a dark polo shirt. *Craw.* None too soon, he thought, and began to burrow toward him when three men off to his right registered as being different, somehow not part of the crowd. He couldn't put a finger on it and he was eager to get Craw's attention, but they were all three lighter skinned, carrying bundles that struck Alan as *wrong.* Some kind of tension. He hoped they had only swords or cudgels. The rest of the crowd seemed to keep them a little distant, too; he could see they were not 'with' anyone.

'Craw!' he yelled – pointlessly, as it turned out. There was too much noise. He kept burrowing. The three men were still there, just off to his right, and they were all looking at him now. *Great.* 'Craw!'

35

Craw was standing on a step next to a half-Masai guard. The man was ignoring him, and Craw was looking up and down the street. Alan willed him to look a little farther back, and kept pushing, an inch at a time. Suddenly, as if a dam had broken, the crowd began to move the way he wanted to go, and the sound crested and crashed like the noise of the sea. Now Alan had to fight to reach the edge of the street and the human eddy where the Masai guard next to Craw was using a club to keep the crowd from his shop. Alan got clubbed on the shoulder as he struggled to get Craw's attention.

'Whoa, Ben, that's my guy! Cool it!' Craw stuffed a bill into the other man's hand.

'Glad to see you too!' Alan shouted and got up on the step. From his new vantage point he could see the crowd sweeping up the hill out of the square at the base of Fort Jesus and into the park where the British colonial office had been. He couldn't grasp how many they might be, but they didn't seem any less packed in the larger area. They were loud, but almost half were *abya*-wearing women.

'Riot?'

'Protest, I think.' But Alan couldn't forget the three men he'd seen.

At the top of the park, as many as twenty trucks full of what appeared to be soldiers in camo with assault rifles were deploying. Alan leaned past the Masai guard and shouted into Craw's ear. 'General Service Unit. Nasty. Those guys will shoot first and ask questions later.'

The ground rose in a gradual curve uphill from Alan to the park, giving him a dramatic view over the heads of the crowd. The protestors had marched to the park on Nkrumah Road and now it was the only exit. A man with a loudspeaker was bellowing from an incongruous gazebo in the park's middle, and a Kenyan cop with a bullhorn was yelling back at him from the top of a truck cab. The loudspeaker droned on. Alan couldn't catch much of the Swahili, but the man in the gazebo appeared to be using the rhetoric related on the signs – demands for the release of Sheik somebody.

He shouted into Craw's ear again. 'I think we should get out of here the other way.'

'What?'

'I think we should get out of here the other way!'

'What other way?'

'Back through Old Town.'

Alan waved his hand toward the little street from which he had come. A flicker of motion in the second storey across the street caught his eye, and he watched, appalled, as the barrel of a rifle poked from the window and fired. The report was audible over the crowd noise. Alan was trying to point it out to Craw when the GSU officer with the bullhorn was cut off the truck cab and flung fifteen feet. The GSU response was immediate and brutal: a volley of fire swept the front of the crowd. Even from hundreds of feet away, Alan could see the mist of blood as the whole front of the crowd was cut down, and the rising scream of panic and hate that rose behind it. The rifle in the building across the street was firing steadily now. The crowd, trapped in the square, broke from the police guns and trampled their own dead, jammed the two exits, and then seemed to flinch away. The scream rose to an impossible pitch as the guns fired. Alan could smell the copper taint of blood on the air. He wanted to close his eyes. The line of fire from the GSU to the crowd meant that high shots went straight at their position on the step; bullets chipped the doorway behind him, and one creased Craw's arm. Across the street, a group of young men were looking up and pointing, trying to get the crowd's attention on the shooter in the window. The bulk of the crowd, sixty thousand strong, hovered in the cordite-filled killing ground between the choked exit-streets and the guns, and then with a high-pitched cry they charged the gun line. The GSU fired one long burst. Bullets that must already have taken a toll of lives spattered around Alan and Craw. The Masai guard died between them, the top of his head blown off.

Alan was down, huddled over the helmet bag, and Craw was lying flat on the step, but Alan couldn't stop raising his head to watch, despite the dreadful rattling of the incoming rounds all over the coral concrete of the shopfront. He had a gun in his helmet bag but couldn't think how he could change the situation.

A gasoline bomb arced over the crowd and exploded against the top of one of the GSU trucks. The wall of bodies hit the gun line and went over it, and all Alan could see of the action was a single reflection, a panga or a light axe, rise and fall, redder with every motion, set in isolation at the top of the carnage, and then the trucks were overrun. There were more trucks at the top of the square, and they were firing now, too.

But there were no longer rounds slamming into the concrete around them.

'Come on!' he shouted. Craw raised himself and followed.

Right under the peach walls of Fort Jesus Alan saw a trio of foreigners, obviously sailors, with open-necked shirts, khaki shorts, hats. One was black and another lighter, maybe Indian, but all were clearly Americans.

Alan's mind started to work again. He thought that the inside of Fort Jesus, with its five-meter-thick coral walls, might not be a bad place to ride out the riot.

Craw touched his arm and pointed wordlessly at the three sailors. Alan nodded, and in that moment accepted responsibility for them. The sailors were huddled against a wall fifty feet away. The street in front of the fort was almost clear except for the dead and wounded, and blood was everywhere, running over the cobbles and pooling in the gutters. Alan stepped on several bodies as he dashed across the street, and tried not to look down. There was a young woman dead; the bullet had entered her mouth and shattered her teeth, giving her face a feral look. Just beyond her lay one of the boys from the shop, gutshot, clutching his bowels and moaning.

Alan made it to the three men, who were still under the wall of the fort, with bodies at their feet and desperation engraved on their faces.

'Lieutenant-Commander Craik, Det 424.' They looked at him in shock. 'You Navy?'

'Merchant Marine!' the Indian said. He was green under his tan, young. He looked and smelled as if he had already vomited. 'I am Patel.'

Craw ran up and threw himself against the wall.

'Kenyans have an APC!'

Something burning hit Alan's arm and tinkled to the ground, then another. Shell casings. There were twenty or more on the ground beneath his feet, and he picked one up. They were coming from the top of the wall.

He looked up and saw the barrel of a rifle, matt black and hard to distinguish so far above his head. The shooter leaned out and again his casings fell at Alan's feet.

So much for hiding in Fort Jesus.

'We've got to get out of here!' All the men nodded at him. 'Follow me!'

Alan had a vague idea that the suburb behind the fort connected to the road to the port at Kilindini; anyway, it was the path of least resistance amidst the chaos all around them. There were buildings on the other side of the square that were on fire now; and the wall of noise didn't seem to diminish. He recognized the sound of a heavy machine gun; its bullets raked the wall of the fort and sent a spray of high-velocity coral fragments into the street. The GSU, he thought, had discovered the sniper above him in the fort.

And then the earth shook.

Alan never actually heard the explosion – the screams of the wounded and the long combat wail of the mob drowned it out – but within seconds a fist of black smoke leaped into the sky over toward Kilindini. In his gut, Alan knew immediately that it was the docks – either a ship or the fuel farms. He thought fleetingly of his orders about Mombasa and their vague reference to 'dissident' elements who might resent the US presence.

'Craw, bring these guys along. We're getting out of here.' His voice sounded absurdly steady. He thought again of the pistol in his helmet bag, but he was enough of a target now; he didn't need to become a participant.

The first part would be the worst – left along the wall of the fort, screened from the square only by an old colonial office building too lightly built to stop a heavy military round. Even as he began to scuttle along the front of the fort, he watched puffs of coral appear silently along the front like flowers opening. He went anyway, got to the end of the wall, and dove into the cover of a big acacia tree. Patel appeared directly behind him and stood, confused as to where to go at the end of the wall. Alan hauled him down. The black guy appeared with Craw, and then the white guy, sprinting, and they were a hot, sweaty bundle in the marginal cover of the old acacia tree.

Alan looked for the next cover and their best path to a concrete building some meters off to the left. The effort of lifting himself from the ground seemed to take forever, and more willpower than the actual run. The storm of stray rounds was abating here; there were only a few marks in the stucco of the building's wall. After him, the white guy came first, and then there was a pause so long that Alan feared he was going to have to go back. Then the black guy. Then, almost immediately, Patel and Craw. Craw was bleeding from the crease a bullet had cut in his head, a long tendril of blood that ran over his face, dividing it, and down the neck of his shirt, making his head look like a Mohawk mask.

They crossed the open ground and reached the edge of a neighborhood of lost affluence. Once, the place had been for British civil servants and their families, later for Indian shop owners; now it was up-and-coming Kikuyu. The little cottages had yards and trees and bushes, although the grass was gone now, worn dead by thousands of feet over the years, and the houses were so widely separated that each one offered a line of vision – and fire – back to the park. There was some cover, and a screen of big trees divided the neighborhood from the park and the square where the shooting still went on. Alan expected to start moving quickly here, but Craw grabbed his shoulder and pointed north, where a knot of men with weapons was moving parallel to them. Even as they watched, another knot left the cover of an old gazebo in the park and ran almost straight toward them.

Either the firefight with the GSU was lost or, worse, the wave front of the violence was spreading. Alan suspected the latter; there were still bodies in the road beyond the house where he was crouched, and the wailing noise seemed unabated.

'We have to stay ahead of that,' he said, pointing, and led them to seaward of the first house. There were pilings and a heap of concrete rubble, then a mudflat. The tide was down. Alan thanked heaven for a small miracle. He crawled down the concrete on to the mud, and found that it was firm and held his weight.

'Smells like the ocean,' Craw said. His Mohawk-mask face was strained. Alan had never seen him afraid. He wondered what he looked like himself. *Don't stop to think.* When they had all scrambled down, they began to jog along the mudflat. Mombasa was fifteen feet above them, and it was not until they had gone several hundred yards that Alan realized that he could hear again. The screaming was still there but distant, and his feet made little splashing noises as they slapped down on the wet mud.

Above them was a low cliff topped with trees. He didn't know where they were; couldn't remember having seen trees on this part of the island before.

He looked seaward and across to Likoni; he must be at the southern tip of Mombasa. He clambered up the low cliff, raising his head slowly, but there was no motion at the top except the slow flapping of a flag in the wind. He was looking over a sand trap at a fairway stretching off north; the grass was mostly brown and there was garbage everywhere, but no people. The crowd, far away now, sounded like breakers on a distant beach.

Alan waved the rest of his party to follow him up to the golf course.

He hadn't even remembered that there was a golf course, and he was disoriented by the discovery. None of them had any water and there was none in his helmet bag, but the mental search for water reminded him of other things he did have: a hotel-supplied map of Mombasa and a tiny compass in his Swiss army knife holster. He shook his head, reached into the side pocket and retrieved them both. He opened the map and laid it in the dirt, placed the little compass beside it. He watched it steady down and resolve his problem. North. What he didn't like was that in forgetting the golf course he had forgotten another *mile* of open ground and residential area before they could reach the water at Kilindini.

'If we go that way –' he pointed north and west – 'we should cross Mama Ngina Drive and then Nyerere just above the Likoni Ferry. We can catch a *matatu* there for the airport.'

'You're the boss,' Craw said. The map seemed to steady all of them. Alan noted that it seemed to resolve any doubts the three merchant marine sailors might have had about his leadership.

'Why the airport, sir?' the white sailor asked. 'I'm Matt Jagiello, sir. Engine crew.'

'I have a detachment, a naval detachment, at the airport,' Alan said. He looked at the others. 'I need to know your names. You're Patel,' and he motioned at the other man.

'Les,' the black man said in a curiously high voice. 'Les White. I'm a cook.'

Alan subvocalized *White, Patel, Jagiello*. 'Glad to meet you.'

Craw took out a somewhat mangled Snickers bar and cut it up into five sections with his big folding knife. They sat for a moment and chewed. It tasted like heaven but left Alan thirsty. They would need water soon, and reliable water was not easy to find in Africa. It was almost funny, to be lost and without water in a major African city. Burton would not have been proud.

'Okay, we're underway.' Alan rolled to his feet and started to walk. Jagiello bounced alongside.

'I can read a map and use a compass, sir. I mean, if you wanted me to. I taught orienteering . . .' Alan spared the energy to turn and look at him and noted that his face was very white. Still a little shell-shocked. Every time Alan stopped concentrating on the problem at hand, he saw the broken teeth of the dead girl in the square, so he knew that they were all suffering from it. Too much violence with too little warning.

They needed water. It was easier to concentrate on that. Experience didn't make violence any easier; it just gave the veteran an idea of what to expect, from his own body and from the violence. Alan was a veteran. He forced his mind to dismiss the broken girl and moved on.

They crossed the pale tarmac of Mama Ngina Drive almost immediately and were back on the short brown grass of the golf course. Alan could see that there were squatters under some of the bushes, but they were not moving much. The crowd noise in the distance was getting close, he thought. Alan suspected that they were moving down Ngina from the park and hoped that the Likoni Ferry wasn't jammed.

It was. Nyerere Avenue was packed with burning cars, many turned on their sides or rolled right over, and men and women running. They had to stop at a gap in the fence as a knot of schoolgirls in tartan skirts and white shirts pushed past them into the golf course, clearly frightened.

'We're going right across. Don't stop and don't get separated. If you lose the party, stay on the coast and look for the Yacht Club.' He didn't stop to argue, although he could see that none of the men wanted to cross the road. Alan reached into the helmet bag and slipped a clip into his nine millimeter, then cocked it.

'Ready?' He forced a smile. 'Here we go.'

He swung himself over the golf course fence and waited until he heard the *thump* of Jagiello's landing behind him, and then he threw himself toward the road. Nyerere Avenue was thick with people; some seemed to be refugees from the rioting, while others seemed anxious to take part. They weren't Muslims at all, but day workers or unemployed men. There were fewer women. Alan and his group hit the street in an open spot between two burning cars and, choking on the fumes, plunged across. Alan could hear sirens. He didn't look up or back but kept his legs moving.

They were not going to catch a taxi here for the airport.

There was a small wooded area hard against the Nyerere traffic circle, and Alan pushed into it past squatters, rioters, and refugees. Only when he was safe among the branches did he look back. The rest of his people were right behind, with Craw bringing up the rear.

'This whole city is a war zone,' Craw said.

White shook his head. 'Just a riot,' he said. 'Seen 'em before. Looks worse 'n it is.'

Alan suspected that it *was* worse than it looked, but Patel and Jagiello seemed to brighten up at White's suggestion. He held his tongue.

'How far to this Yacht Club, sir?' Jagiello asked. 'I'm kinda thirsty.'

'We all are.' Alan pointed at the sparkle of water ahead. 'That's Mbaraki Creek. Yacht Club's right there.' His mouth felt as if it was full of sand, and he wanted to sleep. He was worried about Craw's head wound, too; it was seeping blood again, and he didn't have a first-aid kit.

They left the wood and came out in a residential area that was obviously still prosperous. Hundreds of people were on the street and on the bare lawns, most sitting or lying down, none armed. Alan's group attracted their notice, however, and people trailed along after them, asking questions in Swahili and English. They were desperate: he was white and looked like authority. Most of them shied away from Craw and the blood.

'*Pole, tafadhali,*' he repeated over and over. And kept moving.

It took them almost an hour to reach Liwatoni Road and the entrance to the Yacht Club, over two ravines and through a crowd of refugees from the fighting. They could still hear long bursts of automatic-weapons fire and see fire and smoke coming from the town center, but the greatest pillar of smoke Alan had ever seen was rising from the docks at Kilindini, which was closer here. He could see now that the smoke was rising from one of the piers. And then it struck him, for the

46

first time, that the *Harker* and Laura and Admiral Kessler were all supposed to be pierside at Kilindini.

Alan had visited the Mombasa Yacht Club twice for functions, and he recognized it as a haven for oddball expats and round-the-world cruisers. Now its parking lot was packed with refugees, squatting on their heels and watching the smoke rise from the port. Alan crossed through them and pushed the door open and led his group inside.

Hundreds of photos and plaques adorned the walls, memories of happier days and more robust times. Two terrified black kids were behind the bar, and there was a handful of patrons, two with guns, all drunk. One rose from his chair and pointed a revolver at Alan.

'Members only, old chap.' It must have been a rehearsed line.

'US Navy.' Alan glared at the idiot, a fat man whose whole arm shook. He retreated. 'Put the gun down, mister.'

The fat man looked at the gun as if it had just grown out of his fist.

'We can't be too careful —'

Alan ignored him and the other whites, and focused his attention on the two Kenyans behind the counter.

'I need water and a first-aid kit.' Alan spoke to the nearer one. *'Baridi, tafadhali.'*

Both Kenyans vanished and then bottles of water appeared as if by magic. Alan handed them around, watching to see they all drank before he took one for himself, although the plastic Evian bottle was cold and he wanted it with a passion bordering on lust. For a moment the club was silent except for the sound of five men guzzling water. Then a big, sunburned man leaned past the fat man.

'Wha' the *fuck* is happening out there?' Aussie accent.

Alan finished his water.

'Bad riot in Old Town. Lot of dead.'

'*Fucking* Muslims.'

'It was provoked.' He realized that this sunburned Aussie was used to getting his way, but the man's manner drove Alan to antagonize him. 'The Muslims seem to have taken all the casualties, over in Old Town. Seems pretty convenient.' He looked around.

'Any of you here own a boat?' The fat man raised his hand. A woman pointed at the sunburned man. 'I need a motorboat that will carry five men.'

The Aussie looked away, but the fat man pointed to him. 'Dirk, here, has a sweet little inflatable.'

Alan looked at him. 'Good,' he said calmly. 'We'll take it.' He raised his hand to stifle protest. 'Listen up, folks. There is a bit of rioting in Old Town. I need to get these men back to their ship. I'm an officer in the US Navy and I'd like to borrow the boat, and stock her up.' He looked around, unaware that he looked like he had been through a battle or that he was radiating focus and energy. No one in the bar would have stood up to him, anyway.

'I'll help you get 'er started, then,' the Aussie said.

Alan collected another bottle of water from the bar, zipped his helmet bag, and followed Dirk outside to the club dock. Dirk kept up a constant stream of surly comments while Craw checked the inflatable, and it took the combined efforts of the Aussie and all three merchant sailors to get the engine to come to life.

'I know all about guns,' Jagiello said.

'That's great,' Alan said, 'borrowing' some sandwiches.

48

'No, really. I can shoot. I hunt deer. Well, my dad hunts. I mean, I've been with my dad –'

'Sure,' Alan said, now carrying the box of sandwiches out to the boat.

He needed to get going; the pause was costing him his edge. He couldn't lose his own worst-case scenario that the *Harker* was the target of an attack.

Two minutes later, they were in the boat and headed down the creek to the harbor, the inflatable low in the scummy water, with five of them filling every inch of her hull and her little engine pushing them along.

It was less than a kilometer to Kilindini Port, a simple piece of navigation, given that they had only to traverse the creek and turn north, and that their boat drew less than six inches of water. Alan passed the helm to Patel; the merchant marine sailors were actually sailors, with experience in boats that Alan and Craw lacked. Various technical aspects and a lot of creeping, dirty water occupied Alan's mind for the first few minutes, but after that he was a passenger, free to let his mind wander on what might be ahead of him and what he had left behind. And then they left the mouth of the creek and turned north, and suddenly all the devastation of the explosion was visible at once.

The *Harker* lay half on her side in the mud at the end of Pier One, her tops on fire. The gantry crane at her berth was toppled over and afire, and a barge of some sort, probably petroleum from the smoke, was ablaze from stem to stern at a mooring fifty yards out. The smoke from the burning barge was what had made the giant black fist in the sky, and the curtain of black smoke lit with bale-fire cut off Alan's view of the northern part of the port. There appeared to be another fire up by Pier Six, although whether it was a secondary from the main explosion or a separate device he couldn't tell.

Already he assumed the explosions were deliberate.

Jagiello said something in a choked voice. Patel's knuckles were white where he gripped the tiller.

'Holy shit,' White muttered. He looked to Alan for direction. 'We going there?'

Alan thought of the admiral's inspection tour; of how he had dropped Laura at the *Harker* less than two hours ago.

'Yes,' he said tersely.

Patches of oil, some burning, heaved on the water. Alan directed the boat to the empty side of Pier One, whose bulk would protect them from the heat of the burning ship. A ladder ran up to the pier. He could see movement on the *Harker*'s superstructure, probably a fire party, but crouched down now in the lee of the structure.

Craw pointed up beyond the giant cranes and port offices to the blue metal of the main gate. GSU trucks and a crowd – difficult to see whether they were protestors or rioters, but then Alan saw the flash of rifles. The crowd was being swelled from the rear by people coming down Moi Avenue; some in front were trying to climb the fence. The man on the wire fence closest to him wore a Chicago Bulls T-shirt, and his head was bare. He was not a Muslim. The riot had become general.

The inflatable kissed the base of the ladder and sat there, rising and falling in the turbulence of her own wake. Alan tucked his pistol into his waistband at the back and grabbed the ladder with his maimed hand

and hung. Then he reached up with his right hand and took a firmer hold and began to climb as Craw grabbed on below him. He had to climb slowly because his left hand couldn't bear weight – climb, pause, climb, pause. At the top at last, he pulled himself on to the pier. It struck him an instant later that it was a shambles.

Whatever had hit the *Harker* had spread paper and cloth and jagged metal and several waiting cargoes over the pier. Fresh vegetables, probably intended for the battle group, had been stacked here by the ton; now they and their thin-walled wooden crates made a decomposing carpet.

A wave of heat from the burning oil barge struck him, enough to suck the air from his lungs. The stench of petroleum was overwhelming.

The fire crew on the *Harker* was yelling at him, but there was so much noise he couldn't hear them. He turned and helped Craw up the last step of the ladder. Craw's face showed the same shock that Alan assumed his had at seeing the orderly pier they had left that morning turned into a giant garbage heap. Oddly, where the superstructure of the *Harker* had stood between the pier and the blast, a few stacks of pallets still stood as reminders of what the pier had looked like before the explosion. Their survival told him that the explosion had occurred between the *Harker* and the oil barge.

'That's gon' take a damn sight of cleaning,' Craw said, his hands on his hips.

Something whickered through the petroleum-laden air between them. Alan was slow to grasp what it was, and Craw looked up at the superstructure of the *Harker*.

'We got to call the *Jefferson*, Commander. This looks deliberate.' He was taking in the angle of the explosion and its shadow.

Alan heard a high-pitched whine behind him, and his mind, filled with the fire, the damage to the ship, and the chaos on the dock, failed to understand it. If he thought about it, he marked it as another spent round, perhaps from the GSU up at the main gate. He was reaching into the helmet bag, rummaging for his international cell phone, when Craw leaped into the air and fell full-length on a heap of cabbage. Alan bent down: Craw's face was ruined. A bullet had entered at his right temple and taken his lower jaw as it exited. But it didn't matter. Craw was dead. *Martin Craw was dead.* Alan finally grasped that a sniper was shooting at them, had been shooting for three or four shots. His hand closed on the cell phone and it all made sense: the fire crew huddled behind the superstructure, trying to get their attention, the little signs of bullets in the air. He flattened himself in the garbage and a saw-like scrap of the crane ripped into his ribs. White's head came up over the edge of the pier.

'Sniper!' Alan yelled. White ducked. Another round hit just to the right of Alan's head, which he had thought was in cover.

Martin Craw was dead.

USS *Thomas Jefferson.*

The flag communications officer laid his hand on Peter Beluscio's arm and interrupted him in mid-sentence. Beluscio, flag chief of staff and a captain with a recent date of rank and the touchiness to go with it, whirled, his eyes fierce. Beluscio was a tense man, at best; with the admiral ashore, he was right at boiling point. But the comm officer didn't budge; instead, he pulled him away from the intel officer with whom he'd been talking. A rating who was watching expected an outburst but there was none: the chief of staff, seeing the other officer's set, white face, let himself be led aside.

'Maybe a terrorist act at Mombasa.'

The two men stared at each other.

'A US ship called the *Harker* has had some kind of explosion in the harbor there. Comm just got a message from their radio, pretty garbled. Asking for help. Sounds like mass confusion there – something about rioting on the dock, gunfire; it isn't clear.'

The chief of staff's thin face was drawn very tight. 'The *Harker*'s the ship the admiral was supposed to visit today.' His face had lost its color, too. 'You heard from him?'

'You were the last one to talk to him – 0600 or thereabouts? Since then –'

'Jesus. Check with his hotel. Bilton's with him, flag lieutenant. See if he knows anything.' He shot his lower jaw forward, always a sign he was near panic. 'Jesus.' He looked up quickly. 'What kind of help they asking for?'

'It's still coming in. Radio guy said there's wounded. Something about being hit by glass himself, plus there's a sniper – it's a real mess –'

Beluscio wiped his hand down the sides of his mouth. 'Jesus. Oh, Jesus –' He strode out of his office and along the passageway. 'Walk me down to Flag CIC.' He put his head in a doorway. 'Dick! Come with me!' Then he was out again and moving, his presence opening a path before him. 'Get everything you can on this ship, why it's there, the ball of wax. Get intel to prep a brief on known threats in the area, in case this was really terrorism. Also local facilities – Jesus, what's the hospital situation there? – better put our hospital on alert in case we have to bring wounded here. Jesus, with AIDS and all, what're the local hospitals like? There must be an advisory on that.' His face was a deep scowl. He was thinking that he was six hours' flank speed from Mombasa; should he order part of the BG there for a show of force? Christ, his ass would be grass if he did that and he was wrong. He needed information, more information, lots of it. 'Check for local contacts – didn't there used to be an air force unit there? And the naval attaché at the embassy, but, shit, he's in Nairobi. He may have something, though. Now, this ship, the *Harker*, what's the crew size? How many potential wounded we looking at? Get on it –'

Mombasa.

Alan raised his head and tried to take his bearings. The pier stretched away like a nautical garbage dump in front of him and, although the first crane was a wreck, toppled by the direction of the blast, the second and third still stood. Even as he looked at the cranes he saw a flash of movement in the cab of the crane by berth number two. The sniper. He was changing magazines. Alan rolled over the edge of the pier and grabbed the ladder with his good hand and found himself on the same rung as White.

'Down.'

'Where's Mister Craw?'

'Dead. Now, *go down*!'

Alan followed him down the ladder and fell awkwardly into the boat. He turned to Jagiello, now at the tiller. 'Farther down the pier. Opposite berth three, if there's a ladder.'

The little boat chugged into the shadow of the warehouse that dominated the north end of the pier and cut off any view of the main port. There was a ladder below berth three; the crane at Pier Two was invisible now on the far side of the pier. Alan set himself to climb the ladder; this time, he barely thought about it. White and Patel made to follow him. Alan waved them back.

'Stay here. Try to raise somebody on the cell phone; I've got numbers for the *Jefferson* in memory.' White nodded; he already had the phone in hand. 'If I don't come back in half an hour, get back to the Yacht Club and hole up there.'

'Our mates are on the *Harker*.'

'The *Harker* is on fire and your mates can't reach it because of a sniper. You can't help them unless you can find a way to get them off.' Alan looked up the ladder. 'Frankly, if I'm not back in half an hour, I don't really give a shit what you do.' He started climbing. *Bad command style.*

He raised his head over the edge. He was on the other side of the sniper's crane now, and unless the man actually read minds, he was unlikely to switch his focus from the *Harker* to the empty end of the pier. Alan moved as quickly as possible, headed for the base of the third crane. As he rounded it he saw motion, and without volition he had his automatic in his hand and on the man's center of gravity, and then he froze and forced the muzzle up and away from him. The man had a fixed smile on his face and everything about his posture said 'no threat.' He was big and very black, almost blue, naked to the waist, stinking of sweat even above the petrol fumes.

He put his hands up, but he smiled. '*Hakuna matata, bwana!*' he said through very white teeth. 'No problemo, man! I ain' got no gun.'

He didn't, either, or if he did, it was very cunningly

hidden. The man didn't look dangerous. He looked excited, even interested.

'Who are you?'

'I da crane man, *bwana*.' He bobbed his head. 'Big blast come, *booom*! An I get down real fas'. Then crazy man start shootin' an' I stay down.'

'Does this crane work?'

'She mine an' she work fine!'

Alan took the plunge. 'I have to get the sniper up there. From this crane.'

The other man looked at him and whistled. Alan ignored him and started up the ladder inside the crane's pedestal, but the other man caught at his leg.

'Where you get him from?'

Alan looked up the interior. He had never been in one of the giant cranes, and he had no idea how to get around one. He had intended to improvise.

'I don't know.'

'I get you into the cab. You go out the arm, yeah? And maybe I give you a little help from the crane. It still have powah; I can feel it.'

Alan shrank against the side of the ladder and let the big man go by. It was odd, because the big man's plan sounded much better, but Alan missed the surge of adrenaline that had carried him this far. He wanted to get it over in a rush. He followed the man up into the cab, another long climb that made his left hand ache.

The cab had had Plexiglas windows, but they were long gone, probably ripped out by the operators when the airconditioning failed. Alan ducked as soon as he got into the compartment; he was at the same level as the sniper now and could see him clearly less than fifty meters away. Close enough for a good man with a rifle to kill them both in two or three shots, even through the metal sides of the cab, and far enough away that Alan's pistol had no realistic chance of hitting him.

Alan's only consolation was that the sniper was not terribly good. He had fired at least four times before he hit Craw; that argued for a poor shot. *But Martin Craw was still dead.* Alan didn't want to face the fact that he had probably got Craw killed. Not yet.

He moved cautiously up to the bow of the cab, where a small door let out into the triangular structure of the arm – two beams below with metal plates for flooring, a single beam above, the three joined by a spiderweb of cross pieces that left a central opening wide enough for a man to walk stooped over. The arm pointed ninety degrees away from the sniper's crane.

Alan looked back at the operator. 'Will the arm reach crane two?'

'Fully extended, she will, *bwana.*' He smiled and hit a button, and the arm started to extend, internal engines powering a second, inner arm out of the first. Alan nodded and moved out along it. He felt the energy again. He was moving. He caught up with the back of the slowly extending inner arm and clambered on it, banging his hip and almost losing his grip. Now he was moving out under power, and he had to watch to keep his feet on the angular braces between the beams. The inner arm didn't have a floor.

Lateral motion shocked him, and he grabbed overhead struts convulsively, suddenly and painfully aware of how high above the ground he was. The arm was swinging, slowly at first and then faster, until he began to fear that the impact would break the arm or throw him clear. He wrapped arms and legs around the supports and clung, no longer worried about fire from the sniper; that seemed like the least of his concerns.

The arm slowed. He could see only poorly up the length of the arm, but very clearly out the sides and *down*, where it was a twenty-meter drop to the pier. Now the arm was pointing almost directly at the crane at berth two and extending steadily, the diesel engine that powered it chugging along so that Alan thought his target must hear him coming. Through the open sides, he could see the barge on fire and the *Harker*, and Craw's body lying still on the dock. He looked back along the tunnel into the cab, but he couldn't see the operator anymore. Instinct told him it was time to make his move.

He crouched over with the pistol held in the ruin of his left hand and his right hand ready to catch at the supports and began to move as quickly along the arm as he could, trying to run on the supports. It was an odd, quirky run, and twice he missed his rhythm and sat heavily, bruising his legs and only just holding on to the pistol. But now he was almost at the end of the arm. It was swaying violently, and the intense heat from the burning barge was creating a wind; his own antics made it move even more. From the end of the crane to the other cab was a ten-foot gap, and the other cab was smooth plastic and steel, with nothing to grab, turned now so that even if the sniper could see him, he had no position from which to shoot. Nor could Alan see him. He wiped sweat away with the back of his right hand.

Then his crane began to move back to the right. It moved only a few meters before the inner arm started to slide out again and Alan realized that the operator must have seen his dilemma; now this arm was moving to cross the other crane's arm. Alan threw himself to the end, regardless of consequences; he had to be there when they touched, because if the sniper was unaware up until now, he would know he was under attack the second his crane was hit by the other crane.

Alan stood in the triangular opening, his legs straddling the cable that ran the heavy winch, and watched the other arm get closer and closer. He would have to leap between the struts into the interior of the other arm only twenty meters from the sniper and fire immediately down its shaft into the cab. He took a deep breath, didn't look down, and leaped just before the cranes touched.

He went cleanly through the opening in the struts, caught himself on the deck plates, and rolled to a crouch, changing the gun from his left to his right now that he was stable and he could see a blurry form over his sights. Then he fired, double tap, and ran forward. He didn't feel himself yell, but someone was screaming as he pounded down the crane arm, firing as he went, and into the cab, where he tripped over the sill and went flat behind the console.

When he raised his head, the sniper was a little above him, slouched over the console, quite dead. Later, Alan would find that he had put six rounds into the man. Just at that moment, he was grateful to be alive, and sorry, so sorry, that he had lost Martin Craw.

2

Mombasa.
Jean-Marc Balcon had got to the port's gate before the riot started, and he had scolded and bullied his two-man crew into setting up a camera position where they could cover the event. The cameraman was as cynical as most of his sort, a Serb who had been kicked out of Kosovo and was now bouncing around the world, freelance and usually stoned, and he said that for stock shots of a fucking nigger port, he could put the fucking camera anywhere.

'The ship,' Balcon had said, 'I want good shots of the ship there.' He had pointed at Pier One and the gray Navy supply ship that floated there.

'What the hell for?'

'Because I say so.' Balcon had sworn to himself for the tenth time that he'd get rid of the Serb as soon as the shoot was over.

Then the dhow had come in and the bomb had gone off, and Balcon had started running with his crew behind him as soon as the rain of debris was over. They couldn't get really close because of all the crap on the dock, plus a small tanker was on fire and Balcon was afraid it would blow, too, and then shooting had started and the Serb had said he was getting the hell out of there, he'd had enough of this shit in Kosovo, and Balcon, because he needed him, had promised him an extra fifty and had said they could pull back some toward the gate.

And then an incredible guy, whoever he was, had gone up the crane, and Balcon had directed the filming of him as he went out the long arm and jumped – actually jumped a gap between two cranes, twenty meters in the air – then walked up behind the sniper and blasted away with a handgun. Balcon had seen it on the camera's viewfinder, zoomed in tight, incredible stuff for which he'd do a voice-over the instant they were done. And the shooting had stopped. Balcon was thinking that he'd be famous, getting the credit for this shot, and somebody in the crowd said the guy was CIA, another that he was US Navy, a SEAL or a Marine, and Balcon thought of the man in Sicily saying 'the fucking US Navy,' and he made a face. He wouldn't say it was the US Navy on air; that way, the man in Sicily wouldn't get enraged at him.

By then, the riot in Old Town had spread, and the street outside the gate was filling. Part of the crowd had been driven through the gates to keep from being mashed; now they milled around Balcon and his little crew, curious as people always are and hoping to get their faces put up on global TV. Balcon paid no attention to them except to push one kid out of the way of the camera lens; he was calculating right then how much he could get for the film and how soon he could get it on a feed. He was walking around the camera, talking on his cell phone to his agency, watching the guy start down from the crane and twice stopping to do a ten-second bit into the camera – silver-blond hair blowing a little in the hot breeze, blue shirt open, safari jacket casual and perfect. Very blue eyes.

'He's down,' somebody said in African-accented

English. The crowd pushed around him and moved toward the hell of the dock.

'Get it, get it!' Balcon shouted at the Serb. He got in front of the camera and pushed to make a path for it, and now the camera followed, bouncing, almost spinning. Balcon was panting, 'That is him – that is him –', and he half-turned to wave the Serb on, pushing his hair into place with one hand and fending off a heavy woman with the other, his microphone hand. Then they were as close as they could get and the people around him were cheering and clapping: the gunman who had gone up the crane had just come out of the cab and was walking toward them along the dock.

'Eh, Rambo!' somebody shouted, and the crowd laughed and applauded.

'Use the fucking *telephoto*!' Balcon screamed at the Serb. 'Zoom in, you moron –! Frame him, for God's sake – I want just him, not these goddam –'

He switched his microphone on and his voice got crisp. 'Jean-Marc Balcon, here on the dock at Kilindini, Kenya, where we have just witnessed this heroic moment by a special-forces agent. Here he comes – An incredible feat – this man climbed a dockside crane and took out a terrorist sniper, armed with only a pistol – Here he comes –'

Balcon tried to push through the last fringe of the crowd so he could climb up on a truck that had been overturned by the explosion, but somebody pushed back and he stumbled. 'Eh – *merde* – Hey –!' The Serb kept zooming in, kept walking forward, lifting the camera over the heads around him and looking up into the finder, and the heroic CIA specialist, or whoever he was, held up a hand – perhaps a greeting, perhaps an attempt to block his face – and the hand was clear, silhouetted against the rising smoke, three-fingered, maimed.

Then there was shooting from the street behind them and everybody scattered.

Mombasa.

Three General Service Unit trucks came down Moi Avenue side by side, herding the people in the street ahead of them like birds. The trucks were moving slowly so that the people could stay ahead, their goal not to run them down but to move them. Even so, a man was run over when he tripped and fell, the driver too excited to notice the bump among the other bumps that the already-dead made; hyper-ventilating, the driver stared wide-eyed through the windscreen, looking for men with guns, looking for the bullet that would shatter the glass and kill him. Like the other drivers, he drove bent over the wheel like a man in pain.

Black smoke was rising from the far end of Moi Avenue. Closer to them, two cars had been pushed into the street and turned over, and men in *kanzus* and white caps, men in shirtsleeves, men in T-shirts that said 'Ball State University' and 'AIDS Sucks!' were waiting behind them. Three men were siphoning gasoline from other cars into Tusker Beer bottles, and a boy was stuffing torn strips of rag into the mouths. The running men ahead of the trucks reached the overturned cars and dodged behind them, and a woman carrying a baby, coming more slowly behind the young men, looked over her shoulder at the trucks and wept and tripped on the curb as she tried to reach a doorway. Pulling herself to her knees, she scrambled out of the road. As the nearest truck missed her feet by inches, somebody fired a shot and they drove on.

The drivers stopped the trucks fifty yards from the overturned cars as Molotov cocktails began to fall. They scurried out of the cabs. Soldiers erupted from the rear of the trucks and began to fire through the flames.

Washington.

Fat-eyed, fleshy, scowling, Mike Dukas stood naked in his sublet living room. The television burbled about the problems facing the US administration. A cheerful woman was trying to make news where none existed, contrasting the incumbent with his predecessor to suggest differences that would be all but invisible to, let's say, a European leftist. Dukas watched her, suffered through the views of two experts, one from the far right, one from the center-right (so much for balance), scratched his belly.

'I hope they both lose,' he growled and headed for the shower. He had first heard it said by a black woman happening on a televised football game between Alabama and Mississippi: *I hope they both lose*. Right on. The upcoming election disgusted him. *Two rich jerks*, he thought as he turned on the water. The likely choices had nothing going for them but their limitless ambition – and their pedigrees. *How is it*, he thought as he stepped into the hot water and winced as it hit his chest, *that in the biggest democracy in the world, the two best guys we can find are both from private schools and the Ivy League?* He soaped himself and bowed his head under the water as if praying. Reaching to expose an armpit to the spray, he winced again: only weeks before, he had taken a bullet in his collarbone, and he still had trouble raising his arms. Out of the shower, he wiped fog from the mirror and stared at the scar, which started just above his breastbone and circled his lower throat like a bubblegum-pink necklace where the bullet had split and plowed two paths along his clavicle. Above the scar, a dissatisfied face stared back at him, pouchy around the eyes, getting lines around the mouth.

'Not a happy camper,' he muttered and reached for a towel. He ambled back into the living room, an ugly brown space with nothing of his own about it: he had sublet it, spent as little time there as possible. Still drying himself, he punched his answering machine, and an adolescent-sounding female voice said, 'Hi, Mister Dukas, it's me.' She giggled. Dukas winced. The voice belonged to a smart, naive twenty-year-old named Leslie Kultzke, who was his assistant and who had begun, he was afraid, to hero-worship him. 'How are you this morning?' she said. She giggled again. 'I got in early and brought some Krispy Kreme donuts; I know you like Dunkin' Donuts, but I think you should just *try* Krispy –'

But Dukas had cut her off and was staring at the television, where CNN had dumped the doldrums of politics and got itself a red-hot story that was happening in real time. Dukas heard 'US Navy' and saw a picture of chaotic motion, a street, a surging crowd, and, as the camera panned, a distant ship half-sunk by a dock, its superstructure tilted away and smoke rising from its far side.

' – *Kilindini Harbor in coastal Kenya, Africa!*' a French-accented voice was saying, his panting breath audible. '*A ship has been bombed here – nobody quite sure what has happened yet; sources dockside say it is –*' pushing somebody away, breathing heavily – '*a US vessel and that the bomb was timed to coincide with Islamic demonstrations in this port city.*' The shot zoomed in on the crippled ship. '*I am at the scene now but –*'

Some stringer, Dukas thought, his reactions flashing past as he switched off the answering machine. *Some guy just happened to be there with a camera crew.* And then he thought, *Nothing just 'happens,'* and he moved closer, squinting at the set to make the picture clearer, because he was an agent of the Naval Criminal Investigative Service, and if it was a Navy ship there would have to be an investigation. And this was evidence. The scene was frozen while a studio newswoman blathered and a line of type moved across the bottom of the screen: *Bomb blast in Africa sinks US ship –*

And then the guy with the French accent was back on screen. *'Jean-Marc Balcon, here on the dock at Kilindini, Kenya, where we have just witnessed this heroic moment by a special-forces agent. Here he comes – An incredible feat – this man climbed a dockside crane and took out a terrorist sniper, armed with only a pistol – Here he comes – out of my way – hey, you –! Hey –'*

The camera moved, bouncing as the cameraman pushed forward. The French commentator's breathing was louder as he started to run. The telephoto lens caught several figures moving toward it along the dock. In the lead, half-trotting, was a tall, slender man in casual clothes, carrying a rifle.

'Holy shit –!' Dukas mumbled when he saw the man, and he bent down even closer to the screen.

The hurrying man was heading for the ship. The camera zoomed in. Another figure, back to the camera, ran toward him, and now the camera followed, the shot bouncing, the frame teetering, almost spinning. The newsman with the French accent panted, *'That is him – that is him –'* and the running figure ahead of the camera half-turned to wave the camera on, and it was clear that it was the newsman, running toward the man who had come down from the crane. The newsman reached out to stop the tall man and somebody body-blocked him out of the way, and his muffled *'Eh – merde – Hey –!'* came from the TV. The camera, however, kept moving, and it had almost caught the oncoming figure with the rifle when he thrust out an arm, then held up a hand to block the lens. There was a moment when his hand was clear, three whole fingers and the stumps of the two that were gone, and then the screen went black.

'Holy shit,' Dukas said, 'Al Craik!'

He grabbed the telephone and punched the NCIS number up from the memory, and when the duty officer answered he shouted, 'Dukas, special agent. Now listen good! There's some shit going down in Kilindini, that's the harbor for Mombasa, Kenya. Got it? Kenya! I want fifteen minutes with the deputy in –' he glanced at his watch – 'half an hour, no bullshit about he's too busy. Number two, I want to know if we've got a ship calling at Mombasa. Get on it.' He'd seen enough of the crippled vessel to know that it was not a fighting ship but some sort of transport, probably USNS, but still within his responsibility.

He looked back at the television. The anchorwoman was trying to make sense of what they had just seen, but she was stalling while somebody offscreen was no doubt trying to get data from the Navy or the Pentagon.

Somebody else, Dukas knew, would be going down a list of Africa pundits to see who would like to put his or her face on national TV at seven in the morning. In half an hour, they'd have a line on it and a story that, if not accurate, would at least have punch and legs. *They're a hell of a lot faster than we are*, he acknowledged. *But we get it right*. Then they played again the clip of the French-accented stringer and the dock and the hurrying man with three fingers.

'Al Craik! Jesus. Here we go again,' he muttered. He had recognized Craik hurrying down the dock, recognized, too, Craik's maimed left hand. Unconsciously, Dukas rubbed the still-red scar on his collarbone; he had got the wound from the same shooters who had hit Craik's hand. *Here we go again. Do I want to go that way again?* Then the telephone rang and he picked it up, and it was the duty officer with the word that USNS *Jonathan Harker* was scheduled to call in Mombasa as of day before yesterday, leaving tonight, local time.

Here we go again. Do I want to get shot again?

He called his own office, and Leslie picked up on the first ring. When she heard who it was, her voice changed from brisk to tender, and she said, 'Oh, Mister Dukas,' in a way that made him wince again. 'Did you get my call about the –?'

He cut her off. 'Put a message in the deputy's box; mark it "urgent". Here's the message; take it down and read it back to me when I'm done. "Special Agent Dukas *urgently* requests assignment to investigation of bombing at Kilindini, Mombasa, Kenya. Important that we move quickly and have a team on-site no later than tomorrow. Dukas will be *very* unhappy if he is turned down.' Read it back. Good. You're doing good, Leslie.' He didn't give her time to hero-worship; he hit the fourth number in the phone's memory and got a house in suburban Houston, where it was only five a.m.

'Hey, Rose, wake up, babe,' he said, making his voice falsely light, 'your husband's on CNN. It looks like I got to go save his buns again.' He spent two minutes telling Commander Rose Siciliano that her husband was alive and well and on CNN; then he stared at the wall, as people will when they are in the middle of a mess of details and they want a moment of clarity, and then he put his hand back on the telephone and dialed another number at NCIS.

'Hey,' he said. 'It's Dukas. Hey, Marie, check and see if a lieutenant-commander named Alan Craik was issued an international cell phone, will you? He was doing a favor for us and the FAA, checking out security in Nairobi, Kenya. I want to know if he got a phone and, if so, what the number is. Can you do that? You're a sweetheart. I love you. No, it's real love – Romeo and Juliet stuff. It may last, oh, until lunch.' He made a big, smacking kiss noise.

On his television screen, Al Craik shot the sniper for the fifteenth time.

USS *Thomas Jefferson*.

Jack Geelin, Marine captain of the *Jefferson's* thirty-man detachment, had a message thrust into his hand in the p'way as he made his way forward toward the flag deck. 'On the double, Jack – Captain Beluscio wants you there ten minutes ago.'

'What the hell –?'

'Read it!' The lieutenant-commander was already hurrying down toward frame 133 and the intel center. Geelin broke into a trot, trying to read as he went, dodging people hurrying the other way. Three sailors had flattened themselves against the bulkhead to let this explosion of activity go past. *Whatever it is, it'll be all over the boat in three minutes*, Geelin thought. He managed to make out words of the message: *Mombasa harbor . . . USNS ship . . . possible terrorist . . . immediate help being requested for . . .*

He ducked into the next doorway and grabbed a phone. 'Gunny! Captain Geelin! Roust 'em out – full combat gear, on the double! Yeah, the whole goddam detachment – I want 'em on the deck, ready to go ASAP – move 'em! –'

One Mile from USS *Thomas Jefferson*.

LCDR Paul Stevens brought the S-3 to eight hundred feet as if he was parking it there and glanced down and around. Soleck, despite having his own tasks for the landing, was able to watch him, admiring the man's competence despite himself. Stevens was so experienced, so good, that what to Soleck was thought and work was to Stevens a set of habits, yet habits that had not grown tired: Stevens seemed always ready for the unexpected in the flight – another aircraft too close, a change of wind, a turning of the CV. Always bad-tempered, he actually seemed calmer in emergencies.

Now, Stevens rattled through the landing checks, Soleck hardly able to keep up with his responses. The wonder of it was that Stevens was actually checking the stuff that he seemed to be hurrying through.

'Fuel –'

'Right tank uncertain –' Soleck started to say.

'Eight thousand,' Stevens said, and went into the break. 'Going dirty,' he muttered, hitting slats and flaps, and the big, fat aircraft slowed as if it had been grabbed by the tail. Around it came, settling into the approach as steady as a kite towed behind the CV, losing altitude and speed and touching down to catch the two wire. Soleck thought how it must look on the Plat camera, how the LSO would rate it – another okay –

and all the guys in the ready rooms saying, *Nice job. Jeez, that guy can fly.* 'Nice landing,' he said.

Stevens watched the yellow-shirt below him as they rolled to a stop. 'Hey, coming from you, that means a lot to me.'

Three minutes later, loaded with helmet bag and kneepads and MARI tapes, Soleck was heading over the nonskid for the catwalk and a slider.

Why does Stevens have to be such a prick? he was thinking.

To his surprise, Stevens was waiting for him at the hatch. 'Been thinking about your wetting-down party,' he said. 'Just buy everybody a beer.' And went into the light lock without holding the door for the over-burdened Soleck.

Mombasa.

'We need goddam muscle!' Alan shouted into his cell phone.

'Get us some cover, for God's sake!' He had managed to raise LantFleet intel in Norfolk – a number he knew by heart – on his new, supposedly international, cell phone, but the signal was weak and the reception spotty. On the other end, a confused duty chief was trying to figure out why somebody was shouting at him from somewhere in Africa.

'Sir, this isn't a secure line –'

'Fuck security! We're dying here!'

'Sir, I got no authority.' Over the satellite, it came through as *Sir – got – o – auth – ty.*

'Chief, pass the goddam message, will you? Mombasa, Kenya; USNS *Harker*, hit by an explosion and under fire, I have a Navy admiral and an NCIS special agent missing –'

'There's ships in your area, sir –'

'Chief, our comm is down to one mayday frequency! Pass the fucking word for us, will you!'

'I can notify Ops –' *I ca – tify – ps.*

'And then call the naval attaché in Nairobi; he's got to get us some onshore support here – cops, the army, whatever – we're pinned –'

'Choppers and Marines, sounds like what you need.'

'Choppers're just more targets until we can secure a perimeter! Chief, we're a decoy – we're helpless, we draw in choppers, they shoot them down. *No* choppers yet!'

Then he really started to break up: 'You telling me the – sage – to – there, sir? Sir – me get – straight –'

At that point, his voice faded and the line began to crackle. Alan shouted, 'You're breaking up!' and he heard incoherent babble from the other end. He punched the phone off, watching the battery signal flash at him. *How much time left?*

He looked at the *Harker*'s radio man. 'I've gotta have a radio link.' He threw the cell phone on the tilted desk. It had been shoved into his hand, still in its plastic wrapping, when he had left Norfolk – memory empty, ability to find satellites untested. Now he was concluding it was a piece of crap.

The communications man looked barely out of his teens. He had come through the explosion with a forearm slashed by flying glass, had stayed at his post, put out his calls for help. 'I'm working on it. Can't you make a local call someplace?'

Alan thought of local friendly assets. There used to be an air force unit at the airport, but they had been pulled out, and it was their abandoned hangars that his detachment was to use. The British had had a regiment up the coast for decades, but they were gone now, too. He thought of the two Kenyan officers he had fought alongside in Bosnia – what the hell were their names? And where were they now? And how would he reach them? The last thing he wanted to have to depend on was a third-world cell-phone network in the middle of a citywide riot. Would rioters tear down cell-phone towers? he wondered. Why not? As useful as burning cars, wasn't it?

Suddenly, he said, 'The Kenyan Navy – Jesus, they've got to be here somewhere! There's got be a Kenyan naval facility at Mombasa!' He picked up the cell phone and punched in a number that he hoped was right. 'NCIS, Washington – they can find the Kenyan Navy for us. Shit –!' He looked around a little wildly; the cell phone wasn't connecting with a satellite. 'All this fucking metal –!' He stared at the communications man. 'You got any local telephone numbers?'

The man opened his hands in helplessness, then gestured around them. The comm office was a mess; the ship had tilted, and what hadn't been shaken by the blast was now tipped on the floor – pubs, gear, a cup of long-forgotten coffee.

'What's your name?'

'Uh, Hansen – Joe.'

'Hansen, we've got to get a number for the Kenyan Navy.' He punched the numbers for NCIS Washington into the cell phone. It was ridiculous: he was halfway around the world and he was calling home. 'If it doesn't work, try a local operator. Try directory assistance, whatever the hell they call it here. Try our embassy; that's in Nairobi. Try –'

A dark head popped in the broken door. 'Fireboat is pumping water in – they think they got the fire limited now –' It was Patel, the Indian who had come down from the riot with him.

Alan ran out to the catwalk that curved around the superstructure. Water began to fall on him like rain: the fireboat.

'Great –!'

A bullet pinged off the steel bulkhead.

'Oh, shit –!' Instinctively, his wounded hand contracted into what was left of a fist.

Somebody had started shooting from one of the warehouses along the dock. Not a very accurate shooter, but real bullets. The few men available to do damage control on the *Harker* were belowdecks, thus safe from sniping; the wounded were up on the main deck now, protected for the moment by the ship's list to port. But up here on the superstructure, they were exposed.

Three levels above him, Jagiello, another who had come with him from the city, was supposed to be sitting with the rifle Alan had taken from the sniper. He was a deer hunter, he had said. He'd drill anybody who tried anything.

Well, why wasn't he shooting?

Alan crouched behind the solid starboard rail. 'Hansen!'

'Sir –?'

Alan looked up, waved him down. 'Get down on the deck –!'

'Get out here but keep down!' When the younger man appeared, ape-like on toes and fingertips, he shouted, 'Get down! Way down – that's it. Try that cell phone out here.'

'I've got to get a radio hookup.'

'Try the cell phone – that's an order.'

Neither of them was sure that Alan had official authority on the *Harker*, but Hansen seemed to recognize that Alan had authority of a different kind. He rolled on his elbow and began to punch the phone.

Alan drew the H&K and tapped two quick shots in the general direction of the sniper. 'Fat lot of good that'll do,' he muttered. *Where the hell was the guy with the sniper rifle?* He peered out through the gap between the steel plates of the bulkhead. The warehouse had a long row of clerestory windows, the glass blown out of every one by the blast. The shooter could be in any of them. It hardly mattered; the range was ridiculous for a pistol, anyway. Still – He saw movement, aimed quickly, fired. Behind him, Hansen was muttering into the cell phone, his long hair plastered to his head by the falling water.

'Got them?'

Hansen held up a hand, shook his head. Alan looked again at the warehouse, saw a silhouetted head, aimed more carefully and fired. Hadn't there been some famous pistol shooter who enjoyed shooting at gallon jugs at a hundred yards? Oh, yeah. *Do better throwing wads of Kleenex.*

'They won't talk to me,' Hansen said behind him. His young face was red with anger. He held out the phone. 'They're asking me for ID.'

Alan grabbed the phone. 'They still there?' He slammed the cell phone against his ear. 'Hello! Now listen up. This is Lieutenant-Commander Alan Craik, US Navy.' He rattled off his service number. 'I'm under fire and I need help and who the hell are you?'

'Uh – sir, this is Special Agent Gollub, NCIS Washington. Uh, sir –'

'Goddamit, Gollub, don't dick with me! I'm on a

ship that's been hit by an explosion, people are shooting at us, and I've got one goddam pistol! Get me some fucking help!'

'Sir, we're the Navy's investigative serv –'

'Then fucking investigate! I want the contact info for the Kenyan naval facility, Mombasa, Kenya. Right now! Do it!'

'Uh, sir, your language is not –'

'Do you know Mike Dukas?'

'Uh, yessir, I know Special Agent Dukas by sight and repu –'

'Well, if you don't find me that information *right now*, I am personally going to have him tear your fucking throat out, because he is my asshole buddy! You follow?' He put his eye to the gap in the steel plates, saw the head again, and fired. 'Did you follow me, Mister Gollub? Hello? Gollub? Goddamit –!'

'You want the Kenyan Naval Maritime Patrol Center, Kilindini, Kenya. The telephone is 596–987. They communicate on the following frequencies: a hundred and –'

'Don't tell me; tell this guy.' Alan handed the phone to Hansen. 'Get the phone number; screw the frequencies.'

He looked through the gap again, saw the head, fired three shots. *There! Bang-bang-bang – body, body, head! Right? No, missed with every one.*

Gallon jugs at a hundred yards. *Jesus!* 'Where's that guy with the sniper rifle?' He tipped his head back, looked up the side of the superstructure. 'Hey! Yo!' *What the hell was his name?* Jagiello! 'Jagiello, what the hell are you doing?'

He scuttled into the comm shack after Hansen. 'You get the number?'

'That guy said he was going to report you.'

'Right, I'm really worried about that. Did you get the number?'

'Yessir. What you want me to say?'

'You say that Lieutenant-Commander Craik, US Navy, is asking – *asking* – for their support and cooperation. He is under fire on USNS *Harker*, hit by an explosion thirty minutes ago. We are in a hot zone – use those words, "hot zone". They got a problem, give me the –'

Both men lifted their heads as the unmistakable sound of a rocket engine whooshed closer. Hansen's eyes were wide. 'Hit the deck!' Alan shouted, but the missile was already by them, the sound decreasing, and then there was an explosion.

'Sir, sir –!' It was Patel, the lookout on the bridge. He came scrambling down the catwalk, half-fell into the room, still on all fours. 'Sir, they are shooting missiles at the fireboat! Now *it* is on fire!'

Houston.

Rose Siciliano Craik was accustomed to waking with first light. Mike Dukas's call had come a little earlier than that, but now, fifteen minutes later, she was up and moving quickly through the habitual motions of the morning. Brush teeth, shower, turn on television; dress in T-shirt and jeans and slippers, make coffee, watch the clip on CNN, check e-mails; feed the dog, check the kids (both still sleeping), drink coffee. Try not to think about where her husband was. Make lunches while standing at the kitchen counter, a book of engineering drawings of the space shuttle open in front of her, because she was beginning astronaut training.

Try not to think about her husband.

Try not to think about her mother.

Her father had called her last night. Her mother, he said, had 'gone funny.' It had taken her a while to get him to explain what he meant. Her mother was forgetting things. Had been, he confessed, for some time. *I didn't want to worry you.*

Thinking, when she wasn't thinking about her mother, of that three-fingered hand coming up on the television screen, knowing how much the wound dismayed him. A proud man, perhaps vain, hating disfigurement; former wrestler, too aware now of holds he couldn't make. *Stupid little things really throw us*, she thought. *Poor guy.* His first lovemaking had been awkward, hiding the hand. At dinner, he had kept it in his lap.

Her mother had got lost walking to the store, her father had said. She had been walking the route for twenty years. She worried that black people were coming into her house. He had found her nailing the windows shut.

Rose wrapped the lunches, hers and Mikey's and the baby's for day care. She flipped from channel to channel, looking for more news. Most of them had the story now, but CNN had the most, the best. Still, there wasn't enough to know what was going on.

She worried. *He could be dying. Dead.*

She worried about him because he was a risk-taker, impetuous. A glory hound, some Navy people said. No. More like a poet with balls of steel – idealist, hardcase.

She had a tough day ahead. Two hours in the astronauts' gym for VO2-Max and heart tests; an hour underwater in mock-zero-gravity, two hours hands-on on the engineering of the shuttle. Plus, just thrown at her by Mike Dukas, an obligatory half hour with NASA security to plan protection for her and the kids.

'For what!' she'd protested. 'What am I being protected from, for God's sake?'

Mike knew her temper and wasn't phased by it. Mike was in love with her, but he wasn't afraid of her. 'From whoever blew up that ship, babe. Listen to me! The family of every man on that ship is going to get the same message today – maximum alert, get security, protect yourself! It's Uncle's standard OP when there's terrorism.'

'But why me? Mike, I'm up to my ass in work as it is!'

'Because your husband's on the ship now and because he put his face on TV for every goddam terrorist in the world to see. Babe! Trust me!'

'Oh, yeah.' She had pretended to argue, but she saw the point. If not for her, then for the kids. Dukas was to get on to NASA security as he soon as he had hung up from talking to her; she was to warn Mikey's Camp and Bobby's day care.

She wasn't afraid for herself. But she'd kill to protect her children.

Reminded, she went back into the bedroom and slid open the drawer on her side. There, in a locked metal box, was her armpit gun, a Smith & Wesson Model 15. A revolver. Some guys had laughed at her for picking a revolver. But she liked the feel of it and the no-bull-shit simplicity of it, and she liked the .38 Special plus-Ps that she shot in it. 'Not a lady's gun,' the fat man in the gun shop had said to her when she bought it, and she had said, 'I'm not a lady.'

She aimed it at a spot on the wall. The sights lined up as if they had been programmed. She dry-fired every day, hit a range at least once a week, shot fifty-yard combat courses for fun.

There's an old saying: Be careful of the man – or woman – who owns only one gun. They'll really know how to use it.

Two empty speedloaders were in the box with a carton of plus-Ps. She took them back to the kitchen and loaded them while she watched the news.

Nothing really new. Her husband was suspended in time and space, his three-fingered hand held out to the camera, trotting toward risk.

She worried. About him. About her mother. She didn't even like her mother; what was she worrying about? Her father, whom she loved, and the effect on him? Or was the link to her mother too strong for 'liking' to even matter?

She worried.

She wanted to talk to her husband. She wanted to hear his voice. To know he was alive.

She went back to the television.

USS *Thomas Jefferson.*

Captain Beluscio's voice sounded strangled with tension. 'Now what?'

The comm officer had just been handed a message slip and was reading quickly. 'A message from the *Harker*. "Mob action in city and at dock gates. Local fireboat hit by shoulder-fired missile or grenade. Recommend send no air or surface help until situation resolved. Signed Craik."'

The captain stared. 'Who the hell is *that*?'

'Unh, the O-in-C of the S-3 det is named Craik. The guy they had to fly out of Pakistan a few weeks back, he lost part of his –'

Beluscio made an angry sound. *Friend of Rafehausen's*. The chief of staff and Rafehausen were cat and dog – too close to each other in rank, with Rafehausen having only days of seniority; too different in temperament, the CoS tense, quick, Rafehausen laid back. And the two men too often treated as opposites by the admiral, who liked competition among his officers.

'Craik,' the chief of staff growled now. 'I remember. What the hell is he doing in Mombasa?'

The other man dared to grin. 'You can watch him on CNN, sir.'

Mombasa.

Alan duckwalked along a line of wounded men, six in all. Cook White had patched them up, but there was blood on the deck, and one man was pumping blood from an almost severed leg despite a tourniquet.

'I got to get medical help!' White was saying.

'Nothing's going in or out of the docks.' He looked down at the blood that was spreading slowly over the chipped gray paint of the deck. 'Anyway, we can't use local blood. Navy policy.'

The black man stared at him. What Alan had said didn't register. 'They could send in a rescue chopper!'

'Yeah, they could, if people weren't shooting at us.' He glanced back toward the dock, but the tilt of the deck hid everything; he saw only thin, gray cloud.

'This man gonna *die* if he don't get help!'

Alan gripped his big upper arm. 'Save the ones you can save.' That was the moment when he realized that they all might die there. It hadn't occurred to him before – but here they were, cut off from the city, easy targets, with Alan the only shooter. He was carrying the sniper rifle himself now, because Jagiello, it turned out, had panicked and forgotten to take his safety off when the shooting started.

Alan looked up at the blown-out windows of the starboard wing of the bridge.

'Patel!'

The dark head of the lookout appeared. 'Sir!'

'What're the Kenyans up to?'

'Very active in aid of finding the missile launcher! Twenty or more guys running about! Some shooting!'

Hansen had got on to the Kenyans twenty-five minutes before. Now, two hundred feet beyond where the *Harker's* sloping deck met the water, the crippled fireboat, its radars shorn off and its deck littered with metal fragments, had stopped pumping water on the *Harker* but had stabilized itself. Alan had to be grateful for the hit on the fireboat, because, without it, the Kenyan Navy wouldn't have come out.

Beyond the fireboat, a Kenyan Nyayo-class Thornycroft cruised slowly between the docks; beyond it, eighty yards from where he stood, he could see the tiny figures of Kenyan sailors swarming over an anchored dhow. He guessed that they were searching the ships there – too late – for more snipers and missile launchers.

It occurred to Alan that the hundred-foot Kenyan patrol boat carried a potent surface-to-surface missile that he hoped they wouldn't decide to use in these close quarters. As if in answer, the boat could be heard to back its engines, bringing it to a stop, and at once a 20mm repeating cannon opened up. Instinctively, Alan ducked, but he heard the rounds hit behind him and knew that the Kenyans had solved the problem of the sniper in the warehouse: they had taken out what was left of every window in the wall – and the wall, as well. (*And collateral damage beyond?* he was thinking as he ran to a ladder and started for the bridge.)

It had turned out that the Kenyan Navy had a facility two docks down from where the *Harker* lay. They had gone on full alert when the explosion had gone off, putting their three boats to sea and hunkering down for some kind of assault, but they never explained why they had not at least sent somebody to gather intelligence on what had happened. Alan suspected some sort of wrangle between the Navy, a minor part of the Kenyan establishment, and the army, with the GSU thrown in on the army's side. More to the point, perhaps, was the huge fuel depot that sat behind where he now knew the Navy installation was: they were guarding that, they said, because if the explosion that destroyed the *Harker* was repeated there, all of Kilindini, maybe all of Mombasa, could be afire. At least that was the explanation the government would give later, although by then there were rumors that somebody had ordered the Navy to stay in barracks to keep them from helping the *Harker*.

Alan ducked as he came out on the bridge's wing. He glanced aside, saw the shattered roofline of the warehouse.

'Done nicely,' Patel said from the windowless bridge. 'Very nicely.'

Alan went up one level to the communications space, where Hansen was still trying to patch in a secure transmission unit.

'How you doing?'

Hansen had established a radio link to the *Jefferson*, but it wasn't yet secure. Until he had secure communications, Alan couldn't tell the CV anything but the bare bones of what was happening. He had been trying to raise LantFleet, Norfolk, on his cell phone again, but, as soon as he got somebody on the line, he'd lose the connection. He tried once more, waited two minutes, then gave it up. He laid the cell phone on Hansen's table. 'If they call back, tell them I tried.'

There was firing far up the dock. Presumably, the Kenyan sailors had found the missile launcher.

If they could secure the area – *if*, the Big If, and *if* the Kenyans would stay with them – he could call the *Jefferson* and tell them to fly in Marines and medics. It was an irony of the situation, of course, that when he could do that, they would already be more or less secure.

Twenty minutes later, Alan was heading below to check on damage control when a snappy-looking black man in a pale blue uniform shirt and body armor came striding over the deck toward him. He was smiling, but he was clearly not going to kiss any white man's butt.

'Ngiri, Maiko, lieutenant, Kenyan Navy.' He gave a partial salute. 'You are in charge?'

Alan nodded.

'You are civilian?'

'Craik, Alan, lieutenant-commander, United States Navy.'

'Oh!' Ngiri snapped to, really saluted, put on his helmet and fumbled with the chin strap. 'Sorry, sorry, sir, they said this was a civilian ship –'

Alan waved all that away, pulled the man into the shade and relative privacy of a bulkhead. 'What's the situation up the dock, Lieutenant?'

'Neutralized.' He got the buckle fixed and snapped to again. 'One shore party, under my direction, sent to neutralize missiles launched against our fireboat: mission accomplished, sir.'

'What'd you find down there?'

'Two Islamic terrorists, sir. One launcher, I think a bazooka. Bazooka?'

'Yeah, could be – bazooka-type, yeah, could be one that hit your fireboat.'

'And two surface-to-air missiles.'

Alan stared at him, stunned. A SAM could have taken out a helo – of course, that had been the intention. The explosion on the *Harker* was supposed to bring in help; the SAMs and the snipers would then destroy the help. Alan thought that through, then jumped back to something the lieutenant had said. '*Islamic* terrorists. You sure?'

The lieutenant smiled. 'Nothing else they could be, sir. We have a so-called political party, the Islamic Party of –'

'IPK, yeah, yeah –'

'You know? Well, then!' He squared his shoulders. 'I am a Christian.'

Alan decided to let that pass. 'You *killed* both of them?'

'We did.' With some satisfaction.

'We'll want to examine the surface-to-air missiles, if we may.'

'They are the property of the Kenyan Navy, sir.'

Alan stared at him, nodded sharply. Embassy business. 'Can you tell me what kind of SAMs, lieutenant? Country of origin, manufacturer –?'

Ngiri bristled because he did not know. 'I am not an expert, sir. You must ask my superiors.'

Above, on the superstructure, Hansen was waving at him. 'Come with me,' Alan growled.

'I have been ordered back to my base, sir.'

Out in the open water, the Kenyan patrol craft was

still idling between the docks, its guns threatening the shoreline. Alan pointed at it. 'Your guys are still out there. Hang on for a couple of minutes, okay?' He guessed that Hansen had got his secure comm link at last. Could he now order in helos, with the possibility that a couple more SAMs were waiting somewhere in ambush? 'Lieutenant?'

Ngiri's face was blank. 'I will ask my superiors.'

Alan started away, turned back. 'What's it like out there on the end of the dock now?'

'Very quiet.'

'Room to bring in a helicopter?'

Ngiri had never brought a helo in anywhere, he guessed. Still, the lieutenant said, 'Oh, yes, maybe – perhaps –'

Alan took a step closer to the Kenyan. 'Lieutenant, *Mwakenya na mwamerika ni rafiki – kweli?*'

Ngiri wasn't taken in by the white-man-speaks-Swahili ploy. He lowered his head half an inch to acknowledge Alan's feat, but he didn't smile. 'Yes, we are friends,' he said, using English as if he was closing a door.

Alan didn't give up. '*Rafiki yangu, nitaka saidi yako.*' It was pretty bad Swahili, actually – he never could get those agreements of the prefixes – but it got across his plea for help. '*Tafadhali.*' That meant 'please.' In Arabic, sucked into Swahili by the force of convenience on this coast that had been trading with Arabs for two thousand years.

Ngiri gave a flicker of a smile, held up a long, thin hand like an Ethiopian saint. 'I will try.'

Alan started for the superstructure at a trot. He passed the wounded men sprawled in the shadows. The man who had been bleeding was dead.

Bahrain.

Harry O'Neill tried to ignore the knock on his office door. His house staff knew better than to trouble him when he was on the phone in his home office. He shuffled his slippered feet in annoyance.

The caller, a rich Saudi with a lucrative security contract to give, required careful handling, and any interruption of the conversation would almost certainly be taken as an insult. O'Neill, a black American with a security business in the Middle East, had learned to be careful with every nuance of courtesy.

'Harry?' Dave Djalik, ex-SEAL and Harry O'Neill's best contract operative, was leaning in the door to his office.

'Busy, Dave.' Harry waved his hand and hardened his voice to convey the seriousness of the situation and went back to his telephone call.

'Harry, you're going to want to see this.'

'I'm on the phone with an influential –' Harry looked up and caught the expression on Djalik's face. He leaned down to the phone and murmured an apology in Arabic. The response made him wince, and then he hung up. Djalik was already gone, and Harry followed him out of the office space in his house and through the foyer where a fountain played on ornamental rocks under a clear dome, and down a short hallway to the one room in Harry's compound that held a television.

'I've already watched it twice,' Djalik said. He laughed.

On the screen, a slender man in shorts was climbing out on what appeared to be the derrick of a dockside crane. The yellow lettering at the base of the image said 'CNN Mombasa, Kenya.' The camera panned across wreckage and then back to the crane.

'*The man on the crane is unidentified, but CNN sources suggest that he is a member of the US Navy,*' a hushed voice from the television said. Djalik laughed again.

'A member of the US Navy! Wait till you see who it is, Harry –'

One of the cranes was moving, the man on the derrick a passenger, the tension of his grasp on the supports around him clear even at a distance. The crane swung until its arm neared another crane, and the passenger was up and moving, jumping from one to another. A circle appeared around the man.

'*We think he's firing here, Jean,*' one of the reporters said. In the background, Harry could hear somebody talking in French. The camera zoomed in, and he could see the man firing one-handed. Moments later, there was a close-up of the man as he walked along the dock, and Harry saw the man's maimed hand and it all came together for him.

'Alan Craik,' he said aloud.

'Bingo,' Djalik said.

USS *Thomas Jefferson.*
Captain Beluscio stood in the Tactical Flag Command Center with his left hand on his hip, his eyes on a television screen that showed the CNN tape, right forefinger pressing a miniaturized headset to his ear. Listening intently to the headset, he was nonetheless giving orders to subordinates with his hands and eyes. Standing in front of him now was the Marine detachment commander, a wiry, muscled man whose short-sleeved shirt already revealed goose bumps on his arms from the frigid air-conditioning. Crew cut, scowling, the Marine looked like a boxer waiting for the bell. Beluscio held up a finger of his free hand to tell the

Marine to hang on one more second.

Beluscio listened. 'But –' he said into the headset. 'But –' Then, 'Goddamit, no, but –'

He threw his head back and rolled his eyes; clearly, somebody was really giving him an earful. He looked up at a wall clock. Reaching a hand forward as if he was going to touch the Marine captain's cheek, he said softly, 'Okay, suit up and join your boys. But nobody goes until I give the word!'

The Marine was gone as soon as he stopped speaking.

Beluscio glanced at the TV screen, now back to a talking head, and turned his attention again to the headset. 'I know that, sir –'

He waved over an aide and murmured into his ear. 'I want to know how fast *Yellowjacket* can put her Marines into Kilindini Harbor – at least a company.' USS *Yellowjacket* was a Wasp-class gator freighter – a small aircraft carrier with VSTOL aircraft, choppers, and nine hundred Marines. Beluscio had decided to send the *Jefferson*'s Marines to Kilindini; the idea was that the helos could stay off the coast for at least an hour if need be, then divert to Mombasa airport if the landing zone was still hot. The chief of staff held the man from running off. 'Tell them my Marines are on the way as advance guard; *Yellowjacket* is a lot farther away, and what I want to know is how fast they can be there *in* force, *with* logistics for at least a week. Go!' He locked eyes with a female officer across the room and, eyes open in a question, mouthed the name: *Craik?* The woman shook her head, shrugged, palms up.

The captain swung around and pressed his whole hand against his ear and all but shouted, 'No!' He listened, eyes wide, mouth open. 'I don't care who you are, you're not giving me that order! No!'

He gestured savagely at a lieutenant-commander a few feet down the space. He made equally savage writing motions; somebody pushed a message pad into his left hand. He was so angry that his handwriting became a tangle of points and edges as he wrote: *Message to CNO URGENT. Get these assholes off my back! CIA – FBI – whoever!*

He pushed the pad at the lieutenant-commander and returned to the headphone. 'Sir, you do that! Go right to the White House! You tell them you're going to override Navy authority in this area! I hope they ream your ass good. Until then, I'm in charge here, and I'm in charge of the situation at Kilindini! The *Harker* is Navy responsibility, and the Navy will investigate, and the Navy is in charge! Now get off my comm channel so I can do some real work!'

A sailor materialized in front of him. 'Comm has a secure link with Lieutenant-Commander Craik on the *Harker*, sir.'

'Well, thank God, finally –'

'And, uh, sir, Captain Rafehausen is on channel four for you.'

Beluscio had an instant realization that everybody, even this sailor, knew of his and Rafehausen's rivalry, and then he was on channel four and trying to sound neutral. 'Captain Beluscio.'

'Hey, Pete, Rafe. What's the situation?'

'I'm up to my ass in alligators, but everything's under control, okay? We're on top of it up here.'

'What's the word on the admiral?'

Beluscio hesitated. They were both thinking the same thing, he knew: if the admiral had been badly injured, the BG would need a new commander, and

Rafehausen had the seniority. 'Nothing as yet. We're assuming that he's alive and well until we hear otherwise.'

Then it was Rafehausen's turn to hesitate. 'Keep me posted, will you?'

Beluscio repressed a bitter answer and said something neutral. Switching channels, he snarled, 'Get me this Craik – now!'

Washington.

Mike Dukas strode up the corridor toward his boss's boss's office, his face severe, hardly acknowledging the hellos and nods of passing people. The meeting he had asked for early this morning was going to take place three hours late. Not really his boss's boss's fault; he had been summoned to a meeting with the head of NCIS and reps from both the CIA and the FBI, and he had decided that meeting Mike Dukas was probably less important.

Dukas had spent his time finding out who was available to go with him to Mombasa and what sort of support he could hope for. He had tried to raise Al Craik half a dozen times on the supposedly international cell phone NCIS had given him, without success; two of the times, at least, Craik's phone had been busy, so he was probably still alive. Otherwise, news from Mombasa was iffy, to say the least, that coming from the television increasingly so, as the stations went more to spin and less to simple fact. There had been a couple of long camera shots of the city, with distant smoke that the voice-over said was from the crippled ship, but who the hell knew how accurate that was? As with most TV news, what you had to look at most of the time was the newspeople themselves, who seemed to believe that they were really what was happening. Dukas had been particularly taken with a blond Brit who had worn a bush jacket and said he was broadcasting from 'the edge of Mombasa city,' although Dukas, who knew Mombasa a little, believed the guy was really at a tourist lodge about fifty miles away. Palm trees are palm trees, right?

NCIS had nothing in Mombasa. Neither had the Navy. The nearest presence was the naval attaché in Nairobi, and he didn't seem to know squat until ten a.m. Washington time, when he called to say that 'an asset on the spot' said that there was rioting by the Islamic Party of Kenya, which the General Service Unit was putting down with maximum violence and minimum concern for human rights. (Actually, he hadn't said the last part; that was what Dukas had added from his own experience.) The attaché added details over the next hour: hospitals filling; some people with gunshot wounds, a rarity in Kenyan demonstrations; firing heard from Kilindini, some of it described as machine guns; the dock area closed off; the big fuel dump by the docks safe so far. (The closing of the docks explained the end of the CNN coverage of the *Harker*, Dukas thought – also the disappearance of the French newsman who had tried to interview Alan.)

By eleven, Dukas was getting itchy. He wanted to go. He had even managed to get a tentative promise of a forensics team and an aircraft they called the Flying Trocar, an airborne forensics lab bundled into a 747. But only if he moved fast; in a few hours, somebody else would have a better claim on it.

Almost running now in his eagerness to get going, he nonetheless diverted from the straight path to Kasser's office to put his head into one of the cubicles

93

where the special agents spent their days when they weren't on a case. A bright-looking, tousle-headed woman named Geraldine Pastner was sitting there, surrounded by photos of dogs.

'You in?' Dukas said.

She grinned. 'Better than DC. We going for sure?'

He shook his head. 'I'll know in a couple minutes. Meantime, do me a favor? The clip on CNN – I want to know how they got it and who shot it. Get us a copy if you can, unedited if it's available.'

'Ask or order?'

'Ask, ask, Jesus! We don't want to get crosswise of them. Anyway, you can't order media to give up sources, you know that.'

'I know that.' She smiled; he smiled; the smiles meant that under certain conditions you certainly could lean on the media, but this wasn't one of the conditions.

Then Dukas pushed his heavy body to Kasser's office, summoned by a phone call that to him was three hours late. He didn't smile this time but shook the other man's hand, took note of the wall of citations and certificates and trophies without acknowledging them, and sat. He preferred Geraldine Pastner's dogs.

'Okay,' Kasser said, 'it's this ship at Mombasa.' He was sixty, a career NCIS man, deputy to the overall honcho.

'Right. I left you a mes –'

Hand held up to stop him. 'I got it. You got bumped by CIA and the Bureau.' He sat back, joined his hands, looked up at Dukas. 'They want it.'

'Like hell.'

'That's what my meeting was about: they want it. "Major international incident, part of worldwide move-

ment, big picture; NCIS lacks the facilities, the personnel, the experience, the –"'

'That's bullshit!'

Kasser smiled. 'Not the word I used.' He had been
a special agent for a long time. Now he was polished
a lot smoother than Dukas, but he was still a Navy cop.
'Make your case, Mike.'

Dukas hadn't thought he'd have to do so. He thought
the case made itself. Still – 'This is a Navy service ship,
considered as Navy property. In this situation – any
war or combat situation – it falls under the command
of the local authority, who in this case is the
commander of BG 9, now the flag on USS *Jefferson*.'
He tapped the desk. 'I checked with legal.' Kasser
nodded. Dukas went on. 'Explosion, cause not yet
known, but TV says a bomb, and we got no better
information. But that's what we need to investigate,
right? No, this is *not*, repeat not, an Agency or a Bureau
matter! They'll get the reports; we'll share with them
just as generously as they share with us –'

'Now, now –'

'They think information comes in suppositories and
should go up their ass for safekeeping.'

Kasser grinned and then got serious again. 'There
was also somebody from State at my meeting, plus two
guys from the Joint Chiefs. *They'd* rather work with
the Bureau.'

'They've got nothing to do with it!'

'They say they have. They're saying what everybody
on the TV is saying – Islamic fundamentalists, Islamic
extremists, whatever. There's already pressure to carry
out a punitive strike.'

'Without an investigation?'

'Osama bin Laden. They've got a contingency plan.'

'This only happened a few hours ago!'

'It isn't just this one – there's a whole string of stuff. They want to use this one as motivation to make a punitive strike.'

'They call for a punitive strike before there's proof, and they're wrong, this country looks like shit! What'd they do the last time – they blew up a pharmaceutical factory in Sudan! We're not goddam Nazi Germany!'

'The Agency and the Bureau say they can have the proof in seventy-two hours.'

Dukas banged his fist on the arm of his chair. 'This is a Navy ship; we're a Navy investigating unit; we do our own work. CIA and FBI stay out.'

Kasser looked at his hands again. 'Tell me why I should send you.'

'Because – Because I don't belong in the office doing routine.'

Kasser nodded. 'And because you got shot and you want to prove to yourself that you're okay.'

Dukas shrugged.

'You refused counseling, Mike.'

'So would you have. What do I need counseling for?'

'Post-trauma.'

'Bullshit.'

'Statistics show –'

'I'm not a statistic! I want a job!'

Kasser swung around to look out his window at the tops of trees, blowing now in a warm wind. He sighed. 'Okay, you got the case for now – for as long as I can fight off the Bureau and the Agency. What's your plan?'

Dukas, suddenly sweating, ran through it: team, schedule, forensics, support. 'I can be there tomorrow,' he ended.

Kasser nodded, but he was frowning as if the most important thing hadn't been said. 'CIA will have somebody onsite before you get there – they've got a station there, can't be helped. The Bureau, too – they're international now. We can insist that you're in charge for a while. But if you find something that doesn't go along with what they want to find, you're going to have a hell of a time.' He pointed a finger. 'You go, and go as fast as you can. You hit the ground running. I'm not going to be stampeded, Mike, but I think we can hold the line for only a few days. Maybe a week. Okay?'

Dukas jerked his head. 'Okay.'

He held out his hand. 'Go.'

Dukas went.

Houston.

For Rose Siciliano Craik, the television sets were like needles some malign power had left to jab her with. She'd manage to forget her husband and the idea that he might be dead, and then she'd pass a TV and would see some part of the Kilindini footage, and he'd be back at the front of her mind.

She had dropped the kids off and spoken with their teachers, and she had come on to NASA and spent her obligatory time with a woman in security. The idea that somebody who had blown up a ship in Africa would also reach into a day-care center in Houston seemed absurd. Dukas had said they had to 'take precautions.' Whatever that meant. Arm all the six-year-olds? String razor wire around day care?

'I've got a weapon in my car,' Rose told the security officer. 'NCIS recommendation.'

'Not on the base, I hope!'

'It's locked.'

'That's against the rules, very much against the rules, Commander.' Rose thought that was a peculiar view for a security officer to take, but she was only beginning to glimpse the culture around her. It was more about rules and conforming and looking good than she had suspected. Or, a traitorous voice whispered in her mind, than she liked.

The security officer said that Rose was safe on the base and there was no reason for a gun. Rose volleyed back with an offer to check her handgun in and out every day at the gate. She would be a good little astronaut, but off base she wanted the gun. The security officer frowned and said that unfortunately she had no control over what Rose did off the base, but she advised against carrying weapons.

'I'm not carrying it.'

'Semantics.'

The security woman got on to Rose's boss, a Colonel Brasher, and made an afternoon appointment to meet with somebody whose title was Director of Personnel Education, although she'd already learned a lot about the educating that went into the making of an astronaut, so she concluded that 'education' in this case probably meant something else. Like fitting in or getting along.

'Fine,' she said with a bright smile. She could feel the phoniness of the smile, like something she'd glued on. She hated that smile.

She was in the gym when they pulled her out for an 'urgent' phone call. She thought at once of her kids – a kidnapper? an attacker? – and then of Alan, and then of her mother.

It was Rafe Rafehausen, calling from the *Jefferson*.

'Nothing yet, Rose, but I wanted you to know we're trying. We can't get a secure channel.'

'Thanks, Rafe. Any idea how he is?'

'I figure no news is good news. He's tough, Rose.'

They were all tough. That was what they got paid for. Life was tough; they were tough. Rafe had a paraplegic wife who was pregnant; she was tough, too. She thought of her mother, who was not tough, who was a whiner, who couldn't see beyond the end of her own comfort.

'Keep me informed, will you, Rafe?'

'The minute I know anything.'

Walking back to the gym, she decided she'd get a book on Alzheimer's. Not for her mother's sake, but for her father's, because he was the one who was going to have to be tough.

Mombasa.

For the old silversmith whom Alan had visited that morning, who was not really old but was an 'old man,' an *mzee*, because he owned his own shop and had three sons, the hospitals were hell. He had always stayed away from doctors, cured himself with traditional remedies, avoided the clinics where Western medicine and modernity were doled out together, and now he was in a hospital and it was, as he had known it would be, hell.

This was his third hospital today. He had let his second son lead him through the streets from hospital to hospital, allowing himself to be pushed into doorways, pulled down behind a barricade, urged into a trot to escape the trucks and the soldiers. They had walked or run everywhere; there were no taxis, no cycle-jitneys, no *matatus*. Chaos. He wanted to go inside his house and shut the great wooden door and wait until it was over.

Instead, he was in hell. Hell had green walls, scuffed and nicked and stained, marked today with new blood in smears and spatters. Hell had a slippery floor where there was hardly room to place his small feet because human bodies had been put down everywhere. Mostly men's bodies, young men, but some women, some children. Bleeding. Bandaged, some of them, with cloth torn from garments and now sodden.

Hell had four one-storey buildings with signs outside that said, in English and Swahili, 'Maternity,' 'Outpatient,' 'Surgery,' and 'Wards.' The signs meant nothing today, because the floor of every building was covered with human bodies. The wards were full; the families who had come to feed relatives who were regular patients shrank back around the beds as if protecting the sick from the wounded. The sick who were not already in the wards sat or lay in the shade of the acacias between the buildings and waited, their cancers and tuberculosis and AIDS and childbirth pushed aside by the inhabitants of hell.

The old man plodded between the lines of the wounded. He had small feet shod in heel-less slippers; he pulled up the skirts of his *kanzu* with his fingers to keep them out of the blood and dirt, thus revealing the feet and the slippers. His fingers wore silver rings, because he was a silversmith. He looked into faces as he stepped over ankles, shoes, bare feet.

Every young man looked like his son but was not his son. When, at last, he found his son in the Maternity building, his son was dead.

3

USNS *Jonathan Harker.*

The *Harker* lay at a twelve-degree angle, canted away from the dock with her portside deck edge awash, bow-down, a third of her keel on the mud of the bottom. More than six hundred feet long, she had been breached two hundred feet back from her bow, her slightly forward superstructure taking much of the force of the explosion. The portside wing of the bridge was now tangled steel; her radars were shorn off; her forward boom had broken at the hull so that it had swung up and back and pitched down again on the dock. Steel cable writhed along the deck, its whipping path marked by smashed boats and, at one place, a pool of blood, dried now to the color of oily rust.

Alan Craik, on what had been the starboard wing of the bridge, was looking down into this metal snakes' nest. His face was streaked with smoke and dirt now, his knit shirt black with sweat. A Navy-issue compress was taped over his right side. After four hours on board, he looked both exhausted and eager, worn out and yet still keyed up.

It was three-quarters of an hour since the first SH-60s had arrived with the *Jefferson*'s Marines and medics, touching down at the far seaward end of the dock under Kenyan Navy cover, the Marines boiling out to secure first the landing area, then the dock itself, in leapfrogging moves that took them to the *Harker*. Now four Marines in combat gear guarded the deck below him, while medics worked to bring up bodies and what they hoped would be living sailors from below. The smell of burned rubber and hot metal still gripped the air. In the shade of the superstructure, the fittest of *Harker*'s crewmen crouched like refugees, spent from fighting the fire down below and trying to save their ship. Their wounded comrades had already been lifted off in an SH-60 heading for the *Jefferson*'s shipboard hospital.

Halfway along the *Harker*'s starboard side, a companionway had been jury-rigged back into usefulness, connecting the ship again to the dock. Aft, a damage-control assessment team were working their way forward, compartment by compartment. Outboard of the drowned port rail, two SEALs were in the water where the damage was worst.

'What's the situation down there now?' Alan said, jerking his head toward the chaos of the deck. Next to him, the engineering officer of the *Harker* was just back from a tour below.

'No electric, so no lights; water to level three everywhere forward of frame seventeen on the port side. Damage to the starboard side not assessed, but the senior chief from your carrier thinks there's whole frames twisted down there. Two compartments are still too hot to get into. There's some smoke – I was coughing like crazy down near the anchor locker. Something burning down there smells like truck tires. We got a Kenyan guy with acetylene from the dock; he's trying to cut into the compartment where we think the, uh – where we think –' He swallowed. 'Where they may be.' He meant the admiral and those with him.

Alan had ordered a search of every space on the ship they could safely go into. *They* – the admiral, his lieutenant, the ship's captain, and Laura Sweigert – hadn't been found. The other ship's officers were thought to be ashore, but nobody was sure; of the crew of twenty, six were known dead, a half-dozen more injured badly enough to need hospitalization, five still working.

To Alan's right sat the dock, littered with debris. On the far side, a Toyota pickup that had been chained to the deck of the *Harker* was upside down. Steel cable wound from the ship to the dock and back as if it was growing there, a gray vine; two corrugated-iron sheds on the dock were crushed front-to-back; a crane had been swiveled on its base and tilted at an angle away from the ship; meat and vegetables were everywhere, rotting now in the heat. Windows had been blown out all along the dock. Far up to his right, the Kenyan Navy had moved two trucks across the chain-link gate at the entrance to the docks and had taken up positions there, blocking the crowd outside from entering. Behind him, far beyond the cranes where the sniper had lurked, the remaining helo from the *Jefferson* was waiting, rotors turning, ready to take off at the first sign of trouble. With the other SH-60, it had come in over the water, avoiding the land areas where somebody with a shoulder-fired missile might lurk. Six body bags were lined up in its shade. In one of them, Alan knew, was all that remained of Master Chief Martin Craw.

'How soon will they know whether they've found them?' he said.

A head appeared over the rail one level above them. 'Hey, Commander!'

It was Hansen. He was still trying to make sense of

the ship's communications. He had rigged sound-powered phones aft and down where the damage was, their lines adding to the confusion of the deck. Alan now had one headset that was more or less patched into Hansen's radio link to the outside, another that was more or less patched into shipboard phones, although sometimes one worked and sometimes one didn't.

'Sir, I'm catching shit from your carrier. They say Washington's trying to reach you and we got no secure channel. I'm working on it as fast as I can! They're gonna have to go through the carrier, is all –'

'Fine – that's fine! Do the best you can.' He turned back to the ship's officer. 'Sorry – where were we? Oh, yeah – how soon will we know something?'

'Can't say.' The *Harker*'s engineering officer was a short, middle-aged man who had been far aft when the explosion had happened. He was uninjured but in shock, Alan could see; he was trying to act normal, but he kept giving himself away with a forced casualness that was grotesque in the presence of the body bags and the wreckage.

'I want you to go see a medic, Mister Barnes.'

'Hey, no way! This is my ship. I'm fine!'

'You've done great, but I want you to get yourself looked at.' He deliberately kept his tone light.

'Hey, no problem. I just –' Barnes's careful cheerfulness vanished as his head snapped around: somebody had just started up from the gaping hole in the deck. But it was only one of the medics, coming up to cool off in the Mombasa heat. 'Oh. I thought – you know –'

The comm man's head appeared above Alan, one level up on the superstructure. 'Mister Craik, I got the

STU patched in. Can you talk to the *Jefferson*'s chief of staff on six? He's hot to trot, man.'

Alan waved and pressed the earphone to his right ear.

'Craik here, sir.'

'Stand by for Captain Beluscio.'

He had already had two nonsecure conversations with the chief of staff. Alan had heard the man's tension even over the raspy radio link, remembered Beluscio's reputation for nerves. Beluscio had been an F-18 pilot, and a good one, they said; the tenseness hadn't showed until he had got a squadron command. Then it had got worse with each promotion. Odd.

'Craik! Captain Beluscio.'

'Sir.'

'Are we finally secure?'

'My comm man says so, sir.'

'Christ, at last. Any news on the admiral?'

'Negative.'

'What's the situation?'

Alan told him pretty much what Barnes had told him and added that the Kenyans now had the gate under control and the sporadic firing out there had quieted.

'That's only local,' Beluscio said. 'We've got reports of massive rioting elsewhere in the city. Naval attaché says intel there is sure this is local Islamic fundamentalists – something called the Islamic Party of Kenya.'

Alan wanted to laugh, didn't, and too late realized he should keep his mouth shut, because by then he was saying, 'Pretty unlikely, sir; IPK isn't fundamentalist and they aren't the kind of –'

'These people are experts, Craik! Don't argue with me.'

'Yes, sir.'

'I want the area cleared of everybody but my Marines as soon as humanly possible. Evacuate people to your det area at the airport if you have to, otherwise, send them back in the choppers. You in touch with your det? I want them back here, too.'

'Sir, they're in a secure area at the airport –'

'Goddamit, I said don't argue with me! I'm dealing with the big picture here! You get your ass out of there and organize removal of all personnel but my Marines, period! Got it?'

'Yes, sir.'

Then Beluscio made him repeat it all. Alan didn't say that he had secret orders to stay in Mombasa from a level higher than Beluscio's. Well, he'd deal with that when he'd got himself to the det spaces at Mombasa airport. One thing at a time.

'*Anything* on the admiral?' Beluscio said.

'They're cutting in with acetylene. They should know something soon.' He didn't bother to say that if the admiral was in a space so close to the blast that they had to use acetylene, he was gone. Well, maybe he wasn't there. Maybe he was – somewhere. And Laura?

Nobody was sure where they had been on the ship, but a wounded sailor had seen the admiral, an aide, the captain, and a woman heading down a ladder one level up and slightly aft of what was now the point of maximum damage. Where there was now a large hole in the hull; where, two levels up, the side was bent in as if a fist had punched it; where, along the deck, rivets had popped and steel plates had been lifted into the air, to land on the dock and in the water, dozens of yards away. Where they had found the mangled bodies of two crewmen.

When he spoke now, Beluscio's voice was bleak, the voice of a man who knew that he was in over his head. 'Keep me informed.'

Alan started to say something then, because he saw activity around the hatch by which the medics were getting down to the worst area. He started to tell Beluscio to hang on, that some news might be coming, and then he decided it was better to wait. No point in adding to the man's tension. Instead, he handed the comm set to Patel, and he went to the forward rail of the bridge and looked down at the scene below. Overhead, a Kenyan Navy 'gunship' – an ancient Westland Wasp retrofitted with gun pods – whupped and chuffed its way landward, hunting for shooters.

Beside him, Barnes was leaning a lot of weight on the same rail. Trying to follow the chopper's progress, he looked distinctly worse – eyes hot, skin pasty, sweat only a thin film despite the Mombasa heat.

'Patel!'

'Sir.' Patel's cinnamon skin seemed chiseled, his lean face intent.

'Take Mister Barnes aft to the medic station and get him immediate attention.'

'Hey –' Barnes protested.

'Do it!'

Below him, a black medic had pulled himself out of the distorted hatch opening. He glanced up at Alan, then looked away as if guilty. Another man was looking down into the hole, reaching forward. A third medic appeared, and together they began to wrestle a litter up from below. It held a body bag.

The black medic, the one with the guilty look, made his way to the ladder and began to climb toward the bridge. Alan watched the litter and the body bag come out. Two men were straining from below, two lifting from above. Finally, they got it over the edge of the hatch and hauled at it until more than half was beyond the edge and the two on the deck could rest, part of the body bag still sticking over the open hatch, and they stood there, bent over, panting, looking at each other, waiting for the others to come up from below.

'Commander Craik?' the medic said behind him. He knew what they had been looking for and what finding the admiral would mean. Only a young man, maybe twenty or so, he had seen blood and injuries, and he knew what death was; like a nurse or a doctor, he had a manner to protect himself from other people's pain. But now he was moved, barely able to speak. He said an odd thing, holding out a hand for Alan to see: 'I'm sorry.'

Alan thought it was a piece of wood, then realized it was too thin to be wood. Leather, maybe – the sort of thing they bought for the dog to chew on. Then he touched it, and he knew it was cloth, blood-soaked cloth. Half of the collar of a Navy warm-weather uniform shirt that had been khaki and was now deep brown. Hidden by the medic's darker thumb, as if he didn't want them to exist, were two silver stars.

'Shit,' Alan said. He looked at the medic. 'I'll have to identify him.'

'No, sir.'

'I have to –' his eyes went to the man's name tag – 'Green.'

Green shook his head. 'Nothing to identify, sir.'

'I'll be the judge of that.' And, because it had sounded harsh, he said, 'I have to try. They can't just take my word for it.'

He moved past the medic and went down the ladder

to the deck. They had marked out a safe lane with yellow tape, and he went along that, stepping over cable that they hadn't had time or hadn't been able to remove. The smell of fire was stronger, the smell of the sea, too, the offshore breeze shifting as the end of day came near. The four medics who had pulled the body bag out stood a little away from it. As he came near, one stepped forward; he checked the man's tag: Hyman, First Class.

Alan indicated the body bag. 'The admiral?'

Hyman's shoulders rolled, a kind of shrug, maybe a suppressed shiver. He was wearing a T-shirt that was brown with rust and smoke. 'We got what we could. We think there's, um, parts of four people in there.'

He absorbed that. 'Is there more to get out?'

'Well – not without – Maybe with a – special tools, like that.'

Alan nodded.

'Open it.'

Hyman unzipped the bag. A smell of overcooked meat burst up. Most of what he saw was unrecognizable, but he made out the shape of a skull, the hair burned off, the skin black. Teeth plain where the lips were gone. He saw a hand. Ribs.

'You sure there are four people in here?'

'Sir, I'm not sure of anything. There's at least three, I know that. We tried to count, you know? but there isn't enough – you know? There's pieces of metal everywhere – sharp as hell – they were cut to pieces.'

Alan jerked his head. Hyman unzipped the bag the rest of the way. At the bottom, another hand, browned, shriveled, seemed to reach up from the mass. Above the wrist, it was wearing the stained remains of Laura's pink shirt.

'Okay, close it up.' He turned away and took deep breaths. Suddenly, saliva poured into his mouth, and with it the taste of salt. He looked for something to support himself on.

A black hand appeared just below his nose. The sharp odor of ammonia filled his nostrils, and his head cleared. 'You okay, sir?'

'Yeah.' The ammonia had helped. 'Yeah.' He put a hand on Green's shoulder.

'Breathe deep.'

'Yeah.'

'Okay now? It gets to everybody.'

He nodded. 'Send that bag back on the next helo and mark it. They're going to have to do some kind of forensics on it to be sure. Where'd that piece of collar get itself to?'

'I got it, sir.' Green was still standing close to him, as if waiting for him to faint. He held up a plastic bag. 'We know the drill, Commander. Always gotta do ID.'

'Right.' He tried to breathe slowly, deeply. 'Mark off the area where you found them – put up some kind of sign, whatever. I don't want anybody in there until we get some forensics.' Thinking, *It'll be my career if we screw up the ID of a dead admiral.*

He made his way up to the bridge again and stood there, trying to sweep the stink of cooked flesh out of his nostrils with the sweet, damp breeze from Mombasa. When he was better, he got on the comm to the Marine captain and told him to post a guard on the space where the bodies had been found.

He was thinking that the situation was bad and getting worse: a ruined ship, an American island in a rioting city – now a dead admiral. Could they hold on here to the little they had left?

Far down the dock, they were loading the body bags into the chopper.

USS *Thomas Jefferson*.

Pete Beluscio winced when he looked at the wall clock. It was too late, he knew. There had been too much time. If the admiral was alive, they'd know by now: more time, likelier death. He felt a queasiness in his gut. He'd have a hell of a night now, no matter what happened after this. He'd be up, taking pills, sitting on the can, feeling like hell. *The perks of command.* Yeah.

Fuck command, he thought. Some people were born to be flyers, not to take command. Nobody knew better than he did himself that he'd reached his max when he was an exec. But the Navy said, 'Up or out,' and he'd kept moving up. Now –

A face he distrusted appeared at the far door; it took an instant for him to realize it was Rafe Rafehausen's. He felt that momentary hatred, suspicion, fear that came from seeing the face of a rival, then almost relaxed as he admitted that maybe Rafehausen was about to take the whole problem off his hands. Bitter, bitter though that loss would be.

'Pete, what the hell's going on?'

Beluscio was pleased to see that Rafehausen was stretched tight, too. 'We're keeping you informed, Rafe.'

'Jesus, it's more than four hours – they must know something!'

'You're on the links, what do you think, we're holding back?' Beluscio had let his own tension show; his tone had been harsh. A second class at a terminal looked around at them, looked away. Beluscio lowered his voice. 'The moment I hear anything –'

111

'Lieutenant-Commander Craik on four, Captain!'

Beluscio clapped his right hand over the earphone and swung away from Rafehausen. 'Yes!'

Rafe Rafehausen was puzzled by Pete Beluscio, who seemed to him tricky, overcomplex. Rafe himself was a fairly simple man, one who believed that the best direction was always straight ahead. Beluscio seemed to him always to be going one step sideways for every step forward. Like now, getting antsy over nothing, turning away when he might be getting the word at last.

Not a cynic, Rafehausen was still capable of suspecting that Beluscio might try to hold on to his temporary command of the battle group by demanding some absolute, legalistic confirmation of the admiral's death long after it was clear the man was gone. If he did –

'How long ago?' he heard Beluscio say.

Rafehausen moved closer; at the same time, Beluscio swung back to look at him.

'This is confirmed?' Beluscio's head was down now, his eyes not meeting Rafe's. He listened for what seemed far too long, then muttered, 'All four?' After a few seconds, he said, 'Well – the collar seems pretty, um, definite. Yeah, yeah, we'll have to have the legal eagles confirm, dental and all that, but –'

Beluscio looked up then and met Rafe's eyes. Switching off his mike with his left hand, he said softly, 'Craik has evidence the admiral's dead.'

The two men looked at each other. Rafe felt his heart surge with adrenaline, then with relief that Beluscio was going to do the right thing. He held out his hand. 'I'm taking command of the BG, Pete.'

Beluscio hesitated and then, nodding, pulled off the headset and handed it over, as if it was a crown he was passing on. 'I, uh – you know I'll back you all the way, Rafe.'

The two men's hands touched. Rafe took the headset and, putting it on with his right hand, grasped Beluscio's arm with his left and squeezed.

'Alan!'

'Hey, Rafe –' They were old friends.

'Fill me in, the short version.'

'Medics brought up parts of three, maybe four bodies in one bag, all cut up from shrapnel. One was an NCIS female agent who was known to be with the admiral. They found a Navy collar with two stars, same location. I've had the bag loaded for transfer to the *Jeff* so your guys can make a real ID, but – there's no place left to look, Rafe.'

'Okay. I'm assuming command of the BG, Al. What're your orders?'

'Beluscio ordered us out, including my det – the embassy told him the city's rioting, something about Islamic fundamentalists – but that's bullshit, Rafe. The Kenyans –'

'No time. Answer me one question: you want to stay or fly back?'

'I've got a mission here.'

'Good. New orders: continue as before, your det to hunker down at Mombasa airport. I'll send your second bird as soon as Stevens can have the guys ready. Okay, listen up, Al, I gotta go, but I'm depending on you there. You're the Navy's point man until you hear otherwise, you hear me? One, I want to know what happened to that ship; two, we want the bastards who did it if it's a terrorist thing; and three, we want you to protect your people and the ship. Got it?'

'You authorizing me to investigate?'

Beluscio had handed Rafehausen a quickly scrawled note. He scanned it and said to Alan, 'NCIS is putting a team together, but that'll take time. You're on the spot – make the most of it. I'll support you every step of the way. For now, hang on there. As far as I'm concerned, you're in command of the *Harker*. Can you hack it?'

Alan tried to laugh. 'I think the Navy'll say I don't have the right designator for command at sea.'

'Yeah, well, you aren't putting to sea, are you?'

'It would help if I could contact my det at the airport. We can't raise them.'

Rafehausen scowled. 'Neither can we. All we can figure, they don't have their comm on. We'll keep trying.' He glanced at the clock, then at the men and women around him. They were all looking at him, he realized. *They knew.* 'Marines are to be attached to your det, under your command. Dispose them as you see fit. What else have you got for defense?'

'One nine-millimeter handgun and a sniper rifle and some maybe-maybe support from the Kenyan Navy. They saved my ass from a missile attack, Rafe, so if you can send some sort of message of thanks, it'll help. Right now, they're back in their bunker. *Maybe* they'll come out again to help us if things get bad and I say "please" really nice. But the situation's iffy.'

Rafehausen made a face, glanced at the clock. 'We'll turn the choppers around as fast as we can; one should get back to you by –' he squinted – 'maybe 2200 local.' He looked at Beluscio's note again. 'Captain Beluscio has been prepping the gator freighter to send in more support, but it looks like tomorrow before they can get there. Can you hold out?'

He heard Alan give a wry, small laugh. 'We've made

114

it this far.' He hesitated, then said in a rush, 'Martin Craw bought it.'

'Oh, jeez.' Rafehausen, Alan, and Craw had been in the same aircrew in the Gulf War. 'We'll be praying for you, Al.'

Rafe switched off the mike and squared his shoulders. Raising his voice, he said, 'Ladies and gentlemen, we have good reason to believe that Admiral Kessler was killed this morning on a visit to USNS *Harker* in Mombasa. As senior officer on board, I'm assuming command of the battle group. I'd like to meet at once with Captain Beluscio, Lieutenant-Commander Byng, Commander Nesbitt, and Commander Manfredi.' He turned to a jg standing with Beluscio – the flag lieutenant's gopher. He lowered his voice. 'Dick, contact the chaplain, schedule a memorial service for tomorrow, subject to positive ID of the remains. But first, get ship's captain on comm and let me speak with him personally, please.'

Going out, he grabbed Beluscio's arm again. 'Pete, Metro mumbled something to me about a tropical depression that's coming the wrong way south of Sri Lanka; get a clarification and see what it means for us, will you?' He let go and turned to the flag intel officer. 'Get us a contact at the embassy in Nairobi; I want to be able to reach them twenty-four hours a day. Tell them to get my guy some protection at Kilindini – they need to lean on the Kenyans – tell them I don't want to have to bring the BG off Mombasa to make the point – okay?' He grabbed somebody else. 'Dick, we're going to have to refuel the gator freighter's Seahawks for the trip to Mombasa. Here's how I see it –'

Beluscio, left to follow in his wake, had already fallen back into the role of subordinate. He liked Rafehausen no better but felt a painful gratitude to him, as if, in over his head, he had been rescued by a stronger swimmer.

USNS *Jonathan Harker.*

Alan handed his comm set to Patel and ran his hand over his sweaty, spiky hair, thinking about Rafe Rafehausen as acting commander of the BG. *A hell of a lot better than Beluscio.* Far away, fire sirens wailed, and a seabird sailed on the wind above him, swung back as if to look again at the crippled ship, then soared away. A distant gunshot sounded.

Alan's and Patel's eyes went to the shoreline. The shot had been a long way away, Alan was thinking – somewhere up in the city, even. He heard a police hooter. He looked at Patel.

'They won't get in here again,' he said more confidently than he felt.

'I am not worried, sir.' Patel's lean head lifted. He looked like a Roman aristocrat. Then his eyes flicked over Alan's left shoulder and he made a small motion with his head.

'Sir,' Alan heard behind him. Geelin, the Marine captain, was standing there, looking truculent. 'You wanted to see me, sir?'

'Yeah, thanks – you got my request to post a guard below?'

'Haven't got the men, sir. Sorry.'

Alan thought about having called it a 'request.' He grinned. 'Something else has come up. You probably know – it looks like Admiral Kessler is dead. The acting commander of the battle group has ordered me to take command here. You and your Marines are being attached to my det.' He smiled again.

'I gonna get that in writing? Sir?'

116

'In time, I'm sure you will.' He smiled for the third time and lowered his voice. 'Geelin, I need a guard on the space where we think the admiral died so that there can be an evidence chain. Okay?'

'I'll have to take somebody off the dock.'

'Do what you gotta do.'

'What're we looking at – Arab mobs?'

'More like a few real badasses and maybe some street action, demonstrations, like that. This isn't Palestine, Geelin, and it isn't Somalia. We're not at war.'

Geelin looked down at the damage. 'Somebody is.'

'Yeah, well, that's what we're here to find out. You with me, Geelin?'

'Call me Jack. I'll get a man down below – sorry, I didn't understand before, the way it came to me –'

Alan was starting to speak when Geelin whirled about and leaned over the rail and shouted, 'What's that goddam woman doing down there! Bring that woman up here! On the double! On the double –!'

Woman? His thoughts jerked to Laura Sweigert, as if she might still be alive –

Alan looked down at the dock and saw that there *was* a woman down there. But not Laura. Foreshortened by the angle from the bridge, she still looked too tall, too pale, too – what? Sort of limp, as if her bones were made of something softer, like plastic. His respect for Geelin went up: he had never known anybody before who had eyes in the back of his head.

A Marine began half-dragging, half-coaxing the woman up the ladder.

She was white, red-haired, a little overweight, and she was, surprisingly, laughing her ass off.

She raised one white arm and reached across her own head to pull some hair out of her eyes. 'Hi!' she said.

Geelin was all but gritting his teeth. He thrust his helmeted head at hers, 'What the hell are you doing inside a goddam military perimeter –?'

Alan put out a hand. 'Hey, hey –'

'She could get killed! She could get my men killed!'

'Hey, Geelin – easy –'

'I haven't got the men to nursemaid women!' He whirled on the woman. 'Are you a goddam *journalist*?'

'Belay that, Captain Geelin.' Their eyes met. Geelin's shifted away, as if he had remembered rank and discipline. Alan said, 'I'll take care of the lady.'

Geelin's eyes swung back. 'I'll do my job, then, sir.' He nodded – a substitute for a salute? – and went around the woman without acknowledging her and started down the ladder, calling over his shoulder for the Marine to follow him.

The woman was again laughing her ass off. Alan wondered if it was nervous laughter, maybe even something near hysteria. In the movies, you always slapped the woman at this point, and she broke into tears and fell in love with you. Bad move.

'ID, please?' he said.

She used that same gesture, the raised arm reaching across to mess with her hair, the arm a frame around her head, her armpit bare and dead white, and she said, 'I'm Sandy Cole?' Squinting at him from slightly pop-eyes as the last of the sun splashed golden light on her from behind him. Then she was scrambling in a huge shoulder bag that was full of junk – he saw address books, checkbooks, lipsticks, tampons, maybe a pair of panty hose, pens, coins, combs, lists, keys – and tossing out phrases, half-finished sentences. She gave him an embassy ID badge. Her passport. A State Department card.

'Uh, Miz Cole – what are you doing here?'

'Oh, I came as soon as I saw it on TV. To investigate? I'm the Legat!'

Legat, legal attaché – from the Nairobi embassy, must be. Okay. Meaning that she was also FBI. *Not so okay.* He studied the documents, which looked authentic enough. 'Were you ordered here, Miz Cole?'

'Oh, no, God –' She started laughing again. 'I just got into my car and drove.' She held a hand over her eyes and squinted. 'You want me to look at the body or the engine first?'

He hesitated. 'What engine?'

'The boat engine. There's a V-8 –' She made a sweeping gesture toward the dock with an arm; the other was over her head again, the hand in her frizzy hair, head tipped. That way, she looked like a dancer or a model, her flexible bones bending and willowy despite her size. 'An old car engine with a propeller shaft, I think from the dhow.'

He felt stupid but wary. 'What dhow?'

'The dhow that carried the bomb.' She looked back at him quickly. 'It came in from over there –' Pointing with one hand, pulling hair off her face with the other. The hair business was getting to him, driving him a little nuts. 'It looked like it was going to the other dock, but it came very wide and then –'

'How do you know this?'

'There's an eyewitness? They have him over at the Kenyan Navy base? They also have somebody, he's totally in shock and really out of it, but I think he's either from the crew here or maybe he was even on the dhow, although they would have been suicide bombers and, you know –' She shrugged, gave a smile with her mouth closed. Played with her hair. 'The eyewitness says he thought somebody jumped off the dhow before it hit, so maybe he's a bomber? And he was in the water when the bomb went off, and he's suffered concussion or whatever?'

'You *interviewed* an eyewitness?'

'No, the Kenyans are being real selfish. They *told* me that's what he said.'

Alan was thinking that they hadn't told him any of this, but maybe Lieutenant Ngiri hadn't known any of it. Or maybe he had, and that's the way the ball was bouncing. He remembered the Kenyan sailors who had been searching the ships on the opposite dock. Of course they'd found eyewitnesses. He looked again at her documents. 'How'd you get in here?' he said. He looked up the dock at the blocked gate.

'Oh, I came in through the tank farm.' Pointing again with one of those white arms. 'I got an embassy shield on my car. Special plates. You know, they're very hierarchical here – special plates make a big difference.' She scrabbled in the big bag again and came up with the sort of leather case that cops carry shield and ID in. She was laughing. 'And I used this.' It had a courtesy card from the National Association of Sheriffs, unimpressive except for the big embossed eagle, and a shield that said 'Special Police' and '007.' 'I got it on the Internet,' she said, laughing and playing with her goddam hair and showing him her armpit.

'You're lucky you didn't get shot.'

She shrugged. 'You want me to look at the body or the engine first? They say you shot a sniper. Wow.' She waved toward the crane. 'I better look at the body first. He'll be pretty ripe in this heat. It is a he, isn't it? I'd hate it if it was a woman.'

'What do you want to look at the body for?'

'I'm trained to look at bodies. I took an extra twelve hours in forensics. After law school?' She wrinkled her nose and looked at the sky. 'I don't want to do it in the dark. But I brought a flashlight? So maybe I could. I don't know –' She laughed. 'Or I could look at that engine. Engines have numbers, you know.'

It was just what he needed, he thought – a pale woman in a long dress. A perfect target. Well, nobody was shooting. And dusk was falling. And Rafe had told him to investigate, and she said she knew how to investigate. Oh, he believed her credentials well enough, and he believed her story about using the patently fake police stuff. He'd been tempted to get himself just such crap, in fact – a badge, any old badge, went a long way in some parts of the world. 'I think I'd like you to start with the body,' he said. He smiled, not entirely pleasantly. If she worked inside the crane, at least she'd be protected, and the smell was her problem. 'You can examine the engine with your flashlight later.'

'Oh,' she said, 'cool!'

Right.

Half an hour later, he had a call from Harry O'Neill.

'Hey, *Harry*!' Alan shouted. For this man, Harry O'Neill, he was able to be *truly* hearty. 'How the hell'd you find me?'

'Al, you're into some bad stuff, man.' Harry O'Neill had not picked up his tone; instead, he sounded severe. The cellphone connection was suddenly lots better, he thought, if he could recognize severity. 'This is bad, *bad*, Al.' Harry had been a shipmate during the Gulf War, then had left the Navy and joined the CIA, jumped from that when he had lost an eye on a mission; now he ran a private security company in Africa and the emirates.

121

And he had converted to Islam.

'I'm not getting you, Harry.'

'It's all over the TV and the Net, Al – Islamic terrorists have hit another US target, all that *shit*. It *isn't* Islamic terrorists!'

'How do you know?'

'I *know*! No, I don't know, but – fuck, Al, not everything bad that happens in the world comes from Islam! The TV is jumping at it like dogs, like – wolves. It makes me sick.'

Alan turned to look aft. The long sweep of the deck was empty of people, only the containers, jumbled by the explosion, breaking the straight lines. 'Harry, you're way ahead of me – I don't know what you're saying, man. I'm standing on a ship that's had a hole blown in it; I've got a bunch of people killed, a bunch more injured. What're you telling me – it didn't happen?'

'I'm telling you everybody's jumping to conclusions.' There was one electronic break in the sentence, so that the word 'to' had to be guessed.

'Okay – but why you telling *me*?'

'Because you're *there*, man!'

'Harry, I've been running my ass off since this happened; I don't know what the hell you're talking about!'

'Alan, every time there's an incident, the first people you come for are Muslims.'

'The first *I* come for!'

'You know what I mean.'

'No, I don't know what you mean, Harry. What? Why are you saying this to me?'

'Because you're there! Because you're all over the television!'

It was the first he'd heard of it. He'd hardly noticed

the newsman with the camera; now Harry told him in detail of the scene that was on every television news show in every country in the world. A worrying fact registered – *I was on TV; I can be ID'd* – and was put aside. At the same time, a cautioner in his mind was saying, *This man is a Muslim now; how far can you trust him?*

Harry finished by saying, 'Do you even know it was a bomb?'

Alan thought fast – about friendship, about prejudice, about trust. 'Harry, you know the position I'm in. You've been in the Navy.'

'Okay, okay, I understand. I'm on the other side now, right?'

'Wrong. I'm not saying anything, because I don't know anything yet.' He was standing as far to the port side of the bridge as he could get, looking past where the water lapped at the ship's deck. One of the SEALs surfaced and raised his dive mask, and Alan could hear him blowing air into it.

'*Was* it a bomb?'

'I don't know.' Had the Kenyans told the LegAt the truth about the dhow? If so, of course it was a bomb. The SEAL replaced his mask and dove again.

'What's the evidence for Islamic terrorists?'

'You'd know better than I would, Harry. What're they saying on the TV?'

The SEAL, or perhaps it was the other of the pair, surfaced and slung a net bag into their inflatable. He hung on the side, and the other SEAL surfaced a few yards away.

'I feel very strongly about this, Al.'

'I know you do.'

'No, man, I don't think you do. You don't get religion,

Al. No offense – we're old friends; I can say that. You're not religious. You go to church, that's it. I *feel* my religion. Islam has saved me, Al. From bitterness, from, oh, shit, just indulging myself, just – I went to Mecca last year.'

'I know.'

'But you don't know what it meant to me.' He began to sound far away; was the sound of his voice changing because of his seriousness, or was the cell phone going? 'Okay, I can't explain it. It's just – it's important to me, okay?'

'Okay.'

'I don't think this was Islamic, Al. I've got a lot of ears. I'm in that business – a lot of ears, a lot of eyes. I made some calls before I got you. Everybody's in shock. It *isn't* the usual suspects, Al!'

Alan had been thinking of the Oklahoma City bombing, the way they'd all jumped at 'Islamic terrorists' the moment they'd heard of it. There was nothing wrong with basic caution in any case; what Harry was saying was only good sense. And if Harry had reason to believe this wasn't the work of Muslims – well, Harry, as he said, knew a lot of people, and he lived in that world.

Or, on the other hand, they could be using him.

'Harry, the best I can say now is I'll keep an open mind, okay?'

'What? I'm losing you –'

'I said I'll keep an open mind!'

'You're running the investigation, am I right?'

Harry knew the Navy, all right. Alan grinned. 'Not for prime time, Harry.'

'Let me help.'

'You know what my security people would say?'

'Fuck them. Al, I'm a source for you. I'm a voice from the other side of the wall. How about it?'

In one pan of the balance, friendship; in the other, religion, habit, security. 'No bullshit?'

'No bullshit.'

Alan watched the SEALs flutter-kick the inflatable parallel to the *Harker*'s side until they disappeared behind the superstructure.

'When I have something, I'll let you know.'

He thought he could hear a smile in Harry's voice, but there was static now. 'Allah be praised. You're a good man, Charlie Brown.'

'You're breaking up, Harry – I'll make it short. Do two things for me, haji – one, call Rose and tell her I'm okay; two, check out the IPK here in Mombasa and see what the skivvy is on them.'

'Shit, I can tell you about the IPK right now – Sufi – [*static*] much oriented – Aga Khan, not as much [*static*] as a lot of Islamic parties –' There was a lot of noise, and then: '– call Rose. In fact – already called me – morning – her you must be – Hello? Al –? Hell –' Pops and a rattling hiss, and then, clearly, as if from somewhere else, Harry's voice saying, 'You're my best friend, guy.'

The battery indicator told him that the phone was dead. He dropped it into his helmet bag, wondering what he had done with the backup battery – with the battery charger, for that matter. He put on the headset, checked that Hansen was still getting him. There was a moment of quiet. He might have been in some other place, standing on the bridge of a healthy ship in some peaceful harbor. Suspended in that moment, his body had the chance to tell him how tired it was: aching, shoulder-bowing fatigue.

'Last fucking chopper's leaving.'

It was Geelin. He turned and looked down the dock. He had time to see details in sharp focus: two Marines in combat gear out there, lying prone, weapons ready; the chopper rising, rotors churning up a sparkle of water drops that looked like golden sparks in the late-day light. With it went their last physical link with the battle group.

'There could be a goddam SAM out there anyplace – anyplace!' Geelin stared at the distant green shore beyond the harbor as if he'd like to nuke it. 'We gotta secure this place.'

'The Kenyan cops? Can you coordinate something?'

'*Coordinate* something? I don't even have a fucking *map*! How am I gonna tell some fucking African where I think a fucking SAM could be if I can't even identify it on a fucking map! And I'm not sending my guys out there to do it all alone!'

Alan said to himself that he wouldn't let Geelin send his guys out there even if he wanted to; no matter what he felt, you didn't send American Marines down foreign streets as if you owned them. The fatigue settled like a heavy, heavy bird on his head. He made a mental note, *Maps*. 'Right, I understand –'

'You *don't* understand! I'm not sending my guys out into some urban warfare like goddam Mogadishu to get them fucking shot up by A-rabs who hide behind women and little kids!'

'Right.'

'My mission is to protect this ship and you and the rescue choppers, and that's what I'm fucking well doing!'

'Geelin, I'm with you –'

'I had ten minutes to get intel before we took off

from the boat. I go to CVIC, you know what they gave me for a map of this shithole? The fucking *liberty kit* they give every sailor when he goes ashore! You think I'm gonna send my guys to fight with nothing but a fucking *liberty kit*?' Geelin stuck his lower lip out. His eyes were hot and hard, his face red. 'I just want you to understand!'

'I do.'

Geelin nodded. 'Get me some local plug-ins for our GPS, maybe we'll talk about cleaning out some of this rats' nest – *when* we've secured this area!' He looked around. 'Where the hell's that woman that was here?'

'Looking at the body in the crane, I hope.'

'Jesus – I don't even wanta know.' Geelin hit his hand-held again and told somebody to check for a woman in the second crane down the dock. He was still scanning the ships across the water. 'She a reporter?'

'Unh-unh. Embassy.'

'Shit. How we gonna feed her?'

'Feed her? Oh, right –'

'She's locked in here with us now, we gotta feed her. Bitch.' He laughed. 'I hope she likes MREs. You eaten?'

Alan thought about it. He'd had what was called breakfast on the plane before they'd landed in Nairobi. And then? My God, was that all today? He'd flown to Mombasa; Craw had got killed; he'd got the sniper. Laura. The admiral. 'No, I haven't eaten.'

'MREs for them as wants them at 1900 hours. Bring your own beer.' Then Geelin was on his handheld again, shouting at the gunnery sergeant to keep those goddam Kenyans out of his line of fire.

Alan saw a single star in the steel-blue sky.

Mombasa.

In the slum behind the fuel depot, where the smell of sulfur and oil was so strong it flavored the food, men looked at the evening sky and watched the reflection of fire. *Mombasa is burning*, they said, but they knew that only part of the city was burning, because where they were there was no fire. Here, in alleys laid out between shacks made of flattened oil cans, men gathered in clusters, looking at the sky and telling each other how terrible the day had been.

'Tomorrow will be worse,' a young man said. He said it with pride.

The women were in the tiny shelters. Some stayed near the doors, looking out to watch the men. A naked child, thumb in mouth, stared.

'I won't go out tomorrow,' a fat man said.

'Yes, you will.'

'I won't! It isn't my business! What's the good – you wreck the city, you burn the shops, where are the jobs?'

'This isn't about jobs, you fool.'

'Everything is about jobs. I need a job. You need a job. Allah be praised, this will be over by tomorrow and we will go looking for jobs again.'

'Tomorrow –!'

Somebody up the street yelled that the GPU trucks were coming, and the men scattered, pulling closed the doorways of the tin shacks with doors made of pieces of chipped plywood and, on one house, the door of a burned-out car. A GPU truck came down the alley more slowly than a man could walk, its sides grazing the flattened-tin walls and shaking the earth.

Houston.

Rose Craik had had another call on a STU from the

Jefferson, this time from a Captain Beluscio, who was calling for Rafe and simply wanted to tell her that they were in touch with her husband and he was okay. She had already talked to Mike Dukas again by then and learned that he was off this evening to join Alan. She had wanted to shout, *Take me, too!* But she knew she was where she had to be. Then Harry O'Neill had called – elegant, handsome Harry, who always smelled wonderful and wore the most beautiful clothes she had ever seen on a man – and he, too, had told her he had talked to Alan and he was okay and everything was going to be fine. 'You should try to call him, Rose. I'll give you the number.'

'Mike gave it to me. But no.'

'Duty calls, right?' Harry had been in the Navy; he seemed to understood this bit of Craik family ethos. You didn't play the worried spouse when things were tough.

'I'll let him call me,' she said. If he could, when he could.

In fact, it wasn't just the family ethos that kept her from calling. She didn't want to load her troubles on Alan, and she was afraid that if she talked to him she wouldn't be able to keep her mouth shut. Her mother, yes, that was part of it, but also her boss, Colonel Brasher and the 'Director of Personnel Education,' with whom she'd met ten minutes before and whom she'd despised. One of those smooth, glossy men, half corporate geek and half would-be makeout artist. He'd in effect given her a dressing-down, his eyes all the time giving her an undressing, and although he'd use words like 'team player' and 'the NASA image,' what he'd meant was *Get in line, bitch*.

'We don't want you carrying that gun.'

'I do want me carrying that gun.'

'I don't think you understood what I said.'

'You got kids?'

'We don't want to give the impression that the Space Center is the set of a cowboy movie, Commander.'

She had tried the same smile she had used with the security officer. Submissive, pert, bright-eyed. Little Miss Cheerleader. After that, she let him talk, and she smiled.

And when she got into her car, she made sure the gun was still there under the seat, with the two speed-loaders and the extra cartridges.

4

Near Mombasa.

The hotel lobby was glossy and clean and looked, quite deliberately, like hotels in Rome and London and Atlanta and Honolulu. 'International' really meant 'Western,' or even 'white.' This hotel, like three others along the strip of white beach nearby, was close enough to Mombasa that you could shop in the city's colorful bazaar, but far enough away that you wouldn't feel overcome by what one Brit had called 'miles and miles of bloody Africa.' A lot of American military people stayed here.

A handsome, light-haired man, who might have been recognized as the French-accented journalist who had scooped the *Harker* disaster, walked with the ease of the international male – whiteness, Westerness – to the marble-topped reception desk. He was dressed in the sort of casual clothes that would have allowed him into any restaurant or office – a dark blazer, an open but good shirt, blue jeans, running shoes. He had a leather laptop bag slung over one shoulder. Without his journalist's intrusive microphone, and in his fresher, better clothes, he looked quite different from the morning.

His sun-wrinkled eyes scanned the clerks behind the reception desk, settled on a young black man. Producing a French passport, he laid it on the marble in front of the young man and then laid an American twenty-dollar bill on top of it.

'I am looking for a friend,' he said. His voice had the same slight French accent as on CNN. He gave the twenty a little push with a finger. The young man looked aside and put a hand on both the passport and the bill. 'Sir?'

'My friend has been on television all day. The *matata* at Kilindini. Maybe you saw it? On CNN?'

'Oh, yes, yes –?' *The Land of Yes.*

'My friend has only three fingers on his left hand. He is in the American Navy. I thought he might be staying here.'

'Oh, yes.'

'He is?'

The young man slid his eyes to his right, toward the other clerks, to see if they were listening. He pocketed the twenty. 'I was not here, sir – but my friends here, they say that man he did check in early-early this mornin'. They talk about him when the TV come on.' His voice was soft.

The journalist said, equally softly, 'I'd like for you to find the man's name.'

'You say he is your friend, sir. How come you –?'

The journalist smiled. It was quite a fine smile, crinkling his eyes and putting creases in his cheeks. 'It is a way of speaking.' He produced another bill. 'Could you find me his name, ah – Thomas?' The young man had a plastic name tag on his maroon lapel.

Thomas bent into a computer terminal. He was a very intent young man – good at his job, the journalist supposed. He let his eyes hunt through the lobby. A woman with a tight backside and impressive breasts was crossing toward the elevators. *Look at me*, he said inside his head, and she looked. She, too, had been hunting in the lobby, so there was no magic to her looking at him. She smiled. He smiled.

'Lieutenant-Commander Cra-ik, sir. Christian name, Alan.' Thomas spread a slip of paper on the marble. The journalist took it, laughing – at what, he didn't say – and slipped it into his shoulder bag. He thanked Thomas and hesitated, looking again for the woman. She was standing by the elevators. She raised an eyebrow. He decided that he couldn't indulge himself that way, because it was dangerous to leave tracks.

'Thank you, Thomas,' he said, and, with a look of admiration and regret at the woman, he turned away. The man in Sicily was waiting for a call.

USS *Thomas Jefferson.*
Most of the det had seen 'the skipper' on TV enough times that they didn't even turn toward the set now, but to Soleck and Stevens and the aircrew of 902, it was all new. They saw the burning ship, the littered dock, the figure hurrying toward the camera that turned out to be Alan Craik (not really a skipper, only a detachment officer-in-charge, but Soleck and a lot of others called him 'the skipper' anyway), and then the brutalized hand held up to ward off the camera.

Seeing it, Soleck sucked in his breath.

Seeing it, Stevens said, 'The glory hound bites again.' He pulled himself out of his armchair and headed for the door. 'Bite mine!' he called to the room at large.

Soleck, never really ready for cynicism, was shocked. 'How can he – how can – *say* that?' he sputtered. He had *been there* when they had flown Craik out of Pakistan, that wound new and bleeding, his life dripping out on the deck of the S-3. But Stevens had been there, too! Stevens had flown the goddam aircraft and had flown it, well, brilliantly – had saved Craik's life! And now –

'How can he *say* that?' Soleck asked.

'Forget it.' Reilley was a few years older, already a lieutenant. 'He can't help himself.' Reilley had been a Stevens supporter when Craik was new and Stevens had tried to turn the det against him, but Craik had turned things around and now Reilley, too, was on his side. 'Stevens is his own worst enemy.'

'But, Jesus –' The news that Admiral Kessler was dead in the explosion on the *Harker* had hit Soleck hard. He thought that Stevens should control himself out of respect, at least – show some sign of mourning. The death of an admiral was a big thing to Soleck, for whom the admiral had been an eminence, somebody glimpsed but never known, part father figure, part hero, embodiment of the idea of 'the flag,' not the national flag, but the flag of the battle group's command. To have him snuffed out was like – he thought of it as being like the death of Kennedy, which he'd heard his parents talk about. The reality of Admiral Kessler, who had been a political string-puller and a manipulator of his officers, had never reached him.

But Stevens had no respect for the admiral and he had no respect for Craik. It made Soleck angry. It made him determined that when the det's other bird flew off to Mombasa to join the skipper, he was going to be on it.

Washington.

It was one in the afternoon at Washington's Navy Yard, and Mike Dukas hadn't had lunch. He took food seriously, considered it a sovereign remedy for illness, lost love, depression. He was also a good cook.

'You call this food?' he said to the younger man who had put take-out Chinese in front of him.

'Yeah. Shit, yeah! You don't like Chinese?'

'I like good Chinese. This is dragon puke; I can tell by the smell.' Dukas was known for his ability to eat his way through a box of a dozen Dunkin' Donuts, an entire pizza, other people's leftover burgers-with-everything. 'This is full of MSG and fifty-five kilos of saturated fat per carton.'

'You didn't tell me you wanted the gourmet health-food special.'

'You speak Italian?' Dukas gave him the arm. The younger man rolled his eyes and walked away, and Dukas called after him, 'Hey, thanks! I'm just in a bad mood!'

His mouth was full of stir-fried vegetables and pork by then, and he was opening another container and sticking his nose into it, and then another that proved to be full of white rice, which he began to mix into the vegetables and pork. 'Too much cornstarch,' he muttered. 'They don't even *have* cornstarch in China.' He dialed a number. 'Now they probably do – they probably *make* cornstarch.' He took another mouthful, swallowed quickly, and said into the phone, 'Hey, Mario! Hey, man, you coming with me?'

Mario Delahanty was a forensics specialist. He liked the idea of some time in Africa, it turned out, but he couldn't leave that day, no way.

'Come tomorrow on the Flying Trocar. Yeah, Andrews at two p.m. is the current schedule. Hey, can you get that woman in the glasses to go? What the hell's her name – Shirley? Shelley – Sheila, yeah -- uh

– right, Ditka, that's the one. She's really good. Yeah, I want her. Don't be a smartass; she's the best explosives analyst in your lab. So can we have her? Put her on the plane with yourself. I'll see you in Mombasa day after tomorrow.' He started to hang up, heard something, put the phone back to his ear. 'Yeah, you heard right: they're shooting at each other there. No, we'll be out at the airport. Secure, man! Marines! Navy air! It'll be absolutely safe. I guarantee it.'

He was back into the food, his mouth full and rice dribbling back into the carton, when the telephone rang. He picked it up and said, 'Dukas,' which sounded like *oo-kush* because of the food.

It was his immediate boss. He had had an idea. Dukas's face darkened.

'I don't need any more good men, Don. I got all the good men already.' In fact, he had put together a hell of a team: in addition to Mario and Sheila Ditka, he had Hahn, the best of the newer special agents; Mendelsohn, who had been to Africa before and even knew a little Swahili; Geraldine Pastner, a pit bull with evidence, who bit and never let go; and Keatley, who had been a Marine and believed that God had put him on earth to enforce rules. All good people, all reliable, all smart. And all eager to go because the word had reached them that Special Agent Laura Sweigert had been killed.

Now his boss said, 'I'm giving you Bob Cram.'

Dukas swallowed so much food his eyes bulged. 'No, you're not!' he tried to say. He looked around for water, saw only tea, gulped it. Too late; his boss was already talking. 'You'll get along fine; Bob's a real people guy. What you need to hold your team together, Mike – guy with people skills, always sharing.'

The tea was scalding hot. Eyes watering, Dukas said, 'He's a worthless asshole.'

The opinion was widely shared but seldom voiced. Cram had been on loan to the Drug Enforcement Agency in the early 1990s (even then, people were trying to get rid of him) and he had got picked up off a Colombian street and tortured for four hours by one of the cartels. The torture had given him a certain status, even a certain heroism, and, even though he had remained a worthless asshole, he was to a great degree untouchable. After the torture, nobody had ever dared fire him – but nobody wanted him around, either.

'I won't take him,' Dukas said.

His boss laughed as if that was a really good one. Laughed and laughed. 'I've already told him he's on your team.'

'No –'

'He's on your team, Mike.' Said with a certain forcefulness.

'Aw, no, Christ –'

'Liaison. That's what I'd use him for – liaison. Perfect for dealing with those people over there.'

Dukas thought of Bob Cram with the Kenyan police. Actually, they might get along – a shared experience of torture, although from different perspectives. 'What if I say no?'

'You can't say no. Unless you want to lose Mario and Geraldine. Okay?'

Later, when he had eaten and his mood was no better despite the food, Dukas walked to the other end of the building, where Files and Archives hid itself. Cram had been assigned there for a while to keep him out of the way of agents who were actually doing work. Dukas saw him across a room that was mostly file

137

cabinets and desks, all but two of the desks empty – at one a fiftyish black woman, significantly located as far as possible from the one where Cram sat. She had a perpetual scowl, probably more from years of bureaucracy than from closeness to Cram; anyway, it was clear that pleasantness was not what she would serve up if challenged.

Dukas studied Cram. Like a caricature of a cop: pushing fifty, hair already white, face red shading to purple, gut defying gravity only because of a leather belt. Dukas felt disgust, not at the physical man, but at the waste Cram represented – an agent slot made useless. At the same time, he felt a grudging respect, the residue of the torture.

'Cram!' he said.

Cram looked up. Big, shit-eating grin. 'Hey, Michael O'Dukas!'

'A higher power has put you on the team. We leave from BWI at eight, British Air. Be there.'

'Yeah, I heard. I'll come on tomorrow – not enough time –'

'Tonight.' Dukas wanted to say, *Give me an excuse to dump you, please*, but he felt constrained. The common experience of superiors who tried to deal with Cram.

Cram got very sincere. He reminded Dukas of the political reporter he had watched that morning. 'I'm a family man, Mike.' There were rumors that Cram liked to hit on young women – the younger and dumber the better. Dukas had been careful to keep him away from Leslie, his assistant.

Dukas ignored the 'family man' bullshit. 'You'll handle the press, okay? You'll need two words – "no" and "comment." Other than that, you'll hold down our office at Mombasa airport.' *And try not to give yourself*

AIDS while you're thinking about your family. The woman was scowling at them. From the look of her, Dukas was glad they hadn't forced him to take her, as well. 'Take tropical clothes. It's hot and sweaty there. Get to medical for shots – you got three hours. You'll need a flak vest and a sleeping bag; call this number and talk to Sergeant Bally and then get your ass down to Building Nine and draw them from Marine stores.' He threw a piece of paper on the counter between them.

'I'm allergic to shots,' Cram said.

'Oh, too bad! Maybe you better not go.' Dukas tried to smile. 'Tell the boss.'

'Well – no-o-o –' Cram sighed. 'I'll put up with it.' He smiled a martyr's smile.

Back in his office, Dukas found that Leslie had pasted yellow stickies on the empty Chinese-food cartons, mostly about calling people who wanted to go with him but whom he didn't want. There was one, however, about a man he very much wanted and hadn't been able to find, Dick Triffler. Triffler was a too-precise, straight-arrow man whose performance on a recent case with Dukas had made Dukas want him around for every hardball that came his way. Now Triffler had been bumped upstairs to a post with the Bright Star advance guard in Cairo (doing the ground-work for the annual US-Egyptian naval whiz-bang), and the Bright Star office hadn't known where he was when Dukas had started calling at eight that morning. Now, it was eight p.m. in Cairo and Triffler was in his hotel.

'Dick!' Dukas shouted. *Too loud*, he told himself; Triffler liked quiet.

'This is Richard Triffler speaking.' Melodious voice, calm.

'Dick – it's Mike Dukas!'

Pause. 'Oh, hi, Mike.' A distinct lack of enthusiasm, perhaps because Dukas had beat it out of town in the midst of an investigation and left Triffler to clean up.

'Hey, Dick, uh – how's Egypt?'

'Unbelievable.' That could have meant anything. 'The dirtiest place I've ever been.' Clearer.

'How's Bright Star?'

Pause. 'Some of the people are okay. Some are quite different from the way they behave at home.'

'That bad, huh?'

'I was saying to my wife only this evening – by telephone, of course – that I've seen things in the last three weeks that make the Ugly American look like the Osmond family.'

Dukas smiled. He put his feet up. 'Well, jeez, I'll bet you can't wait to get out of there, huh, Dick?'

Triffler's tone grew warmer. 'If I told you that I have twice asked for a transfer, you'll get an idea of how I can't wait for this to end! I spent the whole day at the embassy trying to get somebody to pull strings and help me. It's supposed to be an honor to be here – living in a fancy hotel, traveling in a special car, everything on the tab – It makes me feel guilty, Mike. I hate the dirt and the disease and the poverty, but I hate it, too, that I'm supposed to be enjoying myself by ignoring it. Man, I can't wait!'

Dukas smiled more broadly. 'Dick, it just so happens that I got a proposition for you. Have you heard about the explosion in Mombasa, Kenya, this morning?'

Triffler wanted to go back to Washington, not Mombasa. Still, after ten minutes of hemming and hawing and digging one toe into the hot sand, Triffler admitted that he'd rather be working on an honest-to-

God investigation with Dukas than swanning around Cairo with a lot of pampered bureaucrats.

Dukas hung up with a satisfied smile on his face. He made a note to have Kasser spring Triffler from Bright Star, and he was shoving stuff into an attaché in preparation for going home to pack when he noticed another yellow sticky, way off by itself on a pile of files. It said 'Inter-Agency Relations' and gave an extension number.

That would be CIA Inter-Agency Relations, which would have heard that NCIS was serious about no-divvies on the investigation, and which would be trying to use the grail of inter-agency cooperation to horn in. Dukas frowned.

He called to Leslie on the other side of the office. She came around the divider that gave them both some sort of privacy. She was wearing what she called 'appropriate dress,' which meant that she didn't look as if she was headed for a rave, but Leslie remained essentially a teenager with really bad taste. A fast learner, but a lot to learn.

'Hi-i-i-i,' she said. She grinned. She grinned all the time now, he realized. Dukas thought that the signs were not good. She had invited him to her place for dinner, and he was still finding excuses to put it off.

'Got a job for you.'

'Great!'

Coming to his desk and standing too close. Dukas wondered if he should point out that he was forty and she was twenty. He decided not. He was already getting jokes about that from some of the other special agents. 'I want you to call this number.' He held up the yellow sticky. 'It's CIA Inter-Agency Relations. Tell them Mister Dukas is too busy right now, and he's on a case, but

141

if they'll put it in writing and send it over by messenger, he'll try to get to it next week.'

She beamed. 'O-ka-a-a-y!' She swayed out, turning to look over her shoulder at him.

The trouble was, Leslie was also cute. And sexy. A little overweight, but that had never bothered him before.

As he swung a laden attaché off the desk and got ready to go home, he wondered what he was going to do about her. *Nothing*, an inner voice accused him: *You'll use the Mombasa thing as an excuse to leave town and not deal with her, you shit.*

And that's what he did.

USS *Thomas Jefferson*.

Rafe Rafehausen was using his CAG office as a temporary BG-commander's headquarters, unwilling yet to take over the admiral's office. He'd never move into the flag suite to stay, he knew, not because of how it would look, but because of some innate sense of propriety that was odd in a man so usually brash. He also suspected that his time as acting commander would be short; once Kessler's death was confirmed, some other two-star would be sent out. So, for now, he was doing the admiral's job in his own office and trying to wear the CAG's hat, too, although if the job lasted more than a day or two, he'd have to move to the flag deck so flag staff didn't have to keep running to the CAG's office.

He had just got off the radio-linked phone with the American ambassador in Nairobi. The news that he had to pass to Al Craik because of that call was not good, and he pulled at his lower lip as he thought about how to tell him. 'Get me Craik on the *Harker*,' he muttered into the phone.

He scanned a printout on squadron fuel consumptions and then pulled out another document and looked at it to see what the Texaco had in reserve. Sticking out at an angle and deeper in the paper pile was a message from Beluscio on the coming week's weather. He was reading about the depression southwest of Sri Lanka that might become a typhoon when a voice told him that Lieutenant-Commander Craik was on.

'Hey, Alan.' He pushed the papers away.

'Hey, Rafe.' Craik sounded tapped out.

'You holding up okay?'

'We're alive and well and living in – if it's Tuesday, it must be Mombasa.'

'Give me a status.'

'Second helo lifted off half an hour ago. Ship's Marines have secured our dock, and we've got the Kenyans to keep a patrol boat in the water nearby. City sounds quiet, whatever that means. We've got food for three days; water's iffy. No telephone lines, no off-ship electric. SEALs tell me the ship's forward third is on the bottom, apparently stable. Fires out. Minimum water coming in beyond the flooded compartments, but no pumps operating. Summary: we're stable, but we're stuck here.'

'Yeah, well, that's what we need to talk about. First off, the Kenyans want your Marines off the dock.'

'Like hell.'

'Restricted to the ship. They acknowledge the ship is US territory, but the dock is theirs. You *will* restrict all American personnel to the ship.'

'Rafe, Jesus –'

'That comes straight from the ambassador, Al. He doesn't like it; I don't like it. But here's the deal: the

Kenyans say they have eyewitnesses plus evidence, plus maybe one of the terrorists, and we can't see anything or talk to anybody until we give them back their dock. Period.'

'All we're doing is maintaining our perimeter!'

'A Kenyan general or some such complained to the ambassador that Marines threatened Kenyan Navy personnel.'

'Like hell. A couple of them were in the potential field of fire. We waved them off.'

'They're very touchy. Pull your people back.' Rafe heard Alan's weary anger, guessed that Alan would have to deal with an even angrier Marine officer. Couldn't be helped. 'You with me?'

'I hear and will comply.' The ironic tone was not lost on Rafe.

'Okay. Then we gotta have an evacuation plan I can lay out for the ambassador ASAP so he can tell the Kenyans we're "lessening our presence" – his words. Here's the bad news, Al: he wants you out of there before tomorrow. You can leave ten men on the ship. It's a done deal with the Kenyan military.'

'What the hell is this? These guys have been busting their asses to save this ship! We can't abandon it –'

Rafehausen rubbed his forehead. He wanted a cigarette, and he couldn't smoke in there. 'The Kenyan view is that they've busted their asses to keep a mob from tearing the ship apart, and you with it. I only know what I'm told, Al. The word from the ambassador is that the Kenyan mil have arrested hundreds of people today, and they don't want us looking over their shoulder. The hospitals are full. There's at least forty people dead in Mombasa – that's the official total, so

144

it's probably a lot more. They think they've got a revolution on their hands and they're paranoid and I think the real truth is they don't want American Marines all of a sudden coming out of that port and messing up whatever it is they're doing.' He rubbed his eyes. 'I heard Mogadishu mentioned three separate times. The Kenyans think we're cowboys.'

'*We're* cowboys! You should see what I saw today. The Kenyans are using automatic weapons against their own people. And funny you should mention Mogadishu – that's exactly what the Marine captain doesn't want, too.'

'Okay, so the sooner you get out of there, the less chance of it.'

'Rafe, you're telling us to, to – retreat.'

'I'm telling you to do what's best for the US right at this particular moment.'

'But, Jesus – All we need is a rooftop and a couple of choppers, we can do the Fall of Saigon.'

'You want to whine, do it in a corner someplace. I want an evacuation plan – for tonight, for all but ten personnel to be restricted to the ship! Now give it to me.'

Craik hesitated, probably dealing with his anger, Rafe thought. The guy would be pretty strung out; who wouldn't? He'd done well and now he was being told it didn't matter: get out. Yeah, Rafe would have been mad, too. But when Craik's voice came on again, emotion had been erased from it. 'We'll evacuate to the det spaces at the airport. We can't go by sea; we don't have the boats, and anyway we'd land someplace and still have to make our way to the airport, meaning we'd need vehicles. And we can't just call a taxi – am I right that there's still fighting going on?'

'As I understand it.'

145

'And you don't want US Marines shooting their way down the road to the airport – right?'

'Yeah, yeah –'

'Plan B. You could fly in, say, fifty Marines from the gator freighter, and enough Humvees for them and ourselves. They drive from the airport here, pick us up, and we drive back. I don't think anybody'd stop a convoy of that size.'

Rafehausen had been wincing. 'That's Mogadishu revisited. Negative that. Anyways, we couldn't get all that gear to the airport before forty-eight hours, minimum, and then there's gotta be route planning, co-ordination with the Kenyans – negative that. Air, Al, it's gotta be by air.'

'This is still a hot zone.'

'How hot?'

'How would I know?' Alan sounded angry again. 'I can't see beyond our dock. We can't coordinate with the Kenyans, except the Navy, and they've gone tough on us. For all I know, there are SAMs in every building around us, not to mention the point of land opposite Kilindini. Not to mention it's night and we don't have a chopper pad and you're talking about at least two, plus they'd have to have extra fuel tanks to get here in the first place. No.'

'They won't need extra fuel; I've got your det working on fuel at the airport. They fly off from here – two SH-60s and maybe a gunship – and they fly to the airport, refuel, and come in at the same place the first choppers landed. Where's that?'

'End of the dock. But anybody who's been watching knows that's the landing place. They have it targeted by now. They don't even need to be able to see it. No.'

'How long since they've been shooting at you?'

'We still hear shots.'

'*At* you, I said.'

Al Craik paused. 'Three hours.'

'That's not such a hot zone.'

'Rafe, they could be waiting for us! How do we know that the Kenyans haven't leaked the word that we're going to have to leave tonight?'

'Now *you're* paranoid.'

'Yeah, come stand on this ship, you'll be paranoid, too.' Then, almost at once, 'I'm sorry I said that, Rafe. That was out of line.'

'Understood. Okay. Your recommendation is no air evac.'

'Yes, sir.'

'We leave you there.'

'For now, yes.'

'Even though the ambassador has promised we'll get you out, and the cooperation of the Kenyans depends on it.'

Craik hesitated. Then, 'Yes.'

Rafehausen blew out his breath. 'Overruled. I have to make the call, Al. Choppers will take off from here as soon as crews can scramble. EMCON throughout. Have your gunny drop lightsticks around the landing area, and it'll be pick up and go – your people there, ready to pile in and lift off. ETA –' he squinted at a clock – 'three hours and a half.'

'I object.'

'Noted.'

They both waited for the other to say something. Then Craik said, 'EMCON all the way is no good, Rafe. They'll have to coordinate with the Kenyans; best do it through control at the airport, plus whatever contact you have with Kenyan military. Can you do that?'

147

'It's already been done.'

Craik took time digesting that – a done deal. Then: 'I want the right to wave them off if things go bad. I don't want to be the one who blew away two helos and thirty people because he couldn't tell the helos there was shooting going on.'

'I'll have intel set it up.'

'That it?'

Rafehausen felt the other man's coldness. 'We'll get details to you. Al, we'll make this work.'

And because they were old friends and Craik had some idea of the spot Rafehausen was in, he said, 'Not your fault, Rafe. Hey, my det out at the airport finally got in touch. Thanks for goosing them. Hang in there.'

Houston.

Rose, never good at controlling her temper, had managed to turn a growing anger into coldness. Fire into ice – not bad, she thought. She had managed not to take it out on her kids, and she thought she had managed to hide it from other people in her training sessions, but the rage she had felt in her meeting with the 'education' wonk was still with her, even if chilled down. *It's so unfair*, she thought and caught herself. *'Fair' doesn't get you anywhere.* So maybe it was unfair that Dukas had told her to get her gun and NASA was telling her to ditch it, but so what? Maybe it was unfair that her husband was gone and she had a full plate plus two kids and a lot of unpacked household goods, but so what? Maybe it was unfair that her mother's mind was going and her father had the burden of that, but so what? Was God laughing? Was anybody having fun yet?

Home at last, she played with Mikey and the baby,

walked the dog, got out things from the freezer that other astronauts' wives had brought over when she'd moved in. *Wives*. Not the astronauts, but their wives. There were women astronauts, of course, but either they didn't cook or they didn't make house calls, and if they had husbands, the husbands didn't, either.

'We're a family,' one of the wives had said to her. A decent, pretty, nice woman. Wife of an Air Force officer.

'Just one big happy family,' Rose said to the dog. He thumped his big, black tail on the kitchen floor. He didn't fool her – he wanted his supper.

After she fed him, she looked for news on the TV, found she was too early. CNN was showing the same footage, with some new clips of black mobs and military vehicles. Talking heads made serious babble. She turned it off and decided to bite the bullet and call her father.

'How bad is she?' she said when they'd got past the greetings. Her father loved her, perhaps adored her; he couldn't just say 'Hi' and move on. He even had to sing a line of 'Rosie, she is my posey,' and she knew that if he'd been in the room with her he'd have danced her around while he sang. He was a small, slender man, still kind of good-looking in his sixties, a machinist who'd gone down with the rest of Utica's working stiffs when the factories failed, surviving now on Social Security and savings. And now he had a wife who was losing her marbles.

'How bad is it?'

'Well, Rosie, she's getting on, you know. Getting to be an old lady, what the hell.'

'Dad, how bad is it?'

'Well – I tole you, she had out my hammer and nails

149

she got God knows where and I find her nailing up a window.'

'That's all?'

'I thought it was funny, you know? I still do. I mean, funny if she isn't your wife. Or your mother. Somebody else's problem, it's funny. I told you she thinks the colored are gonna get in.' He would never learn to say 'African American,' usually not even 'black.' On the other hand, he didn't say 'nigger,' although the word was often heard on Utica's streets. 'Then there's little things.'

'Such as?'

'She cries. You know – you'll see her sitting some-place, you think she's just daydreaming, whatever, and you go close and she's crying. 'About what?' I say. She don't know. She looks at me like I'm the one who's nuts because I don't know what there is to cry about.'

Rose chewed her lower lip. 'I think I better come up there.'

'Nah, Rosie, what're you talking? You got kids, the job –' She could hear a smile in his voice. 'My daughter the astronaut. I tell you there was an article in the paper?'

'You told me.' Did he know about Alan? He would have said something. 'You been looking at TV today, Dad?'

'Your mother got a lock on it. She's got her soaps, her shows – who knows what crap she watches? She sits there with her face turned toward the TV, and she cries.'

She told him about Alan and CNN. He liked Alan, but his concern was always for her. His daughter, his Rosie, suffering the pain of a husband in danger.

'I think I ought to come up there,' she said again.

150

'Nah. Rosie, what could you do? Nah, I can handle it.'

'I thought I'd bring the kids. Maybe they'd pull her out of it.'

He was silent again. 'It breaks your heart, kiddo.'

'Oh, Daddy.' She understood then how bad it was.

After she hung up, she went on the Internet to look at airplane schedules, and then she sat in front of the TV and watched the early news. She wondered if, like her mother, she should cry.

Mombasa.

They came up the dock in the darkness, hurrying, each man touching the back of the one ahead, trying not to slip on the rotting vegetables that should have gone to feed the BG but were now blown all over every surface. The air stank of rot and sea and burning; the night air was heavy and warm, hardly stirring. Mombasa reflected yellow-gray on the low cloud. Far up the hill, a light in the Seamen's Mission seemed to stare down at them.

Alan and Geelin came almost last with a Marine on each side, backing the length of the dock and covering the rear. As they moved away from the ship in the darkness, armed Kenyan sailors filled in behind them; they saw them only as shapes. 'Jesus, don't shoot,' Geelin muttered to the man on his right. He and Alan had discussed what would happen if somebody started shooting: US Marines and Kenyans blasting each other with automatic weapons. It would be bad, very bad. And the Marines wanted to shoot, because they were angry and frustrated. They had left nine of their buddies and Patel and Barnes on the *Harker*, and the Marines believed deep down that the ones left behind were hostages as much as they were protectors of the ship. They were itching for the chance to shoot.

The two SH-60s were down at the end of the dock, their rotors turning. A Kenyan gunship whupped along the shoreline to the south, two hundred yards out and high enough up to have a jump on anything that came at them from the shore, or at least that was the theory. It was only a sound out there, showing no lights. Alan believed that if anybody along the shore had a SAM, he'd be saving it for the SH-60s. A terrorist with a SAM probably couldn't tell one chopper from another, but he'd know which ones had just touched down on the dock and taken on passengers, and he'd know enough to wait until they lifted off again full.

He slipped, put his hand out to catch himself, felt the slime of something already gone bad, spinach or lettuce. Nobody slowed, nobody made any comment. He could just make out Sandy Cole's long dress thirty feet ahead of them; she had a Marine on each side, their instructions to carry her if she stumbled or even got short of breath. Two other Marines were walking sideways, weapons ready, one scanning the water, one the ruin on the landward side.

'Keep moving, keep moving –' he heard the gunny saying over the sound of the helicopters. 'Get aboard – move your ass –' The gunnery sergeant sounded angry.

He hit an ankle on something hard, stumbled, felt Geelin's hand on his elbow like a pair of pliers.

The group ahead slowed, then stopped. They had reached the helos.

'Second chopper!' the gunny said. 'Break here – Morton, you're the last one on the forward chopper – go, Christ, what are you waiting for –?' Then, hidden behind the bodies ahead of him, the gunny began shoving people toward the second helo. 'Go, go – hustle, goddamit –!'

Against the barely lighted cloud, he saw the first helo's rotors start to turn faster.

In the right-hand seat of the SH-60, Lieutenant Pat Blessing of the *Jefferson*'s chopper squadron scanned the instrument panel, its lights in the darkness like the lights of a city from the air. The sweep was habitual – altimeter, barometric altimeter, vertical speed indicator, vert instrument display –

Beside him, the pilot glanced out his side, then looked over. 'Hanks?'

The aircrewman, seated facing out behind him, muttered, 'Yo,' his voice raspy over the comm.

'You got 'em tucked in back there?'

'Sitting on their helmets and praying, sir.' The Marines were, indeed, sitting on their Kevlar helmets – protection from ground fire when they got into the air.

'Okay, guys, I'm going up fifty and straight out three-zero-zero and hold on for jinks. Here we go –'

The VSI moved and Blessing felt the aircraft rock and soar as the engine seemed to burst into its full throb and growl, and the horizon dropped as they jumped the fifty feet; to his right, the lights of a Kenyan patrol boat swung past his window. He was hitting switches and scanning the instruments, taking time to glance over his left shoulder at the aircrewman's panel, the silhouette of Hanks's arm and helmet.

Then they were over the water, and Hanks, staring at the AN/AAR-47, seemed to jump, and he shouted into the comm, 'Missile bloom three-three-five, three

153

hundred yards, water level!' and the world spun as the big helo tipped hard to the right, turning its cold belly to the heat-seeker that was after it. Blessing was shouting, 'Chaff and flare, goddamit –!' his fingers flying, Hanks's hands moving to switches behind them, and they heard the thunk of the flare pods.

Alan saw the helicopter rise, the thunder of its engine and the blast of its rotors making him duck and wince. They were shuffling forward toward the second chopper, his hand on a Marine's back and Geelin's hand on Alan's shoulder because Geelin was determined to come last. The gunny was three men ahead, pushing Marines into the blackness of the door, hectoring them.

He looked past the dark bulk of the aircraft and saw the first helo disappear behind it and then appear again out over the water, silhouetted against that sickly sky, and then a line of fire was drawn from the shore to his left out over the water, and he felt his gut drop as he recognized a missile. The chopper tilted violently right, its belly seeming to burst with light, and he thought it had been hit, but the missile was still away to the left, moving over the water, drawing its pencil streak of fire longer and longer. The flares burst into hot light, and the missile's pencil line became an S-curve as it found heat, then other heat, and the curve became a wiggle, and the missile twisted in an agony of indecision and blew up.

The helicopter was well out over the water by then, turning north.

Then a rough hand was trying to force him inside, but he pushed the gunnery sergeant's hand off and shouted, 'I'm the commanding officer here, Gunny! Get in!' and there was a fraction of a second's meeting of eyes, the faces only inches apart, and the gunnery sergeant threw himself through the door. Alan gave Geelin a shove; a blow started his way, was pulled back, and they stared at each other.

'Come on! Come on!' the aircrewman shouted at them.

The gunnery sergeant grabbed Alan and the aircrewman grabbed Geelin and they were pulled aboard, nobody ever sure who was the last man to leave Kilindini. The last voice was Geelin's, however, shouting angrily, 'We'll be back! We'll be back —!'

Seconds later they were over the water.

Dulles Airport, Washington.

Dukas had all his team in the departure lounge, except for the two who were coming in tomorrow on the forensics aircraft. It may have been a first: everybody on time, everybody with a valid passport, only three without the required shots or pills, which they'd get from a medic when they stepped off the plane. They had three hundred pounds of excess baggage, but that was the government's problem; they had to have laptops, evidence kits, sleeping bags, flak vests, all the basics. Plus several steel thermoses of booze, five cartons of cigarettes, assorted packets of condoms, one extra set of false teeth, GPUs, handguns, cell phones, MSR two-way radios, and a compact barbecue that Special Agent Mendelsohn thought he was going to set up on their hotel balcony.

Everybody knew everybody else, and everybody was pretty much at ease with everybody else, except Cram. Cram was always the specter at the feast, which may have been why he was always laughing. When he wasn't laughing, he was telling jokes, or stories he thought were jokes. Right now, he was telling Geraldine Pastner about two female officers he'd investigated who'd turned out to be lesbians.

'We didn't ask! They didn't tell! So guess how we found out they were gay!'

It occurred to Dukas that Geraldine was unmarried. And unamused by Cram. 'How?' she said. Being polite, nothing more.

'They picketed in Vermont to get married!' He waited for appreciative laughter and got it from two of the men. But not from Geraldine, who said, 'Civil union, not marriage.'

'Whatever! But isn't that something? Here they're naval officers and they know they can't be lesbos, and they go someplace to get *married*!' He cackled. She did not. Unsatisfied, trying for the laugh, he pushed harder: 'And would you believe it, one of them had *been* married? I mean, really married – to a guy. Not once, but twice! To guys! Married twice to guys, and she turns into a lesbo. How about that!'

Geraldine smiled. 'Some women are slow learners,' she said.

Cram looked puzzled. Geraldine gave Dukas a small, complicit smile.

Mombasa Airport.

Alan had arrived at the det spaces at Mombasa airport to find that what awaited him was not a solution but a problem: no food, no beds, and morale shot to hell.

The space that had been assigned to his detachment had two side-by-side hangars and a tatty Quonset hut that had already been taken over for EM sleeping quarters. They had no beds and no bedding, but they had scrounged tarps and a roll of filthy foam rubber, and they had made mattresses of a sort. The Quonset also had a studio-sized kitchen, but they had nothing to cook and no pans to cook that nothing in.

Each of the hangars was big enough to hold a couple of S-3s and then some, but now only a lone aircraft sat under the inadequate lights, big and bulbous and not threatening the way a warplane should perhaps be. It looked polished, and Alan guessed that it had been wiped down for the admiral's visit.

A long time ago, it seemed now.

A second level ran along one side of the hangar, with a metal stairway down to the concrete floor. A pile of prefab plywood bulkheads rose at the far end; from this, the det had already made a detachment office and four other spaces on the upper level. Two wire-mesh storage cribs took up part of the lower level; the maintenance chief had installed himself in one. At the back were pallets of plywood and precut two-by-fours left by the air force for the next tenants.

Next to the det office, two egg crates of comm equipment from the S-3's belly pack had turned into a communications center, including an FS200 and a Pacer Bounce radio set with an RF-3200E transceiver and a compatible AVS card. The result was a flexible, powerful setup that gave them secure voice, image, satellite, and patched telephone comm – so long as they had things turned on and manned, as they had not for most of the day because everybody had been too busy getting ready for an admiral's visit that had never happened. This partial comm failure had made the det personnel touchy – some sense that they had not only missed the action but had screwed up their end, as well. And then, one of the first things they had learned once they had communications was that Master Chief Craw was dead.

They had already been cranky because of the matter of food. The det's sailors had planned to be there only that day, so they had brought hotel-packed box lunches, and then they were supposed to go back to their hotel. They had been willing to make do for one day. But there was the matter of drinks, too: it was a mile-and-a-half walk in wet heat to the civilian terminal, so, until word had reached them of the explosion and the deaths, they had been fraternizing with the Kenyan Air Force guys in the next hangar and using their Coke machine. Cohen had wisely stepped on that as soon as he had – belatedly – made contact with the CV, so then there was no Coke machine *and* no food, and the water was tepid and, according to some of the men, polluted.

These conditions and the comm mistake had made the det people edgy and supersensitive, and, when the loaded helos had arrived after midnight with the retreat from the *Harker*, these feelings had combined with the Marines' sense of betrayal to kill whatever had been left of morale. It was as if they had lost a battle.

Now Alan and what he thought of as his lead team were sitting in a circle of folding chairs under a work light at the far end of the hangar. It was after one in the morning and everybody was drooping, their faces old and hard in the cold light. Alan was aware of his own smell and thought they must all be like that. He was so tired he could feel his eyes trying to close, his body crashing toward sleep no matter what his mind wanted to do. Three cups of awful coffee from the detachment pot (brought from the boat with the maintenance gear) had done little for him. And yet he knew that he had to drive them and himself, or the feeling of defeat they had brought from the *Harker* would become their reality.

He forced himself to focus. 'If I could have your attention –' His voice was raspy, thick. He cleared his throat. 'We'll make this just as short as we can.'

Geelin was standing opposite him, looking mad as hell. He was apparently refusing to sit, as some sort of demonstration of – what? machismo? protest? pride? *The hell with you; stand*, Alan thought, too tired to assert so trivial an authority. Next to him, Lieutenant Cohen, a good pilot who now believed he had blown his first shot at even temporary command, and who had been in the hangar for eighteen hours, looked shell-shocked. He had, to Alan's surprise, taken Craw's death particularly hard.

Next to Cohen, a big, shaven-headed SEAL named Fidelio was sitting with arms crossed and big feet pushed out into the middle of the circle. People who knew him called him 'Fidel,' which was thought to be drop-dead funny. Alan thought the man had a chip on his shoulder but couldn't yet tell why. Briefly, he and Fidelio stared at each other, the SEAL's look seeming to say *I can take you with one hand*, but Alan thought this might simply be habit – SEAL culture. He looked back with a look that he hoped said *So what? I'm the CO*, but he was so tired it may simply have said *Do what?*

Sandy Cole was sitting on his left. Fatigue didn't do anything more for her than it did for the rest of them. Her slightly popped eyes seemed to float on swollen, flushed lids; deep lines had been driven downward from the corners of her nostrils, and it was possible to guess now how old she was. *Maybe thirty-five? Thirty-eight?* The long dress was stained with oil and old vegetables, and her bare feet were dirty. Her running shoes, neatly lined up by one leg of her chair, looked brand new by comparison. She smelled a little of the decomposed body she had been working on.

On his right was Bakin, the det's chief petty officer in charge of aircraft maintenance. With Craw dead, he was now the ranking enlisted man. Alan wanted him there to hear what was said so he could spike some of the rumors that must already be floating around.

Alan thought of standing to speak and decided against it. He might fall over.

'Folks, it's late, and we've all had a hell of a day.' Nobody so much as smiled. 'We're going to have a worse day tomorrow.' No response. 'But we're going to pull up our socks and come out of this winners.' Doubt, gloom. 'Okay, let me tell you where we are. If you already know, just hear me out, because different people here know different things.

'As of several hours ago, we are the US Navy presence in Mombasa. As commander of the detachment, I've been tasked to guard the *Harker* and start the investigation of what happened to it.' Fidelio guffawed, not very loudly, but certainly audibly. Apparently it was obvious to Fidelio what had happened to the *Harker*. 'The lady on my left is Sandra Cole, the legal attaché of the embassy in Nairobi. I'll ask her to talk in a couple of minutes about what she's found on the dock at Kilindini, including her analysis of the body of a sniper.' He looked across at Fidelio, who was scowling again. 'Before that, I'll ask First Class Fidelio to report on what the SEALs found in the water and on the outside of the ship. First, however, I want to square away some practical stuff that will affect us all.'

He looked around at them and tried to smile. 'As of right now, you are all restricted to our two hangars, the Quonset hut, and the space between. *Nobody* will leave our perimeter for any reason whatsoever without a written order from me.' He heard Chief Bakin's sharp intake of breath and the scraping of the man's feet as he suppressed a move to jump up. 'On my right is Chief Petty Officer Bakin of the air detachment. Okay, Chief, say it.'

Bakin was quite a young man. He took himself fairly seriously, but he was good at his job; tall and good-looking, at least by his own standards, he was accustomed to being listened to. 'Detachment personnel were told they would be returning to their hotel tomorrow morning at the latest, sir!'

'Negative that. Hotels are off-limits until I give the word.'

'But –!' The posh beach hotels were the reason that this was supposed to be good duty – sun, beer, women, American-style living. 'With all respect, that isn't fair.'

'No, it isn't. But I'd rather they were alive here than dead in a high-rise that's been hit by mortar fire. Or stuck at a barricade somewhere in Mombasa and not able to get out of it.' Bakin was going to object, and Alan held up a hand. 'Chief, you and I'll talk about it later, okay? For now, that's the word – We're all here; we're all staying here. I'll do my damnedest to get some sort of bedding and food in here before tomorrow night.'

'Can't we just fly them back to the boat?' Cohen said.

'My orders are to stay.'

The SEAL asked about tents, and Alan said that maybe tents would be along in good time; there was some fruitless discussion of tents versus hangars in the Mombasa humidity. He let them go on for forty-five seconds and then cut them off. 'Okay, enough – we're not getting anywhere. Geelin – by the way, that's Captain Geelin of the Marine detachment standing over there – check with me in the morning about tents, okay?'

Geelin wasn't having any of it. 'Tents suck if there's mortars.'

Alan nodded, unable to see anything wrong with the statement. *Tents suck if there's mortars. Right. Canvas not much protection, absolutely.* The Marines, who had brought sleeping bags, had already glommed on to an equipment cage and a lot of plywood tables to sleep on; several of them were snoring, way up at the far end of the hangar.

'Here's our situation.' Alan rubbed his eyes, blinked. 'Eight Marines, a Marine officer, and two civilians have been left on the *Harker*. Kenyan navy and army are providing security on the dock.'

'So they *say*,' Fidelio said. He had a surprisingly high voice for a big man, and the statement came out more as a whine than a sarcastic snarl.

'Belay that.' He looked around at them. 'Kenyan navy saved our buns out there today. They're being a little shitty about sovereignty, but remember – how would we feel if a foreign ship went down in an American harbor and the other country sent in *their* helos and marines and navy? Please, folks, *please* – get your people to see it that way. The Kenyans are basically our friends.'

'With one of the most corrupt governments in Africa,' Sandy Cole said. 'Which is saying a lot.'

Another four-way chat room formed itself on the subject of African corruption, and Alan almost had to shout, 'Can we talk about that later, please?' They shut up, and he said hoarsely, 'We're not here to discuss politics. I was simply making a point: the Kenyans are not the enemy.'

'Who is?' Geelin said, sticking his jaw out.

'Goddam ragheads,' Fidelio said in his high voice.

'Lotta Kenyans are ragheads –' Bakin started to say.

'Stow it!' Alan stood up, knowing now he should have stood from the beginning. He hauled the folding chair around so he could lean on the metal back. 'Geelin, sit down!' He waited. Geelin sat, having hesitated long enough to show he objected, but not so long he'd get called on it. Alan looked at them. 'It's one in the morning and I'm about out of patience, and if you want to practice the art of conversation, do it on your own time. All of you: if you don't have something useful to say, shut up!'

It got very quiet. Down at the far end, a Marine snored, three ascending snorts that ended in a long sigh.

'Now! Situation: eight Marines, one Marine officer and two civilians on the ship; Kenyans on the dock. We will resupply and transfer personnel once a day – our helo if it gets back here from the boat, Kenyans' if not. Marines on the *Harker* are currently supplied for a three-day stay.

'Thirty more Marines will get here from the gator freighter tomorrow – that's today – ETA noonish. They will also be under Captain Geelin's command; they will bring tents and will set up inside our perimeter but out of the way of our aircraft; if there's space in the tents, the troops sleeping down there right now will also move outside. We need the space.'

'Objection!' Geelin shouted.

'I said we'll talk about it in the morning. Next – an NCIS investigative team will be here by tomorrow night. They will also stay *here*. That means they will have to be fed and housed, so it's going to get crowded. By the next day, their airborne forensics lab will be here with two *more* agents plus at least four forensics people; they may be able to sleep on their aircraft, but the agents will be in the hangar with us. Two of them are women.' He looked down at Sandy Cole. 'You'll have company.

'The second S-3 will join us from the boat. Aircrew of four.' He looked up at the upper tier of offices and the narrow balcony that connected them. 'As of now, all female sleeping quarters to be on the upper level; there's a head up there for their exclusive use. Far end of the upper level is off-limits to male personnel.'

'Air-conditioning,' Bakin muttered.

'It would be nice to have, but we don't.' Bakin sighed, one of those loud sighs that is meant to show how heavy the world is. Alan rode right over it. 'Get your minds up to speed: we're in a combat situation. *This is not America.* We are not welcome guests. But we're here to do a job, and by God we're going to do it – and we're going to put up with the heat and MREs and people shooting at us! I'll go to the mat for you and your people where it's appropriate, but damned if I'm going to listen to a lot of whining about no Coke machine and no fried chicken, and damned if I'm going to give in because we got our butts kicked today! We are here to do a job and we're going to do it!'

He felt wetness on the metal chair-back where his hands rested, realized he was sweating heavily.

'Mark –' He looked at Cohen. 'I want Campbell to fly up to Nairobi tomorrow. Don't file a flight plan until the last minute – I don't want anybody out there knowing when we're taking off and landing.' He didn't have to remind them that the airport was surrounded by small houses, *bandas*, and that any of them could hide somebody with a shoulder-fired SAM. 'The embassy will meet him with thirty sleeping bags and some fresh fruit and maybe even some Coke; I'll give him a purchase order.' He didn't say that it would be drawn on his own account, and if the bean counters in Washington decided to be shirty, he'd be paying the tab.

'Chief Bakin, I want you to get on the phone first thing tomorrow morning and get us a four-by-four from a rental agency. Toyota preferred, pickup okay. It's to be brought to the airport security gate, then through airport security *after* the locals check it, and then you and Fidelio and whoever you need will take that thing apart until you're absolutely sure it hasn't been booby-trapped. Then you bring it here. Understood?'

'How do we get over to the gate?'

'We'll try to scrounge a ride from the Kenyans next door.' He didn't say what he wanted to: *For Christ's sake, walk!*

'I thought we had to stay inside the perimeter, sir.'

'I'm making an exception, okay? In writing. We need a vehicle.' He looked around the circle again. 'But *nothing* else comes in here. Don't let anybody get cute – no cutting out for beer, no running to the fence to buy tourist crap from somebody who just happens to be there. Bombs come in all sorts of packages.' He looked around at them, met each one's eyes and satisfied himself that, yes, they had got the message: they were staying and it was going to be rough, but his will to do the job was bigger than anybody's objections. 'And no cell phones. All communications are to be from the comm office *only*. We have one local phone line and it's to be considered insecure and not for personal use. I'll try to set up personal calls to families through the boat ASAP, but nobody, *nobody* makes a call himself; I don't care what the crisis is!'

He gestured to Fidelio. 'Okay, the floor's yours. Tell us what you found in the water.'

Fidelio looked around and decided to stand up. Sitting, he had seemed menacing; standing, he was majestic – a big, big man with iron-pumped shoulders and arms, which he folded over his massive chest. Again, however, the voice was surprisingly, even comically, high. 'Two of us spent three hours diving just off the hole in the *Harker*. What we found was damage from your typical Islamic bomb. That's what we found.' He started to sit down.

'Hold it.' Alan was leaning his elbows on the metal chair-back now, trying to stretch his back. 'Please, folks, no conclusions yet.' His back arched, he had to look up to meet Fidelio's eyes. 'Skip the Islamic part. Give us some detail.'

'Lots of pieces of wooden boat – they call them your dhows – and most of the rear end floating around over by the next dock. We found part of a propane cylinder on the bottom, which I'm not saying came from this dhow, because there's all kinds of crud down there, but it has the kind of damage you get from explosives. We brought that up.'

'I want to see it,' Sandy Cole said.

Alan waved a hand to tell her not to interrupt, never taking his eyes from Fidelio. 'Good. And?'

'Hell of a hole in the ship, as you know. This was a big, *big* bomb. We figure plastic explosive, probably C4 with maybe the propane tank for ignition.'

'Propane tanks are an *IRA* specialty,' Sandy Cole said. Again, Alan waved a hand at her.

'Have you got anything that could have bomb residue on it?'

'We brought up lots of junk. Lots of residue on the ship, I figure. But you put it together, the dhow, the type of bomb, the MO, you got your usual Islamic –'

'That's a conclusion. Premature.' Alan straightened. 'That it?'

Fidelio stared at him. 'You want more detail? I gave the high spots.'

'Let's save it for tomorrow. You catalogued what you brought up?'

Fidelio nodded.

'Thanks.'

Fidelio sat down. He looked around as if challenging anybody to say he'd been less than perfect.

Alan turned to the woman. 'Okay, *now* you can talk.' He tried to smile.

'Well –' She started to slip one dirty foot into a shoe and apparently thought better of it and remained seated. 'You want the sniper's body first? I'll do the body first. Uh –' Her left hand went to its usual resting place over her right ear, the pale arm framing the hair and face. Seeming to find inspiration in the open bracing of the ceiling, she kept her eyes fixed up there. 'Dead man was a black male, young, I guess, but hard to say because of decomposition and wounds. Pretty swollen. But I think under thirty, don't hold my feet to the fire on that. Shot six times, I'm told with a nine millimeter, died pretty quickly. No ID. Nothing in the pockets, anything like that. No labels in the clothes. Not circumcised.'

Bakin made a little intake of breath, expressing what every man was thinking: *She had the balls to strip a corpse?*

Sandy Cole stopped playing with her hair and leaned forward. 'The only other thing was an MP3 player. It was in the booth. I don't think he was listening when he was killed, so I don't think he was listening when he was sniping. Or maybe. Anyway, he didn't have the earphone on, but it was connected, so I think he was listening sometimes, okay?' She shook her head. 'Some kind of wailing sort of music, nothing I recognized.'

'Another A-rab,' Geelin said.

'There're black Arabs?' Fidelio said, as if he and Geelin were two guys sitting in a bar with nothing to do.

'Well, yeah –'

'That'll do!' Alan growled. He looked down at Sandy. 'That it on the body?'

'There's the gun, but I understand you guys took that. I picked up the casings; we can check headstamps, but I think it's Yugoslav ammo, and that's everywhere.'

'That it?'

'There's the engine?' She was squinting up at him, hand over eyes, as if she was looking into the sun. 'The dhow engine?' She dropped the hand and looked at the others. 'The dhow came in under motor power. We know that courtesy of the Kenyans. The explosion apparently blew the engine up on to the dock – at least, there's an old Ford V-8 engine up there with part of a propeller shaft attached. I got the numbers, also some script that I think is Arabic.' She turned her attention back to Alan. 'I got photos but I haven't uploaded them yet. Digital.'

He was thinking about Harry O'Neill and Harry's insistence that the bombing hadn't been Islamic. It was pretty clear that the bombing had, in fact, been Islamic – Arabic writing, the dhow, the method. Still, Harry might be able to do something with the engine numbers. 'Can you get the numbers on a jpg file?' he said to her. 'Tonight?'

'Tonight?' she said, as if she had never heard of anything called *tonight*. Not that there was much left of tonight. 'Well – I suppose so.' She sighed, a dramatic exhalation that told everybody how put upon she felt. 'Then there's the possible terrorist the Kenyans pulled out of the water. Last I heard, he was alive.'

'Can we interview him?'

'Ha, ha, ha.' That was the way she said it – ha, ha, ha. As in har-de-har-har. 'They'll have him in a hospital in town by now, surrounded by cops, and if they haven't beaten him to death, they'll be trying everything short of a tongue transplant to make him talk. They won't want any Americans around studying their technique.'

'He's got to be interviewed.'

She shrugged. 'The only people who can make that happen are the ambassador and the chief of station. It means saying in clear English that Kenya is a small nation of corrupt shits, and the US is a big nation that can clean their clock without breaking a sweat. The ambassador doesn't like to be that honest because it isn't *tactful*.' She was slumped down, her arms crossed over her breasts. 'They'll do it if you get somebody to goose them from Washington.'

Alan made a note. 'Good.' He straightened. His back complained. 'Okay, anything else? If not, I'm going to give us a chance to get at least a little sleep. Fidelio, I'd like a written report – you're making one, anyway, am I right? Sandy, same goes for you.'

'I report to the embassy,' she said.

'Yeah, and I'd like a copy. Mark, remember that you're

taking off for Nairobi early, let's say 0700, so set it up tonight. Bakin, you're getting us a vehicle and you're going to sterilize it. We both clear there? Okay. Captain Geelin, I'd like to meet tomorrow a.m., let's say 0830, to talk about the incoming Marines and perimeter defense. Okay, that's it – see you all in the morning.'

They all sat where they were for several seconds, and it was only when he turned his chair back to its original position that they moved. Then Sandy stretched, Geelin jumped to his feet, Fidelio yawned, and Mark Cohen stood up and shook himself like a dog who'd just climbed out of the water. Alan wondered where he was going to sleep and remembered something about a plywood table that had been pointed out to him. He started toward a distant stair, and the others moved off into the darker world beyond the work light.

'You really want those photos now?' he heard Sandy say.

He remembered that he had decided to send the engine data to Harry O'Neill, and he said, 'Mind?'

'Of *course* I mind,' she said, and disappeared into the gloom.

'Sir?' The voice was behind him. He turned. Bakin was silhouetted against the light. 'Uh, could I talk to you, sir? Only a sec.'

He would never be allowed to sleep, that was what they were telling him. Okay, so be it. 'Shoot.'

Bakin came closer. 'Uh, sir, the men want to do something about Craw.'

He had to remind himself that Craw was dead. Too much had happened too quickly. And what did the man mean, 'do something'? It was too late to do something.

'They want to do a memorial service, sir.'

170

Ah, that kind of something. 'I'm sure there'll be a service on the boat, Chief.'

'Craw was very popular, Mister Craik. The men'd like to sort of say goodbye. They were planning on having a man of God here, somebody local, but if you put the kibosh on anybody coming in –'

'Negative anybody from outside.'

'Well, I thought that was the way, yessir. Well –' Bakin cleared his throat. 'I've done a certain amount of lay preaching myself. I'd volunteer to do that. Pray, and so on.'

'Good. Okay.'

'Fidelio would sing "Danny Boy."'

'Craw wasn't Irish.'

'Fidelio says he's sung it at a lot of Catholic funerals.'

'Craw wasn't Catholic.'

'Well, no – but the men think very highly of Fidelio's singing. They want it.'

This suggested a life in the EM spaces that Alan had hardly guessed. It made him feel guilty and a little angry. He told himself that he was wiped out, that he would see it differently in the morning. 'Okay,' he said.

'Basurto is writing a poem.'

All Alan could do was nod. Basurto was nineteen and until that moment had seemed to him a kid who lived only for pop music. *I'm their CO and I don't know anything about them!* 'Okay,' he said.

'I thought we'd do it down at the far end of the hangar – we can rig up two tables, sort of where a casket would go, you know –' Alan let him talk and then said that that was fine, everything was fine, good, he was glad the men were so thoughtful, and, wishing he'd had the idea of a memorial service himself, he staggered away toward the stair.

171

Sandy Cole was waiting at the bottom. She had a laptop and a digital camera.

'Ready?' she said.

He'd forgotten about her. He looked at his watch. After two-thirty. 'Yeah.'

It took her twenty minutes to get three photos out of the cameras and up on the screen, and then, because he wanted his own copies, it took another fifteen minutes to hunt down a floppy she could use. He found one at last in the comm office, where a bright-eyed second-class named Belk was monitoring the equipment and making adjustments that only an electronics freak would have understood. 'Hey, Belk,' Alan said.

'Hey, Mister Craik. Hey, I'm really sorry about Master Chief Craw. Really.'

'We all are.'

He dug out a floppy and carried it to Sandy Cole, who was asleep in a chair in the det office. She woke up long enough to make the copy and then crept away, her languid bones bent so far she almost flowed along the floor like water.

Alan booted the images up on his own laptop and then e-mailed them, PGP-encrypted, to Harry O'Neill.

Thirty seconds later, he was stretched out on a plywood table with his head on his helmet bag, and a few seconds after that he was asleep.

Day Two

5

London.
It was raining over London. The small windows of
the aircraft wept ribbons of water, and Dukas, leaning over from his aisle seat to look out, saw only the
grayness of cloud below and mist at eye level. He had
actually slept for an hour between the movies and
the snack, and now he stretched and decided to visit
the head, but only in time to hear that seat belts and
tray tables and all that were now more important. He
sank back into the seat, felt the knees of the woman
behind him, grunted. Her knees had been a problem
all night.

They came out of the clouds at a thousand feet, the
air around them seeming to brighten. Then they were
rushing down, and the wheels slammed and the
engines screamed, and in only slightly less time than
it would have taken him to walk, they were at the gate
and the bin doors were crashing and luggage was raining down. Dukas signaled his people in nearby seats
to stay put; only when the plane was all but empty
did he pull himself up and, with the slowness of a
patient man, take down his laptop and his raincoat and
head for the front of the aircraft.

They gathered in a knot in the exit area. Cram had
enjoyed the free booze and now looked like hell; several
of the others had the look of men who hadn't slept,

but Geraldine Pastner looked good, a little too bright-eyed, but amused and alert.

'We'll find a place to settle in at the outgoing flight lounge,' Dukas said. 'Nobody goes through immigration or customs. You guys aren't seeing London this trip.'

'Holy shit, Dukas.' It was the ex-Marine. 'We got eight hours.'

'Life is hard. Use it to read the briefing stuff.'

'I didn't get any briefing stuff.'

Dukas held up a CD-ROM. 'You will.'

'How about breakfast?' Geraldine said. 'I don't eat on airplanes and I sure don't drink.' She looked straight at Cram. 'It leaves me healthy but hungry. Who's for breakfast?'

Dukas started to say that he was, partly because Geraldine really pinged on him, but before he could speak he felt his left arm gripped hard, and a voice said, 'Dukas, listen up.'

It was somebody he knew but couldn't immediately place; he had turned and seen the big, pale face quite close, registered blue eyes and thinning hair and then stepped back to get a better look, thinking, *NCIS, served with him someplace, where?* The man pulled him back, mouth to ear again, and said, 'There's been another bombing. Come on.'

Dukas felt himself marched along a corridor, his gut dropping, heart banging, his inner voice whining, *Oh, no, oh, shit, oh, man, oh –* He waved for the others to follow. *Biggle. Biddle. Biddler, that was it – Biddler. Jesus, on the* Jackson, *that was umpteen years ago –*

'Biddler, right?' he said.

'Yeah. Been a while. Wasn't sure you'd remember me.'

'What's going on?'

'Not here.' He relaxed his grip on Dukas's arm. 'I'm in the London office now. I thought you were in Bosnia.'

'I was, I was – long story.' They were going so fast that Dukas was puffing. Next to him, Geraldine was charging along like a racehorse. Or a model, he thought. Yeah, she looked like a model – long, long legs, coat open, good color in her face, even though it wasn't even a pretty face, too much mouth, too much nose, but –

'So tell me –'

'Not here.' Biddler waved at a door up ahead, muttered something into a handheld, and the door opened, seemingly by itself. Once inside, Biddler led him into a corner where there were dark chairs and sleek tables and telephones and modems – some sort of VIP business place. The others were shepherded to a table with coffee thermoses and plates of killer sweet buns and, for some reason, a dozen bananas. Geraldine looked at Dukas and raised her eyebrows – *What's up?* – and turned gratefully to the coffee.

'Get me some!' Dukas called. Then, back to Biddler, 'Okay, what's going down?'

'Car bomb, they think. Cairo. The AID office.' AID was a US agency supposedly devoted to international development, but suspected in other parts of the world of something more sinister. But was it suspect enough to get itself bombed?

'Cairo! Shit, I've got a guy in Cairo! You sure it wasn't –'

'I'm not sure of anything. They told me yesterday to meet you out here and make nice; I get here this morning, and fifteen minutes ago there's this call,

Cairo's had a hit. That's about all I know.'

Dukas made a face – tongue between teeth, lips pursed out, eyes looking aside. As Geraldine put coffee in front of him, he said, 'Two in a row. They gotta be connected.' Then, less certainly, he said, 'You think?'

Biddler's eyes went to Geraldine and signaled to Dukas, but Dukas said, 'Oh, Christ, she's fine. They're all fine. What d'you think we're here for, golf?' He waved at the others, who were munching sweet buns and swilling coffee and looking hollow-eyed. 'This place okay?' he said to Biddler.

'We use it all the time.'

Dukas stood. 'Hey, people, listen up –! We just got the word, there's been another bombing.' Winces, a curse. 'Cairo this time. Geraldine, plug the STU in, get the office and find out what's up. Mendelsohn, I want everything on baddies in Egypt; it should be on the CD, but when you've got that down, double-check State and the Agency stateside. Keatley, find out what you can about AID in Cairo – where it is, what they were doing, what their security was. Hahn – hit the Internet, we got four chat rooms on our list, so see what they're saying.' He looked at Biddler. 'Right off the top of my head, I don't get hitting an AID office.'

'AID isn't our business,' Cram said. His face, purplish and swollen from the free booze, looked a little crazy. His eyes were swiveling about as if he was looking for a way back to the States.

Dukas held up two fingers. 'Two bombings. One Navy-connected. Therefore both our business, because when these things come in twos and threes – Jesus, pray God there isn't a third – then they're connected.' He swung back to Biddler. 'I need a secure phone.'

Biddler put him in a small office nearby, with a

phone he was assured had been vetted that morning. He called Triffler's hotel in Cairo, where it was two hours later and the entire Bright Star team were probably all eating breakfast in the same upscale place, and another car bomb could do a hell of a job on US-Egyptian planning. The woman on the other end sounded a little excitable, he thought – the bombing? Or maybe just local manner. Whatever the reason, she had trouble with the name Triffler, which she pronounced *Tereefeller* and wasted a couple of minutes finding the room.

'Dick?'

'Who is this, please?' Triffler was a cautious man, to be sure, even when he was waking up.

'Dick, it's Dukas, come on!'

'Oh, hi.'

'You heard?'

'Heard?'

'Dick, come on –! We've got a report the AID office there has been hit.'

'Oh, yeah.'

'"Oh, yeah!" *Yeah*! You heard.'

'Oh, yeah, I heard. I was headed out and they told me to go back to bed. In fact, I've been ordered to stay in the hotel until further notice.' Triffler sounded hurt. 'I was going to see the pyramids today.'

'You been there three weeks, for Christ's sake!'

'I've been working.'

'Dick, look, I need you to go to the AID office. Now.'

'I've been ordered to stay in the hotel.'

'By who?'

'My boss.'

'I'm your boss, as of midnight last night DC time.' He had a horrible moment when he thought it might

179

in fact not yet be midnight in DC; he tried to figure it and then thought, *The hell with it*. 'Get your ass to the AID office! Or what's left of it.'

'You're ordering me?'

Dukas sighed. 'Yes.'

'I'll never see the pyramids.'

'You'll live. Here's what I want you to do. When you get there, find somebody in security. It's maybe a US Marine, but I suspect it's likelier a local rent-a-cop. He or she'll have a list of employees. You find out what employee didn't come to work this morning. Get me?'

'Somebody who didn't want to get bombed.'

'That's why I asked for you, Dick, you're smart.'

'What if the security people got blown up, too?'

'Then we're fucked.'

'Maybe then I can go to the pyramids.'

'Dick, come on! Now look, you get the name of whoever didn't report in this morning, then you locate that person. Okay? We need to have the person held, so I guess you'll need a local cop. You with me?'

'What's the charge?'

'I don't think that'll be a problem; leave it to the local guy. Okay?' Triffler really was smart. Dukas knew that Triffler had been playing him a little, partly because he was smart and partly because he liked other people to lay everything out, to use all the rope they needed to hang themselves. Undoubtedly, he wanted Dukas to see how thin his idea was. And, as a result, Dukas did. He said, 'I know it's iffy, Dick, but it's all we got right now. Okay? The quicker you move, the better chance you got.'

'Then I'm outta here.'

Dukas gave him the numbers where he was, the contacts in Washington that could find him quickly.

When he was done, he said, 'What'd you want to see the pyramids for, anyway?'

Triffler hesitated and then said, 'Cleopatra was African American, too, you know.' And hung up.

Dukas lumbered back to the big room, where everybody was working at a laptop or a telephone or both, and the sweet buns were gone and the coffee was being refilled. He peeled a banana. 'Cram!'

Cram looked up from an armchair like a dog looking up from a stolen steak.

'Cram, get us all on the next flight to Cairo. Soonest, get me? I want to be there *now*!' He realized that he hadn't given Cram anything to do. Dukas bit into the banana. 'Understand?'

'Cancel the tickets to Nairobi?'

'Get us to Cairo, Cram; we'll worry about the rest when we get there. *Now*, okay?' Cram looked uncertain. Dukas raised his voice. 'Hey, Biddler –!' The London NCIS man looked up from the far side of the room, where he had been bent over somebody's laptop. Dukas waved him over. 'This is Cram, um, Bob? Bob Cram – um –'

Biddler was shaking Cram's hand. 'Del Biddler.' He must have heard of Cram, but he was polite, nonetheless.

'Yeah, listen, you know the local drill, help Cram get us to Cairo, will you?' Dukas sighed. He had just given Cram a responsibility and then taken it away from him, as he could see from the relief on Cram's face. Could Cram really be that lazy? Or was he scared? Of – of what? Of being tortured again? That seemed far-fetched. Dukas stared at Cram so long that Cram, perplexed, smiled at him – the bleary smile of a panhandler. Dukas turned away, pretending to have just thought of something, and then he did think of something that had flashed on him while he was talking to Triffler.

'Hey, Geraldine,' he said, sitting down next to her.

She was on a STU nonstop and said, 'Hold,' and put a hand over the mouthpiece so she could listen to Dukas.

'Didn't I ask you yesterday to check up on whoever shot the TV footage? The Mombasa thing?'

'Yeah.'

'What'd you get?'

'They gave me the runaround.'

'Lean on them. I want a name and I want the unedited tape. The Cairo thing, something gravels me – I dunno –'

'They *gave* me the name. It was the tape I didn't get – hold on –' She was tapping out keys on the smallest laptop Dukas had ever seen, an HP Jornada the size of a book. She muttered, 'Shit,' and then, 'Big fingers, I got big fingers,' and then she stared at the screen and said, 'Jean-Marc Balcon. French guy, I think.'

Dukas moved himself around so he could see the little screen and then copied the name into his black appointment book. Unlike many people, Dukas couldn't use a computer for notes, appointments, jottings. He needed paper. 'You too busy to follow this up right now?' he said.

Geraldine smiled, held up the telephone. 'Am I busy?' she said.

'I want that tape – okay?'

She gave one of those sighs that says *I'm overworked and underappreciated and you're an asshole*, but she nodded and began to bang on the keys of the little laptop. 'This shithole able to receive streaming video?'

she said. She apparently meant the VIP lounge they were in.

Dukas wasn't sure that he even knew what streaming video was, but he said, 'Ask Biddler.'

She hit some more keys, and then she was back on the telephone, talking to somebody about al-Gama'at and links to al-Qaida.

Dukas sat down to draft a message to Al Craik in Mombasa, gazing longingly at the empty plate that had held the sweet buns.

Mombasa.

The runways stretched into haze on either side like desert, flat, sterile, the air traffic so light that it was as if no other life existed. Near the hangar door, the Marines had set up a strongpoint of sandbags from which they could watch the approaches and the airport itself. More sandbags were being filled out back. Off to the right, the EM Quonset sat in its own little scrub of green weeds, the nearest they had to an oasis. Just in case they were tempted to get careless, four of the Marines were listening to a radio version of a CNN broadcast on the Cairo bombing.

'Sir?' a voice said at Alan's elbow. 'They got snakes here?'

Jacklin, a twenty-year-old electronics tech. 'Some,' Alan said.

'Jeez, I hate snakes.'

Alan debated telling him about mambas, which reared up as high as a man's chest and could deliver a venom that killed in minutes. Or yellow cobras. Or various others that were, at best, unpleasant. 'Just watch where you walk and where you put your hands,' he said. 'You'll be fine.' He was watching another det sailor put something on the ground near the enlisted men's Quonset.

'What I like on the boat, there's no snakes.'

'Yeah, but look at how great the food is here, Jacklin.' The sailor over by the Quonset was looking at something in a clump of weeds.

'Oh, yeah. Oh, *ye-e-ah*! When they start putting pizza in MREs, maybe I'll start liking them.' Jacklin hesitated. 'I heard about a guy opened a box of spare parts, there was a *cobra* in there.'

A cat came out of the weeds and moved parallel to the sailor, eyes on the ground near his feet. Alan realized that he'd put part of an MRE down there. The cat came close, sat down. The sailor backed off a step. The cat came closer, sat down. Another cat appeared at the edge of the weeds.

Alan nodded. If they'd started to acquire mascots, morale was picking up. Or had been until the news from Cairo had come through. He was waiting for the morning commercial flight from Nairobi to bring some embassy people for a meet. It was odd, loafing here in the haze, but he was wiped, physically and mentally. Maybe emotionally, too. Of course there was a lot to do, a lot he could have been doing, but he felt wrung out and disassociated, and he thought he had earned a few minutes of doing nothing. Although that was a dangerous idea, that you earned one kind of behavior with another. Like thinking you earned good luck by going through a bad patch, when the truth was you could get whacked again and again and again, and there wouldn't ever have to be compensation for it. Like Job.

'I'll bet you have something you're supposed to be doing,' he said to Jacklin.

'Oh – yes, sir –!' Alan had told the chief to keep

184

everybody busy, even if they had to end up polishing the concrete with their toothbrushes.

So why wasn't he working? Because he was tired and mentally down. He'd called Rose as soon as he'd got up, waking her in the middle of the Houston night, and it had been good – good to talk family talk, good to hear that husky voice. But when he had hung up, he was still tired and mentally low, and he thought she had sounded down, too, although she wouldn't admit it to him.

He heard the aircraft then but couldn't find it in the haze, then spotted it as a silver spark already low and going from his right to left, swinging into its approach. This would be a milk run for the pilot – down from Nairobi in the morning, up again and back the same day. It seemed very peaceful and ordinary and not part of a world in which ships blew up and good men got shot by strangers.

He pulled a handheld from his pocket. 'Captain Geelin.'

'Yo.'

'Craik. Nairobi flight's incoming. Our guests should be here in about fifteen.'

'They're expected.'

The Marines seemed in better shape than the sailors of the det, at least more alert this morning. Geelin was a good CO, Alan thought, good at pumping his men and good at making them feel they had a purpose. They were all still pissed at leaving their buddies behind on the *Harker*, but they were sure they would all be back there in a day or two, and it was Geelin's planning and Geelin's force of will that gave them that confidence. Alan would have to write him a good fitrep for the time he spent in his command – oddly easy

185

when there was a personal antipathy, as if written praise was more straightforward when there was no liking. Maybe a kind of one-on-you: see how swell I am, even though you think I'm a shit?

'That their plane?' It was Sandy, shading her eyes and squinting. 'I hope they brought me some clothes.' She had learned from the Kenyan Navy that her car, with her suitcase in it, had been torched where she had left it outside the fuel depot. Messages had been going back and forth between the det and the embassy and the *Jefferson* all night. 'I *asked* them to bring me some clothes.' She looked at Alan, her hand still over her eyes, as if he had denied the possibility of anybody's ever bringing her clothes again.

'Sorry about your car,' he said.

'Yuh.' She shrugged. 'It's insured. I guess Pan-Afric Insurance, Limited, will pay.' She gave an *Oh, yeah, like cows give pink Zinfandel* kind of laugh. 'I asked the Kenyans about interviewing the guy they pulled out of the water. They said, "What guy?" I talked to four different people. Same answer – "What guy?" We're going to have to lean on them.'

The airbus was far across the field, taxiing toward the thin slab that was the terminal, vaguely gray-green in the humid heat. The sun struck gold and silver lights from the aircraft, and they could hear the whine of the engines. At least three people from the embassy were supposed to be on board, and it was they who were supposed to be bringing the LegAt her clothes. Not a very high item on their list of priorities, Alan thought – or maybe it was. Maybe keeping a crucial member of the staff in clean clothes was right up there with defending America.

'I told them to bring my blue jeans,' she said.

'Don't wear them off the det space.' He looked at her. 'Islamic sensibilities. They don't like –'

'For God's sake! I've lived here for eighteen months!' She wrapped her arms around herself and stepped back into the shade. 'I'm *sick* of Islamic sensibilities.'

Somebody came striding toward them through the gloom of the hangar, and Alan squinted sun-dazzled eyes to make out Cohen, who looked serious and insecure. When he saw Alan looking at him, he bobbed his head and came faster. 'Message from the boat,' he said when he got close. 'Somebody named Dukas sent you a Most Urgent.' He handed Alan the message.

'He's the head of the NCIS team that's due in tonight. Where the hell is he? – London.' Alan read: Early reports were that an AID office had been the target in Cairo; Washington had word that a car bomb had gone off at the side of the building, blowing out three floors and the building across the side street. No casualty figures yet, but Cairo police were already reporting that the nearest hospital was overflowing with people who had glass injuries and had been able to walk there. Dukas was sending Dick Triffler, already in Cairo, to check it out.

Alan looked at Sandy. 'Why would anybody hit an AID office?'

She shrugged. 'Seen as very aggressive "Big America" presence. Maybe resentment because they think it's connected with the World Bank or the WTO – people believe all kinds of shit in this part of the world.'

'You don't think much of this part of the world.'

'Do you?' She squinted off into the haze, played with her hair. 'I'm not judgmental. I just get tired of all their shit.'

187

It was the third time he had heard her use the word *shit* that morning, and he couldn't remember her using it or any other strong word the day before, when things were tougher. Stress? Aftershock? 'Maybe you know them better than I do,' he said, trying to be tactful. He was reaching for his cell phone.

'Oh, Christ, don't patronize me.' She walked away into the cool of the hangar. So much for tact.

Cohen, who had been hanging around, started to move away, and Alan grabbed his arm. 'Pass the word to the *Harker* that we're upping security because of Cairo. They'll probably have it from the boat, but make sure. They should be extra alert. Captain Geelin will probably have something to say to his gunny on board, too.'

Cohen hesitated. 'What should we expect here?'

'If I knew, I'd tell you.'

'I'll be happier when those other gyrenes get here.'

'Maybe.'

'Memorial service for Craw has been set for 1700. Should we cancel it?'

They were walking into the hangar together, heading for the office. The space where the aircraft had been was empty, making the place seem even bigger. The plane would be loading now in Nairobi.

'The memorial service is a good idea. Keep it.'

He already had one of the intel specialists checking Egyptian terrorism and possible links to Mombasa. It seemed far-fetched, the two countries not contiguous, their branches of Islam different, their faces turned in different directions. Like most other intelligence professionals, he resisted the idea of highly organized terrorist networks that spanned national boundaries and were equally effective in very different cultures. It was one thing to speak Egyptian Arabic and work in a nation where a strong Islamic counterculture had long waged a war against the government, quite another to speak Swahili and work in a nation where the Islamic political movement was mostly nonviolent and legal. And yet, intel people also knew that when two terrorist events happened closely in time, they were almost certainly connected. And a third might follow.

What would Harry O'Neill say now?

'Get to CIC on the boat and ask them to secure-fax us everything they've got on Egyptian terrorist groups.' That was merely insurance, however; he knew pretty well what the boat would have: al-Gama'at al-Islamiyya, which had attacked tourists and the Egyptian government and which had an external wing, but which had been quiet for more than a year; al-Jihad, a specialist in high-level assassination, including Anwar Sadat, with a branch in Afghanistan connected to Osama bin Laden's al-Qaida; various splinters of the Palestinian groups, but their real interest was Gaza. Many of them had signed on to bin Laden's hatred of Americans. But why now? And why one day after an attack in Mombasa, where these groups had never operated?

He found Sandy at the far end of the hangar, sitting in one of the chairs of the circle they had made last night. She looked miserable, and he thought that she, too, would benefit from something to do. 'You got any contacts in Kenyan military intelligence?' he said.

'I'm more into police. But it slops over – you know.'

'How about you try to find what they've got on connections with Egypt? Anything – anything at all. Money, intercepts, rumor – what the hell.'

She stared at her feet, which were cleaner this morning. 'They're all Muslims,' she said.

189

'We need *connections*. How about it?'

She heaved herself up. 'Okay,' she said in a voice that suggested that hope was a fantasy. She started to slouch off, then turned back to him with her hand in her hair. 'If you really want to work with people I trust, let's go to the Kenya Wildlife Service.'

'They wouldn't have much on terrorism, would they?'

She shrugged. 'They're their own country. They don't trust the military, they don't trust the cops, they don't trust the crooks around the president – and they're right.'

'So try them.'

She scowled at him as if she was going to say something else, then turned and wandered away, playing with her hair. She seemed to him a different woman this morning. Tough to be married to, if so.

London.
Dukas had gathered his team in front of Geraldine's laptop. People were slouching in easy chairs as if they'd been dropped on them from a height. Jet lag was not being kind.

'Okay, look and listen, please. What we're going to see is the unedited tape of the first stuff on the Mombasa bombing. This is what you saw on CNN and elsewhere. Geraldine?'

She hit a key, and the screen changed color. The television material came up abruptly and, without introduction or editing, looked jerky and disconnected. Everybody leaned closer, because the small screen was hard on detail.

There was no voice-over on the early shots, but there seemed to be sound, even at one point somebody's breathing. The first shot showed a metal gate with coiled razor wire along the top, then, abruptly, a street lined with palms, young men moving on it apparently aimlessly. Two or three looked at the camera. A voice could be heard saying something; Dukas thought he heard '. . . *non plus*.'

Establishing shots.

'Some riot,' Hahn muttered.

Then the gate appeared again, growing jerkily closer, apparently as the cameraman moved toward it. The French-accented voice that Dukas remembered said something like *'venez – venez – vite, vite – pas encore –'* Dukas thought he could see a ship's superstructure on the other side of the gate – had he? No time; another change without transition, and they were apparently on a dock, looking at the open water between it and an adjacent dock. There was a crane. The camera swung left and showed a large, gray ship almost bow-on.

'That the *Harker*?'

'Inutile,' the French voice said on the tape.

More cranes, buildings glimpsed behind them. A slow pan to the right, movement out on the water, the end of the next pier, a small freighter tied up, another small ship –

Complete change – buildings, the tops of palms, smoke at a distance. Then a gate, maybe the same gate as before. Seen now from its other side? The voice was muttering on the tape but it was unclear, certainly not meant for broadcast. Dukas could make out none of it.

And then the scene they had looked at again and again on television, this time with voice-over, ending with Alan Craik hurrying toward the camera and turning, injured hand out.

The screen went blank.

'Show it again.'

They went through it a second time. Then again. People talked over it now. Mendelsohn, whose French was pretty good, translated what he could. '"Useless," is what he said when it showed the *Harker*. "Inutile" means "useless."'

'Why the fuck would he say that? What's useless about a ship?'

'Maybe he was looking for shots of the riot. A ship would be useless if you wanted shots of the riot.'

But Dukas was thinking that if the guy had wanted shots of a riot, he wouldn't be here in the docks. He'd be out in the street, where that early shot had been filmed. On the other hand, a shot of the *Harker* would be useless, maybe, if you knew it was going to be blown up, because it would tell too much about what you knew. Was that just too far out?

'Show it again,' he said.

This time he focused on only the shot with the *Harker*, but he didn't look at the ship that was going to be blown up. He looked at the right side of the screen, the open water next to the *Harker*. It widened as the camera swung right – movement on the water, muffled sound –

'Hold it!'

Freeze-frame didn't work on a computer, but Geraldine managed to back up and stop, which gave them a blurry approximation. Dukas pointed at the pale smudge where the movement was. 'What is it? Anybody see it well enough to know?'

They all strained to see. Geraldine said, 'Well, it's on the water. It's a boat.'

'Could be a bird,' Hahn muttered.

Dukas told her to run it again. Was it a boat? He

listened to the muffled sound. 'Turn it up and run it again.' He watched the camera start to pan, saw the movement on the water, heard a chuffing sound like, perhaps, wind hitting the mike, and the voice, '– *non, non –*'

They shoot the Harker, *and the camera pans, and it sees the boat or whatever, and the French guy says, 'No, no.'*

And at that point, the pan had stopped.

They looked at it again, and this time it registered on Dukas that the final sequences, those that included Al Craik, had started much farther away from the *Harker* than the pan with the movement on the water. At the very first, the camera had started shooting outside the gate; then it had come inside the gate, then had moved closer to the dock where the *Harker* was moored. And then it had gone all the way outside the gate again. But between the last two sequences, somebody had bombed the *Harker*.

'Get somebody in DC to analyze the tape,' Dukas told Geraldine Pastner. 'I want to know what was moving on the water. And I want to know every word that sonofabitch said.'

Geraldine looked at him with raised eyebrows and a small look of fake surprise. '"Sonofabitch?"'

'Yeah, sonofabitch, as in he knew exactly what was going to happen. *That* sonofabitch.'

Ten minutes later, with phones ringing and voices filling the space as if it was a telemarketers' boiler room, Dukas was in the midst of chewing something the English thought was an edible bun when his cell phone went off and, mouth full, he pulled it out and shouted 'Dukas!', which came out as a kind of seal's mating cry because of the bun.

'Mister Dukas?'

'Yeah, oh, hi, yeah, Leslie –' He swallowed. He didn't want to talk to his barely post-adolescent assistant. He suspected he'd jumped at the chance to leave Washington partly to get away from her. He swallowed again. 'Yes, Leslie, what?'

'There's been a bomb in Cairo.'

'I already heard.'

'I worried about you.'

'Leslie, I'm in London. Cairo's in Egypt.'

'Even so.' She waited. Was he supposed to say something? He didn't. She said, 'I want you to be very careful.'

'That's it? You called me to tell me to be careful? Leslie, do you know how busy I am?'

'Now you're mad at me, aren't you.'

Dukas took a deep breath. 'Leslie, what time is it there?'

'About three-fifteen.'

She meant three-fifteen in the morning. 'Leslie, go back to bed.'

'I'm in bed. I can't sleep. I'm worried about you.'

Dukas told her to take two aspirin and not to call him again unless there was something important. She said that this was important. Dukas restrained himself and said it was nice of her to worry and everything was fine, goodbye, *click*, and he turned his cell phone off because he was sure she'd call right back. *What's the matter with her?* he asked himself. *She's usually such a smart kid*.

Dukas had loved a number of women who hadn't loved him back. He'd never experienced things the other way around.

Cairo.

NCIS Special Agent Dick Triffler was tall and slender and more medium-brown than black. He tended toward the sartorially elegant, usually wore expensive suits and heavy silk ties when the climate cooperated. Cairo had frustrated him at first with its heat, which was oppressive even for a Washingtonian, but he had bought a couple of locally made shirts and a local jacket, the shirts like tissue and the jacket a nubby silk so fine it could have been used for a scarf, and in these he was almost comfortable and certainly splendid. The concierge of the first-class hotel where the Bright Star crew were housed approved: the day that Triffler had first appeared in his new clothes, the concierge – a slim, silver-haired, olive-skinned Egyptian who spoke flaw-less English, French, and Arabic – said, 'Ah-h-h!' the equivalent of a standing ovation.

Now, however, Triffler was crossing Cairo in a brutal car that needed a right front shock absorber and had no air-conditioning, and he knew he should have worn short sleeves and no tie and no silk jacket. Sweat was pouring from him and from the Egyptian cop who sat next to him, radiating heat as if he had just been fired up and turned on full. The cop's name was Sergeant al-Fawzi-al-Mubarak, but he had said 'Call me Ali' in a tone that suggested that Ali was not his real name but that he had learned from long experience that 'Ali' was all Americans could manage.

Triffler had decided to call him 'Sergeant.'

Right now, he wanted to say, 'Sergeant, move way over and stop metabolizing, would you?' but of course you didn't say anything like that to an ally whose co-operation would be vital if they in fact found anything at the apartment they were headed for. Indeed, the sergeant was there only because Triffler had already made connections at a fairly high level through Bright Star. As soon as Dukas had rung off from London, he had made three phone calls, standing in nothing but a pair of lime-green jockey shorts with dancing female nudes on them. The first, to a biggie in the military police, had given the number of a somebody in the Cairo police, and that call had given him the sergeant and the plainclothes car and the driver.

And the heat, and his wilting, wonderful jacket and shirt.

'We are there,' the sergeant said. He waved a large, glistening hand at the side of the street. Triffler was momentarily disoriented: where was *there*? Then he remembered: *there* would be the apartment of an American woman named Alice Dempsey, who hadn't reported for work that morning at the AID office.

Just as Dukas had said.

Triffler ducked his head and twisted his neck and looked up. The building had been put up under the French or British and was falling down in its own good time. Monumental columns rose on each side of an arched doorway; above it, pediments and pilasters and deep window bays rose up out of sight. It had once been very grand, indeed.

The driver had scuttled around and was holding the door open. He, too, was a cop, but a small, weasely one. Packing, however, like the sergeant; Triffler could see the bulges under their open-necked shirts. He, of course, was unarmed. (The Egyptians loved the Americans like brothers, but they certainly didn't want them going about with guns, for God's sake.)

On the sidewalk, Triffler stood half a head taller than the sergeant, and six inches more than that above the driver. The sergeant, however, made up for the difference in bulk; he was a wide man, and his short haircut and no-bullshit expression made him look very tough. Now he said something to the driver, who scuttled back behind the wheel. 'We go in,' the sergeant said.

'Let's set some ground rules first.' Triffler looked into the man's eyes. Nothing came back out. 'Rules of engagement? You know – how we're going to conduct ourselves?'

'You want to find woman.'

'Right. But we're not going to bust in – you know, go in big? Noisy? No noise, no guns. We knock.' He made a knocking motion. For some reason, the sergeant laughed. 'This is *investigative*,' Triffler said.

'Woman does not go work, bomb goes off, you *investigate*.'

'Right.'

The sergeant reached under his shirt and tugged his pants upward. The gesture was aggressive, at the same time cautious, as if he was reining himself in. '*Your* investigation,' he said. 'Something wrong, it is *Cairo* case.'

'Absolutely. I just want to talk to her. Okay?'

'Okay-okay.' He barked more Arabic at the driver, who slunk down in the seat like a dog who has been scolded. The sergeant led Triffler through the arched doorway, whose huge wooden doors were propped permanently open by wooden poles as big around as sewer pipes. Inside, there was a courtyard, with balconies rising on three sides; small cars had been jammed in so tightly that Triffler didn't see how the drivers got in and out. An elderly woman was screaming at a young man who was squeezing himself into

197

one of them while two other men waited, and Triffler saw the system: you parked your car, then other people parked all around you, and then when you wanted your car, the old woman screamed until the other cars were moved.

'Is she the concierge?' he said.

The sergeant used an Arabic word, then nodded at a cubbyhole behind the door. No doubt the old woman's lair.

'Ask her if Miss Dempsey is in.'

The sergeant flashed a badge and said something; the old woman stopped screaming and looked terrified; the young man shot the car between Triffler and the sergeant, and the other men got in their cars and gunned the engines. The badge had made everybody in a hurry to be someplace else.

'She say, American woman upstairs.' His big face looked as if it had been oiled; as Triffler watched, a drop of sweat fell from the sergeant's nose.

'Ask her if she has a car here.'

More talk, and the old woman pointed at a green Fiat in the middle of the pack. Triffler squeezed himself between the cars, sucking in his gut and trying to keep his elegance unsmirched – hopeless with the dust of the streets on every surface. He scraped his thighs, shifted, and scraped his butt; he lifted the skirts of his jacket and felt his cordovan loafers lose their shine on a tire. When he got to the car, there was nothing to do but bend down and look in, trying to penetrate the dirt of the windshield so he could see – what? Nothing. The interior of a small, messy car. With what was perhaps a laptop on the back seat, under a lot of paper folders.

Out of the tangle, Triffler dusted his trousers and

wiped his loafers with a tissue and inspected his jacket for dirt or, horrible to think about, oil stains. The sergeant looked disgusted.

'Let's go upstairs,' Triffler said. 'Does the old lady have keys?'

More Arabic, then a 'yes.'

'Bring her along, please.'

There was an elevator that had perhaps been the wonder of the city in 1898; now it made a clanking overhead that suggested bad things to come, perhaps on this very trip. The ride up two storeys seemed interminable, but it gave Triffler time to reflect that it would be quicker to take the stairs, even in the heat, and if you wanted to cover exits from the woman's apartment, you'd need at least four people, because he could see two sets of stairs through the elevator's porthole, and he was sure there was at least one back stair somewhere, because when this place was put up, everybody who had lived here had had servants.

'So,' the sergeant said.

'Right.' Triffler got out and stood aside for the old woman, who, in response, cowered at the back of the elevator. The sergeant reached in and yanked her out. She began to weep.

'That wasn't necessary,' Triffler said.

The sergeant looked at him as if necessity was hardly a relevant concept. He gave the old woman a shove and she plodded along the balcony to their right, weeping and going through her keys as if they were a rosary. She came to a stop outside a tall doorway, holding up a key as if it would ward off the sergeant's evil spirit. Taking Triffler – probably correctly – for the kinder of the two, she jerked her head toward the door and then bobbed the key up and down.

199

The sergeant reached for the keys, but Triffler put out his hand to stop him, and he started to say, 'I'm going to knock,' getting as far as 'I'm going –' when a small-caliber gunshot popped and a woman screamed inside.

The sergeant wrenched the bundle of keys from the old woman's hand; she retreated, holding the hand and bawling; Triffler leaned his ear against the door, and the door swung a few inches open and then stopped on a high place in the floor. Then things happened very fast, with Triffler's brain slowing them down for later sorting: the scar on the doorjamb where the lock had been forced; the semicircle on the flooring where the door had dragged an image of its opening and closing; the feeling of a blow on his shoulder as the sergeant pushed him in and down.

Triffler pushed the door hard and it swung open and he stumbled two steps into the interior, sensing high ceilings and ornate moldings, another door open on the right and the glare of high windows straight ahead, against which were the silhouettes of two figures. He held out a hand, something in him meaning to make the habitual apology for bursting in; something American and coplike wanting to forestall complaint, lawsuit; something warning him that he had no warrant.

One silhouette was female. She was falling backward.

The other silhouette was male. Triffler understood that the silhouette was turning, turning toward him, the meaning unclear, and then he saw between the two figures the hand and the gun, and he knew that the silhouette was going to shoot him.

Triffler hit the floor and the gun spat, and behind

him another gun roared, a big caliber, shot after shot. Triffler's face was in a carpet, his fingers clawing at it, waiting for a shot in the top of the head or the back, one shooter or the other sure to get him, and then the shooting stopped and he rolled to the side and, coming up against the legs of a table, raised his head.

The sergeant was pulling a backup gun from an ankle holster, his face transfigured by an expression of ecstatic concentration. His off hand held a huge automatic.

Triffler swiveled his eyes and saw only the shot-out windows and the glare; bringing his gaze down, he saw a dead man and, behind him and to the right, a dead woman.

'Oh, shit,' he muttered. He got to his feet, motioning to the sergeant to back off. 'It's over, it's over —' The sergeant pushed past him and opened the door on the right in a combat stance and went through. His footsteps, and then Triffler heard another door open in there.

The man on the floor had been killed several times over. He had been hit at least four times, center-of-body hits that had blown blood and tissue over the floor and walls behind him. Triffler's eyes, accustoming themselves to the indoor light, saw the sweep of red, and he smelled the stink of it. He blew out his breath, shook his head. 'Oh, boy,' he said. He looked down at the woman, who, thank God, didn't seem to have any big bullet holes in her, only one small one where her heart was, which had penetrated a pale blue blouse and a pink brassiere and left black powder residue and burns. The shooter had been holding her, he guessed, maybe by an upper arm or a wrist, and he had put the gun right against her breast and fired, and when Triffler had fallen into the room he had still been holding her.

He felt for a pulse in her throat and got nothing. 'Oh, boy.'

The sergeant passed behind him going the other way and Triffler heard another door open.

He had blood on the soles of his loafers now, he knew, and he knelt beside the dead man and got blood on the knee of his linen trousers. He felt in what was left of the man's pockets and came up with a bloody nylon wallet that was more like a card case, hardly big enough for money, but it held plastic cards and what he took to be a driver's license and folded papers. By the time he had that figured out, the sergeant was back, his reloaded cannon again stored in his cross-draw holster. He knelt by Triffler and started wiggling the backup gun into the ankle holster.

'Great shooting,' Triffler said sarcastically.

'Thank you.' Sarcasm doesn't travel well.

'He's very dead. Remember when we talked about rules of engagement, I said we were going to *investigate*?'

The sergeant pointed at the little wallet. 'You *investigating*. Here in Cairo, not good to, ah – play with evidence.'

Triffler stood up. 'I'm not playing.' He dropped the wallet on a table that had bowlegs and claw feet. 'Get this guy's address. Is that a driver's license?'

'Evidence,' the sergeant said.

'My fucking A it's evidence! I'm investigating a fucking bombing; don't talk to me about evidence!' Triffler leaned forward and put his nose almost against the Egyptian's surprised face. 'This guy killed the woman who didn't show up for work! Why do you think he killed her – because he was here to steal the silver? This is a fucking assassination, Sergeant! This guy killed her so she wouldn't be able to talk to me!'

He pulled his head back. The shorter, wider man looked stunned, as great anger will cause even strong people to look when they don't expect it. Triffler already knew what the sergeant had been thinking since they had met: *Thin American black man, no balls, treat him nice and he'll go away.* Now the sergeant was thinking, *Uh-oh, very big balls.*

'I want the dead man's address and I want to go there. Now!'

The sergeant gestured at the mess.

'They're dead. She's dead; what the fuck can she tell me now? He's dead, but his room or his apartment or whatever the hell can tell me something! Come on, come on –!'

'I make report – it is rule –'

'Okay, report, get a forensics team or whatever over here. Then I'm outta here.'

Sergeant al-Fawzi-al-Mubarak headed for a telephone.

Mombasa.
They made a kind of parody of a conference room out of a space between two prefab bulkheads by pushing two plywood tables together and putting folding chairs around them. There was water in a plastic carrier, and yellow legal pads that must have come from the boat, but there was a shortage of pencils in the det and so there was nothing to write with unless you brought your own.

Alan took the head of the table and let the three embassy men sit where they would, with Sandy Cole at the bottom opposite him. She looked like a harpy – hair wild, eyes red, mouth turned down. They hadn't brought her any clothes. They said they hadn't had time, with lots of apologies, but the apologies hadn't helped. Trying to pacify her as they headed for the meeting room, Alan had said, 'Sandy, it's okay, I don't have any clean clothes, either,' and she had hissed, 'I'm having my period! Are you?' Now, she didn't meet his eyes.

The three men from Nairobi wore short-sleeved white shirts and ties, and they had batteries of pens in their shirt pockets. Two of them were CIA officers stationed at the embassy: Patemkin, very dark, intense, pushing forty; Mink, a thirtyish, long-headed ex-jock. The third man was from embassy security and looked distrustful of the whole situation. Maybe it was his attitude that caused Patemkin to take charge at once and say to Alan, 'We're here to help. No bullshit – this is a Navy thing, we acknowledge that, end of story.'

Alan grinned. 'I'm stunned.'

The embassy security man, whose name was Pierce or Pearson and who was older than anybody else in the room by at least ten years, said, 'You don't have the best record of cooperation yourself, Commander.'

Mink leaned forward. 'Did you really tell George Shreed he was "contemptible" in his own office?'

Alan grinned even more widely. 'What can you do for us now, is the question.'

The embassy security man growled, but Patemkin pointed out that Alan already had the LegAt, and they were prepared to join him full-time if he wanted them.

'Here?' Alan said, surprised.

'Absolutely.'

'The best we can offer is a table to sleep on, MREs to eat, and a sleeping bag – if they find some in Nairobi. We've got twenty-two Marines to defend the whole place, and I'm allowing nobody in or out. If you commit, you're here. Okay?'

Patemkin nodded. Mink nodded. The embassy security man said, 'No way.'

Alan smiled at him. 'We'll put you on the afternoon plane back to Nairobi. Okay, let's get down to work.'

Cairo.

Triffler walked through the dead woman's apartment, eye-balling it for the obvious, the big things that would tell him something about the bombing. He saw a man's pants and shoes in a closet otherwise full of woman's clothes: okay, she was getting laid, maybe by the guy who killed her. That would fit: trusted American employee, Egyptian lover, leaked information. He saw a kitchen where nobody ever cooked, a little Swedish refrigerator full of yogurt and orange juice. He went back and looked at the woman's face. Maybe forty or a little younger, a few pounds over the American limit, no wedding ring. He went to the bathroom: birth-control pills, a decorative, lidded glass jar full of condoms. *Cute.* Okay. *Bang me and I'm yours. Bang me and I'll help you arrange to kill my coworkers.* He went back to the bedroom and found her car keys in a purse under the pillow, flipped through her wallet – Alice Dempsey, same face, right woman; no AID pass, so maybe somebody had taken it; photos, including two of a cat – *Shit, does she own a cat?*

'You see a cat?'

The sergeant was standing by a telephone near the bodies, sweating. He had the expression of a cop who has waked up to the fact that maybe he had used excessive violence.

'He shoots at me first,' he said.

'Right. I'm your witness for that, and don't you forget it. I said, did you see a cat?'

'Cat?'

'Oh, shit –' The big door was closed; Triffler opened it a crack and closed it at once because there was a crowd out there. 'You call this in?'

The sergeant nodded.

Triffler went back to the kitchen and looked for a cat bowl and didn't find it, then looked in a couple of likely places for a cat-pan. He was relieved when he didn't find one. He didn't want there to be one more starving cat wandering the Cairo streets.

He heard a police hooter close by. He went to the sergeant and, standing a little behind him, put a hand on his shoulder. 'You ever shoot anybody before?'

The man shook his head. 'Once –' He waved something away. 'Not dead.'

'You better sit down.'

'No! No good.'

'Your call.'

Triffler opened the door to the first knock, and Cairo police poured in. Triffler, who was a straight arrow and who believed that you followed every rule exactly as it was written, was nonetheless a man who knew where his responsibility lay. And he had been exposed enough to Mike Dukas to know that you had to keep your eyes on the goal.

As the cops came in, he slipped out.

He went down the stairs, his slender feet tripping, tapping on the worn marble treads, and squeezed himself between the cars again. There was hardly enough room to get his hand and the keys down where he could put the key in the lock, but he managed to get the driver's door open, and then he used his long, thin arm to reach into the back seat and extract, one by one, the folders that were there. He glanced at them

206

and threw them back – Economic Forecasts; Maxitrends, economy; Boreholes; Nontourism – and wiggled his fingers over the seat until he got the edge of the laptop and pulled it toward him by the pressure of one finger on the corner, until he could grab the corner with index finger and thumb and pull it to him.

He hugged the laptop to him as he squeezed through the cars again. The old woman was watching from her post near her cubbyhole. Triffler nodded as he went by her, reaching into his pocket for a fifty-piastre note.

The plainclothes car with the bad shocks was still at the curb, the weasel still behind the wheel. He was having a vigorous conversation with a uniformed policeman until he saw Triffler, when he sank down into his seat.

'You speak English?' Triffler said to him. 'English?' The man looked terrified.

'English,' the uniformed cop said. He tapped himself. 'English.' Big deal.

'Great!' Triffler took the dead man's driver's license from his pocket. 'Is there an address on this? Address? Street number?'

It took a while to communicate what he meant, but at last he got it across. 'Tell him to take me there. Me.' He pointed at himself, then away into the unknown. 'There. He – take – me – there.'

Seconds later, he was on his way.

6

Mombasa.

Alan briefed the three embassy men on what had happened the day before, from the first sound of the bomb to the nighttime helo flight from the docks. Then they told him what they knew: Mombasa had quieted, but only because of a massive police and military presence; there was still no movement within the city, with a curfew that would be lifted only late in the day for two hours. The hospitals were overflowing.

'What do your contacts say?'

Patemkin made a face. 'Mixed. Not getting good response, you know? Some, it sounds like a preplanned report: "The soldiers came and we were only defending ourselves." Others, it's more like: "We had this demonstration going but it got out of hand." A couple, they were scared but they told us there was outside interference of some kind.'

'I saw a guy with a gun, as I told you. Not a Swahili – lighter-skinned.'

'Arab,' the security man said.

'I don't know that.'

The man grunted. Patemkin got some papers from Mink and spread them in front of him. 'It's all confusion right now. Kenyan government is saying the Islamic Party of Kenya was behind everything that happened, and they're showing pix of the sniper you killed, as if the guy was a known IPK. In fact, we can't find any ID of him yet. Same-same with a guy they say was on the dhow that bombed your boat, but the guy is missing a leg and is in a coma and who knows *what* the hell he is?' He looked up at Alan. 'Now there's this crap in Cairo.'

'Hold the phone,' Sandy Cole said. 'The Kenyans are admitting they've got a guy from the dhow?'

'To us they are.'

She glanced at Alan. 'I got a load of bullshit from them. We need to interview him.'

'They say he's in a coma.'

'I want to see for myself.' She and Patemkin stared at each other. There was some sort of silent communication. Patemkin said, 'Okay, I'll lean on them.' He made a face. 'The Ugly American strikes again.'

Alan leaned in. 'Let's go back a minute. Outside agitation – what if the guy I saw *was* an outsider – if your reports are right and there was outside agitation?' He was thinking of Harry's insistence that Islam was not responsible.

Sandy shook her unhappy head. 'That doesn't sound right. Not the situation here.'

'Well, it would be an *unusual* situation, wouldn't it? If you had outside interference?'

'Yeah, but why?' Patemkin said. 'IPK are a pain in the ass to the government as it is; they don't need outside help.'

Mink spoke for the first time. 'If they wanted to go violent, they might call in, let's say, the Yemenis or somebody?'

'Why?' Alan said. 'No homegrown muscle?'

'It isn't necessarily muscle. You said a guy with a rifle. That'd be unusual here.'

'Damned unusual.'

'Well? So you go outside for it – other Islamic militants –'

'Are the IPK really militants?'

Patemkin was waving his hands. 'Let's do a "what if," okay? What if your man with the rifle *was* an outsider? So what? It doesn't change the facts – big demo, violence, everybody knows the Kenyan cops are out for blood, so you get massive retaliation. I mean, whether your instigators are homegrown or you bring them in from outside, what's the difference?'

'Unless,' Sandy said, 'the outsiders are uninvited.'

Patemkin looked at her. 'Say what?'

'Well, we don't know, do we? *If* there were outsiders, why do they have to be people who were *brought* in? How about if they were *sent* in? By – somebody.' She waved her hands. 'Elsewhere.'

'OBL?' Patemkin muttered. They all stared at the center of the table as if he had scrawled the letters there. OBL: Osama bin Laden. A man who had had such hype and such attention that he was his own acronym.

Alan chewed his lower lip. 'Why would OBL –?' He caught himself, remembering that the Nairobi embassy bombing had been an OBL job. When he glanced at the embassy security man, he found him nodding, his face grave.

'He hit us once, he'd hit us again,' Pierce-or-Pearson said. 'The sonofabitch, I'd like to kill him.'

They all started to talk at once, and Alan shouted them down and said that there was no point in trying to guess at that point. 'We need facts,' he said. 'Let's leave OBL until we know more. We haven't covered the sniper and the bombers – in fact, we haven't covered what sort of operation this was. *If* it was coordinated with the demos in the city, then this was planned and executed with a lot of skill, and it took a lot of people. Sandy's working on the engine number from the dhow, that's a beginning. I've got somebody tracking it from Bahrain; I hope to hear from him today –'

'Somebody *not* cleared!' Sandy snarled.

Patemkin raised his eyebrows but said nothing. Alan went right on. 'And I'd like you guys to get anything you can on the sniper's body and the other guy the Kenyans have. The SEALS brought up some debris that they think has explosive residue on it, plus we'll get more from the *Harker* as soon as the forensics people get here, which should be tonight. With their own lab.' This was a way of saying that if the visitors thought they could take over by saying they'd use the Bureau's or the Agency's lab, they could forget it. Patemkin raised one eyebrow a few millimeters and gave a little shrug. Point made. Alan went on: 'But I want to work on the organization of this thing. If this was all one event, then it took the crew of the dhow, plus advance surveillance of the port and the ship, plus surveillance of the police and the Kenyan Navy and some intelligence about how and when they react; plus all the organization that goes into training snipers – there were at least two – *and* the guys with the missiles, and putting them in place. We're talking at least a hundred people, right?'

Patemkin was frowning. 'Your guys had an admiral killed. How accidental was that?'

'They would have had to time the bomb to go off while he was on the ship – and then know where on the ship he was. I think this part was an accident.'

'But what if it wasn't?' Sandy said.

Alan stared at the blank legal pad in front of him. 'They'd need somebody either on the carrier or on the *Harker* – or maybe stateside at LantFleet, but that's reaching – who knew that the admiral was making a visit. I can find how long that's been scheduled – although it can't be too long, because –' His face clouded. 'Oh, my God! I hadn't thought of that! See, until ten days ago, the gator freighter – the Marine carrier, it's smaller than the *Jefferson*, part assault ship, part carrier for helos and V-STOLs – *it* was supposed to make the port visit.' He leaned toward them. 'When the planning and the intel for the attack would have had to be done, that was supposed to be a Marine assault carrier there, not a freighter.'

Patemkin leaned back, jingled change in a pants pocket. 'That kind of changes the price of fish, doesn't it.'

'Could the bomb have sunk this Marine ship?' Mink said.

'The gator freighter's armored, but – I don't know; I'll check. It would have done damage, real damage. Whether the *Yellowjacket* would have its keel on the bottom like the *Harker* is another question. But think of what it would have meant – Marines on shore, caught in the demo. Maybe *targets* of the guys with guns. An American warship, damaged, certainly unusable for the near future. A real blow to the battle group. Especially if you got a lot of the Marines. There goes your land-based force projection.'

'So maybe the target wasn't your admiral at all.'

'Or maybe, because the admiral was going to be on board, the *Harker* was an acceptable target even though it wasn't the preferred one. But that means that at least some of the goal was to hit an *American* target.'

'An American *Navy* ship, isn't it?' Laura said. 'But if the target is the Navy, then why the attack on AID in Cairo?'

'Maybe they're not connected,' the embassy security man said. Patemkin waved a hand at that, as if of course they were connected.

'Five crewmen of the *Harker* are still missing,' Alan said. 'Plus one ship's officer, but he's turned up in Nairobi. If the admiral's schedule was made available to the attackers, then I think we need to talk to the crew.'

'Islamic?' Mink said.

'Some.' Alan was thinking of Patel and finding that he was grateful that Patel was Hindu, then realized that he was just as guilty as the others of jumping to the Islamic answer. Again, he bent toward them. 'What was your immediate response when McVeigh blew up the Murrah Building in Oklahoma City? Did you think "Christian white guy"?' He looked around. 'I'll bet everybody in this room thought OBL.'

Pierce-or-Pearson said, 'I don't think this was done by a bunch of Christian white guys.'

They talked another half-hour, shifting toward the end to the Cairo bombing, but the talk became mostly speculation and the writing of long lists of questions and lines of inquiry. Patemkin wanted to look for a money trail; he had a line into the Kenyan banks, he said, but he needed names – names of people who had accounts and who might have received electronic transfers. Mink suggested looking at the stock markets to see if anybody had tried to make a quick profit from a temporary drop after the bombing; this was thought far-fetched, but he was welcome to look. Pierce-or-Pearson said he'd put the arm on a couple of Kenyan

214

officials who were 'contacts,' meaning that he had them on the payroll. Alan kept filling yellow sheets, turning the page, starting a new list. Explosives, customs forms, passports and visas, weapons smuggling, cell phones, the MP3 player, telephone calls –

'When I was in the silver shop, just before the bomb went off, the young guys seemed to be expecting something. The old man didn't.'

'Word on the street?' Patemkin said. 'Kids got communications to die for. Can you talk to them?'

'Maybe.' He was dubious. 'Not until we can move around Mombasa.'

'God, it's hot,' Sandy Cole said. The others murmured, growled.

An intel-second poked his head in the door. If he'd knocked, Alan hadn't heard it. Alan scowled, but the young sailor tiptoed in anyway, his body language saying that he wasn't really there at all, and he was terribly sorry, and he was being fucking *quiet* –

'Urgent p-comm, sir,' he whispered to Alan. He put down a message slip. Alan jerked his head toward the door and the sailor ran for it. Alan unfolded the paper and looked at it under the protection of its top fold. It was from Harry O'Neill in Bahrain: *My sources say Islamic Party of Kenya not involved. See for yourself: you can have a meeting with their top guys at two p.m. at the Intercontinental. I'm working on the stuff you sent me.*

He looked around the table. They were all staring at him. The three men had sweat stains under the arms of their white shirts; one of Mink's pens had leaked, and he had a blue-black spot like a target over his heart. Pierce-or-Pearson was the purple-red that can mean a heart attack is coming.

'Let's break for lunch,' Alan said. 'What wine goes

with Spam?' He felt slightly spooky, light-headed because of the fatigue, but buoyed by the morning's work. And now a meeting with the IPK, graciously arranged at long distance by a man who didn't understand that they were under siege.

He caught Sandy Cole on the stairs. 'Go to comm and tell them I said you were to talk to the NCIS team in London or Cairo or wherever they are – priority. There's a woman with them – tell her what you need, clothes and so on.' She didn't give a flicker of interest. 'Then when the embassy security guy goes back over to the terminal, you can go with him. There's a shop in the terminal. You'll have to put up with a Marine standing by.'

Her expression changed but she didn't smile. She took a long time thinking it all over. 'Thanks,' she murmured, pulling hair from her eyes with that long, pale hand.

He went on down the iron stairs and dawdled crossing the hangar, wondering if he really had the balls to try to meet with the IPK in the middle of a revolution. Abruptly, he turned and went back up the stairs to the space that had been assigned to Sandy Cole. He knocked, there was a long pause, and then she came to the door and opened it six inches. She stared at him as if he was bringing bad news.

'How reliable are these Kenya Wildlife guys you talked about?'

She continued to stare at him, then shifted her weight and opened the door another inch. 'Leakey trained them. They wouldn't let you shoot an elephant even if you paid in American twenties. How's that?'

'Think they could get me across Mombasa to the beach hotels?'

'Getting yourself a little R and R?'

'Getting some information, maybe. Would they do it?'

'Why should they?'

He leaned on the doorjamb. He looked at the floor. 'What do they need that they haven't got?'

She laughed. Not a nice laugh. 'Modern weapons, decent uniforms, good cars.'

'You know a lot about them.'

Her face added defiance to its established sullenness. Also, maybe, a hint of see-what-you're-missing triumph. 'I'm fucking one of them when I'm not a prisoner in a hangar. Okay?' She opened the door a little more and leaned back, one hand closed around the knob so she had something to put her weight against, suddenly on the offensive – because she was defensive, he saw.

Alan shook his head. 'Not my business. Except – can you make the contact? I need a vehicle and three or four guys with guns. Two vehicles would be better. I need them in two hours. Possible?'

She shrugged. She stared at him some more, probably wondering what was in it for her and deciding that if he was really going for information, that was what was in it for her. 'I'll make a phone call.'

'Before lunch?'

'You wouldn't believe how having a period without enough tampons takes away your appetite for MREs.'

Houston.

A black man and a white man set up a barbecue grill and a folding table at the edge of a suburban park, even though it was still dark, between a ball diamond on one side and, on the other, a line of trees and, beyond it, a littered, weedy slope that ran down to a suburban cul-de-sac. They had folding chairs and a beer cooler, and, if the sun had been shining, they'd have looked like two guys there for a quiet day in the sun. As it was, they looked like very early birds.

'Can you see her house?' the white one said.

'Of course I can. Clear as day. Jesus.'

'It'd be too early for her to be up.'

'They said she gets up super-early. She takes the kids to day care; it's perfect.'

'Hitting her with the kids in the car is shit. I don't like hitting kids.'

'You think I'm in love with it? But it's today or tomorrow; that's the deal. That's it, today or tomorrow.' He picked up a cell phone that also had a radio transceiver in it and said, 'Mick, you there?'

'Yeah. Anything?'

'Nah, too fucking early. No lights in the house yet.' He sighed and moved lower in the folding chair. He watched the other man reach for a beer from the cooler. 'Take it easy on the beer. We maybe got all day, man.'

The other man shrugged. 'You're the designated driver. Fuck you.'

London.

Cram had got three of them on an eleven o'clock flight, so they were stuffing papers into attachés and saving files and closing laptops when Hahn shouted across the now-littered VIP room, 'Hey, Dukas! Telephone!'

Dukas stared at him over the swirl. 'I'm busy!'

'Dick Triffler says he's in jail and you gotta get him out!'

Dukas pushed his way across the big room and grabbed the phone. 'Dick? It's Dukas!'

'I'm in jail, I'm afraid.' The voice sounded very far away.

'Where?'

'Cairo. I'm sorry, Mike. I've been a very bad boy.'

Dukas was thinking, *Triffler – jail? It's the end of the world!* 'Dick, what the hell for?'

'Suppressing evidence.' He lowered his voice. 'I, uh, borrowed a driver's license and some keys in the course of my investigation. The owners were, uh, recently deceased.'

Dukas began to grin. 'You get anything?'

'I think maybe.'

'Well, call your boss, tell him to bail you out.'

'I did, and he said that you're my boss now, and as far as he's concerned, quote, "I can rot in an Egyptian jail until my asshole falls out," unquote. Anyway, I'm not sure they have bail here. What I think is, if you come down and show your badge and talk really nice, they'll let me go, because a few homicide cops are mad as hell but the rest think it's pretty funny.'

'Dick, I'm seven hours away.'

He heard Triffler sigh. 'I'll try to keep them from getting out the rubber hoses until you get here.'

Dukas started laughing. 'Jesus, Dick – you! Mister Law and Order!'

Triffler was silent for several seconds. At last he said, 'I did my best in a very difficult situation.' Dukas heard him sniff. 'Please wear a necktie and a clean shirt.'

'Yes, Mom.'

7

Houston.

The two men still sat in their folding chairs. A boom box played reggae beside them, and the sun was already bright.

'This sucks, man. Kids.'

'I said, we do it today if we get the chance. You want out? Good. Go. Then you explain it to the client.' The black one laughed.

Two minutes later, the white man groaned. 'Oh, shit,' he said. 'She's going out.'

The black man was out of his chair and staring down through the trees. Below them on the cul-de-sac, next to a tract house that backed up to the weeds, Rose Siciliano was buckling her children into a 4Runner.

'She's going out.'

'She's got the *kids*.'

'Yeah? That's not my fault.' He flipped on the two-way radio. 'She's coming out. You get that? She's coming out.'

Faintly, a male voice said, 'Yeah, yeah. Gotcha.'

The two men trotted to a van that was parked a hundred feet away. When they were inside, the black man at the wheel, he said, 'I think he's stoned. He sounded stoned.'

'He's always stoned.'

'He better not fuck up.' He put the van in gear and drove out of the park.

Mombasa.

During the day, the atmosphere in the hangar changed.

Before the afternoon sun began to slant through the open hangar doors, the empty space was echoing with the sound of hammers. Plywood walls materialized, breaking up echoes and beginning to suggest that privacy could exist again.

The first Marine helo touched down at 1300L. Within minutes, Geelin had expanded his perimeter, assigned billets to his new men, and started his two additional junior officers and a small cadre of NCOs on a tour of the area. A second chopper had brought sandbags, and within twenty minutes two squads were filling them. An hour after that, the Marines were building a sandbagged mortar position in the shade of the hangar. Alan, delighted, calmer, still death-weary, watched from the plywood eminence of the new Det 424 office – four walls, no ceiling, and a folding chair.

'David is on his way,' a voice said at his elbow. He knew it was Sandy Cole, recognized the scent as well as the voice. 'The KWS guy.' She didn't say, *The man at KWS I'm fucking.* He remembered the tone in her voice when she'd said *fucking* before. Despair? Bitterness?

'Right.' He made himself too cheerful. 'The Wildlife Service.' 'Cheerful' was an effort. 'Cheerful' would prove to be a phase before he got a second wind; real exhaustion was hours, maybe days away. He turned to her. 'I don't want to pry, Sandy, but I have to know – you're *sure* we can trust him.'

'He's the Deputy Director for Forestry, for Christ's

sake!' Their eyes locked. She flinched first. 'That's a nice way of saying he's in charge of all the parks nobody goes to, meaning that he's a good guy who busted his ass doing the right thing and got sidelined, okay?'

Alan tried to step carefully. 'Does, uh, your security officer know about, mm, you and him?'

She didn't do one of her characteristic boneless poses; instead, she threw her head back and locked eyes with him again. 'You think I'm going to have intimate contact with a foreign national and not report it? It'd be my career – and I do have a career, whatever all you *guys* think!' She moved her head as if to toss back her hair, but it hung along the sides of her face, heavy with oil or sweat. 'They did a check on him. He's okay, okay?' She waited, exploded. 'Jesus Christ, he's one of the *good* guys!'

Alan nodded his head, kept nodding. Chewed his lip. 'We're letting him into the perimeter. Some lives are going to depend on him.' He didn't say, *Mine among them.* 'Give me something in writing.'

'So you can cover your naval ass? Oh, yes, *sir*!'

'Better yet, have your security officer e-mail me something.' He smiled, trying to do 'cheerful' again. 'Call me when he's here.'

He had reached the point of fatigue where only cleanliness was left as a remedy. He drained his coffee and tossed the paper cup in a can. Then he went into the newly plywood-walled men's room and splashed tepid water on his face, toweled off with his T-shirt and walked shirtless past sailors swinging hammers to a half-finished officers' rack room and threw the shirt on his bedroll. He changed into civilian clothes – a pair of greenish slacks and a crumpled white shirt with a khaki vest that he had worn on the plane. Safari chic.

He found Cohen in the maintenance cage. Cohen was staring gloomily at a scrawled list of parts. Alan saw 'ASAP' at the top. 'Can't be that bad, Dink,' he said.

Cohen had last smiled at his bar mitzvah. 'It's worse.'

'I need two guys to drive the pickup to get the men's gear at the hotels. They'll follow me and the guy from Kenya Wildlife. Better be black guys. Civilian clothes.' Black civilians might look less threatening in Mombasa than white military, he thought. Another hopeful maybe. 'We must be able to scrounge a couple of civilian shirts from the guys, huh?'

Cohen looked out into the hangar as if the hope of finding two black sailors and two shirts was beyond imagination. In fact, a third of the det was African American. 'Marines'd be better,' he muttered.

'The Marines have a job to do. Anyway, they look like Marines, and they'll want to fight if they're challenged.'

'What're our guys supposed to do – kiss ass?'

Good question. Alan had tried to think it through and had come to the same impasse. 'Get them a couple of sidearms, nothing heavier. Yeah, I know – we don't have an armorer and we didn't bring any weapons, but aircrew brought their own, so borrow. Okay?'

Cohen nodded, but his face suggested that the idea was doomed – the det was doomed, the world was doomed; it was already written somewhere.

When Sandy found Alan again, he was out on the apron in front of the hangar, watching an S-3 getting a blivet to carry extra cargo and drinking water from the boat. 'David just passed the main gate,' she said, closing her cell phone.

Alan nodded. Geelin strode up from behind the hangar, flecks of sand trapped in the sweat all along his arms and hands. He gave a salute. 'Permission to speak freely, sir?'

Alan tried to be cheerful. 'Go ahead.'

Geelin glanced at Sandy; she shrugged and backed away a few feet. Geelin lowered his voice. 'I don't like you going out of the perimeter without a guard. I sure as hell don't like you going to meet the same guys who wasted some of ours yesterday.'

Alan smiled without humor. 'Your opinion is noted, Captain.' Trying to do a parody of Spock, failing. Geelin looked as if he wanted to say more, but Alan's response stopped him, as it had been intended to do. Alan no longer cared to hear every opinion offered, even by someone as competent as Geelin.

Behind Geelin, an open jeep covered in red Mombasa dust rolled up to the Marine post. The driver was thin and very black; at this distance he looked like a stick figure in a cartoon.

'Who's this bozo?' Geelin asked, jerking his thumb.

'My ride.' Alan nodded at the markings on the jeep. In the background, a voice was calling 'Gunny, post three needs an escort!' Geelin's jaw got stubborn. They'd been over it twice that morning, but Alan knew that he was going to say again that it was crazy for the CO to go alone into a hot zone with one unknown foreigner, and what he needed was at least the pickup and eight Marines, and – Alan held up a hand. 'Matter's closed, Jack.'

The jeep crept forward from post three, now with a Marine lance corporal perched on the passenger seat, steering well clear of the S-3 and stopping near the mortar position. Alan and Sandy, fifteen feet apart, walked toward it under the pounding sun. Alan could hear Geelin marching along behind.

'Commander Craik?' the black man asked, extending a hand. 'Deputy Director Opono of the Kenya Wildlife Service.' His eyes crinkled. 'My friends call me David.' He smiled at Sandy, but the smile could have meant anything. He looked younger than Alan had expected, perhaps younger than Sandy by a year or two. Alan glanced at Sandy, who was smiling but already drawing back, her hand half-raised. She had wanted to touch him, he thought, if only by shaking hands.

Alan took his hand and shook it. 'Call me Alan. You know Sandy Cole, of course. This is Captain Geelin of the United States Marine Corps.'

Opono shook hands with Geelin and smiled. Sandy had raised her hand again and, when it was ignored, again backed away. 'You ready to go, Commander?'

He'd already thrashed out the acting command while he was away; Geelin had rank on Cohen, so the job fell to him. Alan tossed his helmet bag in the back of the jeep and came around to get in. Opono turned his head to follow him, and as the sun came more fully on his face Alan saw that the man was older than he had thought. There was a weariness in it, he saw now, too, maybe a hard-earned cynicism. 'How bad was your drive here?' he said, to say something.

'Many checkpoints.' Opono's smile broadened, as at a joke. Alan got it: Opono hated the army and the police, the creators of 'many checkpoints.'

'Are you armed?' Alan said.

'Certainly not.'

Alan glanced at Sandy, back at Opono, thought that the man was lying. For her sake? 'Our pickup truck is going to follow so that my men can get our gear from the hotels. Problem?'

Opono gave a soft smile. 'No problem.' A little mocking now because of the trite African expression.

'I'm carrying a sidearm. So are my men. Still no problem?'

Opono's dark face looked pained. 'Showing a weapon makes things worse here.'

'I don't intend to shoot our way through Mombasa with three handguns.' Opono locked on to Alan's eyes, then smiled, but he still looked pained.

Alan got in the jeep, and the Marine escorted them back to guard post three, where the pickup was already waiting. Sitting that close to Opono, Alan realized that he smelled of beer.

Alan started the drive on full alert, watching every oncoming *matatu* and checking out every gathering of men. It didn't take long for him to accept that Mombasa was quiet, at least for the moment, maybe because military and police checkpoints were everywhere, as Opono had warned. A few people, mostly women, were out, probably shopping for food. The streets they went through had been cleared of any bodies and burnedout cars, but these were main roads. No tourists seemed to be coming into old Mombasa from the beaches, although he saw Masai guards on a tourist coach headed toward the airport. *The* wazungu *are afraid*. Behind him, the two sailors from the det were sitting up straight in the truck's cab, looking grim. Still, by the time they were on Mombasa Island itself Alan was almost relaxed, slumped in his seat and trying to make small talk with David Opono.

'Sandy said you went to school in the States.'

'University of Michigan.'

'Like it?'

'I didn't take a degree. White Americans don't take Africans seriously.' That killed conversation for a little. David and Sandy had in common a certain prickliness. Alan made more small talk, got to his own wife and children. Opono had a wife and children, too, it seemed.

'I understand you were in the KWS special forces. I didn't even know the Wildlife Service had such a unit.'

'We killed poachers.' That seemed to be that. Alan looked over, saw the look of pain on Opono's face again. *We killed poachers and I didn't like it*. No, that didn't seem right. *We killed poachers and –* And what?

And, as if to answer the unspoken question, Opono said, 'It didn't solve the problem. The solution was temporary; Africa is forever.' He scowled over the wheels. 'I used to protect animals by killing the poachers. Now I protect trees and I kill time.'

Alan thought he would simply sit silent for the rest of the ride. David Opono was not big on small talk. On the other hand, it was likely that he was very big on big talk – principles, ideals, and their African opposites – self-service, corruption. Not a conversation Alan wanted to have just then.

He looked around at a traffic jam of sweating men hauling carts piled high with produce. It didn't seem possible that a single man could haul so much. Quite near them, a young man was resting with his cart, his muscles standing out like Geelin's. He looked at the jeep and at Alan. No smile.

They broke out of the crowd and went on, and then slowed for yet another checkpoint. Every checkpoint, whether army or police, was the same: when they saw the KWS jeep, they got nasty. Alan's American credentials and sometimes American cash made them put on a gloss of rather ugly courtesy. It was plain to him that Opono lived with their hatred: his principles, expressed as his work, made him a hated man. *Africa.*

Alan turned to Opono as soon as the pickup had cleared the checkpoint and the pickup truck was behind them again. 'Why are they so angry? Do they know? The checkpoint?'

'Know what?'

'That I'm going to meet the IPK.'

'They are more likely angry to find me going to Nyali.'

'Why?'

'Because the police in Nyali take money to allow the trees in the park and the fish in the maritime park to be taken, and I have caught them at it. I'm no friend of the police here, of that I can assure you.' *Or of anybody else*, Alan thought. Was that his attraction for Sandy Cole?

Once out of the last of the urban sprawl near the bridge, the road was flat and smooth.

'Good road!' Alan shouted over the wind noise.

'The best in Kenya!' David shouted back. 'It gets the tourists to the beaches!'

Nyali wasn't so much a town as a collection of resort beaches with *bandas* for the hotel workers in between. The big hotels, he found, hadn't changed except to age a little, with spiderwebs of cracks in the concrete and a certain smell that suggests age in a hotel – mildew, detergent, people. David pointed out big trees as they came up the resort drive. 'That is one of the best mangrove trees on the coast,' he said, like a man talking about a loved child, pointing to a gargantuan tree growing in a little cut near the beach. 'The hotels keep them for their shade.' He shook his head and smiled. Across the road, a small town of cheaper hotels and bars had grown up to handle the overflow from the Intercon. Most of them were busy. And the great, dark mangrove tree had graffiti sprayed on one side.

At the hotel entrance, Alan got out and walked back to the pickup. The man in the passenger seat, Woodrow, a parachute rigger when he wasn't nailing plywood walls together, shook his head and tried to laugh. 'Hairy, sir. I mean, *hairy*.' They all agreed the checkpoints were hairy. Alan made sure they knew where they were going to get the det personnel's gear and that they were coming straight back here, no side trips or stops. He slapped the side of the pickup. 'Piece of cake!' He started away, swung back. 'Keep those guns out of sight.'

They'd already got that message.

David was waiting beside the jeep. 'I'll wait for you on the patio.' Alan started to say that he was welcome to come to the meeting, saw that the idea was foolish, a hollow courtesy – the meeting wasn't a party where you could bring a friend. Anyway, he saw, as a hotel underling led them across the lobby, four edgy young men standing at the entrance to a corridor. A phrase occurred to him from somewhere – *the youth of today*. These were the youth of today. They looked angry, and under the anger was despair.

After they had led him down the corridor to a door, they searched him and took his pistol. Objecting would have been useless. Would he suggest that they would keep it? Did he think they were that stupid? In fact, he didn't think they were stupid at all. So he nodded and gave the man who had taken the gun a thin smile. Then one of them opened the door and he went in.

Four men were in the room, drinking coffee, seated cross-legged on the floor around a low table. Alan recognized one of them, a short, thin man in Western business attire with a silk knit cap on his head, as the proprietor of the silver shop. Alan thought he looked shattered. The other two were clerics; they wore the robes and turbans of religious conservatism, with Western shoes just visible. One was older and heavy, even fat; the other had an intense look, not fanaticism but focus. The youngest was no older than the hard-faced boys outside. He jumped up as Alan entered. 'Commander Craik?'

Alan extended his hand and the young man took it. 'I am Ali Rahman. I serve Sheik Khalid, okay? I'll translate.' He smiled and nodded several times. He pointed at the three seated men, who looked at Alan with dignified interest, and indicated the heaviest man. 'This is Sheik Labala. He is very well known.' An under-statement. Sheik Labala was a Muslim celebrity, for Kenya. He was one of the government's most vocal opponents. 'This is Sheik Khalid. He is the head of our youth movement. Yes? Yes. Our youth movement is very important to us, Commander.' The youth movement, with its implied message from the angry boys outside. *Our youth are our soldiers.* 'And this is Mister Mohamed Nadek. He is a prominent local business-man.'

'I have met the commander.' Nadek inclined his head. 'I see that you survived the unfortunate distur-bances of yesterday. Did you find your friend?'

'I did. Unfortunately, he was killed by a sniper.' Alan

sat carefully, choosing the spot across from Mr Nadek and farthest from Labala. It was natural; he had experienced hospitality from Nadek, and Labala's hostility was thinly veiled. Khalid, the leader of the youth, was curiously neutral. He was the one Alan felt he had to win. *The youth of today.*

'I lost one of my sons,' Mr Nadek said. He said it gravely, as one might discuss important news, but with no personal reference. Alan remembered the young man he had seen lying in the street, and his eyes stung for a moment. The other men around the table were murmuring greetings as Mr Rahman translated what Alan and Nadek were saying. Mr Nadek raised a hand slightly. The small movement seemed as dramatic as a salute; the others fell silent. 'Our losses were much greater than only mine, Commander. At least seventy people are dead. Another two hundred are in hospital, and there are more. Women. Children. My son's fiancée was also killed.'

Alan looked around the table and saw anger there, even rage, just under the surface, so that Labala's jaw worked, his teeth grinding as he listened to something from Sheik Khalid that was not translated.

These men were close to explosion. He knew Mombasa well enough to know where their thoughts were, and how deeply yesterday's events had scarred them. Their community had taken massive losses and was now facing a crackdown that had the potential to kill more. Behind that lurked the specter of a violence that would kill the tourist trade and close their businesses. He nodded. 'I am sorry for your losses. More than a dozen sailors and my admiral were killed by the bomb on the USNS *Harker*.' Alan paused. 'And at least one woman was killed, as well.' He thought about the

232

service that would be held in the hangar. 'I lost a close friend.'

A waiter came in with American coffee for Alan. The IPK men were drinking Arabic coffee from an urn. It might have been meant as a slight; certainly, none of them moved to offer him their own coffee. Perhaps they expected him to prefer the familiar. Alan added sugar to his coffee, the grains audible as they rustled clear of the paper packet. Outside on the patio, her shape just visible through closed blinds, a woman dove into the pool. Alan stirred his coffee, the spoon ringing against the china cup. He had seldom felt so self-conscious while he prepared a cup of coffee, but he made himself continue, unwilling to break the silence because he had nothing to say until his hosts chose to speak their piece. He had a sip of coffee, the cup trembling slightly against his lips as if to remind him how keyed up he was. He took a second sip and placed the cup softly on its saucer and looked each of the three principals in the eye. As he turned to look at Sheik Labala, the big man twitched his eyes away to the interpreter and spoke into the silence in Arabic. He spoke for several minutes. Alan kept his on Labala, willing some personal contact to flow through his gaze, but the man wouldn't meet his eyes, and Alan glanced at the others from time to time, trying to gauge their reaction to whatever Labala was saying.

Sheik Khalid listened passively, although Alan noted his pupils dilating twice; Mr Nadek was clearly uncomfortable with a great deal of what was said. When Sheik Labala was done, the young interpreter spoke. His voice rose with passion as he translated.

'Sheik Labala wants to speak of the injustice of the Kenyan government. He wishes to know why the US government gives money and guns for the suppression of Muslims in Kenya and everywhere in the world. He relates that he was active in helping the US recruit young men to fight in Afghanistan in the 1980s, and yet when he spoke out against injustice later, the Americans had him arrested and exiled to Germany. He talks about how the Kenyan government deals with Muslims, and how they fired on our people in the protest yesterday.'

Alan nodded.

Sheik Khalid spoke. He spoke briefly, and his eyes were on Alan the whole time.

The interpreter waited for him to finish, which he did with a slight smile. 'Sheik Khalid says that he is pleased to meet with you today and happy that your friend arranged this meeting. He wishes you to understand that none of the men in this room would have anything to do with a direct attack on Americans.'

Alan nodded.

Mr Nadek leaned forward, making a little throwing motion with his right hand. 'We need the tourists from the West, or we will starve. No one here with any sense would advocate direct attacks on Americans. None of us would tolerate such talk if we heard it.' He looked at Sheik Labala. 'We are not friends of the regime here. That is true. And we grow angry at the way that America treats Islam in the world. But none of us would tolerate a direct attack on Americans in our city.'

Alan couldn't help but notice how careful they were. *Direct attack. Our city. Enemies of the regime.* He nodded his understanding. 'So let me be clear. Neither you nor your people were responsible for the attack on the *Harker*?'

'Absolutely not,' Mr Nadek said. The young man

translated and the other two men shook their heads, their long beards moving slowly back and forth as if sweeping the table.

Alan sat up straight and turned to face Labala. 'I can't speak to America's mistakes in the past.' He imagined the response he'd get from the embassy in Nairobi if he tried. 'I cannot comment about the politics of Kenya. I have seen corruption in the armed services and anti-Muslim feeling with my own eyes. I wish to be impartial, not to take a side or be on one.' He looked from one to the other and waited, motioning to the translator to repeat what he had said. Khalid looked interested; Labala was openly derisive. Nadek was looking at him, a level stare. Interested but hesitant? He continued, 'Please be clear. This is not a political forum. I am not here to discuss any past before yesterday.' He gathered their eyes and went for his point, his only card of any importance, and he found he was speaking to Khalid. 'I saw a gunman open fire at the GSU yesterday. He was high on the wall in Fort Jesus, and he fired repeatedly at the GSU as their trucks were deploying.' Alan reached into his pocket and tossed a shell casing on the table. 'This was from his gun. If you haven't already heard of this, then ask your people. I wasn't alone in seeing him. He wasn't local; he could have been an Arab or even American. I am not making an accusation you understand? I'm just saying what I saw. I saw this gunman fire first. The GSU return fire was retaliation.'

The three men talked among themselves, rapid talk, with some angry comments from Labala and then from Nadek at Labala. The interpreter added something, his hand pointing at Alan, and Nadek spoke one word. It was clearly reproof. The translator glowered, and all three of them rounded on him. Alan's Swahili was not close to catching the quick questions and replies, but he got the gist – that the interpreter or someone he knew had also seen the gunman on Fort Jesus. Alan wondered if everything he said had been translated accurately.

A waiter tiptoed in and motioned to Alan. 'You have a call.' He pointed at a telephone outside by the pool. He grinned. The four IPK men scowled at him. 'Telephone,' the waiter said in Swahili. 'Very important, the man says.'

Only Geelin and Cohen and Sandy Cole knew where he was going. He supposed the call must be important. 'If you will excuse me?' He stood. 'I must apologize. But I have duties –'

The silversmith nodded, and then first one and then the other of the sheiks nodded as Rahman translated.

Alan followed the waiter out to the patio. He had to go out the door of the room, around a corner and back, so that he was standing now with the picture window of the room on his left – on the outside now, looking in. The telephone was red, standing on a white table. Two oiled blondes lay braless to his right, then the pool, David Opono sitting upright on the edge of a lounge chair. The beach was close, a backdrop for the entire scene, a speedboat rocking gently in the near foreground.

Alan reached for the telephone.

'Down! Commander, down, *down* –!'

It was Opono. Alan knew the tone – the stridency born of combat, half terror, half adrenaline – and he headed for the blue patio floor. Something hot scorched his ear and the glass beside him shattered. Shots echoed in the pool courtyard. The blondes screamed. A semi-automatic rifle was firing.

At him.

Alan found himself behind a flagstone planter as a shot blew a fist-sized hole in the flowers above him and ricocheted for an impossibly long time around the stone box of the patio.

Opono was on his knees with a big Glock 17 in his fists. He had been lying about having a gun. He began firing at the ocean.

Alan reached back for his H&K and remembered that the IPK guards had taken it. The cigarette boat revved its engines to a roar and he heard it move away, from his right to his left. Opono kept firing at it until the gun was empty. He straightened and trotted to Alan. When he saw that Alan was alive, he laughed. 'I might as well have thrown the damn pistol at him.'

The blondes were still screaming. A male voice was shouting for a doctor. Waiters began to run around.

'The waiter,' Alan said. He sat up. 'Find the damned waiter – it was a setup –!'

But Opono had gone to give first aid to the shouting man, who had been hit in his right knee. He seemed to be the only casualty. The blondes were standing in a huddle by the pool, their naked breasts suddenly on display now that they were standing. Their nakedness became an idea that flashed through his mind – how offensive the men inside the room would find it. They had had their backs to the window the whole time he had been with them.

Alan went back into the room. All four IPK men were on the floor, brushing broken glass away, picking sharp shards from each other's clothes. Mr Nadek was helping Sheik Labala when Alan came in. All four looked at him. He pointed at the shattered glass in the window facing the beach.

'You say your people had nothing to do with an attack on the *Harker*. But someone did. Someone got together the protest that covered the riot and provided fuel for the attacks. Someone told that gunman that we'd be meeting here today.' He waved outside. 'If I'd been killed, gentlemen, no power on earth would have convinced my government that you weren't responsible. To be honest, I'm a little concerned myself.'

Rahman, shaking, translated. The three older men looked at each other. Mr Nadek opened his mouth and then shut it.

'Look at your own, gentlemen. Somebody wants war.'

Alan touched his ear, which still felt hot; his fingers came away with blood on them. He looked down. His ear was bleeding on his safari vest and on the carpet. A ludicrous picture of himself sprang into his mind – maimed hand, now a maimed ear, a man vanishing piece by piece. He found the bathroom, jerked toilet paper from the roll, held it to his ear. The bleeding seemed to stop.

When he came back, Labala pointed at him and said something angry in Arabic. The young translator looked at the floor while he conveyed the gist, as if unwilling to be part of the message, his hands twisted together to hide their trembling. 'The Sheik says it takes two to make a war. He says that the oppression of Islam is what makes young men willing to give their lives.'

'Tell him –' Alan walked over until he was standing by the sheik and his blood began to drip on the floor next to the seated man and he put the wad of now-red toilet paper back. 'That's for politicians, Sheik. This is us. I can't change US policy and I'm not sure I would if I could. Right *here*, right *now* we need a little calm before everyone starts shooting and the Kenyan coast becomes Somalia. You guys have a *provocateur*. A man who wants this war. I don't want him. I want you to find him. And stop him. Before more people have to die.'

Sheik Labala said something angrily to Sheik Khalid. Mr Nadek held up his hand, cutting them off. His face was working. They were all slipping into shock; the meeting was ruined. 'We will find him,' he said. 'You should go.'

'I need to move around this city,' Alan said. 'I need to have your word that my men are safe. I need you to spread the word to your people that my people are safe. Can you make me that guarantee?'

'I can,' Sheik Khalid said. 'Give me two hours, and your people will be safe from us.'

Alan nodded. 'I'll do my best to pass your views to my government.' He looked at the toilet paper, pinched it more firmly against his ear. 'Somebody got you and me here. Somebody made the decision to be here at this time on this day. Somebody bribed the waiter to put the telephone out there where the shooter could get at me. Somebody in the IPK.' He looked at the old men. 'Three of you knew where and when this meeting was to be.'

The silversmith was leaning against the wall. He looked up at Alan. 'Four of us knew.' He looked at the translator. 'Please, Commander. I heard what you said. I *understand* what you said.'

'Four of you knew,' Alan said, looking at the translator again. *The youth of today*. He waited for him to translate. The three elders were looking at him, too, and then Nadek said, 'We will find out. You and your men are safe in Mombasa now.'

*   *   *

239

Opono thought his ear had been hit by a piece of stone, not a bullet. He seemed more amused than worried as he dressed it. 'The ear bleeds well,' he said. 'You look quite dramatic. Would you like me to wrap your head with a bandage, like an actor in a movie?'

'I'd like you to stop the bleeding.'

'The bleeding has stopped itself.' He clapped Alan on the shoulder. 'You'll live to fight another day.'

'Thanks,' Alan said and winced inwardly, wishing he could be a little more generous. *Thanks, you saved my life*. He began to tremble, and he lay back against the jeep's seat. They'd roared away from the hotel just as the police had arrived; the place would be swarming with them now. 'They'd have kept us there the rest of the day,' he muttered.

'It was just high tide. The boat could get in tight to the beach that way. Well planned.' Opono studied him. 'The boat went north.'

Alan glanced in the rearview mirror. The pickup was parked behind them, the two sailors looking serious and perhaps scared. They'd seen the blood on his vest. 'What's north?' he said.

Opono shrugged.

'Sandy says you've told her about poachers up north.'

'Told her and *told* her. That's how we met – I went to the embassy to complain because I knew nobody in the Kenyan government would listen. Yes, we have poachers up north.'

Alan's head was splitting. He was in shock. Still, he said, 'Tell me about them.'

Houston.

Rose drove easily and expertly, checking both of her children and the dog, who rode behind her. Seven-

240

year-old Mike was in the front with her, two-year-old Bobby in an infant seat behind him.

'You strapped tight?' she said to Mike.

'I'm working.' He was staring into the right-side rearview mirror.

She reached across and tested his seat belt, keeping her eyes on the road. When she had sat up straight again, she said, 'You answer a question when I ask you, Michael, or there'll be trouble.'

He hunched into himself. 'Yes, ma'am.' He looked aside at her. 'I was checking for surveillance.'

She laughed. 'You're your father's boy, all right.'

'You're carrying your gun!' he said: rigorous seven-year-old logic – if Mom carries a gun, it makes sense to check for surveillance.

'That's just to satisfy Uncle Mike, because I made him a promise. Monday, it goes back into the drawer.'

More seven-year-old logic: 'It isn't Monday yet.'

'That's why I'm wearing it.' It sat on her belly in a pouch, about as inconspicuous as a pregnancy.

'Well, that's why I'm watching for surveillance.' His eyes were on the mirror again. They were driving through sleeping suburbs toward the day-care center, after which she'd turn around and drop Mikey at school and go on to the Space Center. It would take far longer than she wanted it to, but it was supposed to be only for a week and then there'd be room in day care at the Space Center and neither she nor her kids would have to spend an hour in a car each way.

'Mom.'

'What?'

'We're being followed.'

'Mikey –' She sighed. Being the wife of a man who seemed to live at some border-crossing into the world

241

of espionage was sometimes trying, not least when her child made that world his own fantasyland. 'Who's following us?' she said, finding it easier to go along than to squelch him.

'A dark green van, Texas plates.'

She glanced into the overhead mirror. Indeed, there was a dark green van behind them. Well, yes, it *was* following them.

'See?'

'I see it.'

'I saw it yesterday.'

'Mikey –!'

'I did! When you picked me up me at school. I saw it!'

She was a little exasperated with him for roughening the mood of the day, which had started pretty well despite everything. She had promised to bake cookies when they all got home, and she usually hated baking. *Super-Mom*. It had started out to be a good, quiet day, and now her child wanted her to believe that there was a threat behind them. Nonetheless, she shifted her weight and felt the gun on her abdomen and unconsciously touched it with one hand, checking by feel that the speedloaders were in there, too.

'Mom?'

She decided to be patient. 'Yes, Mike?'

'There's *two* cars back there. Right behind each other.'

She started to protest that two things can't both be behind each other, but she glanced into the mirror, and as she did so she saw a second vehicle pull slightly out over the center line and then glide back in behind the green van. It was very close behind, closer than most drivers would get, and if it was going to pass, it could easily have done so, because nothing was coming the other way. Up ahead was a wide curve to the right and then a long straightaway; the car would have had time to pass before the curve, she thought.

And a memory surfaced. An antiterrorism course five years before, and a video of attacks by bicycle, scooter, and car. One of the scenarios showed a two-car assault on a single car, with one pulling up tight behind and the other swinging out and then forcing the victim off the road.

Without thinking, she accelerated.

'Check your seat belt,' she said to Mikey.

'You just did!'

'Young man, what did I say –?'

He muttered, 'Yes, ma'am,' and checked his belt as she turned and reached over the back seat, getting a lick from the dog, and tested the restraints on the younger child, who patted the dog and called it Bloofer, a corruption of its real name, Blue, that had now become its real name. Then she was into the curve, steering with one hand and feeling the tires come just short of squealing; she took her foot off the accelerator and the car slowed, and immediately she accelerated again, halfway around the turn and increasing speed because it was safe there, gaining speed while still in the turn.

And the following cars did the same.

'Mom –'

'Not now.'

She came out of the turn into the long straightaway, still accelerating. The needle moved past seventy. The big 4Runner held the road well.

In her mirror, the van grew suddenly bigger. It was moving up behind her fast.

Her one day of defensive driving at the antiterrorism school flashed. Thoughts cascaded down her brain: the vulnerability of her kids, the weight of the 4Runner, the bumper height of the van behind.

The second vehicle pulled abruptly out into the far lane and came roaring toward her. It was a pickup truck, half a dozen years old, black.

The van was ten yards behind her.

'Hold on,' she said.

The two vehicles moved on her at the same speed, the van closing up almost against her rear bumper and the pickup matching it and then surging ahead to take a position next to her, at first a bit behind so that she was even with its hood, then moving up until she and the other driver were exactly even, and she shot a look across and saw a man grinning at her, a skeletally thin man with ragged hair and a baseball cap. And a manic grin.

She had done it once with an instructor sitting beside her, and at the last moment he had had to bark at her to get her to make the move. Now she had to do it alone, with her children in the car. At more than seventy miles an hour.

And the dog. The dog had no restraints, and, if she crashed, would come off the rear seat like a missile.

'Hold on!'

She floored the accelerator, moved ahead, then sensed in her peripheral vision the pickup's even faster surge; as it came a little past her, she stood on her brake pedal.

The 4Runner squealed, and she felt herself pitched forward toward the wheel. Mikey's head snapped down, and the dog slammed into the back of her seat and the baby screamed. Then the van hit their back bumper with a loud thud.

This was where the instructor had shouted at her.

She swung the wheel hard to the left. Her left front panel caught the pickup, which was still ahead, in the right rear, precisely as this maneuver is meant to do. The pickup was big, but the 4Runner was heavy and powerful, too, and the pickup had no weight in the rear. The impact put the pickup into a sliding spin. Mikey, staring out his windshield, screamed when he saw the truck right there at their front bumper and then swinging, seemingly toward him, in what would become a 360-degree spin. Behind them, the van was late and so still trying to push her forward; it struck her left rear and simply aided what she had already started by grabbing her parking brake and yanking back, while again standing on the brake pedal – a 180-degree turn that ended in a near-stop.

The van flashed past. Mikey screamed again, and there was another bang as the van hit the spinning pickup.

Then Rose was around. She shifted down and accelerated, controlling the turn, remembering the instructor's bellow ('Not yet, not yet – let it spin – Now!') and coming out of it headed in the opposite direction and beginning to move, the car swaying and both children screaming. She asked the engine for power and it responded, and they started back down the highway.

And swayed drunkenly to the left and then to the right, and she knew that the impact with the pickup had driven metal into her left front tire. It shredded with a sound like a power saw, pieces of rubber hammering against the undercarriage. She tried to control the careening car but felt the wheel torn from her hands as it swerved too sharply to the right. Small trees densely lined the road there, and she prayed in an instant that they wouldn't hit, that the airbags wouldn't inflate and pin them in the car for the men in the van to take as they wanted. She got the wheel again, fighting the momentum, fighting the draw of the trees, and the car sloped into a shallow ditch, straightened, and scraped along to a stop, canted like a beached ship.

'Out, get out!' she shouted. 'Mikey, get the hell out!'

'But Mom –!' He was crying.

'Get out!'

She was around the front of the car, knees like jelly with the fear and the shock of it. She had to wrestle Mikey's door open and unbuckle his seat belt. She grabbed his shoulders. 'You've got to take care of Bobby! Can you do it?'

He looked her in the eyes. His nose was running, his cheeks red and wet. A child of discipline, he nodded. 'Yes, ma'am.'

'Get Bobby out of his seat and take him into the woods, honey. Just stay there until I come for you. You hear me?' She had the Smith in her hand, the other reaching for the speedloaders.

The boy was working on the baby's harness, but his eyes were on the floor. 'Mom – Bloofer –'

She had already seen the dog. One leg was broken like a stick, and it lay with its back arched in pain, blood oozing around its teeth.

'Take care of your brother. Now!'

Rose looked down the road. The pickup had come to rest crosswise but upright, its front end pointing to her right. As she watched, the passenger door opened and the driver pulled himself out. His hat was gone. He put both hands to his head and sat down in the road.

Rose threw herself down beside the 4Runner, her right shoulder against the right rear tire. She liked the right-side prone position for shooting, the support for one shoulder and arm. Parting the roadside weeds, she looked up, the corner of her car's bumper giving her protection overhead and perhaps masking her.

The van was coming back slowly past the front end of the pickup. It stopped next to the pickup's driver, who was still sitting on the pavement with his head in his hands. The van sat there for what seemed a long time but was only seconds; she imagined a conversation between the van and the man on the ground. He didn't get up, however. He was going to stay where he was.

Then the van began to roll toward her.

She let it come. She wanted no more than the distance between two telephone poles between them for her first shot.

It came slowly. The front end was dented where it had hit the 4Runner. Above the damage, the two big windows stared like insect eyes. They would be her target.

And it came on, no more than twenty miles an hour, not knowing where she was or how she was.

To the point she had marked.

She fired off all six shots in rhythmic procession, four in the driver's window, two in the passenger's. The first shot hit the top offside corner of the driver's window, a poor bit of shooting, but it got the driver's attention. The van swerved. The second shot was lower and more toward the center and blew out the whole upper quarter of the window. With that, the van accelerated, and the rest of her shots raked across it at closer and closer range, the last one into the right-side window as it careened past her car, hitting the offside of the 4Runner with a crunch and a squeal of metal on metal. The big SUV swayed above her and she felt the tire at her right shoulder move, and she thought, *Killed by her own car*, and it rocked over her and then back and settled again, a smell of hot metal and oil hitting her nostrils as dust billowed around her, and then another squeal and crunch from down the road.

She dug out her cell phone. There was no 911 out here, and she didn't know the state police number. *Stupid.* She dialed the astronaut duty officer at the Space Center and shouted at the EM who answered, giving her name and her location and telling him somebody was trying to kill her. 'Get the police!' she bellowed. 'Police! Horton Road, east of Oak Grove! Do it!'

Then she was lying across the hood of her vehicle with the Smith in a two-hand hold, looking down the barrel at the van, which was on its side a hundred feet down the road, wheels still spinning. A speedloader was in her left hand; a glance told her it was empty. When had she reloaded? She pressed the trigger, and a shot whanged off toward the van and thumped against it, and somebody hollered from inside.

She looked to her left. The driver of the pickup was on his side, throwing up in the road.

Two dark hands appeared on the posts of the driver's window of the van.

'Come out with your hands on your head! If you don't, you're dead!'

'I'm hurt!'

'Not as hurt as you'll be if you try anything, you sonofabitch! Show me your face, with your hands on your head!'

A dark, bloody face rose slowly into view, one hand

behind his head. When he was clear of the windowframe he'd come through and could see, the man pulled the other hand above the car. There was a big automatic in it. A .40 magnum or even one of those .50 Desert Eagles.

She shot him in the face.

Far away, a police siren sounded.

Behind her, the dog whimpered.

Mombasa.

They had left the hangar doors partly open so that the sun slanted in and gave a warmer light to the gloom. The S-3 was back in the hangar, having returned from Nairobi at two with sleeping bags and forty sets of boxer shorts and T-shirts and crates of fresh fruit and Coke and bread, plus two cases of Tusker beer that were waiting for the end of the service. Four Marines guarded the hangar entrance but stayed outside out of deference to the memorial service, which was the detachment's private business.

In the corner, the twenty folding chairs and the plywood table that was neither altar nor coffin but stood in for both seemed dwarfed by the vast space around them. The table had been covered with a black tarp that hung to the floor and had been folded under so that it looked neat. An American flag provided by the Marines had been put over it to hang down the front. A box, spray-painted the dark gray of an S-3, sat behind the flag and made a kind of lectern, with a vase on each side of it made of painted PVC pipe, filled with a spray of acacia branches because they couldn't find anything else. A chief's hat sat on the box. They didn't have a master chief's hat.

LTs Cohen and Campbell sat front and center in their

flight suits; like everybody else, they'd left their uniforms at the hotel. The men of the det sat behind them in T-shirts and dungarees, all but Chief Bakin, who was out of sight behind the dark blue box and the sprays and the plywood table.

Then Bakin stood up. His appearance could have been comic, rising seemingly from nowhere, but nobody laughed. He had managed to press his shirt somehow. He looked somber and handsome as he opened a Bible on the painted box.

'"The Lord is my shepherd; I shall not want. He maketh me to lie down in green pastures; he leadeth me beside the still waters . . ."' He didn't need the Bible. He knew it by heart.

Fidelio sang 'Danny Boy.'

Bakin read from Genesis, '"And unto Adam he said, Because thou hast hearkened unto the voice of thy wife, and has eaten of the tree . . ."' ending with '". . . for dust thou art, and unto dust shalt thou return."'

Cohen gave a short speech about Master Chief Craw, saying that he had been a good man and everybody had liked him. He asked other people to say things, and seven sailors stood up one after the other and told about good things that Craw had done. Cohen recited the Kaddish and went back to his chair.

Bakin read Ecclesiastes, 'To every thing there is a season.'

Electronics Technician Second Class Basurto read his poem, which had neither rhythm nor rhyme but was well received and made three men sniffle, one of them Basurto.

Bakin read the passage from John 14, 'Let not your heart be troubled', which ends with 'I go to prepare a place for you.'

250

Fidelio sang 'The Minstrel Boy.'

Then Bakin asked them to bow their heads and pray silently, and they bowed their heads and some prayed, and some were embarrassed, and some thought about what death was, and several looked at Sharawi, a nineteen-year-old who was Muslim and wore a Muslim cap and actually seemed to be praying, and then it was over, and the Marine who had been minding the comm office brought Cohen a message from the ship saying that somebody had tried to kill Commander Craik.

And then three mortar rounds came in from the houses beyond the airport fence, and they all hit the dirt, and sailors wondered what the hell they were doing facedown in Africa.

Houston.

A helicopter was moving slowly overhead, circling like a buzzard looking for roadkill. She knew it was from one of the local TV stations and stubbornly refused to look up at it and become its next feed. Two ambulances and an EMT vehicle were parked at angles between her SUV and the overturned pickup; two police cars, lights flashing, blocked the road at each end of the scene. Cops and state troopers and sheriff's deputies were standing in twos and threes all over the road, pointing, making notes, unreeling crime-scene tape.

And she was the criminal.

Not really, but she felt that way. They'd taken her gun and her cartridges, and they'd put her kids, scared but unharmed, with another cop, and they'd grilled her in the back of a sheriff's car. The driver of the van had a bullet in his chest and head injuries from the crash, they said; the guy she'd shot in the face was

251

dead, very dead. The driver of the pickup was strapped to a gurney, and the word was that he had at least a concussion and probably unknown internal injuries.

'Do I need a lawyer?' she had demanded after the first couple of questions.

'You're not under arrest or anything, ma'am. We have to know what happened.'

'I feel like I'm under arrest.'

'Yes, ma'am.' The deputy was fortyish, lean, mysterious behind shades as big as coasters. Perhaps because he had been aware of their effect, he had taken the sunglasses off then and smiled at her. He had paler patches around his eyes from wearing the sunglasses so much. 'Ma'am, nobody in Texas is going to charge a woman who was protecting herself and her kids from harm.' He had gray eyes.

In fact, Texas charged and executed women as well as men, and protecting children might be in the eye of the beholder – or a good prosecutor. Rose had shivered, cold from shock. But she had refused to lie down, refused to be taken to a hospital. 'Just keep the media away from me,' she had begged.

By the time she began to feel other effects of shock, she had finished the interview with the deputy and was going through another with two local police detectives. She knew that her story was already out among the cops when she saw them looking at her, nodding now and then. They seemed to be on her side. One paced off the distance from her vehicle to the window in which she'd shot the nowdead man, and he'd turned toward her and given a thumbs up. Still, she felt like the criminal, not the victim.

'Who's in charge here?' she heard a loud voice say. She was in a police car with the detectives. The lead one was in the front passenger seat, turned back toward her, one arm over the back. When he heard the voice, he looked at his partner sitting in the driver's seat, and the other man did something with his eyes. 'Here come de judge,' the partner said. The lead detective, a mid-thirtyish, fit-looking man named DaSilva, muttered, 'Get him over here and out of everybody's way.' The partner, an older man he called Donnie and whose name Rose had missed, got out and slammed the door. DaSilva gave her a smile that was probably ironic. 'Your guy,' he said.

She felt stupid. 'I don't get you.'

'From NASA. PR. He's gonna tell me he's taking you to the Space Center and we can interview you there after they've got the story straight. Right?'

'I – I don't know.'

'You're an astronaut, aren't you?'

'I just got here.'

A shape loomed next to his window and then folded in two and a big face looked in. 'I'm taking Commander Siciliano to Johnson now. You can interview her there this afternoon if there's a need.'

DaSilva gave her the same smile, eyebrows raised. 'See?' He turned to the face. 'And who the hell are you?'

The big shape unfolded again, and there was some fumbling, and a big hand produced a wallet with ID. The face stayed above, out of her sight, the voice floating down to say, 'Hansen, Public Information.'

DaSilva's partner got into the car and looked at her with disgust.

Her door opened. Hansen's big face peered in. 'My car is right down there.' He held the door for her.

Rose looked at the detectives. The partner still looked

disgusted. DaSilva looked unhappy. She said, 'Would you rather I stayed?'

'Oh, no.' DaSilva gave her the ironic smile again. 'We love jumping when NASA snaps its fingers.'

Hansen made the mistake of saying to her, 'Come on, come on – this is a fucking mess enough already –'

Rose grabbed the door by the windowframe and pulled it out of his fingers. 'I'm talking to these detectives.' Too late, she tried smiling at him. 'You'll have to take a number and get in line.'

'Commander –!' He pushed his face into the open window. It was pink, maybe from bending down so far because he was a big man, over six feet and a couple of hundred pounds. He was going bald but fighting it with a haircut so gyrene that he looked almost shaved. Maybe he'd been a jock when he was younger; he still had the look, but a thickened middle. 'We're practicing damage control here!'

'I'm practicing being a good citizen. Just cool it, okay?'

Hansen started to say something, and DaSilva got out. She could see the two men's midsections, close-up, through her window – belts and trouser-tops and shirts, white on Hansen with a bad tie, black knit on DaSilva with no tie at all. Her impression was that DaSilva might reach five-ten if he was stretched on a rack, and a hundred and sixty stripped and hosed down, but he muttered something and Hansen said, 'Goddamit –' and then *But* and then *She*, and then he strode away, saying again, 'Goddamit! God*dam*it!'

'That was nice of you,' DaSilva said when he was back in his seat.

'I want to do the right thing.' Then she added, with

a tentative smile, because what she had said sounded asinine to her, 'I'm scared.'

DaSilva nodded. 'We do have that effect.' He picked up a notebook from the dash. 'If your story checks out, you got nothing to worry about.' He began to ask her questions again. She interrupted him to ask, for the third time, if NCIS had been notified. She'd already told him, as she'd told the sheriff's deputy, about Mike Dukas's warning and why she was carrying the Smith.

'It's taken care of,' the partner said.

'Would you please check?'

'Lady, Jesus –'

'I'm not "lady," I'm "Commander."'

DaSilva jerked his head. 'Go check, Donnie.' He looked at her. 'This is important?'

'Very.'

'"National security?"' He sounded sarcastic. The local cops must have got a lot of that from NASA, she thought.

'Maybe terrorism.'

'All respect, Commander, these types don't look like terrorists. They look like run-of-the-mill shitkickers to me. We'll know when we get positive ID, but my guess is they're homegrown scumbags and they have good old American prison records.'

'For hire, maybe?' It sounded thin, even to her. Mombasa was a long way from Houston.

He took her through it again. The partner came back and said that the nearest NCIS field office was in Florida, so they'd called Washington. Something was in the works. DaSilva asked, apparently quite sincerely, if that satisfied her, and then he said he wanted to walk her through it.

Outside, she felt the dazzle of the sun, saw the police

255

lights still flashing, heard the helicopter – now joined by two others – overhead. Two deputies were measuring skid marks.

'Who *is* in charge here?' she said.

'I am.'

'How come the sheriff's deputies if it's your space?'

'We haven't had the time to shoot them.' By which he meant that they all got along and apparently shared jobs.

Hansen was standing at the side of the road in the shade. He made an impatient gesture toward her. She ignored him. Her chill was replaced by sweating as she walked with DaSilva in the sun. She passed a car where Mikey and the baby were sitting with two police officers, who smiled. Mikey looked frightened. Rose ran to the car and reached in and hugged him. 'You did so good,' she whispered.

'Can we go now?'

'Soon.'

'Is Bloofer dead?'

The pickup was gone, and a tow truck was backing up to the overturned van. Her SUV, however, was where she had left it beside the road. Rose looked at DaSilva. 'My dog –?'

DaSilva pointed at a woman kneeling in the grass beyond the 4Runner. 'Ask the vet,' he said.

Rose went over. The woman was bent over Bloofer. An inflatable splint was on the broken leg. His eyes were closed. Her stomach seemed to twist, then drop; the dog, always so buoyant, looked only pitiful. The woman looked up. 'I gave him a shot.'

'Not –?'

'No. But –' She stood, wiping her hands on her jeans. 'I'll know when I get him to the clinic, but he's pretty busted up.' She had a thin, homely face, wonderful blue eyes. 'I can put him down, if you want. Or –'

'Save him. Please.' Tears were in her voice and in her eyes and she turned away and pushed her feelings back down where they wouldn't bother her.

The woman made a little smacking sound with her mouth. 'I'll try.'

Walking again with DaSilva, Rose said, 'Who called the vet?'

'I did.'

They paced over the scene. When they came back down the road, the van was up on its wheels and the wrecker was getting in position to load it on its bed. Rose said, 'I wish somebody from NCIS was here. To look for evidence. You know – no offense, but they'd know what to look for.'

'Us local good old boys just never do learn what to look for.'

'I didn't mean that. But you're doing a criminal investigation. They'd look for – other things. You know?'

'Sure – fake beards, invisible ink, missile launchers – shit, we'd just miss all that stuff.'

'Oh, come on –!'

DaSilva waved a negative hand at something Hansen was trying to do or say as they walked past, not even looking at the man. At the van, a black kid in coveralls was fastening a cable to the van's rear towing hook. 'Just cool it a second, okay?' DaSilva said to him. 'Have a smoke.' He held out a pack.

'Don't smoke.'

'Good for you. You'll live to be a hundred. Just cool it, anyway.'

'Hey, man, I get paid by the job, not the hour.'

DaSilva paid no attention. He looked in the driver's

window, then went to the front and looked through the shot-out windshield. 'Where you taking this piece of shit to?' he said.

'Police impound lot.'

DaSilva turned and raised his voice. 'Hey, Donnie, you got anything on this vehicle yet?'

'Oh, man –' The wrecker driver leaned his buttocks against his truck and folded his arms. He looked at Rose. 'I get paid by the job, not the hour,' he said. Rose was standing in the sun, and she felt her head start to wobble. She looked for shade.

'Stolen,' Donnie called from the detectives' car. 'Stolen yesterday in Fort Worth. We're working on the pickup.'

DaSilva leaned in through the smashed windshield. He got so far in that his feet were off the ground, the legs not quite together, the left one bobbing gently as he did something inside. He was in there long enough for the kid in the coveralls to say 'Oh, man' twice, rolling his eyes each time. When DaSilva came out, he dusted himself off and rubbed his hands together and straightened his shirt. Chips of automobile glass had stuck to the knit fabric, and they fell sparkling to the road. He raised his voice. 'Hey, Donnie! Bring some evidence bags! And some gloves!' He motioned to the wrecker driver. 'Move this piece of crap out of the road but don't take it away yet.'

'Oh, man –!'

'You don't mind if we try to conduct an investigation here, do you? You don't object if we do the people's business?'

'Man, I get paid by the job!'

'So get a new job.' He turned. 'Donnie –!' Hansen had come up behind him; DaSilva's turn had put the two men almost face to face again.

'I'm taking Commander Siciliano with me now.'

'If I'm through with her, you meant to say. Thank you. Yes, I think we're through with her for now. So nice of you to ask. Commander?'

Rose felt off balance. Shock had gone another step or two now; she felt as if she had no strength in her legs, and her vision seemed poor. Still, she said, 'What did you find in there?'

Hansen came toward her. 'Commander –'

'Detective DaSilva, did you find something in there?'

'It's "sergeant," not "detective."' He gave her the ironic smile. 'I don't know national security from armadillo-doo, but, yeah, I think I saw some things in there.'

'Commander, I have to insist –'

She went by Hansen and stood close to DaSilva, fighting the feeling that she was about ready to faint. 'What? Come on, Sergeant, I didn't mean to bad-mouth you. If there's anything, *anything* in there, let me know. Huh? Sergeant? Please –'

Hansen's big hand closed around her arm. 'Commander, you come with me right now!'

She turned. He loomed over her. She had to look up with her head thrown way back. 'Get your fuck-ing hands off me!'

Hansen let go. 'I only – Damage control –'

She had been a helicopter squadron exec and a CNO staffer, and she had in reserve a voice that made people jump. 'Don't you ever try to tell me what to do! I am a commander in the United States Navy, and you are an overfed bureaucrat in fucking public relations! Do you understand me?'

'I don't have to put up with that kind of –'

'Get out of my sight! GET OUT OF MY SIGHT!'

Hansen's face was red. His jaw went out and seemed to lock in place. He raised a hand, index finger extended, as if he were going to make one hell of a point.

Donnie, evidence bags under his arm, had come up close to him. 'Beat it,' he said. 'You're badgering a crime victim. You want that on TV?' He pointed up.

Hansen looked up. One of the helicopters had a perfect view. He groaned. 'You'll hear about this,' he growled at Rose.

'Jeez, you mean we won't?' DaSilva said. 'Aren't you going to threaten us with the NASA firing squad?'

'Fuck you!'

Hansen strode away. 'God*damn*it!' floated back. DaSilva made an *Imagine that!* face. Donnie said to Rose, 'Good on you.' He smiled. No look of disgust this time.

She was shaking. It was the next stage of shock. She figured she didn't have long before somebody was going to recommend a shot or a sedative. 'What did you find in there?' she begged DaSilva. She was thinking of Alan and Dukas.

DaSilva had lighted a cigarette, and now he blew smoke sideways. 'A lot of glass. Two guns. And three cell phones, two identical, one still in the plastic wrapper.' He inhaled quickly and exhaled again, as if he was trying to suck up as much of the cigarette as he could in a hurry. 'Us local cops aren't very bright, but when we see cell phones piled up like that, we think one-day phones, and we think drug dealers. Big-time drug guy wants communications, he gives his people cell phones good only for twenty-four hours, then they change – new numbers all around. Hard to track, hard to follow. Even though I'm not an intelligence genius from NCIS, I can see where the same scheme might work for somebody that wanted to do a hit on the wife of a naval officer involved in a terrorism investigation. Not that I'm saying that's what it is. Us local cops, naive and uninformed as we are, try not to make statements until we have evidence.'

'What's the third phone?'

'Probably the one the guy uses all the time. We check it, we probably find it's got a local contract.'

It took a while to sink in. Then she got it, and got, too, that DaSilva was perhaps saying more than he seemed to be. 'Will you share?' she said.

'NCIS gonna send somebody?'

'Maybe. Sometime. I was thinking – more like, if I – if you – Look, Sergeant, if there's two phones, that's today and tomorrow. That means they plan to be all wrapped up in two days. That means we have to move really fast.' DaSilva had pitched his cigarette away and was pulling on plastic gloves. She fought her body for clarity. 'How do the cell phones work?'

'What d'you mean, how do they work? They work like cell phones.'

'But – is there any chance there's a number already in the one for today? Because if there is –'

DaSilva looked at Donnie. 'Smart woman. Think we could use her on the force?'

Donnie grinned. 'Suits me.'

'They for sure came preprogrammed.'

'Where does this one go?'

'Lo-o-o-ng number. Osama bin Laden's outhouse, maybe.' He gave her the smile. 'See, I even know some of the names those NCIS guys know. Astonishing! Let's go, Donnie.'

'Can't I –?'

DaSilva turned to her, suddenly serious. 'Commander, you're dead on your feet. Go home. Don't go to NASA; they'll give you endless grief. You and the kids go home. There's a sheriff's deputy standing by to take you. Also two blues to sit outside your house in case these shit-kickers got other buds around. Got any tranquilizers? Take one, lie down. If not, take two aspirin, lie down. I'll call you when I got the stuff downtown.'

'You promise?' Her head was spinning. She thought she just might throw up.

'Promise.' His lower jaw moved a little sideways, his mouth slightly open. He looked her up and down. 'You're a class act, Commander. I'm sorry I mouthed off at you.' He lowered his voice. 'Go home.'

Everything seemed to recede from her. She stood alone in the middle of a vast space where tiny figures moved like ants along the horizon. The distance to the car that would take her home seemed like miles. She took a step. Another. Another. She made it to a fringe of weeds and threw up.

Langley, Virginia.
An analyst in the African Section conflated an agent report and a satellite sighting into a short, nonurgent notice of activity at the main airport in Sierra Leone, West Africa. An aircraft believed to be a Tu-103 had landed and was believed to have offloaded personnel. On another pass of the satellite, the aircraft was gone, then later was on the ground again.

Because of established UK interest in Sierra Leone – Britain was the old colonial power – the analyst flagged the notice and suggested it be passed to MI6. At that point, she suspected only that some sort of support for local rebels might be involved.

Mombasa.
The word had spread through the det that somebody had tried to kill the skipper. When Alan walked into

262

the hangar, work stopped and everybody looked at him. Any resentment that might have resulted from his absence from Craw's memorial service was erased. Alan, aware of the atmosphere, waved and grinned.

Somebody on the far side clapped his hands together. Then somebody nearer him did. People were coming out of the spaces on the second level. There was a whoop and more applause. Alan waved again.

Geelin had been waiting for him at the guard point. He had filled him in on the mortar attack as they had walked toward the hangar: nobody hurt, no damage, three new holes in the dirt beyond the perimeter; no, he hadn't responded, goddamit, because those were your orders, sir (goddamit, unsaid); would he please, for Christ's sake, let them do a sweep of the raghead slum where the mortar rounds had come from!

Then Cohen grabbed his arm as soon as the men stopped clapping. One of the CIA guys was there, too, then Campbell and Chief Bakin. There was nervousness and a need to be reassured that he was truly okay, uninjured, *really* okay. By the time that was over, he was up the stairs, and they gave him a quick briefing right there on the balcony: the Marines from the gator freighter had arrived; there'd been another small riot near the port, now over; Fidelio and Mink and three sailors had been lifted to the *Harker* to study the bomb damage and were due back at 1800.

Patemkin, the CIA man, was smiling a little grimly. 'Kenyan cops are going to let us talk to the guy from the dhow.'

'Ambassador talked ugly to them?'

'*I* talked ugly to them. I told them if I had to go to the chief of station, ugly wouldn't even touch it.' He jerked his head. 'Sandy and I are seeing him tomorrow.'

'Good. Well done.' Alan started into the det office and turned back. 'Is he Islamic?'

'Kenyans say he's Somali.'

Alan thought about Harry and about the IPK. He nodded and turned away.

Later, he went down into the hangar and was surprised to see that David Opono was still there, he and Sandy Cole silhouetted against the open doors. The sun was almost down, the light the color of hot coals. She was leaning toward him; he was talking, her head turned up to his face. Once, he lifted a hand, finger extended, a gesture perhaps of scolding, perhaps only teaching. Then she leancd back and turned slowly and walked away deeper into the hangar. Her shoulders were bowed. It struck Alan like a tap on the chest: he'd dumped her, probably had dumped her before she had ever come to Mombasa. Then another tap: had she come to Mombasa to be near him, to bring him near? Was that why she'd been so willing to bring Opono into the operation?

What had she asked him? To start over? Whatever it was, it was something he couldn't give. To leave his wife? To spend a night with her? To take her back to Nairobi? Alan watched Opono watch her walk away, sensing in Opono's slender solidity a man who didn't care enough. That, of course, was what he couldn't give. He couldn't care enough, not for her, perhaps not for his wife. Alan sensed what he would have called the man's coldness, which was really a passion, an obsession, an ultimate caring, but not for her – egoism focused on a nobler goal, the attitude we used to see in 'the artist,' see still in the occasional hero, the occasional idealist. It is the object of the only caring it can manage.

8

Cairo.

Walking away from the Cairo lockup, Dukas stopped grinning – he had stopped laughing only a minute before – and said, 'I thought for a second there they were gonna keep you. One of those guys really had a yen for you.'

'That's the sergeant who shot the assassin. He doesn't have a "yen" for me; he knows that I'm his only backup in his self-defense case.'

'Yeah, well, he doesn't have to worry; they've already pinned the dead guy as a member of al-Jihad, so they'll probably give him a medal for the kill.'

'How do you know that?'

'The world's gone on while you were in the jug, Dick. I got it from DC when I got off the plane. Home boys think it was a hit to shut the woman up – they were done with her, etcetera, etcetera – so the Egyptians are looking now for the guy who was her lover, who wasn't the assassin, they think – they've already done some hair analysis and shit like that. I'm surprised they're that good, myself. Or maybe they're making it up. Anyway, we were right, the American woman gave away the AID office to her boyfriend and it got blown. Bad – nine dead, they figure three hundred injured.' He blew out his breath, reaching for the handle of his rental car. 'You ever wonder why they hate us, Dick?'

Triffler's face was in shadow, but his eyes glittered in the light from the street. 'I'm black, Mike.'

'What's that mean? Oh – you don't have to wonder, huh? You hate us, Dick?'

'No. But I've hated some white people. But no – I don't hate America, you know that.'

Dukas was still standing with one hand on the car. 'Sometimes I do,' he said. He was tired out. His shoulders sagged, and he sighed. Jet lag squared. 'A city like this – the goddam dogs are all bones; the kids are hungry and make a pain of themselves begging; half the guys have no jobs. And we have everything. Money – muscle – the crap we dump on the world, rock music and goddam soft drinks that rot your teeth and drugs and –'

Triffler put a gentle hand on his shoulder. 'Mike – you're babbling.'

Dukas straightened. 'Yeah.' He opened the car door. 'Forget I said it. What'd you find in the killer's apartment?' He got in the other side and slid behind the wheel and said again, 'Well? What'd you find?'

Triffler was feeling for a seat belt and realizing that there was none. For one moment, he looked as if he might refuse to ride in the car. Then he put a thin hand on the dashboard and braced himself and, staring ahead for the crash that he knew was coming, said, 'A computer. With Windows in Arabic. You ever try to use a computer with Windows in Arabic?'

'What'd you get?'

'I have no idea.' He flinched at something that flashed by. 'I downloaded everything to disk. E-mails. A lot of MP3 files. Couple of folders, but no idea what was in them. You should try downloading the contents of a hard drive when the instructions are in Arabic.'

'Where're the disks?'

'I sent them DHL to the office. We'll have Leslie e-mail them back to the hotel. I was afraid the Cairo cops would seize them when they caught up with me.'

Dukas laughed. 'Dick, you should have been a crook.'

'I used to be a telemarketer.'

Dukas laughed again, then sobered. He was trying to find the team's hotel. Triffler set him right after two wrong turns. When they were on a long, broad boulevard that was crowded with cars, Dukas said. 'Only three of us could get on the direct flight. The rest are coming in three hours.' He glanced at Triffler, whose face showed the strain of his day. 'I'm afraid you gotta stay up for a late-night meeting.'

Triffler looked down at his bloody trousers, his ruined silk jacket. 'I suppose I'll be allowed time to shower and change.'

'I suppose you will.' Dukas flinched and swore and stood on the brakes as a truck darted in front of him. 'So long as you get on the STU to Leslie and get those files back so you can report on them at the meeting.'

Triffler was silent. When he spoke, it was clear that he had been figuring. 'It's almost lunchtime in DC. I'll just have time to shower and change before Leslie gets back.' The car swerved and lurched and Dukas swore again. 'If you don't get us killed before we get to the hotel,' Triffler said.

'Eat mine.'

'I'm almost hungry enough to, but no thanks.'

Dukas stood on the brakes again and there was a solid smack as they were rear-ended.

Houston.
Rose had slept uneasily on the couch and had waked often. She had got up four times in two hours and

checked on the kids, Mikey playing a computer game or staring at the television, the baby challenging his toilet training in a playpen in the dining room. She had taken the aspirin that DaSilva had recommended, but she hadn't really slept. Odd bits of bad dreams flickered through her consciousness. At one o'clock, she forced herself up, again, her head aching, and made the kids some lunch.

'You okay?' she said to Mikey. He shrugged. She hugged him and told him he'd behaved as well as a grown man would have. His stillness seemed to say that he was a child, not a grown man; he was scared and he was confused because he wasn't in school, and he wanted certainty and safety and a house with a father and mother who didn't shoot people or get shot at. He said all that without ever speaking a word. With tears in her eyes, she promised him that things would get better. 'Eat your sandwich.'

'I'm not hungry.'

Then the doorbell rang, and her heart raced. She looked out, standing beside the window, not right behind it. The police car was still out there blocking the driveway, one of the officers visible as an arm and a coffee cup.

'Who is it?'

A female voice called something with 'NCIS' in it, then called her 'ma'am'. *And goddam the police for keeping my gun,* she thought. She put an eye to the corner of the square window that was high up in the door. A young woman and a fairly young man were standing out there, back from the door where she could see them. Both wore casual clothes – jeans on her, chinos on him, shirts – with something else worn loose over the top (vest, golf jacket) that could have hidden a hip gun. They must have seen her eye, because both held up blue wallets with NCIS badges.

'Ma'am,' the woman said when the door was open, 'I'm Warrant Officer Reko and this is Petty Officer Gorki. We're from the NCIS resident agency in Corpus Christi.' She smiled – nice smile, no bullshit, good teeth – and did something with her shoulders that suggested a squaring away for action. 'We're here to protect you?' It sounded like a question, but it wasn't a question.

'You're special agents?'

'I'm an LDO-special agent; Gorki's in the Master-at-Arms program.' She smiled again. 'We're legit.'

'Ah – the policemen –?' Rose's head felt thick and stupid. She made a gesture toward the police car.

'Oh, we checked in,' the woman said, laughing. She turned and waved. One of the cops waved back. 'We really are legit.'

'We'd like to check the house and then the perimeter,' her male partner said. It was a way of saying they'd like to be asked in.

They had a rental car that they pulled in around the cop car and parked next to the house. There were long black nylon bags in the trunk, which they carried inside, and then Petty Officer Gorki, the man, went out and wrestled a STU out of the car and slammed the lid.

Both were already wearing Kevlar vests and carrying handguns, she found. 'We got more firepower, but there's no sense scaring the neighbors,' Gorki said. 'Where's your phone?' She led him to it. The instrument was on its side, the dial tone buzzing, because early on there had been horrible calls from nosy reporters and all she'd wanted was peace. He hung it up and then listened to it and checked it with a device

269

that looked like a pager, then asked about extensions and disappeared. The woman was going from room to room with a bigger black box.

'You think I'm *bugged*?' Rose said.

'Just being careful, ma'am.'

Gorki came back in. 'Phone line's okay. Cops think the bad guys eyeballed you from a park up there – they found some stuff they'd left behind. We thought maybe they'd listened in, too, but they did this quick and dirty.' He looked at Reko. 'Got anything?'

'Zip.'

'Good.'

'Let's get out there.'

The phone, now active again, rang eleven times and stopped, then began ringing again immediately. It might be Alan, she thought. Could he know yet? Maybe. But she didn't want to be meat for the media feast. When the phone stopped ringing, she took it off the cradle and laid it on the table.

On local television, they were showing a tape of the incident as if it was an OJ rerun – overhead shots of the overturned van, her SUV, the vet and the dog, a shot of her and Hansen with his finger raised and her face thrust up, and there was no doubt that hers was the face of a very angry woman, and there was no doubt when Hansen stamped away that he was a very angry man. '*Commander Rose Siciliano, a new astronaut out at Johnson Space Center, was said to have killed one man and injured two others in an incident that police are classifying as an attempted homicide. Johnson spokesman Rick Hansen has scheduled a press conference for five this afternoon, when Commander Siciliano will present her side of the story. Hansen and Siciliano didn't seem to be too friendly when our cameramen saw them duking it out in this –'*

At two, an Air Force major was led to Rose's front door by one of the cops. He had the kind of serious face that undertakers put on when they discuss money.

'From Colonel Brasher, Commander. He's been trying to get you by phone all day.'

'So have the media.'

He shook his head. He had a manila envelope under his arm. He waited, as if she might be about to invite him in, and then handed it to her. 'Orders,' he said.

'Orders to what?' He pursed his mouth up.

The cop was strolling back down toward his car. Warrant Officer Reko walked across the yard and waved.

Rose opened the envelope.

She was being put on leave, effective immediately.

Attached to the sheaf of leave orders was a hand-written note on paper that said at the top, *From the desk of Colonel 'Chuck' Brasher, USAF*. The note said, *Return to the Space Center with Major Gaston at once. You are restricted to the base until further notice.*

Rose asked the major if he had a pen. He did. She wrote at the bottom of Brasher's note, *Thanks for asking after me and the kids. We're bearing up pretty well. We're not up to going anywhere yet, I'm afraid*. She handed him the note. 'Thanks.'

'You're to come with me. Those are my orders.'

'Major, you can't get an order for somebody else to do something. You can be ordered to *bring* me to the Space Center, but I guess you weren't. Were you?'

He frowned, as if the customer had asked why the plain pine coffin costs eleven hundred dollars. 'Colonel Brasher was quite specific.'

271

She nodded. The shock was passing, she guessed – she felt better. Maybe it was adrenaline from despising Brasher. 'You may tell him that the Navy is taking care of me just fine.'

She smiled and shut the door.

At two-ten, she called DaSilva and he told her that all three men who had tried to kill her had records. 'As American as apple strudel. No foreign connections. It's more like a mob hit.' His voice was warmer, no irony. A little sex thing there?

'You got a mob down here?'

'We got twenty mobs. What flavor you like – mafia? Cali cartel? Pachuco?'

'It doesn't make sense.'

She was thinking of the cell phones. Her brain was clear. The baby was sleeping and Mikey had eaten a big lunch, apparently energized by the arrival of the NCIS people, and her world looked better, despite Colonel Brasher.

'Mom?' Mikey had said after he was full.

'Honey?'

'The Navy takes care of their own, right?'

'It looks that way.'

He had grinned at her. 'I guess my mom can take care of herself.'

Off and on, she had been watching energetic people get as far as the police car and then get turned away. Some guy with a microphone had got into the backyard, and Gorki had met him in a combat stance with a Beretta pointed at his face, and he had disappeared.

The Navy takes care of its own.

'Either of those goons talk?' she said now to DaSilva.

'One can't, one says he won't but dropped a few

bits before a pro-bono shyster arrived. Contract hit, that looks good.'

'I've got my phone off the hook. You can't call me, but I may want to talk to you, so I'll call. Okay?'

'Anytime.' Did that sound just faintly personal?

She cut the call off with a finger and immediately released it to get a dial tone before somebody else could get a call in, and she dialed fast. She heard the phone ring on the other end – three, four, five – and she checked her watch. Four in Washington. He had to be there. Where the hell –?

'Ethos Security.' This was the Washington office of Harry O'Neill's company.

'Henry Valdez, please?'

A muttered something about waiting, then the voice, muffled, shouting 'Valdez! Phone!' And, after a long silence, Valdez's voice on the phone. 'Yo.'

'Valdez,' she said, 'Commander Siciliano.'

'Hey, Commander!' Sincerely pleased.

'Don't you guys ever answer your phone on the first ring?'

'Hey, we're geeks, not peons. How are you?'

Valdez had been her personal computer expert for a year, back when he was an EM and she was doing a shore tour. Now he was a civilian who worked for Harry O'Neill in computer security.

'I got a question,' she said.

'You always got questions. Shoot.'

'Cell phones.'

'I heard of them.'

'One-time cell phones?'

'Right. Very big with druggies. Call for twenty-four hours, throw it away.'

'Could you track where the call is going to?'

273

'Not very easy. Not easy at all. Not really my specialty, but unless you're NSA, and maybe even not then, you sort of get dropped at the first tower. Call gets there, zip, it's there with a couple thousand others going all over, you can't follow which one.'

She'd thought she'd had an idea. 'Shit.'

'However,' he said.

'Oh?'

'However, if you could piggyback a signal to yourself from each tower, you could track all over the world. Assuming you got the technology, which you don't but NSA this time does.' She knew he was smiling then. 'I got a buddy over there.'

'How do you piggyback?'

'Hey, this is classified information! No, seriously, you'd have to get the actual, physical cell phone. You go to a drug dealer, you say, "Can I borrow your cell phone for an hour so I can plant an insidious device in it?" and of course he gives it to you, and so you put a bug on it. Simple. That's why all the drug dealers in the world have been arrested.'

They talked a little more, mostly personal things, and she hung up and went back to the couch. She was up again within seconds. She grabbed the phone. 'You mean like a virus?' she said.

'Right. It *is* a virus. A cell phone's got a chip; it's a kinda computer. You insert a virus.'

'How long would it take?'

'Do I get a feeling you're going to lay a task on me?'

'I'm thinking.'

'I work for Harry, remember?'

She called Harry in Bahrain. He asked her if she'd heard from Alan; when she said she hadn't, he told her with some reluctance that there'd been an attempt on him at a meeting that Harry had set up for him with an Islamic faction in Mombasa. 'I've got shit all over me,' he said.

'But you didn't –'

'Of course I didn't, but somebody did! Anyway, he's okay, but you probably want to check with him yourself.'

She told him about the attempt on her own life. And the kids'. Nobody was better than Harry at a moment like that. He could express everything she wanted to hear – outrage, relief, vengefulness, affection. And pride. 'You shot the bastards? Four stars!'

She asked him if she could borrow Valdez.

'Is it connected?'

'Sure is.'

'He's yours.'

Valdez had been thinking, too. Also shmoozing with his friend at NSA, he later admitted. When she got him back on the line, he said, 'How about a virus that propagates itself? You follow what I'm saying? So every time the guy who gets the first phone call makes another call, *his* phone makes the towers ping, and then the phone that picks up at the end, *it* gets the virus.'

'But – it would be endless.'

'Every hacker's dream.'

'What do you need?'

'I need the cell phone. Unless we're just chitchatting theory here.'

'Shit.' She thought about it.

He said, 'I got an IM from Harry to give you the moon if you ask for it. You want the moon?'

'Maybe. How late are you working?'

'The moon's up at night, right?'

'I'll get back to you.'

Cairo.

Bob Cram stood against the wall of a big meeting room in the Semiramis Hotel and tried to look like an important man with an announcement to make. In fact, he knew he was a shmuck with nothing to say, but, as he had said to Dukas only an hour ago, he was the official face of the United States in this particular arena. Dukas hadn't taken that idea seriously enough, of course; Dukas didn't have any respect for him, as Cram perfectly well knew. Dukas was a pompous windbag with an overinflated reputation; well, so it goes. Cram would show him how these things were done.

The room was too big by a factor of about eight for the twenty or so people who were in there, some of them sitting on folding chairs, some standing around like refugees waiting for a border to open. Lots of baggy lids, lots of red eyes. Lots of looking at watches. The room had a high ceiling and acres of red wallpaper, most of it bleeding up into darkness. Smoke hung in thin strata. Cram was wearing a gray suit with a red stripe so narrow it wasn't visible six feet away, a maroon silk tie, and a button-down gray shirt with a white tick in the weave to give it texture. He was the classiest thing in the room, if he did say so himself.

The Cairo police briefing – not a press conference, they'd made that clear several times, a *briefing* – was already twenty minutes late. Finally, a fat Egyptian cop in a suit Cram wouldn't have worn to hose down the dog got up on a box behind a podium where, except for the box, only his scalp would have shown, and he tapped on a microphone, sending thumps like sonic booms reverberating around the walls. People made faces, then jokes. The fat cop said 'One, two, three' in Arabic and then 'Good evening' in English, and people

– all men except for two women too blonde to be locals – drifted toward the chairs and got out tape machines and laptops. One guy in rimless glasses and a moustache with waxed ends even got out a notebook. They looked less expectant than sullen, a universal *Tell me something I don't know* look that proclaimed them as professional journalists.

The fat cop ran through the stats on the morning's bombing and said that thirteen suspects were in custody and further details would be forthcoming. Cram didn't smile knowingly. Neither did the journalists. The thirteen suspects were probably street thugs and old cons too slow to get out of the way when a sweep was made, who got arrested every time there was a need for suspects. They'd all be out again tomorrow.

So many had been killed. So many had been injured. Blood supplies were such and such. The explosive was believed to have been this. The vehicle used was believed to have been that. Credit for the act was being taken by the thus, the such, and the other, none of whom had either the balls or the wherewithal to blow up an outhouse much less the AID building.

Cram listened and kept his pink hands joined over his groin as if he expected an attempt on his privates. He moistened his lips as he sensed his turn coming. He rehearsed his words. 'No comment,' Dukas had insisted he should say. Dukas had repeated it several times. Dukas had no class. When Cram got his turn on the box, he let his eyes roam over the assembled twenty or so, making contact here and there, especially the two broads, and he said in a voice that combined the best tones of a paid political announcement and a plea to support a ministry to God's forgotten ones, 'The government of the United States regrets that it is forced to say at this point in time that no information can be released as to the nature or the cause of the criminal act perpetrated upon its property and its citizens and employees in this city this morning. However –' he touched his tie, straightened, eyed the blonde with the bigger tits – 'we have every expectation that this situation will change in the next twenty-four hours as impending data become available for unclassified distribution.' He put his hands on the sides of the lectern and leaned forward. 'Our policy is an open policy.' He bobbed his head once. 'Thank you.'

There was no applause. Well, what did a bunch of foreign journalists know?

He waited against the wall while people milled around, moaning about having to show up for such crap at that hour. He tried to look deep into the eyes of the blonde with the gazoombahs, but she was too busy making fellatio mouths at a tall TV newsman with a camera crew and an assistant who seemed to be making notes for his life story. They all left together. The fat cop went away without so much as a thank-you to Cram. Everybody went away. Hotel staff started to fold up the chairs.

Cram started out, already headed for the bar, even though it was two flights down and a hundred steps to the right.

'Monsieur Gram,' a male voice said.

One of the media hacks. Cram had seen him in the crowd, remembered him because he had actually seemed to be listening. 'Cram,' he said.

The man smiled.

'Not Gram.'

'Ah, Cram, of course.' The guy had a French accent. 'Monsieur Cram, a word?'

Cram held up a senatorial, even imperial, hand. 'Nothing further to say beyond my statement.'

'I thought perhaps without attribution – on background –?'

Cram dug deep and came up with Dukas's words. 'No comment.'

The Frenchman smiled. Rather dazzling smile. 'Even if not for use now, looking toward the future? Maybe we might chat, become acquainted –?' He grinned. 'One hand washes the other hand. You know?' He made a hand-washing motion, and when his left hand came out of the washer there was an American hundred-dollar bill in it. 'Purely off the record.' He put the bill in Cram's breast pocket, where a less careful dresser might have carried a colored handkerchief. 'Drink?'

Cram, already headed for the bar, didn't see that there could be any harm in that. 'Strictly off the record,' he said.

9

Houston.

Rose tried to get Dukas in Washington but got his assistant, Leslie, who asked how she was, so that Rose realized that of course the Washington NCIS office knew about the attack on her, meaning that Alan probably knew by now, too. Then Leslie said that she couldn't say anything about Dukas over the telephone, but did Rose have a STU? Rose eyed the instrument that had come in with the NCIS couple, said she'd get back to her, and hollered for Warrant Officer Reko. 'In a minute!' floated in through the windows. Then Rose tried DaSilva again.

DaSilva was out, but he had a cell-phone number. She got him in transit; the connection was flirting with breaking up. Still, it was good enough for him to say that no, N-O, absolutely she could not have one of the cell phones from the van. 'That's evidence tampering. That's a broken custody trail. Not even for you.' The last words were *definitely* personal.

She called Valdez and told him she couldn't get the actual cell phone they'd been talking about. He said first that shit happens, and then he said, 'What's the make and model?'

She sighed. 'I don't know.'

She got back to DaSilva. He didn't know either, but it was in a report that was in his computer. Could she wait? Rose thought that she couldn't. DaSilva laughed, swore, and said that somebody would get back to her. Ten minutes later, a policewoman named Kaplan called to tell her that the two identical phones were Norito M707s.

'I ain't got one,' Valdez said.

'Buy one.'

'Pricey. International satellite-capable.'

'Buy one. I'll pay for it myself if I have to.'

'Where are we heading with this, Commander?'

'I'm not sure yet. You get a cell phone and tell me if your virus is feasible.'

'Will do. Better if we go secure from now on, Commander. My bud at NSA says we're walkin' around the edge of top secret.'

By then it was three o'clock. Midnight in Cairo, one a.m. tomorrow in Mombasa. Did she dare call Alan?

No.

Or, rather, not yet.

Warrant Officer Reko said that sure she could use the STU, and she set it up for Rose. While she was plugging in, Rose asked her if she would have any leverage over evidence from the attack on her that morning.

'Leverage? Commander, NCIS *owns* the case.'

'But the local police have the evidence.'

'Sure. They were on the scene; they're going to probably do a local prosecution. But, see, even though we came in late, we say it's a Navy case because you're a naval officer, because you were on duty, and because we think you were attacked as a naval officer or as the wife of a naval officer. So it's federal, and we're the relevant agency.'

'What do the local cops say?'

Reko smiled. 'Sometimes they say, "Get lost," and then there's a hassle.' She narrowed her eyes. 'Why?'

Rose hesitated. 'Rain check on that?'

Reko grinned with one side of her mouth. 'Your nickel.'

Rose got on the STU to Leslie and got Dukas's international cell-phone number. Leslie said in a worried voice, 'You can't say anything, you know, like classified on his cell phone, but he's got a STU with him someplace, okay?' Rose thought that Leslie's worrying about security was new. Everybody must have been told to screw the lid down because of the two bombings. And the attack on her. She was out of shock now and beginning to think of things other than herself and the kids, and she realized that an attack on a Navy family must have thrown the entire Navy into near-panic.

'Great.'

'He's traveling; I haven't heard from him; he was in Cairo because there was a bomb there too, you heard? Anyways, he hasn't been in touch. You think he's okay?'

'I haven't heard otherwise, Leslie.'

'I worry about him.'

Rose smiled. Leslie was twenty and apparently was in the process of falling in love with Dukas. Well, he was lovable. But not a very good bet, because he was also driven and hard-nosed and he had a terrible record with women.

'I'll let you know what I hear, Leslie.'

Dukas didn't answer his cell phone.

Cairo.

Dukas gathered his team in his room, which was big enough for twice as many people and had a view over the city that was as dazzling as one of any big city at night. Darkness is good for cities if you don't have to go down into it.

The room was really a suite, meaning that it had two double beds and a refrigerator and a pay-as-you-go bar, which Dukas didn't open. Everybody was wiped; they had all been mostly awake since the morning before in DC, except for the imitation of sleep you can get on an airplane and the catnaps they'd been able to catch in London. Half the team had arrived only a few minutes before.

'You're a lovely-looking group,' Dukas growled.

'You're a picture of loveliness yourself, Mike,' Keatley muttered. He was sitting on the narrow window ledge; Geraldine and Mendelsohn were on one of the beds with their shoes off and pillows behind them; Hahn was on the other bed, flat, with Triffler sitting beside him like somebody visiting the sick. Triffler looked better than everybody else because he'd had a night's sleep and a shower. But then, Triffler always looked better than everybody else.

'Where's Cram?'

Somebody muttered *Who cares?* and there was a low laugh. 'Try the bar.'

Dukas tried again. 'Anybody seen Cram?'

'He had a press conference.'

'I know, I sent him. Okay, we'll start without him.' Dukas could feel forty-eight hours' worth of fatigue like an illness, a good imitation of the Black Death, made worse by the still-sensitive bullet scar on his clavicle. He had been eating aspirin and he still ached. He found it wise not to look in the mirror. 'Okay, let's catch up. You folks who just got here, listen good.' He recapped what they knew about the morning's bombing. Then he told them about the attacks on Alan Craik and Rose, the reports of which had hit Dukas like sucker punches and had come one right after the other in secure messages from Washington. The one about Rose chilled him, not only because he was in love with Rose but also because it meant that somebody was at war with the Navy, including Navy families. He looked several of them in the eyes. 'Kasser has all your names and promised me he'd make a special effort to protect your families. That's trying to anticipate a worst-case, because so far as we know, our names aren't public and never will be. Still, we're being very, very careful.'

All of them had talked to their families. Everything was fine, they said.

'Rose Siciliano really got *attacked*?' Triffler said.

'Three guys, two vehicles. She took them out.'

Somebody muttered *Jesus*.

'You want to consider getting your families to lie low someplace for a few days. Maybe a good time to visit Grandma. Or Disneyland.' He put his hands in his pockets. His coat was off; his badly wrinkled shirt was bunched up in back from his shoulder holster, whose straps seemed to be pulling his shoulders around to meet each other. He was wearing the pants of a brown cotton suit he had put on in Washington. He looked like a ragbag. 'Folks, this is serious business. Mombasa, then Cairo, then almost simultaneous attacks on Craik and his wife. Craik was on CNN and I think they ID'd him there; it's hard to miss that shot-up hand. But then to go after his wife is goddam scary. And brutal.'

'How much time did they have to set it up?'

'Thirteen hours.'

'Jesus.'

'Yeah, either it was planned ahead of time, which doesn't make any sense, or they were set up for something like it and just plugged in Houston and Craik's wife.'

Triffler said, 'That means they'd preplanned to hit Navy families.'

Dukas shoved his hands way down in his pockets. His pants threatened to come off. 'That's what's got Washington tearing their hair. That's why I'm recommending families get out of town.'

Geraldine folded her arms without moving her head or her legs, still leaning back against her pink pillow. 'Who we talking about, Mike? OBL? Let's get real.'

'We don't know.'

'Can OBL reach into the US?'

'Can dogs chase their tails? You know what the intel says.'

Mendelsohn said to her, 'I don't believe it.'

'You better believe it!'

'Mike, bin Laden is not that well organized! Forget the bullshit the media feeds the public; this isn't Doctor Fu Manchu and his magic mushrooms! *You* know how difficult it is to pull off coordinated attacks from far away! You gotta have people on the ground, an organization, money flow, communications –'

They all started to talk at once. Dukas let them go for half a minute, then shut them up and said again that they had to think seriously about their families, and then he told them that they also had to think seriously about Mombasa and Cairo and what might be coming next. 'We're reeling, folks. We're reacting, not acting. Somebody else is pulling the strings, and we're doing the Oh-My-God tap dance just as fast as we can and we're *reeling*. We're also exhausted. I want to hear any good ideas and then I want us to all go to bed and get some fucking sleep. Anybody? Anybody got an *idea*?'

Triffler looked at Dukas, cocked his head as if to ask permission, and said, 'Muezzin calls. That's the call to prayer you hear five times a day from a mosque. I got files from the computer of the guy who killed the American woman this morning, and they were full of muezzin calls. Anybody got a take on that?'

Keatley scowled. 'I thought there was just one call. Like a song. Everyplace the same call.'

'No, no, every muezzin's different. Like cantors, right? I suppose a guy could be a collector of muezzin calls, an aficionado, but this guy was also a killer who was deep in the bombing, so I look for hidden meaning. Anybody?'

'Signal?' Geraldine said.

Hahn muttered, 'Code?'

Keatley growled, 'Could you set off a bomb with one?'

'What else was in the computer?' Mendelsohn said.

Triffler shook his head. 'They'll analyze it in DC. It's all in Arabic, which is Greek to me. Well, I just thought the muezzin thing might strike a chord with somebody. Sorry.'

Dukas looked around at them. Geraldine was asleep. 'Time for bed,' he said.

And there was a knock on the door.

Everybody except Geraldine went for a gun; she opened her eyes, looked toward the door but didn't move. Keatley was on his feet first. 'Shall I –?' He was already at the door but standing out of any line of fire from the outside, a 1911 Colt in his right hand, safety off. Triffler was off the bed and leaning back against the wall, a sleek Sig .380 in his hand; Hahn and Mendelsohn were crouched at the other side of the room, their guns out. Geraldine stayed on the bed.

'Yeah?' Dukas called.

'FBI.'

They looked at each other. Keatley shook his head. He motioned Triffler to the other side of the door and put his left hand on the knob. Dukas went past him, putting a hand on his arm to tell him to go slow. Dukas stood by the peephole in the center of the door and leaned forward, knowing that if the wrong people were on the other side, he would die of a battering ram of bullets fired through the door. It was metal, but not armor.

He looked through the peephole.

A sallow face looked back. Covering part of the chin was a leather case with a gold badge and an FBI ID card. Dukas read it with great care and stepped back between the beds and knelt, aiming his .357 at the door. He nodded to Keatley.

'Jesus Christ.' The moan came from the man with the badge when the door opened. He was looking at the guns that were pointed at him. 'Don't shoot the fucking messenger!' he shouted. 'I'm FBI! Jesus!'

'Who's with you?'

Another body interposed itself. 'I am.'

He was big, blond, sunburned, and unpleasant, one of those people who see no point in being nice when nasty will do just as well. 'Get out,' he said.

Dukas stood. 'What the hell does that mean?'

The guy came in and stood inches from Dukas. 'That means you're in a place where you're not supposed to be.' He flipped a pale blue envelope out of an inner pocket so that the free end bounced on Dukas's clavicle.

'These are orders to proceed to Mombasa *now*. Do not pass go. Do not collect your laundry. Do take your get-out-of-Cairo-free card. *Beat it*. Capeesh?'

'Who the fuck are you?'

'I'm the guy who's telling you you're outta here. Go!' He bounced the blue envelope. 'You're booked on the seven a.m. flight. Don't piss, don't moan, don't call your boss – this comes from the top. The *top*. Get it?'

Dukas looked down at the envelope. In the upper left-hand corner it said, *The White House, Washington, DC*.

Houston.

Rose decided it was stupid to wait any longer, and, because she couldn't get Dukas, she called Alan. And got no answer on his cell phone, either. Then she spent a half hour going the long way around to get the short way home – a contact at the Pentagon to get to an office in Norfolk to get a direct line to Rafe Rafehausen on the *Jefferson* to get them to set up a secure link with Alan's det in Mombasa.

They'd call her back when they had him on.

Meaning that she had to put the phone in the cradle so he could call her. Meaning that every other asshole in the world could call her. And did.

The connection was poor, and the STU made his voice sound as if he was talking through a toy trumpet in a windstorm. Still, it was his voice, and her heart lurched and she put her forehead against the wall and felt her throat constrict.

'Rose? Rose? Rose, it's Alan.'

She swallowed the ball of feeling in her throat. 'I know.'

'How are you? My God, I've been so worried – when

I heard –' His voice was ragged with fatigue, blurry, a voice that had just waked up and was trying to talk through emotional pain.

She pulled her forehead off the cool of the wall and stood straight, her eyes fixed on the blankness of painted plasterboard where it had rested. 'I'm fine and the kids are fine and Bloofer's probably going to make it.'

'Rose, if anything happened to you –'

'Facts now. Feelings later.' She forced emotion back into its hole. 'If I start to feel, darling, I'll explode.'

He was silent. The wind whistled in the STU. He said, 'I love you.'

'Yes. I know. Yes. More than – anything.' Emotion came scrambling up, trying to get out, trying to leap around the room and shout, and she said, 'Facts.' She swallowed, focused. 'The guys who tried to kill me had three cell phones. The police and Valdez think two of them are one-day phones. For calling whoever made it happen, right? Valdez thinks he can rig one so NSA can track it and we can find out who hired them to kill me. It has to be connected to what you're doing. Doesn't it?'

'Families of every man who's with me are being given protection because of what happened to you,' he said. 'They damned well better be protecting you.'

'I've got two cops and two NCIS gunslingers. What do you think of Valdez's idea?'

'I just –' He was fighting his own battle with feelings. It took him a while. Then: 'How would he do it?'

'No idea; he says it's feasible. But we have to move really fast – the phones probably have only twenty-four hours each, and we don't know when the twenty-four hours start.'

'NSA, Jesus – they're more inscrutable than the Chinese. It would have to come from the top.'

'Local cops say the phones are evidence and they won't give them up. But Valdez says he's got to have a phone because there may be a recognition code in the chip.'

'Wait one.' The wind whistled and her heart ached. She didn't want to be talking about cell phones and danger. She wanted to be lying in bed with him, holding each other. *Let me feel*, she thought, and then, *No – later*. He said. 'Okay, here's what you do. Call Ted Kasser at NCIS Washington. He's the director's deputy – Dukas's boss's boss. He knows me, or he's met me. Tell him what you need and what the time limit is. Tell him you have to get the cell phone away from the local cops, meaning that there will have to be a custody trail. Is one of your NCIS folks a special agent?'

'Yes, Reko – a woman – she's a Limited Duty Officer-special agent.'

'Okay, tell Kasser he has to lean on the local cops. You got a name there?'

'Yes, DaSilva, nice guy, he –'

'Kasser leans on him to turn the phone over to your special agent so there's a custody trail. She'll know what that means. Then you have to get the phone to Valdez. Or he flies out there. How long a trip is that? Six hours – two to four to make a reservation and get to Dulles – Christ, that's a loss of ten hours right there –'

'I'll worry about that. Ted Kasser. Okay. Then I get the phone to Valdez; he works his magic; will NSA follow up if it works?'

'Ask Kasser that.'

'It's important, isn't it?'

'It could be the ball game.'

'Or it could be nothing.'

'I love you.'

'Well – *that's* the ball game.' She smiled at the blank wall. 'I love you, and you're everything to me, and I'm going to give the phone to Mikey and get on with saving the world. You take care.'

He, too, might have had something in his throat. 'You, too.'

She put Mikey on and heard the monosyllabic discourse of a seven-year-old: 'Hi,' 'No,' 'Yes,' and then the inevitable, 'Some guys tried to kill us.' Sounding as affectless as she had tried to. She stood behind him and held his shoulders, and when he was done he passed the phone up to her and she said, 'I love you' and ended the call, and Mikey buried his face in her and held on. She stroked his head. 'Sometimes,' she said, 'bad things happen and we just have to live through them.'

She put the buzzing phone on the table and went looking for Warrant Officer Reko, whom she found taking a break in the kitchen, Coke in hand. 'I need to phone NCIS Washington, most urgent. Also secure. What do I do?'

Reko looked surprised, but hesitated only a fraction of a second. 'Who you want there?'

'Ted Kasser.'

Reko's eyebrows went up, but she passed Rose in a rush and was at the phone. Less than a minute later, she said, 'They're trying to find him. You want to wait?'

'Definitely.'

'I used your name. I wanted to move things along.'

'He doesn't know me.'

'Commander, after this morning, everybody in the Navy knows your name.'

Kasser got to the phone six minutes later. He did, indeed, know who she was, and he asked how she was and how the kids were, and he endeared himself to her by asking about the dog. 'How did you know?' she said.

'I'd say we know everything, but in fact I heard it from Mike Dukas's assistant, who apparently has been watching CNN since it happened.' He had a deep voice, perhaps an old one, she thought; it had a roughness, a kind of scratchiness. But it was a good voice.

'I need your clout,' she said.

She told him everything.

'I've met your husband,' he said. 'He's a friend of Dukas's. Kind of a gunner.'

'You could say that.'

'You think this phone thing could really work?'

'My computer guy says yes. But NSA is vital. They've gotta be on board.'

'Okay.' He paused as if he was making notes. 'Put the LDO-special agent on.'

'Warrant Officer Reko, yessir. One moment.'

Reko held the phone against her ear and nodded. And nodded. She said 'Yes, sir' five times. Then she held the phone out to Rose. 'He wants you again, ma'am.'

'As I understand it, your man has to have this phone in his hand.'

'That's the way I understand it, too.'

'How you going to bring the two together in time?' Before she could speak, he said, 'If I hear you right, the window is twenty-four hours and the clock is running. Yes?'

'Yes, sir. Commercial air is nine or ten hours mini-mum. But, uh –' She thought about her children, the rough time that Mikey must be having since the attack.

293

Didn't they put kids with counselors, even shrinks, when this happened? And she was about to suggest that she leave her kids behind. 'Um, well, if an F-18 could be made available, I could, uh, fly it myself. I'd have to refuel someplace –'

'You're F-18 capable?'

'I've been flying them getting ready for astronaut training.'

'In-air refueling?'

'Well, I've done it –' She gulped. 'But it would mean leaving my kids, and I – they were with me and had a rough time – I don't know –'

'The Navy has other pilots.'

She hesitated, then blurted out, 'I want to do it. I want to help my husband.'

'Stand by.' He must have covered the telephone then, because there was nothing but the stormy silence of the STU. Then his voice was back. 'I need to clear this at ONI and put somebody on it there. What's your active-duty status?'

'I was put on leave. And told to get myself to the Space Center and stay there.'

Kasser was quiet for about three seconds and then he laughed, but without humor. 'Let me see what I can do about that. You keep your phone clear, because you're going to get a lot of calls.'

That was easier said than done, but the media appetite was perhaps wearing off. Or maybe they were focused on the press conference that was supposed to take place at Johnson at five. At any rate, the calls got through.

At four-seventeen, a Navy captain called from the Pentagon to say that an F-18 would be flown from NAS Corpus Christi to Ellington Field for her use.

At four-nineteen, Reko was told to stand by to sign for and secure a package from the Houston police.

At four-twenty-one, DaSilva called to ask her what the hell the Navy was trying to pull.

'It's important, Sergeant.'

'Yeah, "national security," I got the lecture. You're pulling rank on me, Commander – I got my goddam lieutenant shaking in his boots because our chief gets a direct call from the White House! You people are endangering evidence in an important case!'

'It's important to us, too. It's really important.'

'So is justice in Houston, Texas.' He didn't sound friendly anymore. 'Okay, I'm sending out the cell phones – *over my stiff objections!* – but we keep the plastic sleeves because they have fingerprints on them.' His voice dropped, now that he had accepted the inevitable. 'We going to get these back?'

She had her brain back together sufficiently to think about what he'd said. 'I think NCIS will want the fingerprints, too.'

'Then let them ask for them.'

'How about the phones? Did you check the phones inside the plastic sleeves? For fingerprints?'

'No, that would never occur to us.'

'I don't mean to patronize you.'

'Okay, so you can do it without meaning to. It's a skill, right? Look, Commander, you did a hell of a thing this morning, and you behaved in a standup way. But I know my job, okay?'

'I'm sorry.'

'Tell your NCIS people to ask us nicely for the prints. We dusted everything – phones, sleeves, the works – as a matter of course because we're professionals and Houston isn't really Mayberry RFD. Okay?'

'Okay.'

'So I ask again – we going to get the phones back?'

'I don't see why not.'

'I suppose you can't tell me what's really going on.'

'I'm sorry.'

'I'm sorry, too.'

She heard him hesitate, as if maybe he was going to say something like *How sorry?* That might lead back to the personal, but he let it go and said, 'Yeah,' and hung up.

At four-twenty-five, a female commander called from the Pentagon to say that her orders had been amended from 'leave' to 'special duty' with NCIS, Washington, report soonest to responsible authority.

At four-thirty, a squadron exec from Corpus Christi called with her flight plan from Ellington to Andrews Air Force Base in Washington, with refueling by an Air National Guard tanker out of Memphis. 'You'll be met at Andrews, I was told to say, by a car with driver, and you'll know where to go, that right?'

'Yes, sir.'

'Have a good flight. And please be nice to our airplane.'

Then life sped up and two police cars parked, blocking the driveway even more, and two cops came up to the door, and Reko signed for a sealed package they handed over. Phone calls came in for both NCIS people, and then Gorki told her that he and Reko would be bringing her kids to Washington right behind her on commercial air and they would meet in the morning. 'My understanding is you may be there a little while. People upstairs figure you want the kids.'

And they also figure I don't want to be under house arrest at Johnson, she thought. She got Reko and Gorki to sit down in the living room while she told them what Mikey liked and didn't like. The baby was too young to know what was happening, but Mikey had had a brief moment of panic when Rose had told him that she was leaving. Gorki had two kids, he said; Reko said they'd take special care. Rose brought Mikey in and explained it all to him, holding his shoulders and looking into his worried, too-young face.

'This is for Dad?' he said.

'Maybe it'll end what happened to us and what's happening to him.'

'Okay.' He glanced at Reko and Gorki. 'I'll see you in the morning?'

'Absolutely. And then maybe we'll go see Gran and Nana, okay?'

He liked her father. He'd spent a lot of his life with her father, in fact.

'I wish we lived like other kids,' he said.

She held him, tears in her eyes. *The Navy has other pilots*, Kasser had said. But they weren't married to her husband. And she couldn't sit with her hands folded and do nothing.

For which her child paid.

Then she was collecting flying gear and kissing Mikey and listening to the vet say that Bloofer was groggy but coming out of it, and the last thing she did was call Valdez and tell him she was on the way with the goods, to which he said, 'I know.'

'How the hell do you know?'

Laughter. 'Man, I got more Navy people on me right now than the *Constitution*. I'm being taken to NSA. You, too. I talked to your guy DaSilva in Houston. He thinks you walk on water, he tell you that? So he gave me

297

the number showing on the cell phone those guys used today. A number in the Cayman Islands.'

'But I – That doesn't make any sense.'

'Sure it does. It's just a pass-through. From there, the call could go to Afghanistan, Saudi Arabia, you name it. NSA already has the pass-through ID'd in the Caymans. I talked to a guy over there is hot to trot on the rest. They love it. Big challenge!'

'Is your magic going to work?'

'Two more frogs and a psychedelic mushroom and I think I got it.'

Then she was in a military car with a driver, and then she was in the cockpit of an F-18, and then she was cutting a line through chill air at forty thousand feet.

USS *Franklin D. Roosevelt*, Inport Haifa, Israel.

Narc was first in line for the liberty boat, an evolution he had perfected as a junior officer and which now seemed too damned easy as a lieutenant-commander, but habits were habits. He blasted through his paperwork, recommended everyone in his department for promotion, and left it to the skipper to make the tough calls about who wouldn't make the cut. That gave him an hour on most other officers, so he scammed a cheap sci-fi novel from the squadron intel officer (*no Al Craik*, he thought in passing) and headed down to the hangar bay where the line would form for the beach. He was so early that he seemed out of place in his clean Gap khakis and his polo shirt, and he didn't want to sit anywhere and risk getting the omnipresent black grease-soot mixture on his trousers, so he went out to the fantail and scammed the seat that would eventually belong to the senior Shore Patrol officer.

Last liberty before the Indian Ocean, he thought. *Time to party.* He wanted to get this cruise done and get back to real life with a squadron. He had a mental image of the folks on the *Jefferson* getting ready to transit the canal the other way, toward home. Just doing the turnover with them would be a major evolution. He opened the book and tried to tune it all out.

The sci-fi novel wasn't cheap enough and seemed determined to inflict both plot and character on Narc, who resented it and thumbed along rapidly, looking for action. *Jesus, the thing's like* Dune, he thought. *Everyone thinks that's great, too.* As the novel didn't grab him, he found himself looking around idly, watching the first enlisted men and women arrive to form a separate line on the port side of the fantail. He speculated about the first man to show in the opposite line. *What job did he gun-deck to get here so fast?* He watched an IS1 from the intel center flirting openly with a chief from his squadron's admin and shook his head. *Trouble with a capital T.* Narc wasn't always at the head of the ethics class, but he drew his own line at fraternization. He'd seen how it could bite folks in the ass.

The port of Haifa, Israel, had started to envelop the carrier, so that buildings began to appear beyond the fantail on the starboard side. Narc got out of his purloined chair and leaned carefully against the rail so that he could see the shore. Haifa looked like every other Mediterranean port, with a lot of low, white buildings, dirty streets, and too many people, but it was prosperous compared to Egypt. You could see it in the cars and the lack of a shantytown. Israel hid its shantytowns in the occupied territories. He shrugged.

Off the starboard side, a big ferry left one of the piers and started toward the carrier, which had yet to lose her weigh or pick up her buoy and anchor. Narc watched the pier for a moment and realized it had to be the beachhead for the liberty boat, as it was already thick with both Israeli and US security. The attack in Mombasa had made the Navy cautious. For the second time in an hour, he thought of Al Craik, still stuck in Mombasa, and thought of all the crap his old shipmate had apparently endured in one cruise, and how pissed off he must be to be stuck on the beach when his carrier was about to go home.

The big ferry had a bow wave as she plowed the water toward the carrier, which was just in the tricky process of picking up her buoy. Narc couldn't see them, but he knew that, well forward, a party of bosun's mates were doing the real deal, hauling chains and dropping anchor in a manner that Nelson would have understood, despite the technology that drove every other aspect of the huge ship. Somewhere above him, a fairly senior officer would be sweating the process of maneuvering the monster through the congested confines of the port. *Better him than me,* Narc told the bridge silently. He hadn't liked any part of driving a ship at AOCS and he didn't plan to go that way in his career.

He felt the gentle change as the ship took up slack on the buoy and then settled again. Somehow, there was more motion at anchor, not less. He looked across the sun-dazzled sea to the liberty boat that was now slowing as it made a curve to approach the platform being rigged at the stern of the ship. Narc could see that the boat was early and wondered for a moment if it could be carrying a bomb. It wasn't a panicked thought but an idle one, as he noted that the boat was virtually empty and tried to imagine how such a boat could be employed. But then one of the stewards on the boat waved up at him and he saw there were several more behind him, all wearing red waiters' jackets. Narc couldn't bring himself to believe that a dozen men would commit suicide together in silly red coats, so he waved back and started down the ladder from the fantail to the platform.

The chop even in the harbor was enough to make the last ladder rise and fall five feet with each wave, but Narc had years of experience on liberty boats and he waited his moment and jumped to the platform. The big ferry was closer now and Narc thought she still had too much weigh on her. His opinion was a professional one. Every aviator endures years of commanding liberty boats as part of the duties of being a junior officer. He had commanded boats in Fort Lauderdale and Naples, Toulon and Antibes and even Haifa, and he knew that the hired ferry was going too damned fast.

'He's going to hit us,' Narc said aloud. There was only a small party on the platform, because the liberty boat wasn't due for fifteen minutes and liberty wouldn't even open for half an hour. The chief petty officer in charge seemed pained, then looked over his shoulder and his eyes widened. 'Shit,' he said.

'Everybody off the platform. *Off!*' Narc bellowed. He pushed a sailor up the first steps and grabbed another by the collar. '*Off! Now!*'

The chief made a leap for the ladder and caught it, and there was no time for Narc to wait for the uproll. He jumped after, hooked an arm through the chains, and got his feet under him in a scramble that pulled every muscle in his lower back. Then he pounded up the ladder after the rest of the sailors as the ferry annihilated the platform behind him and plunged on like a shark seeking his blood. The whole carrier moved and he heard a noise like a bell sounding. The ladder-well distorted, and Narc was sure he was dead, crushed by a wall of metal, and then he heard metal tearing and watched as the deck above him ripped away from the ladder-well like paper, rivets exploding off the failed seam and ricocheting around him like bullets. One hit him in the shoulder and numbed it, and another hit his hand. One of the sailors screamed.

Then they were all on the deck of the fantail and Narc could breathe again. He bent over, afraid he was going to vomit, and when he stood up, he was looking into the eyes of the ship's XO.

'You okay?' he said.

Narc nodded. He looked past the XO to where the ferry, her bow staved in, was sinking slowly just aft of the mooring buoy and the wreckage of the liberty platform.

'Holy shit,' he said. He wondered if there was a bomb.

An hour later, Narc had changed his clothes and was ready for another try at the liberty line, although he wouldn't be the first and would have to wait like everyone else. By the time he got there, the line ran all the way down the hangar deck. Only the ship's boats were allowed to run, and they were leaving from the small companionway docks built in under the flanks of the stern, slowing the process to a crawl. He twisted and turned at the waist, trying to ease the pain in his back.

'Damn, I'm never getting ashore,' he said to the next sailor in line, a female jg from one of the Hornet squadrons.

'Haven't you heard, sir?' she asked, far too chipper for the penultimate JO in a long liberty line.

'Heard what?'

'The accident bent one of our screws.'

Narc thought of the deep, bell-like note he'd heard at the moment of the crash. 'So?' he said, hope rising within him.

'We're here for an extra two days, at least,' she said, and Narc gave a silent cheer. *Two extra days in port.* The cruise was shorter already.

Cairo.

Dukas and his team, minus Cram, stumbled out of two taxis and dragged themselves into the Cairo terminal as if they were the only survivors of an epidemic. Dukas, coming last with two Egyptian porters and the luggage, felt even worse than he had the night before, although he hadn't thought that possible. Three hours' sleep. Maybe he should just never have gone to bed. 'Here comes the zombie patrol,' he growled.

For the first time since he had known her, Geraldine Pastner looked like hell. Her skin had turned a dirty olive green. Somebody had gouged deep lines in her face while she slept. 'I'd kill for a coffee with sugar,' she moaned. She sounded as if she'd been smoking Gauloises for twenty years or so.

'Where's Cram?' Dukas said.

Mendelsohn raised sad eyes. 'Never showed.' He was sitting on his luggage with his fist under his chin. He was supposed to have shared a room with Cram. 'Never turned up.'

Dukas went off to call the embassy and report Cram missing. He didn't make much of it, really; Cram was the type who'd turn up in a whorehouse or an after-hours club and think it was a hell of a thing to have six a.m. breakfast in what he'd later call 'the real Cairo.' Meaning that you could see Egyptians there.

When Dukas came back, Keatley had checked them in and the baggage was gone. 'They gave me grief about the guns,' he said. 'Grief, endless grief. Why'd that stupid fuck have to put us on a plane so early?'

'To be a stupid fuck. But that isn't the question. The question is, *Who* is that stupid fuck?'

Dukas had read the orders in the blue envelope. They had told him exactly what the blond bastard had said – get out of Cairo and get out fast. And don't ask questions. Signed by the National Security Advisor, whose signature on the document had been confirmed when he telephoned Washington.

So here they were.

Dukas figured that their efficiency had been reduced about eighty percent by fatigue, and that they could have improved that to twenty percent if they'd been allowed to get eight hours' sleep. But here they were, by the grace of a government whose right hand didn't know that its left hand had itself by the dick.

'Everybody sleep on the plane,' he said. 'That's an order.'

At the Semiramis Hotel in Cairo, everything was quiet. The guests slept; the night staff yawned and watched the clock. In the mezzanine bathrooms, called the cloakroom, a sallow Egyptian named Farouk Bazir sluiced down the marble floors with a mop and then polished them with wax and a buffing machine. While he waited for the floor to dry in the ladies', he went to the men's with his mop and his mop-wringer and his cart of cleaning chemicals, and he parked the cart and went from stall to stall to make sure that nobody was asleep in them. He flushed each one, because late-night guests were given to doing animal things in them and then stumbling out without flushing. In the third stall from the end, he saw that something solid was mounding up out of the toilet and he muttered to himself because he'd be expected to clean it out, with his hands if need be. Then he leaned over the toilet and looked in and realized that he was looking at a small amount of human excrement and, under it, a human head.

Bob Cram had been found.

Day Three

10

Mombasa.

'Eerie.'

Mombasa airport in the after-dawn lay like a wilderness plain. The morning air was cool, smelling of dust and a hint of the sea. The eastern horizon was almost white, but the sun was not yet above it, and in the west he could still see the brightest stars.

An animal roared distantly.

'Lion?' Bakin said.

'Elephant, I think.'

They listened. Alan heard the rising whoop of a hyena. Beside him, Chief Bakin frowned. They were standing at the outer perimeter, two Marines in battle gear fifty feet on either side of them. It was silent, magical. Then the magic broke: the sun appeared over the horizon and the first brightness touched the terminal building across the airfield, and, as if on that signal, the doors of the hangar behind them rumbled.

'Aircraft,' Bakin murmured.

They watched the S-3 rolled out. The crew were early, maybe nervous. Campbell started to do his preflight.

'This is the third day,' Bakin said. 'These things come in threes, I guess.'

'We'll see.' Alan grinned. *'Inshallah.'* As Allah wills it.

Washington.
Rose had turned the cell-phone package over to an NCIS special agent at the NSA security gate, she still holding the package while the silver-haired man signed for it in both her own log book and the Houston custody log. It was he who insisted that the signature be witnessed by another special agent with him – 'We want the cops to like us, ma'am; never know when we're gonna need them.' – and then he had walked away with the package and she had had herself led to a ladies' room where she could change. She had been still in her flight suit, clammy and cramped from the flight. It was a relief to change into a uniform.

NSA security was tighter than a hose clamp. She had to be photographed and thumbprinted; the photo went on a badge that she was to wear *at all times*, the point made with considerable emphasis. The thumbprint was scanned and digitized while she watched, and then an unsmiling black guy no older than Valdez told her that it would be available for comparison at 'all class 1 checkpoints.'

'What's a class 1 checkpoint?'

'You find out when you hit one.'

Valdez and the cell phone were on the fourth floor. She had to be accompanied by a guard to get there, although nobody checked her thumbprint, but she figured she was like the cell phones – she'd been in somebody's custody ever since she'd walked through the door.

The room had no more character than a styrofoam cup. The walls were off-white and unadorned, except for scuffs and knocks where furniture might once have hit them. The floor was gray tile. A long, gray table littered with equipment and laptops ran most of the length of the room. Valdez was sitting at the table, staring through a magnifying lens at something held in a contraption that looked like the arms of a bionic midget. He didn't look up, but the eight other people in the room did, sixteen eyes focusing on her as if they thought she might erupt into flame. Five of the eight were men. The women looked no more welcoming than they did. Two of the men came forward, blocking her sight of the table and Valdez. One even put his hand inside his coat, but maybe he had an armpit itch.

'Commander Siciliano,' her guide said. He was a lanky redhead who had been introduced as Rondeau and who had an accent that could have been Texas or Louisiana. 'Commander Siciliano's cleared.'

'ID,' the bigger of the two men said. Both were big, but he was really big. She touched her badge, but he held out a hand to mean that he wanted her own ID. 'Mmm,' he said. He handed it to his buddy.

'Commander Siciliano's cleared,' the redhead said again.

The very big man checked a laptop. 'Ri-i-i-ght,' he said. He sounded as if he wished it had been wrong.

The big men parted and she was allowed to move toward the table. Valdez glanced up and grinned and put his face down to the magnifier again. A tall, balding man who had been standing behind him stepped back and then came around the group and touched Rose's left elbow. 'Ted Kasser,' he murmured. They shook hands. Rose found herself whispering. 'How're we doing?'

'He's getting ready to download the virus into the cellphone chip. Then we see if it works.' He had a nasal voice and an accent that she thought she recognized as western New York.

Somebody else was whispering on the other side of the table. Rose suppressed a nervous giggle. What were they all being so quiet about?

'Security,' Kasser whispered in her left ear as if he had heard her thoughts. 'They had to get the okay from the White House before they'd let you and me in.'

Good God, she thought, and I didn't even go through a class 1 checkpoint. What must they have on the other side of *those*?

Valdez cleared his throat. People around him leaned away. 'Well –' Valdez said. His voice sounded unnaturally loud. He stretched. 'Hey, Commander, ain't this fun?' Three people looked disapproving. Valdez stood and said, 'Okay, let's download this sucker and see what we got.' He was a small man with muscular arms and shoulders, a head that seemed huge because of thick black hair, a bright-looking face with high cheekbones and dark eyes. He moved down to a laptop that sat half a dozen feet away on the long table, the crowd parting as if contact with him was dangerous. He was like a wizard, indeed, feared by the people he was there to help.

Rose and Kasser whispered together. Kasser knew Alan slightly, knew Dukas well. She asked about the Cairo bombing, but there was little known yet. Dukas was on his way to Mombasa, Kasser said.

'I thought he'd stay in Cairo,' she murmured.

Kasser's face clouded. 'Something came up.'

Everything took longer than she wanted it to. It was after eleven when Valdez said that the phone was ready to use. The first day's cell phone, he told them, the one the men in the van had been using when they had attacked her, was already out of it. Its twenty-four hours were over.

'Who wants to be the birthday boy?' Valdez said. He held out the phone. Everybody frowned and looked somewhere else. 'Jeez, I got to do everything myself?' Valdez laughed and winked at Rose. 'You ready there, Freddie?'

A very young woman with a red NSA badge was hovering over another laptop. She hit a key and gave Valdez a thumbs-up.

'Okay?' Valdez held up the cell phone. 'And uh-one, and uh-two, and uh-three –!'

He hit the call button with his thumb.

The cell-phone beep, amplified by a speaker on the table, sounded like a baby's shriek. A man flinched; a gray-haired woman in a dark suit and draped scarf frowned as if somebody had broken wind.

The sounds of the call bounced around the little room. The beeps became static, then utter silence, and then a single rattling ring sounded.

'Cayman Islands pass-through,' Valdez said. The speaker began to emit clunks and knocks. 'Passing through,' Valdez said. He almost sang it. The noises stopped. 'Here we go – satellite – transfer – *now* –!'

The room was charged but silent, as if everybody was holding his breath. Rose knew that she was, and beside her, Kasser was leaning a little forward, and she couldn't hear him breathing, either. Down the table, the woman who looked hardly out of her teens was staring at her laptop, and suddenly she muttered, 'Hit.'

Valdez was still looking at his own computer. He said, 'Oops.'

'Jakarta, Indonesia,' the young woman said.

Valdez put the cell phone on the table. 'Well, back to the old drawing board.' He grinned around at them. 'Sorry about that. There's a digital answering machine at the other end. I configured for an analog. Little glitch.'

The feeling in the room changed. Rose felt a wave of relief and then annoyance from the others; suddenly the room was filled with voices, still low, but no longer whispering. Kasser made a sour face. 'Win a few, lose a few.'

'How long?' somebody with an NSA red badge said.

'Maybe half hour.' Valdez was sitting again, staring at his screen. He turned to the young woman at the other laptop. 'Wha' d'you think, Mave?'

'Twenty minutes, half hour.' She wasn't pretty, but she had a bright, felinc look to her, and Rose wondered fleetingly if she was Valdez's girl. Geek meets geekette?

Somebody said he needed a cigarette and somebody else said he'd buy that. The room started to empty.

Mombasa.

Alan was leaning over the shoulder of an electronics mate who had one of the detachment's five laptops open in front of him on the plywood table. Around them, extensions and cables squirmed across the floor and two other tables. Every surface held electronics equipment, most of it a gray or black metal box – big, small, narrow, wide. They were getting a feed from the NSA office where Rose had been watching Valdez.

The laptop in front of them had just had its blank screen replaced with a long line of numbers.

'What's that?' Alan said.

'Uh, I think – frequency –' The young man touched the screen where a block of numbers ended. 'Then this here should be coordinates of the cell towers, I guess – UMG probably, let's see –'

Alan knew the universal military grid better than

he did. He studied the numbers. 'East of India, west of Hawaii,' he said. 'South of the equator – where's a map, for Christ's sake?' He looked around. The electronics tech didn't even bother to respond; maps weren't his line of work. Alan poked his head out the door to look along the balcony above the hangar. He shouted at the first sailor he saw. 'Grab me a world map! Anything with UMG coordinates on it!'

'Uh, sir – we didn't bring –'

'Find something!'

When he turned back to the room, the laptop had two new messages below the numbers: *Jakarta, Indonesia* and *Reconfiguring*.

'What the hell's that?'

'They're reconfiguring, sir.'

'Reconfiguring what?'

Washington.

'Is my husband getting this?' Rose said to Kasser.

'We sure hope so. We've gone way out on a long limb for this.' He didn't look happy. He looked, in fact, old and tired – a man nearing retirement, who needed sleep to deal with the pace he had to keep. A late night in a room at NSA was not doing him any good, physically. Still, he was gracious. 'Want to meet some people?' he said.

'Oh – well, if –'

'Anyway, they want to meet you.' He smiled. 'You're famous.'

It helped to learn who some of the people in the room were. One was from the National Security Advisor's office, a short, balding man named Saffron, who kept snapping his fingers as if he wanted to hurry things along. A taller, thinner woman with gray hair

315

that looked as if it had been sculpted from aluminum proved to be a senator who sat on the Intelligence Committee. The two security men she'd already met, although now, in this more relaxed atmosphere, one grinned at her and asked if she'd really shot a guy dead with a revolver at a hundred feet.

'Bad news travels fast,' she said.

'One-shot kills ain't bad news, ma'am, 'less you on de receiving end.' She didn't understand what the fake Southern accent was for, hoped it was not some sort of African-American parody, and settled for smiling at him.

A black man in a sweater and an open shirt turned out to be a CIA executive, no office or branch specified; a Latino woman was a specialist in inter-agency relations; two middle-aged men who talked only to each other were from FBI antiterrorism.

'This a first?' she murmured to Kasser. 'All these folks in one room?'

'First chance most of us have had to watch one of NSA's new toys in action.'

Then Valdez was standing again. He picked up the cell phone. Aware of the change, people began to move toward him; somebody leaned out the door and called, and the two security men went to guard the entrance.

'Gonna try this again,' Valdez said. 'Sorry about the glitch. Had to choose, made the wrong choice. Shoulda flipped a coin.' He looked at the young woman. 'Mave, you ready?'

An NSA man with a red badge cleared his throat. 'We've, uh, added a visual cartographic display that we hope will show graphically what's going on.' He waved a hand at a twenty-five-inch flat-screen monitor that had been set up on the end of the table. A Mercator

316

projection of the world in spiderweb blue lines filled the screen. 'It will graphically represent the grid co-ordinates that the, um, system –' He looked at another NSA man as if checking if it was okay to suggest that they had anything resembling a system. The other man closed his eyes in what seemed to be agreement. '– um, presents as numeric values. If this experimental effort works, you will see each – what will those be, Mavis, cell-phone towers? – okay, each tower represented by an orange dot. All calls between towers will be represented by red lines.'

Kasser leaned close to her. 'He knows damned well they're cell-phone towers. He just hates to tell us.'

The man stopped speaking. Valdez said, 'Okay?'

Nobody said it wasn't.

'Okay.' Valdez flashed Rose a smile. 'Showtime!'

His thumb pressed the send button again.

Mombasa.

Two sailors had piled charts on a cleared space across from the laptop. Alan had had time to locate Jakarta on one, but the charts were in different scales and weren't continuous. One sailor was standing over the charts; the other was sitting next to him. In theory, at least, they were ready to plot positions. If any came in.

'They're up again, sir.'

Alan crossed to the laptop. A single word was on the screen: *'Calling.'*

Washington.

'One ringy-dingy,' Valdez said. He waited. 'One ringy-dingy's all we get – it's picking up – Mave, you got a fix? Jeez, maybe we need more time –'

On the big screen at the end of the table, an orange dot appeared about where Jakarta was.

Everybody waited.

'Well, it's sitting there,' Valdez said. 'This time, it took.' He watched his own screen, leaned forward and hit several keys. 'Yeah, we're in. Line is still open. Virus has to be in place; that's microseconds to get in, no more. Lookin' good.'

The NSA man, standing with his hands joined just where his trousers' zipper ended, said rather grouchily, 'What are we waiting for?'

'Waitin' for somebody else to call. It's an answering machine, right?' There was an uneasy stir around him. Valdez said, 'Hey, folks, I'm just the head wizard here; I can't make the dudes out there in Jakarta or wherever do our work for us. We're in. Now we gotta wait for them to do their thing.'

Kasser said, 'What if they call in only once a day to pick up messages?'

'Then we got a long wait.'

General unhappiness. Movement, muttering, even a female voice – the senator's – saying pretty clearly that somebody could have warned them. Rose, siding with Valdez because he was an old friend, resented the irritation around her, the implication that the important parties missed, the contacts foregone, the gossip given up to be here in this stupid office were all Valdez's fault.

He, however, was unfazed.

And then he said, 'Bingo.'

At the same time, a red line sprang to the screen to connect Jakarta with the eastern end of the Mediterranean, somewhere in Israel or Lebanon.

'Where the hell is that?' the CIA man said. 'That Beirut? Can't we have a little more detail there?'

Mavis looked at him with the bored weariness of a world-class call girl talking to a Brownie scout. 'The map's too small.'

'I want those coordinates –' He began to push toward her.

'Second gotcha,' Valdez said.

A line flashed from Jakarta across half the world, jagged for an instant as individual towers registered, then straightened to a mean that ended at the southern tip of Italy.

'That's a surprise,' Kasser muttered.

'What's it mean?' the senator said.

'It means the virus works,' Valdez said.

Mombasa.

Alan looked over a sailor's shoulder, silently urging the man to work faster but knowing he'd only slow him down if he spoke. The sailor had already got the coordinates of the first two hits and made a dot on Jakarta and one on the Bekaa Valley, in Lebanon. At the same time, the electronics rating at the laptop began to read off a new set, and Alan, looking at the edge of the map, called out, 'This one's farther west – get the map for the western Med – Valvano, you got that –?'

'Yessir, yessir –' Valvano was too eager to please – young, insecure, anxious in the presence of the skipper. 'Got it right here someplace –' He went past the correct chart and burrowed in the pile. Alan saw him do it, bit his tongue.

'Got another,' the electronics tech called. Alan put a hand on his shoulder. 'Just hold it. Let them settle down.' He watched the numbers stack on the screen. Unless Valdez and NSA were crazy, the virus was scoring hit after hit, and in places that so far made no sense. A part of his brain whispered. *Why all the traffic? Who talks that much?* He filed the question away as unanswerable at that time, although he was thinking, too, that people who committed acts of terrorism didn't communicate unless they had to. And what he was seeing suggested that, however horrific the bombings in Mombasa and Cairo, something bigger was surely going on.

'Sicily, sir,' Valvano called. 'It's in Sicily!'

No sense at all.

Washington.

'Sicily?' Rose said.

'Like your name,' Kasser said, smiling. *Siciliano*. He looked worn out. Rose suspected that she did, too. The day had been full, a twisting, turning day with surprises and changes.

On the big screen, the red lines were weaving a new red spiderweb over the pale blue one. What Valdez had said he would try to do was now proven: both the eastern Med and the Sicilian dots had sprouted other red lines, meaning that the virus had caused the phones at those sites to mark their outgoing calls. And as she watched, one of the sites that had been called from Sicily, a dot on the Italian mainland south of Naples, shot a red line northward into Switzerland.

The CIA man was standing next to Valdez. He shook his head. 'What the hell have you wrought?' he said.

'I wrought like I ought, is what I wrought.'

'You wrought cool, man,' Mavis said. She high-fived Valdez. They grinned at each other, and Rose thought she could see the sexual sparks the two gave off. She smiled. She guessed she knew what they'd be doing when the job was done.

320

It was going on midnight. Nearly ten in Houston. The kids and their NCIS guards would be in the air.

And her husband?

Mombasa.

Alan grabbed Cohen by an elbow. 'We need a world map,' he said. 'Even a kid's map would be better than what we got. I got three guys in there now, they're like the Marx Brothers with a roomful of flypaper.'

'Get it from the boat?'

'I need it *now*.' He stared down into the hangar, where sailors in T-shirts and jeans were carrying crates from the morning run to Nairobi. He saw more Tusker pass below him. Well, at least they remembered the essentials. 'Call the embassy in Nairobi. Tell them we need the biggest world map they can find, on tomorrow's flight.'

Back in the office, some sort of order prevailed, worked out by the men themselves. They'd divided the world among them; they'd go one at a time to the computer, pick off the next item that fell within their UMG parameters, and head back to the improvised plotting table.

'Menendez's like a chick with hot pants,' one of them said. They laughed. Alan looked over the shoulder of Menendez, the man handling the Middle East, and saw that he, indeed, had more hits than the others. Four lines radiated from the Bekaa Valley site now and, to Alan's surprise, one of them connected it to Malindi, a port only eighty miles up the coast from Mombasa.

'Valvano, how you doing?'

'Good, sir, not too much action now. Stuff going out from Sicily, but slow. See, over to, um, Salerno, I guess it is, then they called somewhere up in, I guess, Switzerland. Like that.'

'Can you give Menendez a hand?'

'Uh, yessir, I guess.'

'Don't get in his way, just figure the location and let him enter it and draw the lines. Okay?'

'Yessir.' Valvano's tone suggested that he felt he'd been demoted.

'You're doing good,' Alan said to him. Did that help? Apparently not.

He looked at his watch. After ten. Dukas and his team were due in on the noon flight. The forensics people were supposed to ETA with their 747 at one-thirty.

Cohen put his head in, found Alan and hurried over. 'Can we talk?' he murmured. Alan led him out to the balcony. Cohen kept his voice low. 'Boat says they're planning a flyoff in case the typhoon hits. Our other S-3 is coming in this p.m., but between the lines I read that we're gonna be on our own until that storm is over – no more Marines, no more choppers after today.'

No lifeline. Alan grimaced. 'Better make up a wish list. For sure, I want some firepower on our S-3.'

'Kenyans won't like it.'

Alan ignored that. 'Plus a better medical kit and some big cooking pots. We're all sick of MREs, and the planes can get us fresh stuff from Nairobi.'

Twenty minutes later, Patemkin and Sandy Cole came in. They looked pleased with themselves. She signaled with a look that they had something. Alan huddled with them in the dead corner outside the det office.

'The guy from the dhow talked.'

'And?'

'He boarded in Kismayu. They picked up the explosive somewhere on the coast.'

'Somalia.'

Patemkin was leaning back against the metal railing, the elbow of one arm in the fingers of the others, his chin held between thumb and finger as if he were stroking a beard. 'Maybe Kenya, actually. He didn't know. Or so he said. They picked up the explosive and sailed into open water and he could see Lamu Island.'

'That's Kenya.'

'Yup. That's Kenya.'

Alan turned back to the maps. Menendez was drawing additional lines beside the first one wherever there were repeated calls between sites. There were now three lines between the Bekaa Valley site and Malindi.

And one new line northeast from Malindi to a nowhere spot where a tangle of tiny islands marked the eastern end of the border between Kenya and Somalia.

Alan looked at it.

Jesus Christ. South of Kismayu where he could see Lamu Island.

He grabbed Cohen. 'Find out what we've got in the det in the way of photo equipment. The longer the telephoto, the better. Then schedule both aircraft for a two-plane mission tomorrow, full crews with MARI gear up and ready. Schedule me on the flight.'

He looked at the map, the single line angling northeast from Malindi.

Maybe – maybe –

Washington.

'What does it mean?' Rose said. The room was emptier now; she and Kasser, Valdez and Mavis were still there, along with the security men and the CIA man, but the others had drifted away. It was one in the morning, after all; most of them would be up again at six.

Kasser stretched. 'It means NSA can do something I didn't know they can do. And it means your man Valdez is a genius.'

'Oh, we already knew that.' She smiled at Valdez. 'But I meant the map.'

Kasser looked at it. His shoulders sagged. She wondered if perhaps he was sick as well as tired. He had a look of resignation that she thought might go with one of the slow, inexorable diseases. 'Well,' he said, 'I think it means we have a real oddball problem. I don't see a single call yet to the places I'd expected to see – Sudan, Afghanistan, Iran. A Lebanese connection is a little strange, too. If we're talking some sort of connection with the attempt on you, I mean. Palestinian groups in Lebanon really focus on Palestine and Israel. They don't normally connect with things like these two bombings and trying to kill you.

'The other oddball is the site on the African coast. That's north of where your husband is, but close enough to be suggestive. Then there's another little tick north of that. Right up tight against Somalia.' He made a face. 'I hear Somalia, I get uneasy.'

'Everybody's saying al-Qaida,' the CIA man said.

'You buy that?'

The man sighed. Shrugged. 'I *want* to buy it,' he said. 'But so far, that's not what I see.'

'So what do you see?'

'You tell me.' He put his hands in his pockets. Another line flashed on the map, this time from Sicily to the Kenyan coast. 'What's got one foot in Sicily, one foot in Lebanon, and one foot in Kenya?'

'I didn't like riddles, even as a kid.'

11

Mombasa.

Dukas and his team stumbled off the aircraft and looked around as if they were at the end of a magical, miserable mystery tour. Mombasa airport steamed under a near-equatorial sun now; concrete runways stretched away into rippling haze backed by trees that congealed into a smear like green algae in the sun-dazzle. An American who said he was CIA attached to the embassy led them to a cinderblock-walled room where a customs and an immigration officer gave them a cursory look and waved them on. The only one they gave any grief was Triffler. 'Racial profiling,' he muttered when he caught up.

Two Marines in battle gear were waiting beside a Toyota pickup that was parked in a cargo area. Dukas looked at it and said, 'Geraldine rides inside,' because Geraldine hadn't slept on the flight and looked as if she might already have died.

'Like hell,' she rasped. She sniffed back what might have been tears but was probably the beginning of a cold. 'You're not going to treat me like some goddam woman, Mike.'

'You are some goddam woman. Get in the truck.'

She climbed up on the back bumper and fell over the tailgate into the truck bed. When she didn't reappear, Dukas said, 'Keatley, ride in the goddam cab. Don't argue.'

Everybody else got into the back, including the two Marines. 'This is how illegal immigrants travel,' Mendelsohn said. Nobody cared. They arranged themselves around the supine Geraldine with their backs against the sides of the bed, their legs stuck out. Triffler sat with his back to the cab and scowled at the landscape.

They drove around the runways on a service road. The two Marines had their weapons pointed over the sides, and the CIA man rode standing behind the cab with a 9mm Sigarms in his hand. Dukas thought it looked a little like grandstanding, but maybe the guy had never had a chance to ride in a pickup with a drawn gun before. Maybe he needed more stories from his Africa tour. Rommel in the desert. He should have brought his hat and goggles.

'You're sick,' he said to Geraldine.

She was lying full-length with her head on her laptop, and she kept snuffling as if she couldn't breathe. 'Speak for yourself,' she said. The remark made no sense to Dukas, but little did just then. She blew her nose on a tissue that had already been used too often. 'I've seen that guy who threw us out of Cairo,' she said.

'I've seen him, too. I wasn't more than six inches from him.'

'I mean, I've seen him before.'

'Where?'

'That's what I'm trying to remember. It kept me awake all the way from Cairo.'

'Well, Jesus, remember, will you?'

Hahn said she should stop thinking about it and then it would come to her.

326

'Oh, shut up,' she said.

'That was uncalled for!' Hahn shouted.

'Better than kicking you in the head, which was my first thought.' She coughed. She shut her eyes, then popped them open. 'DEA,' she said.

Dukas, who was sitting with his back against the tailgate and his feet even with her waist, her head another half-body length beyond them, sat up and tried to look into her face, but what he saw mostly was the underside of her nose. 'Okay, I give up. What?'

'DEA, the guy was from DEA.' She rolled to her left side and blew her nose and looked sadly at the result. 'Christ, I *am* sick.' She looked at Dukas. The truck was going slowly but bouncing, nonetheless, and her head bobbled. 'I was at a meeting a couple of years ago, and he was there, and he was DEA.'

'See,' Hahn said. 'I knew if you stopped thinking about it, it would come to you. You started thinking about mouthing off at me, and it came to you.' He grinned happily. Geraldine put her head back down on her laptop and said to the world in general that Hahn was an asshole.

'You're sure he's DEA?' Dukas said.

'He was then. He could be the bouncer for the Cairo Planet Hollywood by now, for all I know. Or care.' She cleared her throat, a sound that would have suited a male truck driver. 'Jesus.'

'DEA.' Dukas tried to figure what the Drug Enforcement Agency was doing in Cairo and why they had thrown Dukas and his team out. Well, turf, he thought, of course it's about turf, but how come Cairo is suddenly DEA turf? DEA must have an interest there, but it can't be much; Egypt isn't a big drug producer. So how come the big red-haired sonofabitch had a letter from the National Security Advisor telling Dukas to go suck eggs? His eyes met Triffler's. Triffler, whose normally russet-brown skin looked gray, with blue in the shadows, shrugged.

'Everybody out,' the CIA man said a little reluctantly. He had to put his pistol back into his shoulder holster. End of fantasy. The Marines were already on the ground, and a sailor was opening the tailgate. Dukas fell backward, was kept from falling out by two strong young men, and allowed himself to be helped down from the truck. He felt bad about the performance until he saw the others getting down and thought that he hadn't done too badly.

'Bed,' Geraldine said as she passed him. 'If somebody doesn't show me a bed, I'm going to act out.'

A pale, rather large woman wearing a long dress appeared. She went right to Geraldine. 'Hi, I'm Sandy Cole. Did you bring some things for me?' She was squinting into the sun to talk to her, and she put a hand up over her head to give a little shade. 'We talked on the phone yesterday?' she said.

Geraldine held up a plastic bag from an airport shop. 'Can you show me where I sleep?'

Sandy grabbed the bag, actually grinned as she clutched it to her. 'You're in with me.'

Geraldine put a hand on her shoulder. 'You got a deal.'

Dukas was walking into a huge, shadowy hangar behind the sailors. Keatley was beside him. 'You still alive?' Dukas said.

'More or less.'

'Geraldine says the guy who threw us out of Cairo is DEA. Can you stay awake long enough to send a message to Kasser and ask him to check it out?'

Keatley didn't say that he had been a Marine, but he might as well have. He had been sucking in his gut and walking tall since he had first laid eyes on the two battle-geared kids in the pickup. He wasn't about to say he was too tired to pick up a telephone. 'What about Cram?' he said.

Dukas stumbled over an uneven place in the concrete floor and swore. 'The other's more important. Cram is –' He shrugged. 'Cram is Cram.'

Alan was coming toward him down a metal stair along the hangar wall. He was already smiling and waving. Dukas smiled, but the effort showed. When they met, Alan embraced him and Dukas sagged into him like a fighter who can't hold his arms up anymore. 'I'm dead,' he muttered. 'We're all dead.' He told him they'd been thrown out of Cairo and it might be DEA.

'Cheer up. We got a breakthrough.' Alan was leading Dukas toward the metal stair. 'Wait until you see it – Rose got two cell phones from the car that tried to kill her, see, and then Valdez – you remember Valdez, her EM computer whiz? – anyway, he –'

Dukas gave up trying to follow it. He had thought maybe he was being led to his suite at the Mombasa Ritz, but no, they went up and the other men plodded behind a sailor toward several doors in plywood bulkheads back on the ground level. At the top of the stairs, Dukas looked to his right as Geraldine and the willowy woman vanished through a doorway at his level down at the other end of the hangar.

'Sleeping rooms up there?' he said.

'Women up, men down. Three guys to a room, sorry. No beds, but we got sleeping bags and pads.'

'Right now, I could sleep on a coil of razor wire.' Alan led him into an office where four enlisted men were working at tables cluttered with electronic gear and cables, much of it pushed into disorder to make room for big charts. Alan pulled him along to the middle table and pointed over the shoulder of the sailor working there.

'Black dot is a beginning or end point for a phone call. Lines are calls to or from – we can't tell which, they go so fast. But look!' He let Dukas look, then said, 'Get it?'

Dukas was stupid with fatigue, but he got enough. Lebanon to or from Malindi, up the coast; fucking Sicily, of all places, to or from Lebanon. Plus other lines that criss-crossed like a messy game of tic-tac-toe.

'Stay with me, Al, I'm wiped. Go back. What am I looking at?'

Alan told him again about the cell phones and the virus.

'So Rose's guy called where first?'

'An answering machine in Jakarta.'

'Answering machine. So does everybody call that answering machine?'

'Negative. Sicily calls it every four hours – that's from Washington, where they're monitoring it closer than we can. So –'

'So Sicily's the center.'

'At least it's some kind of comm center.'

'And then everybody else calls Sicily?'

'Not everybody, not at all. But Lebanon does, and Sicily calls Lebanon. Notice the lines – only a few between Sicily and anybody else. So we think that Lebanon is maybe some sort of operational center.'

'If this isn't just the Middle Eastern version of telephone sex.'

When Alan was finished briefing him, Dukas

walked through the door, heading for sleep. Outside on the balcony, however, he stopped and leaned on the railing. Nobody was close, so it was as good a place as any to talk privately with Alan. 'We've worked a lot together, Al, we get along. But let me lay it out right up front. I'm in charge of this investigation.'

Alan nodded. 'Understood.'

'The *Harker*, everything resulting from it; the Cairo bomb; all this telephone stuff. Mine.'

'Understood.' Alan crossed his arms. 'But I'm in command here. The *Harker*, the Marines, any action that's taken to further the investigation, any reprisals – mine.'

They looked at each other. Dukas smiled the smile of a man falling asleep on his feet. 'Understood.' He looked around as if afraid he'd be overheard. 'It's Day Three. No third bombing yet.'

Alan shook his head. 'No, and it's funny that –' He was going to tell Dukas about his belief that too much traffic had shown on the cell phones to be normal, but he looked at Dukas's face and knew it would be wasted talk. 'You're dead on your feet,' he said.

They went down the stair with Dukas's hand on Alan's shoulder, and Alan led him into a room where two of the three plywood tables were already occupied by snoring men. He pushed Dukas gently down on the third table and swung his feet up and began to pull off his shoes.

'Hey –' Dukas growled.

'Shut up and lie down.'

Alan unzipped the sleeping bag and pulled it half over Dukas and, smiling, went out.

Washington.

Rose woke, wanting not to but knowing that she was fully awake and unable to do a thing about it. She stared at the bedside clock, realized it was not where she expected it and then remembered that she was in a Washington hotel. She rolled over. Ten minutes of six, said a bar of red-orange numbers.

There was another bed. With Mikey in it, his breathing a soft, sweet sighing in the room. The baby was in a rented crib in a corner.

She remembered. They had a suite. Gorki and Reko were trading watches in the sitting room. A hotel security man was posted in the corridor.

She rolled on her back and stared at the ceiling. The hours at NSA had been exciting. Worth the trip.

But now she was out of it.

She got up and checked Mikey and then the baby, who was sleeping on his back, his fists on each side of his head like flower buds. She felt a sudden and surprising urge to weep, an emotion somehow merging her love for this frail creature with her own sense of letdown. How fast it had all come apart! A week ago, she had been riding high on the rush of astronaut training; now she was two thousand miles from Houston, and the people there thought that she was a liability. She could hear the words – uncooperative, grandstanding, aggressive. Violent. Self-centered.

Not a team player.

She went softly into the bathroom and closed the door and cried.

Bahrain.

Harry O'Neill's office had a big teak desk and, behind it, a matching table with a computer; three pages from a Persian manuscript were framed on the walls, their colors picked up by a blood-red kilim on the floor. At the other end of the big room, more comfortable chairs and tables were clustered in a conversational area. Harry sat there easily in a leather chair, but he didn't sprawl and he didn't shove his legs out so that the soles of his feet showed. Bad form in Arab culture. He sat like what he was – a powerful man who was at ease with himself and his world, wearing a silk T-shirt and a linen jacket and black slacks, Bally shoes with thin soles. On his head was an Islamic cap of embroidered raw silk.

'And so?' he said in Arabic.

The man across the low tea table from him was older but showed the respect that, if age were the only factor, should have gone the other way. He was dressed in a good but not pricey European business suit, but with a Saudi headdress covering part of his head and neck. 'The tea is most excellent,' he said. He held a handle-less cup in his right hand; with the left, he wafted the tea's aroma toward his nose. 'India,' he said. He sipped, then nibbled on a cake no larger than his two thumbnails. 'I traced the dhow's engine number to Sri Lanka. Jaffna. Not a stronghold of the Tamil, but –'

'Tamil presence.'

The man nodded. 'The dhow was sold there four months ago. To a European. For cash.'

Harry frowned. 'You are sure?'

'My friend!' The man spread his hands like wings over the tea service. 'For you, I have to be sure.' He smiled, perhaps a little sadly, perhaps only wisely.

'A European.'

'But not an English speaker. Or he did not speak English with the seller. He had a translator, but he did

not himself speak English, which the seller under-
stands. He said the buyer might have been French, but
you know the use of "French" to mean any white who
does not speak English.'

'Description? Name?'

'It was not that kind of sale, my friend. On the
papers, the buyer is something called the Baranjee
Trading Company, Limited, which, so far as I can deter-
mine, does not exist.'

They sat together in silence. Both sipped tea, and
the air-conditioning hummed and the cooled air moved
between them like an invisible servant. Out the large
window to Harry's right they could see part of a
skyscraper and then desert and then, far away, bright
blue water.

'So – Sri Lanka, a European, a nonexistent company.
Nothing after that?'

The man put down his cup. 'He thinks that a skel-
eton crew was picked up on the docks in Jaffna, but
maybe he was only telling me this as decoration.
However it was done, the dhow was taken out of his
yard five days after the purchase cleared, and he has
not seen or heard of it since.' He spread his hands
again. 'The seas are full of dhows.'

'You did well.'

The man inclined his head, neither a bow nor a nod.

'I will remember you when the new contract comes
up,' Harry said.

The man inclined his head again. They talked briefly
of other things, drank tea, and completed gracefully
the ritual of ending their business. When the man was
gone, Harry stared out his window for several seconds
and then moved to the computer terminal. A keen eye
might have detected the bulge of a weapon just in front

of his right kidney, but perhaps not; he was a muscular, fit man with the slender waist of somebody much younger.

He sat and began to type an e-mail:

To: Alan Craik
CC:
Subject: engine
Item was bought by presumed non-English mzungu in Sri Lanka three months ago. No hits since. Will be traveling.

12

Cairo.

Sergeant al-Fawzi-al-Mubarak had caught the case of the head in the toilet. An aficionado of American cop shows, he used words like 'caught,' translated into Arabic – 'he caught the squeal.' He even used a translation of 'squeeze' for girlfriend. *Is she his squeeze?* He didn't have a squeeze of his own, but he was thinking of getting one as soon as his oldest son graduated from his private school. A matter of expense.

He had caught the head in the toilet because the head belonged to a European and it had been al-Fawzi-al-Mubarak who had whisked around Cairo with the black American naval cop and blown away (useful phrase, but not very graceful in Arabic) the man who had killed the American woman from AID. Now, his lieutenant said there might be a connection, so al-Fawzi could fold the severed head into his case.

The sergeant was not sure he was pleased. Flattered, yes – it was a prize. But maybe, as the American shows said, more a trick than a treat? (He had had to have that explained to him, had in fact had to go to the USIS library in the embassy to ask about it, and still didn't really get it because he'd never seen an American Halloween.) A responsibility and a risk – always a risk when the big foreign nations were involved.

The head had been beaten before death, the medical

examiner said. Also burned with a cigarette on the eyelids and in one ear. Also perhaps strangled, as part of a ligature mark showed on as much of the throat as had come with the head. Decapitated afterward with at least two tools, a sharp but short-bladed knife and perhaps a hacksaw.

'Nice guys,' al-Fawzi had said. The Arabic for 'guys' really meant 'men of the people.' The medical examiner didn't get it and didn't care.

Now the sergeant was in the bowels of the Semiramis. Two levels lay under the hotel, the lower even grungier than the upper. He had long since got over being disenchanted by the backstage areas of restaurants and hotels; the concrete floors, the dirt piled up in corners, the harsh lighting were now merely what he expected. Still, they were less pleasant than the fake grandeur and comfort of the public spaces and the rooms above, all of which had already been searched, nothing found.

The sergeant believed that the head belonged to an American named Robert Cram, because the American group with which Cram had arrived had checked out but Cram had not. The group had flown out of Sadat, headed for Mombasa, Kenya, but Cram had not. Cram's clothes and suitcase were still in his room.

'Therefore, we need a body with no head,' he had said. Therefore, he and four Cairo cops were searching the lower levels of the hotel. Therefore, he was not quite astonished when a slightly queasy cop with the regrettable name of Farouk (fat king of not-so-recent memory, playboy and spendthrift) found him and said that he thought he had found 'the remains.'

Al-Fawzi looked at the young man. Leaned forward, sniffed. The boy had just vomited. There was even a fleck on his uniform. 'Where?'

338

The young man jerked his head. 'Storage room. Behind the, I think it's air-conditioning fans. We almost missed it because there was a ladder and a tarpaulin covering it.'

The sergeant smelled it before he saw it. Even with air-conditioning, even two stories underground, the Cairo heat did its work. 'Dead since last night, what else?' he said out loud. He pushed past another cop who had been posted at the door, as if crowds of news-people, perhaps tourists, were going to go flocking in. 'Get the scene-of-crime people and the ME.'

'Already called, sir.'

'I don't want anybody coming into this whole space.' He waved his hand at the vast fan room, which was like a concrete cave with the abandoned relics of another civilization in it – curious fans with bat wings, a mesh cage piled to the ceiling with indecipherable metal shapes. 'I want photos of this place, not just the room where the body is.' He scratched his lip under his luxuriant moustache. 'A black light examination of the entire place? Maybe.' He wiggled his eyebrows. 'Maybe.' He was suddenly ashamed of himself. So Hercule Poirot. Not at all his usual style.

He went in. The stench was remarkable. Blood had run over the floor to a mesh-covered drain in the corner. Even down here, flies had found it and were thick on its congealed surface. The body, pretty clearly lying where the decapitation had taken place, was stretched across the platform from a painter's scaffold. The wooden bars were thick with old paint in cream, gray, and purple – a history in color of the hotel's refur-bishings – over which, near the headless torso, blood had also run.

Al-Fawzi denied himself the luxury of putting a

handkerchief over his nose. *Bad example to the kids.* He tried to take shallow breaths, keeping the air high up in his nostrils. It never worked, but it gave his nose something to do. He stepped carefully over the headless body and looked into the room's corners. No sign of weapons, but many cigarette butts. He went back to the body and knelt beside it. Burn marks on the arms, on the shirtless back.

'Poor bastard,' he said.

He put two fingers in his not quite clean pocket handkerchief and put them into the left rear trousers pocket and lifted out the wallet he found there. Robert Cram. Driver's license, library card, three credit cards, photos.

No money.

He shook his head. All this – murder, torture, decapitation – and some shithead had also robbed him. But put the wallet back so they'd know who he was. The sergeant had no doubt that the body was in fact Cram's, although he would insist in his reports that the ID was unproven until they had other evidence – teeth, fingerprints, visual. Although who would recognize the face after what had been done to it?

Significant. Whoever had killed him wanted him to be found. Wanted him to be ID'd. Knew he would be. The head first. A gesture of – what? Contempt? Bravado, certainly.

He walked out of the room. The scene-of-crime people were just coming in through the far door of the fan room. Al-Fawzi pulled a clean plastic baggie from a pocket and prepared to drop the wallet in. It fell open to reveal a picture of a pretty, slightly overweight woman. He saw the young cop at the door looking over his shoulder at it.

'His squeeze,' al-Fawzi said.

Mombasa.

The 747 that housed the forensics lab landed in mid-afternoon and taxied to the det's hangars, dwarfing the two buildings. The two NCIS special agents on board were rested and bright-eyed and then vastly amused to hear that all the others were sleeping off a couple of very bad days and nights. They were less amused when they heard about the food and the security rules.

'We're better off sleeping in the plane,' the woman agent, Sheila Ditka, said. She had introduced herself as 'the bang expert,' meaning, Alan gathered, that she was an explosives specialist.

'You got beds?' Alan asked.

'Well, no, but my God, at least it's clean!'

It was, indeed, spotless. Unfortunately for anybody who wanted to sleep aboard, it was a laboratory and as tight and crowded as a ship's galley. It was capable of anything from a postmortem on a corpse to an electrophoresis run on a complex organic, but a hotel it was not.

'Give us a try,' Alan said. 'What we lose in comfort we make up in togetherness.'

The male agent, Delahanty, made a face as if he'd bitten into a pickle. 'Swell.'

Alan walked them around the facility and gave them a quick rundown on the perimeter and security. Within half an hour, he had them in his own office for a briefing, most of which he did himself, with Sandy Cole sitting in.

'You got any explosive residue?' Sheila said.

Sandy nodded. 'Still attached to metal, mostly.'

'Well, I'll start with that. I'll take some samples, do a run for DMDNB and see if I can sort out what it was and where it came from.'

'We're not even sure it was C4,' Sandy said. Her voice was sour.

'Yeah, well, I'll know that, too, pretty soon.'

'How soon?' Alan said.

'Well – if we bust our asses, maybe six hours –'

'There was another bomb this morning in Cairo. I want to know if they're connected.'

'I've already been on to the Washington lab to get a reading on it. Somebody's got to get a sample of the residue up there and run an analysis. Egyptians are cooperative but so far slow. We're working on it.'

'FBI?'

'They're there, but there's some screwup.'

Alan thought about Dukas's team's getting tossed out of Cairo and the hint that it had been DEA that had done it. If DEA somehow had clout in the Cairo bombing, they might be trying to end-run around the Bureau, too, although that would be a lot harder than kicking an NCIS team out of town. He explained their communications to her – everything had to go through the boat – and agreed that it was worse than a pain in the ass that they couldn't deal with Cairo directly.

'All I need's an analysis; I don't need the stuff itself. Can I smoke in here?'

Alan shook his head. Chief Bakin was adamant about not allowing open fire of any kind in the hangar. 'Have to go outside. Just don't be surprised if a Marine moves you along. They're trying to keep any snipers from targeting us.'

She groaned. Delahanty asked for the second time if it could be true that there wasn't a bar anyplace. 'Not that you can get to,' Alan said. 'We're restricted to the perimeter. We get beer once a day from Nairobi – two bottles a man, if we're lucky.'

Delahanty clutched his throat and made it a joke, but Alan wondered if the man had a more serious need for booze than he let on.

'Well,' he said, standing, 'let's get to it. Anything you can tell us is a plus.' He turned them over to Sandy and Fidelio to start an analysis of the debris from the *Harker*.

Alan had decided that Dukas and his people were to be allowed to sleep as long as they wanted, with coffee and MREs to be kept ready for them whenever they woke up, but that plan went galley-west when a third-class weapons specialist who was doing double duty as a yeoman caught up with him in the electronics office.

'Urgent message, sir. Comm office. They wouldn't even let me hand-carry it.'

'How urgent?'

'They told me to run, sir.'

So Alan ran the length of the hangar and pulled himself up the stairway two steps at a time, one hand hauling at the metal rail as if it was a rope. He hit the comm office still running. LT Campbell was already there, called as communications officer to ride herd on a message that was headed 'Top Secret' and 'Recipient's Eyes Only – Most Urgent.'

'Came on the link encrypted. Decrypted it myself.'

Alan read it and stepped to the balcony and grabbed the first sailor who went by. 'Go down and wake Mister Dukas. He's in the bed nearest the door in the third room. Don't wake anybody else. Got that?'

'Yes, sir.'

'Tell him it's urgent and I said so.'

Dukas came bulling along the balcony three minutes later. His clothes looked as if he'd slept in them, as of course he had. Next to the T-shirted sailors, he looked like an animated laundry sack.

'Never rains but it pours, right?' he said. 'Jesus, do I need a toothbrush! Okay, what's the crisis?'

Alan handed over the message. Dukas read, groaned, said, 'Oh, Jesus –' in a despairing voice.

'Who's Cram?' Alan said. He had pulled Dukas into a dead area where nobody would walk close and where they wouldn't be overheard so long as they kept their voices down.

'A loser who got attached to my team because he's useless. Aw, shit.'

'Tortured.'

'Yeah – again.' Dukas told him the story of Cram's one distinction. 'Jesus, they found his head early this morning. Why are we getting this now? Shit. Oh, I get it – they didn't ID him until early afternoon. Still, Jesus – five hours!'

'Probably went up the chain at Cairo police HQ, who kicked it around until they'd figured out how bad things were, then they called the embassy; the embassy kicked it around until they figured out how to make sure they weren't involved, then told Washington; State kicked it around and finally decided to tell NCIS, and Kasser finally told us. Always the last to know.' Alan shook his head. 'Kasser seems to believe the guy was tortured to get the names of your team.'

'At least that.' Dukas rubbed his face with both hands, holding the message above the back of his left hand with two fingers. 'He says he's got people already with the families, but I have to wake everybody and tell them.' He looked at Alan with sad eyes. 'Think I ought to give them the chance to pull out?'

'My people didn't get that option.'

Dukas nodded. He needed a shave and knew it, his right hand passing over the stubble on his cheeks and jaw. 'I'm not going to take this lying down. Cram was an asshole, but he was *my* asshole, and fuck DEA!'

Dukas started out, turned back. His face was ugly. 'You better know now – I'm mad, and I'm going back into Cairo, and nobody's going to stop me – including you.'

'I've been waiting for you to say it. Go for it, Mike.'

Alan directed him to a kid who knew the airline schedules, and then Dukas went down to the cubicle in which he'd been sleeping and looked for Triffler but didn't find him, then put his head into the next and finally found him in the last one down and shook him awake. 'Mister Triffler, come here, I need you.'

Triffler opened his eyes to slits. 'Who're you, Don Ameche?'

'Shut up,' a rough voice said from another table.

'You, too, Keatley. I need you both awake and alert.'

'Like shit.'

Triffler was still lying down. He rolled on his back and folded his hands over his chest. 'You're going to make an unjust demand on us, aren't you.'

'I'm going to give you both an order, and you're going to obey it.' He leaned his buttocks against the edge of Keatley's table and put his hands on his knees. 'Cram's body was found in Cairo. Tortured, strangled, and decapitated. You leave for Nairobi soonest, and you *will* be on the red-eye to Cairo.' He scowled, not waiting for an objection. 'And if you tell me we got thrown out of Cairo, I'm telling you we're going back. Don't argue.'

Keatley was groaning. Triffler was still lying on his back with his hands folded over his chest. 'Sometimes

I think you hate me as a person. Other times I think it's just good old American racism.'

'The Cairo cop who's heading the investigation is the one you already worked with. Was that only yesterday? Jesus. Triffler will be the lead, Keatley – he knows Cairo better than you and he knows the Egyptians.'

'I *don't* know the Egyptians!'

'Three weeks there working on Bright Star, you're a fucking expert.' Dukas stood. 'Wash and shave in the men's head on this side. MREs and coffee in twenty minutes in our office, which is at the far end of the hangar. Briefing in three-quarters of an hour.'

'Guns?' Keatley said hoarsely.

'Guns and vests, definitely, take two guns if you got them. I quote from the urgent message from Ted Kasser – "identify and deal with the perpetrators." Okay?'

Keatley swung his legs down. 'Okay. As soon as I can walk.'

Triffler still lay there. 'I want to go home,' he said.

'We all want to go home.'

'I have a wife and two children. You know what Cram probably told those people who tortured him?'

'Yes, and so does Kasser, and your house and your kids and their school are already being protected. What're you going to do, stand out in front with your shotgun? You're going to Cairo.'

Triffler sat up. He sighed. 'Yes, I am. I was just venting.' He put a hand on Dukas's arm and pulled himself up, actually taller than Dukas when he was vertical, but thirty pounds lighter. 'This is a fatiguing profession.'

But when Dukas dragged himself back to the det office, his mind was not on Triffler or how little sleep they'd had. His face was rigid, scowling, hard. He spoke to nobody. In the det office, he said to Alan, 'I need a STU and privacy and I need it now.'

Alan looked at him, registered the hardness, and barked out a command to a rating. Minutes later, the otherwise empty NCIS office next door had a STU set up to communicate via the boat, and two minutes after that, Dukas was alone waiting for Ted Kasser in Washington to pick up his phone.

'Kasser,' the nasal voice said. The sound was spooky, as if it was coming through a pipe with water bubbling somewhere in the middle.

'Dukas. I'm sending my guys back into Cairo.'

'Hold it, Mike.'

'Fuck that. I got thrown out. I left a man behind; he's dead. We're going back.'

'This is more complicated than that.'

'Yeah, DEA. I don't care if it's God and his angels and archangels. We go back and clean up our own mess, or I'm out. Right out. I'll leave NCIS today.'

Kasser took several seconds to think that over. Dukas had clout – not position, but the clout that came from having just come off a big intelligence score. Two of them, in fact, 'Nobody's indispensable,' Kasser said.

'No, and nobody's worthless, which is the way we're treating Bob Cram unless we go back and find out what happened, *because he's our guy*. Is that what you want? Is that what you want everybody to see – that NCIS doesn't care shit about its own people?'

'You'll really resign?'

'Yeah, and I won't do it quietly.'

'Don't do anything until –'

'Triffler and Keatley leave here in two hours for Cairo. Period.'

The connection sighed and gurgled. Kasser took his

time again. Finally, he said, 'I don't know myself what's going on, Mike. But it's very high-level. Director of Naval Intelligence would have to take it up with the White House.'

'I don't care about that. We go, or I go.'

Maybe Kasser sighed. Dukas couldn't hear well enough to be sure. Maybe it was only an electronic hiccup in the link that connected Mombasa, the boat, a satellite, and Washington. What he said was, 'I'll get back to you.'

'Two hours.'

He hung up and sat there, seeing the plywood walls and the gray floor like projections of his disgust. The air was filled with sounds, none clear, but all overlapping and changing each other – somebody hammering a piece of metal, voices, a toilet flushing, the chuffing sound of a bird in the metal trusses above him, all swirling through the ugly room that had no ceiling. Dukas shook his head and stood, pushing himself up with the help of the gray-topped table. His brain was slow from fatigue, he knew. Maybe resigning would be the best thing. He felt no excitement in the investigation, no sense of purpose, only disgust and a desire to laugh or maybe cry because Cram had been such a worthless shmuck and still they had to go back and find who had killed him. And why. Because not to do so – forget what Cram was like; it didn't matter what he was like – was to become a time-server, a bureaucrat. Work to rule and take your pension.

There was a knock. Dukas shuffled to the door and opened it and found a young sailor standing there.

'Mister Craik would like to see you, sir.'

Dukas grunted and headed toward the det office. Alan was there with a clipboard full of messages. 'Bad news,' he said. 'We're losing the 747. It's been ordered to Cairo.'

Dukas was beyond reacting. 'When?'

'Be there 0600 tomorrow.'

'Who's getting it?'

'Isn't specified. "Report to duty officer, US embassy, for assignment."'

'DEA,' Dukas said. He stared at a wall where somebody had put up a photo of the det and one of the S-3s on the deck of the *Jefferson*. Everybody was smiling, Alan in the center.

'You okay?' Alan said.

'Yeah, yeah. No. What the hell.' Dukas took the message, read it.

Alan said, 'Pilot wants to leave at 1930. I say, let's send Triffler and Keatley with him. They'll be there in four hours and they'll be able to get some sleep. Your woman agent – what's her name, Ditka? – she's working on the explosive analysis now. She can work on it in the air, maybe. At least we may get something on the bomb residue out of it.'

'At least. Or at most.'

Half an hour later, they gathered their people in the otherwise empty NCIS office. Again, a circle of folding chairs sat in gloom. Alan and Dukas sat side by side, Geelin on Alan's other side, then Sandy Cole, Geraldine Pastner, Triffler, Keatley, and around to Patemkin, sitting on Dukas's left.

'What do we know?' Dukas said. 'No jokes, please. Sandy?' She was part of his team now, not Alan's.

She looked better, her face less puffy and less angry, and she had been able to change out of the grubby long dress into a tank top and somebody else's blue jeans. She had big hips, it was now clear. She drew both her upper and lower lips in, and then she said, 'Well, mixing what we know and what we think: assuming the information is trustworthy –' a glance at Alan – 'the dhow that hit the *Harker* seems to have come from Sri Lanka to Somalia, taken on some of the crew in Kismayu, and then sailed south and taken on the explosives someplace on the coast. We also know at least one of the cell-phone calls ended up on the coast someplace up there, plus I have a source that's been telling me for two or three months about a lot of poaching up there, which I think may be relevant. We got anything on the explosive yet?'

Geraldine shook her head. 'Sheila's working on it.'

'Meanwhile,' Alan said, 'there've been attempts on me and my wife, and telephones have been ringing all over the world, apparently as a result.'

'How's that going today?' Patemkin said.

'NSA says the hits are down more than ninety percent. Either we tapped into an atypical day yesterday, or something happened to set off all that activity.'

Dukas looked around the circle. 'Anybody got any ideas about that?'

'Not about the activity,' Triffler said in his flute-like voice, 'but I'd like to go back to the attempts on Al and his wife. I think it's really odd – odd, I mean, in terms of terrorism – to personalize it like this. First the big hit, the *Harker*, then two attacks on individuals, then Cairo. Then Cram. That isn't normal.'

Keatley groaned and muttered, 'Jesus, *normal*.'

'What're you getting at?'

Triffler folded his arms. He was wearing a striped, button-down blue-and-white short-sleeved shirt, chinos, and no tie. He still looked as if he was about to model for a Land's End catalog. 'Well, two things, aren't there? One is, identifying Al and Rose and Cram, and so maybe our families. The other is, it's anomalous.'

'Well, if they ID'd me, they could ID Rose,' Alan said. He looked grim.

'Yeah, but how?'

'The television report,' Dukas growled. 'Al was identifiable.'

'The French guy doing the report said he was CIA.'

Keatley shifted as if his chair was uncomfortable, as of course it was. 'They could have found out. Ask around.'

'Ask around where? Al had just got to town.'

'The hotel,' Alan said. 'Everybody knows where American military stay – out in one of the big beach hotels. "You got a guy with only three fingers, US Navy?"'

'Or he showed a photo. He could make a photo from the TV stuff, right?'

'Not a bad idea,' Dukas said. 'It cuts both ways. Al, you got somebody who could print stills from a – what the fuck is it called – screaming TV?'

'Streaming, not screaming,' Triffler said. He looked pained. 'Streaming video. Actually, that's a good idea.'

'Thank you.' It was Dukas's turn to look pained. 'Al?'

Alan made a note. 'Where's the video?'

Geraldine waved a hand, completed the gesture by scratching an ankle. 'My laptop. You got fleas here?'

'We got everything here.'

Alan left the room. When he came back, they were talking about the Cairo bombing and Cram's death, and what Triffler and Keatley would do in Cairo.

'I'd like to go,' Patemkin, the CIA guy, said. 'With you guys.' He must have sensed resistance, because he said, 'I think I can help you with DEA and the embassy. I'm not trying to horn in on your case, honest.'

'You just want to sleep in a hotel bed,' Triffler said.

'Alan?' Dukas said, because he wasn't yet clear who belonged to whom. Patemkin seemed to have signed on with Alan.

'Suits me, if you think you can be useful and we don't need you here. Sandy?'

She shrugged. 'Mink can represent the Agency here, if that's the question.'

It wasn't the question, but it was agreed that Patemkin could go. Then Alan told them that he'd be flying up the coast to see if there was anything in the area where the dhow supposedly took on the explosive. 'We'll do a MARI run on anything we see, plus I've got a digital camera from one of my guys.'

'I'm still puzzled about the attacks on you and Rose,' Triffler said. 'I think they're anomalous.'

'Could say the same thing about Cram,' Keatley said. 'Why Cram?'

'Because he could ID us,' Dukas said. 'And our families.'

'But why?' Triffler demanded. 'This isn't like terrorists, Mike! This is a vendetta.'

'Against the Navy,' Alan said.

'DEA isn't the Navy,' Patemkin offered.

'But the rest of it is.'

'But why?' Triffler persisted.

'Scare us off.'

'But scare us off from what?'

'The investigation?'

352

They looked at each other. Alan said, 'I think that's at least part of it. Certainly the attempt on my wife looks like trying to scare *me*. And killing Cram looks like trying to scare you guys.'

'But that's not like terrorists. So –' Triffler leaned forward – 'who?'

'You ask great questions, Dick.'

Patemkin scowled at his shoes. 'I don't get what Sandy said about poachers. What've poachers got to do with terrorism?'

She was immediately defensive. 'I just meant it's something that's going on up on that stretch of coast!'

Alan raised a hand. 'We don't know what it means; we don't know what any of it means. But Sandy's source is solid, and I think it's worth looking up there. Maybe somebody's financing terrorism with poaching, who knows? Anybody object?'

Everybody looked at everybody, and Dukas moved into the silence to say, 'The cell-phone calls up there went out of Malindi. I think it's important enough that we check. Somebody take Malindi and hit Al's hotel along the way to find out if anybody asked to ID him there. Geraldine, want to go to Malindi?'

She gave him an ambiguous half-smile, head tilted. 'What you got in mind?'

'Well, you go to a strange city, you can't trust the local cops, you got no friends, what else can you do? You spend the day with the whores.'

Geraldine's eyebrows went up; she cocked her head the other way, like a bird eyeing a worm. 'I think we say "workers in the sex industry" now.'

'Not in my hearing, we don't. Would you please-I-beg-you-be-good-enough, O goddess of PC, to interview some whores for me tomorrow?'

353

Sandy swayed forward. 'I speak the language.' She looked at Geraldine. 'Shall we both go?'

'Sounds good to me.' Geraldine looked at Dukas, no smile, and shook her head. She was saying that he was a stupid, troglodyte horse's ass. Dukas already knew that.

At that point, a young black rating brought in copies of the TV shot of the French journalist, and Alan passed them around as the discussion started to disintegrate. As he handed one to Sandy, Alan said in a low voice, 'I'd like to have David Opono if I'm going to take a look at this poachers' camp.'

She looked suspicious, then half-turned her head away. Her reply was almost inaudible. 'He'll want to come.'

'Please ask him to be here at first light, or even earlier.'

She still didn't look him in the eye. She nodded, her mind on something else.

Bahrain.

Harry O'Neill was being driven through the streets toward the old souk, what there was of it now, his Mercedes and its Arab driver hardly noticed among all the other luxury cars. Behind it, a smaller BMW tailed him, two stern men in the back looking out like hawks perched on a telephone pole. Up ahead was another car with two men doing the same. When they came to an opening in a street of shops, the Mercedes slowed without Harry's saying anything; it purred to a stop, and Dave Djalik materialized from a shadow and nodded, and when Harry got out Djalik was waiting in the sun. 'No sweat,' he said.

Harry nodded. He was wearing a nutmeg-colored

linen jacket and the black silk T-shirt, chinos, and Bally shoes, on his head an embroidered Muslim cap. He carried a small black suitcase. He went through the opening between the shops and down a covered passage and across another street, Djalik following with the same raptor's look as the men in the cars. Harry went into a shop that dealt in antique rugs and brasses, where the proprietor stroked his beard and nodded, and O'Neill went through a curtained doorway and out the back and into a garden.

A man in a Palestinian headscarf was sitting at a table in the shade of a fig tree. A small fountain played at the base of a wall. On the side opposite the door through which O'Neill had come, another man in a headscarf leaned against a patch of shade. Behind O'Neill, Djalik did the same.

O'Neill and the seated man murmured courtesies. A small tray already stood between them, on it sweetened tea and four honey cakes the size of walnuts. Each man took one. Each chewed. Each swallowed.

'I'm looking for a person in Lebanon,' Harry said in Arabic. 'I think he is dirtying the name of Islam.'

The Palestinian said that if true, this would be a terrible thing. He called O'Neill *haji*, because it was well known that he had been to Mecca.

'I think he used Islam to attack the American Navy.'

'I wouldn't weep for the American Navy.'

'I would weep for Islam if its faithful were exploited in the name of another cause.'

The Palestinian gave him a sharp look. 'You know this?'

'I *think* this. If you find the person, you can decide for yourself.'

'*You* are American, haji.'

'I am also a Muslim. My support for the families of martyrs is well known.' The Palestinian made a movement that could have been the beginning of a bow.

Harry boosted the small suitcase to the table, careful not to disturb the tray or the tea. 'The person in question uses a certain cell-phone tower. We have traced it that far – a town in the Bekaa called Tel-al-Makouf.'

The Palestinian's eyes flashed. 'A Christian village.'

'Just so.' Harry patted the suitcase. 'This will allow you to listen to calls to and from that tower on the frequencies I will give you. I think it wouldn't take you long to find the man. He has conversations every day with Italy and with the town of Malindi, in Kenya.' The Palestinian's face showed concern, then puzzlement. Harry went on. 'I think you would need an Italian speaker to translate.'

The Palestinian hesitated. He explained that he would not, himself, do such a thing, but he knew people – he meant Hizbollah – who might. What would they get in return?

O'Neill mentioned a figure. He mentioned American gratitude.

The Palestinian sniggered. When he was done showing what he thought of the concept of American gratitude, he said, 'It is not a question of the price. It is a question of the cause.'

'I think this person has betrayed the faithful by exploiting them. Next time, maybe he will betray them by selling them – to Israel? I think your friends would be happy to discover him and deal with him.'

The Palestinian put his hand on the suitcase and called to the man behind him. He spoke to him quickly in a dialect Harry could hardly follow – something about opening the case. The man disappeared through the far door with it and was gone long enough for Harry to realize that he had taken it to some bricked-in nook to open it, in case it was a bomb. When he came back, he put it on the table again, open. The Palestinian gave Harry a thin smile. 'Forgive me, haji.'

Harry held up his hands. 'A careful man has no enemies.' He sipped his tea. They talked about the equipment in the suitcase, how it worked, who would be needed to operate it. The Palestinian closed it and signaled to the other, who came and carried it back to his patch of shade. 'What do you want to know if the person is found?'

'What his part in the ship bombing at Mombasa was. Whose money he is using. What else is going to happen.'

The Palestinian tried his own tea. 'And afterward?'

'I have no interest in what Allah wills for such a person.'

Four minutes later, Harry and Djalik were on the street again. 'They had six guys around that building,' Djalik said. 'Nice playmates you pick up.'

O'Neill laughed. 'Dave, we had *ten* people around the building.'

'Yeah, but we're the good guys.'

Two hours later, when the 747 had disappeared into the soft night, Alan said, 'Look on the bright side.'

'There's a bright side?'

'No bomb today.'

'Today isn't over.'

'You're such an optimist, Mike.'

Mombasa.

Geraldine and Sandy Cole shared Geraldine's spoils of civilization – her cosmetics, her shampoo, her bars of soap. They didn't particularly like each other yet, but they'd known each other only a few hours and they were the only women there. Geraldine sat cross-legged on her bedroll and Sandy paced in her bare, dirty feet, wanting a smoke but not wanting to leave. They shared a Coke.

'What was this guy Cram like?' Sandy said.

'Like you wouldn't want him to wind up a dead hero. A loser. An asshole.' Geraldine sipped her Coke, sniffed experimentally, trying to see if she really was sick. 'Meet you one minute, try to hit on you the next.'

'Anybody nice in the bunch you came with?'

Geraldine shrugged. 'They're okay.'

'You got somebody in DC?'

'A guy?' Geraldine gave her a one-sided smile that tilted her eyes. 'Well –' She shrugged again. 'Actually, I get along pretty well without one.'

Sandy slumped into one of her boneless poses. 'Lucky you.'

A few minutes later, Geraldine decided she wasn't really sick and said she was going to engage in some forgery in preparation for their trip to Malindi. Sandy – the embassy's Legal Attaché, after all – should have looked shocked but instead looked interested. Then again, she was the one who carried the phoney police badge.

Utica, New York.

Rose, the kids and the two NCIS guardians had flown up from BWI in late morning. Rose, restless, had wanted to get out of the house almost as soon as she was in it. Now she was driving a rental car through what had been the Italian neighborhoods of her childhood.

'Jesus,' she murmured at one point as she drove through what had once been familiar streets.

'Changed?' Warrant Officer Reko said beside her. Gorki was with the kids at Rose's parents' house, a Utica patrol car also parked outside. Proud city defends local girl against baddies.

'I haven't really looked at it in years. I –' She started to say that she'd hardly been there and then stopped herself, embarrassed to admit how little she'd been back since she'd got away. When she had come back, it had been overnight, and she'd had no curiosity about a place where she'd been mostly miserable, and it had been to visit her father and tolerate her mother – and, she admitted, to leave her kids with them. 'This was the Italian part of town. Up ahead a few blocks were the Greeks. The Poles were the other side of Genesee – that's the main drag.' She was driving slowly through a neighborhood where urban decay had spiraled down into collapse. Plywood covered the windows of empty houses; vacant lots stared where once houses had stood. 'When I was a kid, these were all two- and three-deckers. There were people everywhere. Now –!'

The streets were almost empty. The few people who could be seen were black.

Rose turned and turned again and headed back down toward her father's house. A stone wall loomed on her right. Wrought-iron gates filled the gaps in the wall; behind them, a big brick building was closed and empty. Grass grew in the cracks of the concrete courtyard.

'My God.' Rose stopped the car. 'I went to school

there!' She tried to grin, felt the corners of her mouth tremble. 'Until they threw me out.'

Saint Catherine's of Siena. Rose had been bounced near the end of tenth grade for fighting, disruption, smoking, and – unsaid to her parents but fully understood by Sister Anthony – precocious sex. *Rose the bad girl.* 'This was a big school!' she said. It grieved her that it was closed, even if the place had rejected her and she had hated it.

'No students, I guess,' Reko said. She meant the empty streets.

No students, no money. The Italians had moved out of their two-and-three deckers and fled to the suburbs. All but her father and a few diehards like him.

Memory was like a lash. She had changed to a public high school, where she had been a bad girl for the rest of the tenth grade and then, her voice already made permanently husky from screaming her way through life, looked around that summer and seen that she was either going to shape up or she was going to join the young women pushing baby carriages along the tree-lined sidewalks. She had thought she was pregnant, had fought through that alone and in ignorance, going on hearsay and such information as she could glean from the public library. When she had begun to menstruate again and knew she wasn't pregnant, she saw through her relief to a hard truth: if not this time, then the next. She didn't, as she might have, take the reprieve as a sign that risk was okay.

I was lucky, she said to herself, but it wasn't luck that made her see that she had to shape up. It was a kind of intelligence, and a terrible egoism, and a fear of ending up like her mother.

That had done it. Her mother was to her like a prisoner – a woman locked into a life too narrow and a mind too empty. Rose had wanted out.

The Navy had shown the way.

She drove down to Bleecker and took Reko along the remaining two blocks of what had once been a vibrant Italian commercial street. Now there was an Oriental grocery and a Thai restaurant mixed in with remnant cafés and restaurants and tailor shops and empty stores.

Rose didn't talk. She was thinking about Houston and what she was going to do next. Her mind had made some connection she couldn't articulate between her past and her immediate future, something about the woman she might have been and the one she was. She knew she had paid a price for not having become one of the women with the baby carriages who, in her generation, had moved out to New Hartford and Deerfield. She knew that part of that price was her behavior after the attempt on her life – the use of the gun, the abrasiveness toward Hansen, the single-minded focus on the cell phones.

'I'm heading home,' she said.

'Suits me.'

She made lunch for her father and mother and the kids; Reko and Gorki were on per diem and wanted junk food. Her mother, she found, was flustered by her being there but somehow pleased; her father smiled a lot but looked weary. *He's got old*, she told herself with the surprise every child feels at that realization. He watched her mother constantly, fussed both at and over her. *Worried sick*. After lunch, he hugged Rose and whispered, 'She's better with the kids here. Like her old self.'

Rose didn't say that her mother seemed to her

frightened and confused. She didn't say that she didn't believe her mother had a self, only an emptiness, a lifelong dissatisfaction.

She put the kids to bed in her old room and lay down on her parents' bed. How strange, to lie there where she had been conceived, to stare at the same ceiling. *Houston*, she thought. *What am I going to do about Houston?*

A different voice sounded inside her head. Tom Hanks at the end of *Apollo 13*, for years her favorite movie: 'All from the confines of mission control and our house in Houston.' He meant, that's how he'd see the moon, because his crippled spacecraft hadn't made it that far.

The confines of mission control and our house in Houston.

The word *confines* stuck like a fishbone in the throat. She hated confines. *Maybe I'm more like my mother than I think – never satisfied.*

Houston. Endless suburbia. The NASA family. Being a good team player. Fitting the image.

She'd hated another movie about the space program – *The Right Stuff*. It had made the astronauts seem in-authentic, constructs of public relations and hype; by contrast, the test pilot Chuck Yeager had been made to seem heroic. She'd disliked him, thought him a kind of outcast, a cowboy loner.

Not a team player.

'The confines of mission control and our house in Houston,' she said aloud.

She thought of a scene in *The Right Stuff* she'd never understood: while the astronauts are being turned into corporate lookalikes in Houston, Yeager takes the X-15 to the edge of space, and the aircraft flames out and goes out of control; the crash crew drive toward the smoking wreckage and, as a figure emerges from the smoke, one says, 'Is that a man?' It is Yeager. Another voice says, 'You're damned right it is.'

You're damned right it is.

But Yeager had been rejected by the space program. 'Doesn't fit the profile – too independent,' the recruiter had said.

Not a team player.

For years, she'd thought that all she wanted to be was an astronaut. Now –

The confines of mission control and our house in Houston.

Washington.

'Jason, this is not about your budget!'

Ted Kasser stared at a picture of his wife and wondered for the thousandth time why she had worn so much eye makeup to a picnic. He was exhausted, but that was normal. He wished he had a good old-fashioned secretary, some trustworthy guy he could send out for coffee. Real coffee. 'I don't care,' he said quietly into the phone. He tapped a pencil on the desk and tried not to stare at his wife's picture. Then he swiveled suddenly in his chair, clearly angry, and tossed the pencil so that it stuck in the ceiling tile.

'Look, Jason, I don't give a shit about your protection budget. I'll get the director to sign. I mean it, I want twenty-four-seven protection on the families of everyone on Dukas's team, starting as soon as this call started. This isn't a fucking drill!'

An analyst from the counterterrorism section came in looking guilty and dropped a message on his desk, then pointed at it with his pencil. Kasser looked up, met his eye, nodded, and pointed to the door. The analyst made a quick exit. Kasser read the message and then started it again.

'Okay, Jason, there's a disconnect here. I'll just call the director and it's your ass. You had your chance.' He hung up. He wondered if, given the air of crisis since the attacks in Mombasa, he could send an analyst out for coffee. Then he placed another call.

'Sir? Ted. Yessir. There have been some developments. Yes, we can link the attacks in Kenya to the attack on Commander Siciliano. Yes, sir. That's what I thought, too. Could you ask Jason yourself, sir? He didn't think his budget would cover it.' He listened to the sound of swearing for two seconds.

'Yes, sir. Yes, sir.' He took a deep breath. He had made up his mind as soon as he had hung up the phone from talking to Dukas. 'Sir, I think we should go for broke on this. I think we should ask to be top dog in the investigation, with Mike Dukas as lead. Dukas has a big rep out there, and we've broken a big one with this cell-phone thing. Right. And if CIA and FBI and DEA are going to squabble over it, my thinking is they won't give an inch to each other, but they might accept us because – Right. They might all settle on a little guy like us. I'd like you to take it all the way to the top. Yeah, I know – but –' He looked at his watch. 'I can sack out here if I have to. And I guess that there's things worse than keeping the President up late in a good cause. Yes, sir. I'll be right here.'

Kasser put the telephone in the cradle. Once, long ago, he'd been a cop.

Mombasa.

Ted Kasser didn't get back to Dukas until two hours after Triffler and Keatley and Patemkin had left in the 747 for Cairo. Dukas figured that by then Kasser would have called if he'd had any success. It was over. He was still awake, sitting in his empty office and thinking of the immediate problems he would face by resigning – getting out of Mombasa, cleaning out his office in Washington, dealing with Leslie. Maybe he'd just go away someplace and leave all that for later.

'This isn't over,' Kasser's muffled voice said in the STU.

'It is for me. I'm sure you tried, Ted.'

'No, no – it isn't over. Right now, you're going to get half a loaf.'

'Which half?'

'You can go back into Cairo.'

That's what he'd asked for. So wasn't that the whole loaf? 'What's the other half?'

'DEA will still be there, and it's their investigation.'

'The Cairo bombing maybe is theirs; Cram is ours.'

'Well, by implication.'

Dukas was in a fog, but he could make out some landmarks. 'By implication' meant that there had been a shouting match and his side hadn't lost. Meaning that DEA wasn't sitting on top of the world.

'Who's refereeing?' he said.

'National Security Advisor and Director of the FBI, near as I can make out. DNI has been over there for a couple of hours.'

'Any idea what DEA is after?' Dukas said. If the DEA position wasn't rock-solid, why not? Because they weren't supposed to be in Cairo at all? Because they'd blue-skyed something and not told all the right people about it?

'We think that's what the FBI is starting to ask. I've been looking around since you said it was DEA, and nobody knows anything, but there's some off-the-record gossip that a DEA team is missing. Only gossip.'

'In the bombing?'

Kasser didn't answer. Dukas remembered wondering why a terrorist would hit a set of AID offices. 'Ted, you got any friends at AID?'

'I might know somebody.'

'How about asking if they did a sublet in Cairo to DEA?'

He heard Kasser chuckle. It sounded over the connection like a hammer tapping an anvil, ker-lunk, ker-lunk, ker-lunk. 'You think I'm too dumb to come up with that by myself?'

'You're on it, right?'

'I'm on it and I'll let you know.'

Dukas was thinking of what it would mean if DEA had had a team in the Cairo building that had been hit. If the target had been the DEA team and not the AID offices, then maybe the bombing was more than an act of terrorism. More than an attack on Americans and not an attack on the Navy. More like what the cell-phone lines on the map showed.

Who blows up drug enforcement agents?

Silly question.

'Thanks, Ted.'

'You're not going to resign, right?'

Dukas took a big breath and let it out. 'I guess not.'

'I almost let you do it. I don't like to be blackmailed. Even in a good cause.'

Dukas nodded, as if Kasser could see him. 'And I'd do it again. In a good cause.' He took another deep breath, as if he was oxygen-starved. Maybe that's what fatigue did. 'Ted, I want more, but I'm not going to resign over it. Call it clarification. We were supposed to have the flying forensics lab for at least a week; it got taken away a few hours ago and ordered to Cairo.

I want it back. It can sit in Cairo, but it's got to be ours, and Sheila Ditka can do the tech work for everybody.' Before Kasser could jump in, he said, 'There's no reason DEA should have sole use. They're hiding something, but they can't go on getting away with it. I'd like that case made tonight to whoever's making decisions there. Then I'd like it clear that the lab is ours, and we'll of course share it and welcome their techs, but it stays ours. And we run our investigation in Cairo and DEA shares with us fifty-fifty.'

Kasser wasn't pleased, but there was an odd mixture of anger and respect in his voice. 'You never stop, do you?' He sounded tired. 'Anyway, hang in there – I may have more before tomorrow.'

At midnight Mombasa time, a message was relayed from the 747, already on the ground in Cairo, to the det's hangar. Per orders, the duty officer – in this case. Chief Bakin – waked Dukas. It was from Sheila Ditka: *Explosive checks out as C4. DMDNB taggant analysis corresponds to explosive manufactured in Switzerland in 1996. Checking for batch and history.*

She had already copied the NCIS lab in Washington, with a flag for Kasser.

Dukas lay back down on his sleeping bag, trying to tell himself that it was cooler at night and going back to sleep would be easy. He was still awake two hours later, trying to put together the bombs and the phone calls that connected Sicily and Lebanon and Malindi, and the murder of a loser in a hotel toilet in Cairo, and enough involvement with drugs to get a lot of people blown up.

At five in the morning his time, a sailor waked him to take another call from Kasser. It was eight at night in Washington and Kasser was still in his office, he could tell, calling on his STU. He sounded exhausted but triumphant.

'It's yours, Mike.'

Dukas didn't get it. He was still half-asleep. 'My what?'

'Your investigation. NCIS owns everything having to do with both bombings, plus anything coming from the cell-phone tracking. You're our man.'

Dukas grunted. He was waking up. 'The Bureau? The Agency? DEA –?'

'They see the light. You're in charge.'

'Who'd you have to kill?'

Kasser's chuckle was hollow. 'Some arm-wrestling at what's called "the highest level of government." The big guys wore each other out and we came in at the end and won. Go for it, Mike.'

Dukas actually smiled. He couldn't stop himself. 'Ted, you're a great man. I'll never threaten to resign again.'

Kasser gave the same death's head chuckle. 'Yeah, you will.'

Day Four

13

Mombasa.
The intermittent rain of the squall line ahead of the
storm beat down on the tin roof of the hangar. It actually made sleeping easier, and Alan was deep down
when one of the duty intel guys woke him at 0115
because the det's other plane was coming in. The
second det plane from the carrier landed at Mombasa
at 0130 local. A helicopter landed a few minutes later.
Grumpy, pouchy-eyed ground crews rolled out of their
bags and ran out into the rain to get the planes tied
down and their contents into the hangar. Alan waited
in the hangar to greet Soleck and the others, shook
hands all around with the helicopter crew that would
keep him linked to the *Harker* if the storm cut comms
with the boat, and went back to his sleeping bag. Before
he could get back to sleep, he noted that the rain had
stopped.

Three hours later he was up again, this time gulp-
ing coffee while he read meteorological notices sent
from the boat in message traffic and tried to guess Rafe's
intentions. The storm was huge, and Rafe would take
the *Jefferson* east to meet it and to get more water under
his keel. Alan thought that if he needed anything from
the boat he'd better get it in the next twenty-four
hours.

Opono drove up to the line of Marine posts before

the sun had risen. This time he had four armed men on his vehicle. Alan saw them arrive under the bright white lights of one of Captain Geelin's posts and then went back to his preflight, expecting Opono to join him. When fifteen minutes had passed and the man still hadn't made the short drive to the hangar, Alan walked out to post one, noting that his hangar had sprouted a Marine platoon with a mortar section, two S-3s, and a helicopter. He had an army and an air force.

'Corporal, where did the KWS team go?'

'Sir, Captain Geelin passed them. He was with them when they drove off.'

Alan shook his head and walked back to the hangar, where he found Geelin and Opono drinking coffee. Opono shook hands, and Geelin nodded. Was there an element of warmth to the nod?

'Good morning, David. Care to go flying?'

'Yes.'

Alan looked a question at the two of them.

Opono explained, 'I brought some men who know the ground here very well. I thought they could help. There are people who live out there in the flat ground beyond the runway.'

'We've already run into the squatters a couple of times,' Geelin said. 'Could have gone wrong.'

That was news to Alan, and he thought, *You should have told me*, but he let it pass. His focus was on the mission.

'Any trouble coming out here?'

'The GSU is putting a cordon around the airport later today. They say it is for your protection. I think it is to keep your men from seeing what the GSU plan to do in the city, yes?'

Alan was leading Opono to the briefing room, a

plywood shack at the front of the hangar where the flight gear hung. It had eight folding chairs on the concrete floor and a piece of plastic screwed to the wall, a black felt-tip pen hanging from it. A tactical pilotage chart with a plastic cover was glued to another wall. Cohen and Campbell were sitting in the chairs, trying to create a comm card, something that was usually done for them. Soleck sat with Chief Bakin and two AWs.

'We have to be able to talk to Mombasa tower,' Cohen insisted as they entered. Soleck was shaking his head. They all sprang to their feet as Alan entered.

'Gentlemen, this is David Opono of the Kenya Wildlife Service. He's the equivalent of a bird colonel, so act straight.' Cohen and Campbell shook hands. 'This is Lieutenant Brian Campbell and this is Lieutenant Mark Cohen. He'll be flying our plane.'

'Al, uh, does Mister Opono have any flight quals?' Cohen could find any glass half-empty, if you gave him a chance.

'No. He's going anyway.'

'Have you filed a flight plan?' David waved at the map.

Campbell bounced up. 'We weren't born yesterday,' he said. 'We told them we had to do a check flight for routine maintenance.'

David's face didn't change expression, so Alan had to guess how complex his reaction might be to a foreigner's lying to his country's air control. Justified? But he didn't have to like it?

'We're afraid Kenya would deny –'

'I was going to recommend the same thing.' David smiled and shrugged. 'Let's go to work, eh?'

Alan nodded.

'We've already done a walk-around. We can fly anytime we want to. I've put a mark on the chart, here, for the possibility of a camp. A *potential* camp. Okay, David, what are we looking for? Will you be able to identify it?'

'From the air? I doubt it will look like much. I have never seen it, yes?' Opono looked at Alan and shook his head. 'But I have reports. A metal shed, they say. Probably a clear space for cleaning carcasses. *Vibanda*, little huts of grass, maybe a tent. That's all. A local guy said they were right on the water. There are three small villages in that area, just grass huts, and one abandoned compound.'

'Brian, what I want is good MARI footage.'

'What about digital?'

'Unless I say otherwise, we don't go too near them.'

Soleck nodded and tossed his empty coffee cup into a distant can with élan. Campbell crossed his arms.

David raised his hand. 'If it looks like anything, I'd consider doing something about it. Directly.'

Alan caught his eye. 'I think that's premature.'

'Just thought you'd like to know how the KWS was thinking.' David pointed at the chart. 'I have some information about these people; I think they are poachers.'

'Do we have this "information," David?' *Poachers*. Alan was after bigger game than that.

'Sandy does.'

'Okay. Point taken, David. Can we look at the situation, first?'

'I'm here,' he said.

Alan nodded and started to brief the mission. When he asked for questions, Soleck raised his hand.

'Sir, what are we looking for?'

'We don't know, Evan. David says there's a rumor of a metal shed. That will give a return, something to look for. If they're the folks we're after, I guess they'll have something on the water; maybe a pier, certainly a boat. That's all guesswork.' Alan's reply covered his own doubt. *What were they looking for?* They were going to a reference point provided by the cell data. That's all they had.

'Will there be weapons? Dead animals?'

David Opono answered. 'Maybe.' He shrugged.

Soleck was scribbling on his kneeboard. 'Closed shed ought to throw a good return. Metal?'

'Perhaps.'

Alan nodded. 'Up in Somalia they have metal roofs.'

'Yeah, I think I remember that. That should make a spike even before you image.'

Alan added, 'There may be some sort of pier or dock; the *Harker* witness may have mentioned this place –'

'Airstrip?' Campbell asked. 'Sometimes they show on MARI.'

'Maybe,' Alan said. He could see it in his mind. 'I bet they have fuel, either way. If they aren't in a town, they'll need fuel. Expect a fuel truck, something like that.'

'Cool,' Soleck said, satisfied. 'Can do.'

The Road to Malindi.

Sandy herded Hahn and Pastner out of the hangar before the S-3's were airborne. Getting to Malindi was not like making a trip to the mall. Mombasa itself was still like an occupied city, roadblock after roadblock, streets cordoned off as unsafe, military trucks parked in twos and threes at corners. Traffic was light, or so Sandy said – to Geraldine Pastner, it seemed frenetic – but slow.

'Well, nobody shot at us,' Geraldine said when they were out of Mombasa. Hahn, who was riding with them as far as the Nyali Beach hotels, looked grim. 'We still have to make it back,' he muttered. He was going to check out the hotels to try to find who had fingered Alan Craik. Neither woman said that he had the cushy job, so what was he worried about, but they gave each other a look.

After they'd dropped Hahn at the doors of the International and assured him that they'd pick him up again at five, they both leaned back and grinned as if they'd just got rid of a difficult relative. 'Men are such shits,' Geraldine murmured. 'You suppose he wanted to be the one to go to Malindi while *we* did the hotels?'

'Only if he's never been to Malindi before.' Sandy explained: Malindi was the last stop before the Tana River, where the two-lane road ended. There used to be a ferry across, and more road on the other side; now there was no ferry, and the other side was *upande ya shifta* – bandit country, worse since Somalia had fallen apart and a quarter-million Somali refugees had moved south. In effect, the Tana was the border now; beyond it was a wild and woolly nobody's land where guns wrote the law. Malindi partook of this wildness, a pretty, old city that was an opportunist's playground – money-laundering, drugs, poaching, all the profitable middle-men's activities that modern life could offer. The road to the place, therefore, reflected its semi-outcast status, poorly maintained, heavily roadblocked, haunted by legends of carjackings and ambushes.

Their driver was a short, slender man who made no attempt to hide his nervousness. He insisted that they drive with the windows up.

'For heaven's sake, why, James?' Geraldine said.

'Spears.'

Geraldine looked at Sandy. She shrugged. She lowered her voice, put her head close to Geraldine's. 'Now and then, a tourist gets speared by somebody pretending to sell stuff, but that's when they're stopped. He's just nervous.'

So they drove along, swerving around the potholes, staying under forty to reduce the damage to the shock absorbers, forking out cigarettes and cash at roadblocks. Two hours and fifty miles after they'd cleared Mombasa, they began to see signs that they were close.

James, relieved, said, 'Okay now. Here is Malindi. Where you ladies like to go?'

Geraldine leaned forward. 'Where the whores are. You understand "whores," James? Prostitutes?'

Sandy told him in Swahili.

James was scandalized.

They found a flight suit long enough to cover David, and the det's parachute riggers spent a hard half hour with their ancient sewing machine, tailoring a flight harness to fit Opono's long frame. Alan took David through the cramped confines of the plane, showing him the spreader pin that would ensure the opening of his parachute if he had to eject and demonstrating the harness. The heat of the day was already enough to make him light-headed. He sweated through his flight suit before he was done walking around the plane, and the concrete was warm under his hands as he crawled under the S-3's belly to check his chaff and flare cartridges. He went back to the hangar to get a tape for the back end of the plane and thought of Master Chief Craw. Opono would be in his seat.

At nine thousand feet, it was cold. They all felt the

change at four thousand, when they flew through the local coastal environment and into the cold air of middle altitude. The sweat of the morning turned to icewater, and Alan unstrapped and handed David a heavy leather flight jacket whose sleeves were several inches too short. Alan was clumsy helping him get it on, his hand cramping from the temperature change. Then he served out a thermos of coffee.

'I thought America had all this technology,' David said.

'We do!' Alan pointed at the computer facing his seat. 'We just don't waste it on sailors. Besides, this plane is older than I am.'

Once he had Opono settled, Alan leaned forward between the two front seats and watched the Kenyan coast roll out in front of him. Cohen was on the radio, his helmet mike switched to allow him to communicate with the tower without interfering with communications inside the plane. He kept shaking his head, which led Alan to want to know what he was saying to the tower. He unplugged his comm cord and re-plugged it to the radio. Immediately he heard Cohen telling the tower that, yes, they were on a check flight for hydraulics failure, just a quick hop, and no, they weren't leaving the control area. Well, maybe a quick jog north to see the elephants. Alan nodded, pulled the cord, and gave Cohen a thumbs-up. They couldn't really file a flight plan for visiting poaching camps on the north coast.

Alan got back into his seat and clicked the toggles that fastened his harness to the ejection mechanism. Then he pulled his keyboard out of the locked position to the right above his seat and drew it down across his lap, locking it on to the armrests. He switched his display monitor from standby to on.

He looked over at Opono, who had an unhealthy pallor under the deep black of his skin. Airsick? When Alan thought about it, the whole plane stank of age and JP-5 and burned electricals and sweat, none of them calculated to make a passenger feel comfortable. It was the first time in months that he had flown in a det airplane without Master Chief Craw. He missed Craw, and he realized that he had expected Craw to put a tape in the back end to run the computer. He unstrapped again and went back into the tunnel, a tiny space that was filled with the computers and electrical gear needed to make the plane's MARI system run. He slid the cartridge, roughly the size of an eight-track tape, into the grooves, seated it, and locked it in. Then he went back to his seat and strapped in. Again. The smell was still with him, and somewhere in it was a ghost of Craw. He plugged in his comm cord, still missing the man, the feeling more intense for being in the plane where they had always been a team.

'Jaeger Two airborne,' Cohen said over the cockpit intercom.

'What'd the tower say?'

'Just a nastygram about our last-minute change of flight plan. No biggie.'

Alan reached up and toggled the computer system on, flipping the switch and then counting down on his watch until the system should have reset at sixty seconds.

The word 'system' flashed briefly across his screen in glowing green. He nodded, relieved. He could run the back end alone; indeed, he was a past master of the MARI system, but there was always that moment where the computer either accepted its load or didn't.

Cohen circled north, waiting for Soleck's plane to

take station. The MARI system required two planes radiating from widely spaced angles for the best possible radar image, an image that could be as good as a photograph under the right conditions and in the hands of skilled users.

Alan was inputting parameters as fast as his undamaged fingers could fly, then frequencies so that the two planes could share a secure datalink, a job usually handled by an airborne control plane. As soon as his own plane entered the link, a pixel map of the African coast appeared, replicated on David's screen. He recognized it but showed no sign of surprise. *Way to go, Evan*, Alan muttered. Evan Soleck, his most junior pilot, who fished from the fantail of the carrier and had arrived on the *Jefferson* with tennis rackets, had qualities of genius, and massaging the ancient computers in the S-3 to maximize performance was one. He also excelled at building the datasets necessary to make primitive graphics. David Opono, raised on Hollywood portrayals of American technology, took it all for granted.

Soleck's plane should be well out over the ocean. Alan could see the line of weather to the north and east marking the coming storm and hoped that the storm front wouldn't interfere with his mission.

'Whoa! You gotta see this, Commander!' Cohen said from the front. Alan looked out of his own window and saw mostly sky as the plane was turning west. He leaned out over the central aisle and then unstrapped to look through the windscreen.

Below him stretched the savanna of Tsavo. An enormous herd of zebra had caught Cohen's attention.

'I think I saw lions on a kill,' Campbell said without his usual affected boredom.

'I could fly here all day,' Cohen said.

'You should see it on the ground,' Opono said, the last word coming out as *g-rowand*, as if it had special meaning. 'Perhaps when we are done here I will take you all to the park.'

'Better than TV,' Campbell said softly.

'That'd be great,' Cohen said, impressed. Cohen, who was armored against any kind of happiness, who could sour any conversation, had a broad grin on his face as he followed the zebra herd, his speed slowed to just above stall. Alan let them look while he strapped himself in again. Opono smiled at him and he grinned back.

'Gentlemen, if we could leave the zebras to their grass? I'm ready to image.'

'Whoa, I'm on it.' Alan heard power go into the engines and the nose came up. He changed his radio settings and called the other plane.

'Jaeger Two, this is Jaeger One, over.'

'Jaeger One, I read you loud and clear. Go ahead.'

'Ready to image.'

'Roger.'

'Sector one.'

'Roger, sector one.'

Alan used his keyboard to point the antenna in the nose and started imaging the first sector they had chosen, an islanded stretch just south of the Somali border. The initial returns were difficult to read and disappointing. The sandy soil of the beaches defracted the radar rather than reflecting it, masking the edge of the water and making Alan's job more difficult. He reimaged several times, each time asking the pilots to reposition the planes.

Far out to the east, beyond Rafe and the carrier battle group, now visible in the link as a wedge-shaped series of circles, a mass of low pressure was moving across the Indian Ocean, bringing high winds, rain, and waves. Outriders of the storm were already around them, little squalls of rain that diminished the pilot's visibility and attenuated the radar. Twice, Alan watched his cursor blink and vanish, indicating that the system had dropped its ability to trace the returns from the focused radar in the nose, and each time he had to start again. Given the relative short range to the target, it was frustrating.

The pilots had to fly racetrack patterns, each pattern with a long leg toward the image target to get the best aspect for the radar, followed by a turn away when one or both planes was out of aspect and the system was off-line. Each pattern took them closer to the target, making their images sharper but raising the possibility of discovery if their quarry had a radar of its own – if their quarry even existed.

On the third pattern, Alan got a spike return on his initial run, but he couldn't seem to focus the spike when he switched to image mode. After refinement, he leaned over to Opono, who appeared to be asleep.

'Take a look at that,' he said.

Opono wiped his eyes and craned forward to look at his screen. He shook his head and reached over the aisle to tap Alan's shoulder.

'What am I looking at?' he shouted.

Alan tapped his helmet and then unhooked his harness, leaned across Opono so he could smell last night's beer on the man and pressed his PTT intercom button. 'You have to press the button to make your intercom work.'

Opono shrugged, pressed the button.

'What am I looking at?' he asked.

'See the line of the coast? See the beach here, and here? I think that's a house, and those are *vibanda*.'

Opono looked at the grass huts. Alan cycled back from image to map mode so that Opono could see where they were imaging.

'It might be Guryama. I can't say for sure, Alan.'

If it was Guryama, according to their chart, then they were imaging miles too far to the south. Alan moved the cursor north and got the spike again, a hard metal return somewhere north of Guryama. When he tried to get the spike to image, the attenuation increased and he lost the image. He used the loss as a break, putting the location labeled *Guryama?* into the link so that the second plane and anyone interested out on the battle group would have a common point of reference.

'It's raining up there,' he said, mostly to himself.

'What?' Opono asked.

'It's raining north of Guryama.' He switched his intercom to talk to the other plane. 'Jaeger Two, this is Jaeger One, over?'

'Gotcha, skipper.' *Soleck*.

'I have a hard return north of the point in the link marked Guryama. You copy that?'

'I copy Guryama, but I don't have a return.'

'Tell your Tacco to keep hitting the coast between Guryama and the border.'

'Roger that.'

Opono waved at him and Alan hit his intercom button.

'Why can we not just fly over and look at the coast?'

'SAMs,' Alan said, thinking that he had explained himself. Opono just shook his head. 'Look, David, if these are bad guys, they'll have MANPADs, little surface-to-air missiles that can take an S-3 down faster than you can say "poacher." And it's raining up there; we wouldn't see much, anyway.'

Opono nodded, clearly unsatisfied.

'And if we spook them with big Navy planes, they'll run, and we'll never get them,' Alan said.

Opono caught his eye and smiled. 'That, I understand.'

Cairo.

Triffler and Keatley had become the tail of a tornado that was blowing through the American embassy in Cairo. Patemkin had made three calls to the Nairobi embassy before they left the ground in Mombasa, and he told them that he'd made six more from the Cairo hotel when they'd first got there last night. Nonetheless, he had bounced into their room at seven this morning and dragged them down to an American breakfast before a hair-raising taxi ride to the embassy.

'Early bird gets the worm,' he said. The taxi banged into a pothole, and his teeth clacked from the concussion when they hit bottom. 'I want to blitz DEA before they realize we're here.'

'If we live that long,' Triffler said. He was holding on to the handle above his window and sitting up very straight.

'You got a contact in the cops here, right?' Patemkin said to Triffler. The words came out in bursts as they bounced.

'Detective sergeant, caught the bombing, then –' a terrific slam and a bounce – 'our guy who was murdered.'

'You get on him while I see the chief of station, we may want his – holy shit look out Jesus Christ that

384

was close – his help.' Patemkin grinned. 'Is this fun, or what?'

At the embassy, they had rushed down a corridor to the chief of station's office, then rushed behind him and Patemkin to the chief of mission's office, then rushed behind all three to the ambassador's chief of staff.

And cooled their heels in a side room while a lot of politicking went on next door.

'Good coffee,' Triffler said. It had been served in china cups. With saucers. 'Kenya,' he said. He tasted again. 'You get the hint of citrus?'

'Get a hint of this, will you?' Keatley said. He held up a finger. Keatley was not a morning person.

'You have to be forgiven a lot because you were a Marine,' Triffler said.

'What the hell does that mean?'

'It means you've been drinking Navy coffee so long your taste buds have dissolved.'

'Coffee's coffee.'

Triffler looked shocked.

'Nothing personal,' Keatley said.

Triffler looked as if he wasn't at all sure. He took coffee almost as seriously as high-school football.

'You look – no offense – as if you're going to church.' Keatley was still resenting the Marine comment. Triffler was dressed in a pale gray lightweight suit, a pink button-down shirt with a plum-colored tie, and black tasseled loafers with a shine that made the eyes sting.

'I wouldn't wear this shade of gray to church,' Triffler said. 'Actually, I'm dressed for a hanging. And I hope to be the guy doing the hanging.'

'DEA?'

'Better them than me.' Triffler took the plum-colored

paisley show hankie from his breast pocket and flicked a mote of dust from his left shoe. 'These mah fightin' clothes, dude.'

'The gun bulge helps. Very stylish.'

'You see it because you know it's there.' Triffler sat erect and looked down his right side, holding the arm away. 'Invisible to the untrained eye. I had the suit tailored for it.' He had a .380 Sig 232 in a belt-clip holster, and Keatley had already told him it wasn't enough gun.

'Not enough gun,' Keatley said again now, never one to let a good thing be said only once. He pulled a Government .45 from under the left side of his nylon golf jacket. 'This is enough gun.'

'Never mind that it makes you look as if you're carrying your lunch under your arm. And don't wave that thing around.' They'd already been hassled at the gate by an Egyptian rent-a-cop who had wanted them to turn the guns in; only some energetic appeals by Patemkin had let them bring them into the embassy.

Keatley shoved the gun back into his shoulder holster. 'We're both supposed to be carrying nines, anyway.' He sounded grumpy.

'I have a nine in my attaché.'

'Me, too.'

Triffler smiled. 'There used to be a song, "I Got a Razor in My Shoe." I could modernize it – "I Got a Niner in My Case."'

'What the hell kind of song is that?'

'They were called "coon songs."' Triffler flashed him the smile. 'Keen perceptions of the culture of my people by white intellectuals in the music business, many of them Jewish.'

'I don't get it.'

'African Americans were all supposed to carry razors in their shoes.'

'Why?'

Triffler opened his mouth, closed it, smiled again. 'To shave with.'

Keatley thought about it. 'Oh, I get it.' He frowned. 'Kind of racist, right?'

Triffler nodded several times. 'Kind of.' He poured himself more coffee, and he was standing by a window, cup in one hand, saucer in the other, when Patemkin stuck his head in. 'You're on.' He twitched his head toward the corridor.

Triffler took a sip of coffee and put the cup on the saucer and the saucer on the tray. 'Let me do the talking,' he said. It was said in such a way that it was clear that there was no room for negotiation on the point.

They went ten steps down the green-carpeted corridor, passing a photograph of Jimmy Carter with the wind blowing through his hair, and followed Patemkin in another door, past a no-longer-really-young woman who nonetheless looked well worth making a move on (that was Keatley's response, not Triffler's), through yet another door, and into a large office that seemed to be filled with people, only one of them female – the CIA station chief. The rest sorted themselves out as an FBI agent, the chief of staff, somebody they didn't know but were introduced to as from State Department Security, and the large DEA guy who had thrown them out of Cairo yesterday morning.

Only yesterday? How time flies when you're having fun.

'Herb Geddes,' the CIA chief of station said as she waved a hand toward the DEA honcho. She was a fifty-ish woman named Marjorie Fine, her graying hair cut very short so that she looked like a swimmer just emerged from the water. She was trim and slender in an off-white shift that seemed vaguely Egyptian. 'Mister Geddes is from the Drug Enforcement Agency.' She spoke to Triffler (*The black guy's in charge,* Triffler *could hear Patemkin saying to her*) but directed the last few words to include Keatley, as well.

Triffler put out his hand to Geddes. 'We've met.' He smiled. Not like a man with a razor in his shoe. Geddes's hand came out slowly; it felt cold to the touch and the grip was limp, then too forceful, sending two messages: *I don't want to be here,* and then, *Mine's bigger than yours.* As they shook hands, Triffler beamed his smile over the others, taking in the constellation that had been created: Marjorie Fine as point of contact and first-level gunner, with the chief of mission and the chief of staff and the State Security guy behind her to give authority and weight, and the FBI man scowling at the edges. Diplomatic street cred.

'We seem to have a situation here,' Marjorie Fine was saying. 'I want it resolved. I want it resolved now. I don't want to leave this office without closure. Is that clear?' She addressed most of it to Geddes, but hit Triffler and then Keatley with the finale.

'Maybe a certain lack of transparency,' Triffler said.

Geddes said nothing. Marjorie Fine said, 'Maybe.' She looked at Geddes. It was clear that she was not delighted with what she saw. She waited. They all waited.

'Maybe we'd better sit down,' the chief of mission said.

Mrs Fine allowed a trace of irritation to show in one eyebrow before saying, 'What a good idea.'

They dragged chairs from the walls, Keatley getting his from the outer office. When they were sitting, the early momentum now lost, Marjorie Fine said something again about finding resolution and the need to be forthcoming in the name of cooperation, with a few other words thrown in about this tragic event. 'And a lack of transparency,' she said. She looked at Geddes. 'On the part of the Drug Enforcement Agency.' She was smiling, but you wouldn't want to hand a knife to somebody who smiled that way.

'I'm acting in accordance with the policies of my agency,' Geddes said in the grudging voice of a suspect asked to give his name.

She looked at the State Security man, who handed her a sheet of paper, which she passed to Geddes. 'The policies have been clarified,' she said.

Geddes flushed. He was not liking what he read. 'This should have come to me,' he said.

'It just did.' She crossed her legs. She was wearing ecru panty hose and lightly heeled shoes that matched her dress, and she had good legs. 'The White House directs your agency to clarify itself.'

Geddes's face got redder and set itself in a pattern of furrows and bulges that suggested permanence. He was a good-looking man, or would have been if he wasn't trying to seem like both the rock and the hard place. 'I have secret orders,' he said, as if secret orders were a medal that came with kisses on the cheek and a swell ribbon.

Triffler smiled. 'So have I. Mine are to find and deal with whoever killed our man here yesterday. And that's what I'm going to do.' Triffler was sitting with his right leg over his left, elegant and almost casual. When Geddes started to say something, Triffler raised a hand from the arm of his chair, the index finger up, and said, 'You ordered us out of town. That won't do.'

'I'm afraid that's just tough. This is DEA's investigation.' Geddes turned toward Mrs Fine. 'We have a moral imperative here!'

She made her voice solemn but no less tough. 'We understand you lost a team of seven people in the bombing. Is that right? We didn't learn it from you. We had to learn it from the deputy director of the Central Intelligence Agency, who got it only because of a lot of screaming and desk-pounding. Now, you're not going to do that here, Mister Geddes. You think you are, but you're not. If you can't play in the sandbox with everybody else, you're going home.'

'You can't do that.'

She put her right hand up as if she was going to cup her ear, but moved it farther back, the thumb and finger held out to grasp something. The State Security man put another sheet of paper in it. She handed it to Geddes. He read it and turned purple. 'Okay?' she said. 'The White House orders that this investigation is under the direction of the Naval Criminal Investigative Service – not your agency, not my agency, and not the FBI. Lead investigator is Special Agent Michael Dukas; Special Agent Triffler is his deputy. Now, please tell us exactly what's going on.'

'I need to talk to my agency.'

'No, you don't. It's all there in those two messages. The words are "cooperate" and "share." You just read them.'

Geddes swallowed and puffed out his cheeks. He exhaled slowly and noisily. Triffler found himself feeling sorry for the man, who was, after all, doing exactly what he was doing: working his ass off for his own people in a terrible situation.

'Okay, I'll "share" and "cooperate". I want it clear

it's under duress, and I'll file a complaint.' He scowled around at them. Nobody seemed to be wetting his or her pants. Geddes shrugged himself upright in his armchair and pulled his right ankle up on his left knee and picked at his shoelace. The purple in his face had faded into a deep red, darkest under his eyes, as if it had puddled there. When he spoke, it was directly to Triffler. 'We had a team in Egypt to work with the local authorities on stopping heroin that was coming in through East African ports and up through here and going, well, everyplace.' He stopped, looked around. No applause. He seemed to be hoping that he'd said enough. Nobody else agreed. He tightened his lips together so that the lower lip bulged, turned and looked at Triffler and started to talk again. 'Most of it was coming from Afghanistan. This wasn't the primary route, but enough was coming up this way that we were worried. It was coming mostly out of Pakistan and down along the Arabian peninsula in fast movers – like cigarette boats?' He paused. No good. Everybody still wanted more. He gave a cluck of disgust.

'Then, three months ago, something happened within the team here. We're not sure what it was. Maybe a personality thing. But there was a lot of internal disagreement, infighting. And they were on to something that we think was new. Maybe connected to the East African smuggling, maybe different.'

He looked over at Marjorie Fine and then back at Triffler, his hands now joined over his right foot, fingers laced. He was warming to the narrative, maybe actually feeling relieved to let it all out. 'Frankly, nobody back home made much of this. I mean, I never heard about it. It was just something their bosses in Washington heard or felt and thought they were keeping an eye on. But it wasn't important enough to send somebody out to ask what was going on.'

His look at Triffler hardened. 'Then you guys came in with this Bright Star stuff. We think that our team here battened down the hatches.'

'Bright Star happens every other year,' Triffler said.

'Yeah, whatever. The cooperation between you guys and the Egyptians spooked them, we think. Our agency got a request to ask you to lay off.'

There was a pause. Triffler was expected to say something. 'I don't get it. Bright Star is just SOP.' He thought he saw where Geddes was going. 'They thought they'd get sucked into Bright Star?'

Geddes shifted his weight. 'Not actually. But in terms of cooperation. They were afraid the Egyptians would get too close. They were *on* to something.' He looked around at the others. His eyes moved in quick jerks, giving an odd sensation of fear. His face, less red and less unbudgeable now, looked worried. 'The team called a meeting for yesterday morning. They were scattered – we're not sure where they were in detail, but we know they were in Europe and the Middle East –'

'Where in Europe?' Triffler said.

Geddes hesitated. He looked at Mrs Fine. 'Italy,' he said sullenly.

'Where in the Middle East?'

'We think they had a guy in Pakistan for a while. Also Lebanon. Maybe the Palestinian areas in the West Bank.' He shrugged himself up again. 'So they scheduled a meeting for the whole team yesterday. And the bomb blew.' He looked around again. 'That's what we know.'

Triffler put one long forefinger along his cheek. 'And the woman who was murdered here yesterday? Was she AID or DEA?'

'She was with us.'

'Member of the team?'

Geddes looked grim. 'Deputy head.'

'So – she could have scheduled the meeting. And told her boyfriend. And stayed home because –'

Geddes's head was going up and down, agreeing, agreeing with everything.

'Okay. You got a mess. We have a mess, too. Here's how it goes: we're here to find who killed our guy. You're here to find who killed your guys. We'll give you everything we have and we expect the same from you. We brought in the flying forensics lab and two people to work it; we'll share on that, too, do your work for you if you want. Or you put your own techs in with ours, but all results get shared. *Capisce?*'

Geddes's head bobbed.

'And of course that goes for the Bureau, too.' Triffler glanced at the FBI man, who hadn't yet said a word. He gave his head a little dip. Practically wild applause. 'First thing I want is bomb residue – unless you already did the analysis.'

Geddes shook his head.

Triffler looked at Marjorie Fine. 'Ma'am, I think we're done here.' He smiled. 'I want to thank you. I hope I don't overstep if I say that I like your style.'

She stood. 'Remember, sharing and cooperation extend to my agency and the FBI, too.'

They all smiled at each other. Triffler managed to be next to Geddes when they left the office. 'I want to have a long chat about some telephone calls we've been tracing,' he said. He touched the knot on his tie, checked his reflection in Jimmy Carter's photo as they passed. 'Then I want to have a chat about drugs.'

The Somali-Kenyan Coast.

When Alan finally got an image of the big return north of Guryama, he was sure he had their target. One big building reflected radar so well that it stood out like a beacon on his screen. There were nine smaller buildings and two obvious trucks, one of which might have been a tanker, and a funny little subsidiary return in a narrow channel just east of the buildings. He put the image on Opono's screen.

'Hangar,' he said. 'Something over here. That's a shed, right? Does that look right to you?'

Opono pointed at the biggest return. 'Drying shed. Trucks. Barracks. Yes. Bigger than I expected, but these poaching camps have a sameness to them. What's that?'

That was a reflective blob near one of the trucks. It was large and irregular.

'Dead elephant, maybe?'

'There's another,' Opono said as the image panned to the west and caught another vehicle and another blob. Alan locked his cursor on the new one and tried for better resolution. At high res, it still looked like a blob, a giant amoeba sitting on the ground next to a truck. It didn't look like an elephant but, even at its best, the system achieved only one-meter resolution.

'Jaeger One, what are those things?' Soleck asked from the other plane.

Campbell spoke up from the front. 'Skipper says dead elephants.'

Silence.

Alan ran his cursor to the other side of the camp. 'Bring our nose a little east.'

The view moved too quickly, so he lost his orientation, and then he walked the cursor back to the blobs and then back east again a few meters at a time.

'Bingo. See the pilings?' He was pointing to Opono but talking to the other plane. 'That's got to be a dock. There's a boat anchored in the creek there and another just off, and something with a huge metal return over here in the middle of the channel.'

'Channel?' asked Opono.

'See this black? That's how water, at least calm water, returns on MARI. And this here is rock, so that's an island. So this is the channel between the shed and this island.'

'Rankov says there's something sunk in the channel,' Soleck said from Jaeger Two.

'There's something there, I grant you.' He turned to Opono. 'This look right to you?'

'It has all the marks of a camp. But I'd like to see it.'

'Me, too. But if we overfly it, we'll spook them,' Alan said. 'Let's get it all on tape and think about it.'

Seventy miles to the north of Alan's plane, their soft tissue invisible to the probing beams of the S-3's radars, four men were practicing death in a lagoon.

'Keep your hand steady, Nala,' the older man called.

'Something is interfering with my signal,' Nalakanu said, but he always complained the most. Out in the channel, there were two big, radio-controlled toy boats linked by a rope. Nalakanu's boat was too far behind. The connecting rope was beginning to drag it into a turn.

'Faster, Nala. Faster!'

Nala wanted to shout his frustration, because he was the one always singled out for his father's insults, never his older brothers. It was not fair. He jammed his joystick all the way forward, hoping that his boat would respond, and it did, finally putting slack in the line and drawing even with the other boat until the two toys were side by side, ten meters apart, moving steadily along the flat water of the channel toward a large piece of metal that stuck up from the channel like the prow of a ship.

'Excellent,' their father said. Even that much praise was rare.

The two toy boats swept past the metal prow, but the cable that linked them caught, and both toys swung suddenly in toward the sides of the prow.

'I'm getting a broadcast signal,' Soleck said from Jaeger Two.

'Do you have your ESM up?'

Lebanon.

Harry watched the Hizbollah men on the street, learning what he could of their tradecraft for the day when he was not on their side. They were quite capable, and Harry didn't even have time to note the arrival of two men on motor scooters before the Lebanese, an officer in one of the Christian militias, came out of a house between two bodyguards and slipped into a car. A bearded man on a scooter raced past and both bodyguards turned to watch him and then they were both dead, shot from behind at point-blank range by a man with a silenced Chinese automatic. And then the other scooter rammed the car's open door, tearing it off so that the man inside had nowhere to hide.

Under other circumstances, Harry would have pitied him.

Malindi.

The Malindi prostitutes were concentrated in a pretty little port area and along the highway into town. Geraldine thought the ones around the port were better dressed, but the ones along the highway were, she learned, greener – country girls who went back into the bush on slow days and walked to their villages, mostly Guryama. The ones in the port wore cleverer makeup and arguably trendier clothes, and no wonder – some of the boats in the harbor would have graced any California marina, price tags running into six figures in dollars.

And the girls had professional names.

'Liese,' one said early on.

'That's a German name.'

She covered her mouth and giggled. Did she speak German? Well, she could say 'three hundred shillings' in German, and 'yes' and 'no'. Geraldine didn't ask what the 'no' was used for.

There were also Britney, Cameron, Christiane, and Michelle. And Hannah, Crissie, Oprah, Cher, Stefanie, and Annamaria. Plus Elizabeth, Tania, Biba, and Golda before the Malindi police appeared and wanted to know what was going on.

Long before that, Geraldine had found that she was having a good time. The Malindi prostitutes were a straightforward lot, not much impressed by their trade and not much offended by it, either. They weren't teenaged dopers on the run or anorexic bimbos who got beaten up by pimps. They had families; they were providers. When Geraldine had to pee, they took her to whatever they used, pretty noisome in one case; when Geraldine was hungry, they told her where to eat.

Sandy sat and translated and looked disassociative.

And every one of them, when the interview was over, indicated the driver James and said, 'He want to fuck? Three hundred shillings.'

He didn't. He was a Christian, he said.

And every one of them said that she was a Christian, too, so what was the problem?

Cairo.

Triffler and Keatley were being led down a corridor in the Cairo morgue by their guide, Detective Sergeant al-Fawzi-al-Mubarak. He had greeted Triffler like an old pal, then shaken Keatley's hand and said, 'Good man, good man,' as if Keatley had brought him something wonderful. Keatley hadn't. In fact, he had looked wary.

The morgue was in a nineteenth-century building that seemed to have borrowed its architecture from the Paris Opera: very flossy, with columns and domes and the sort of presence that very large frogs have in very small puddles. Down in its bowels, however, it was utilitarian and banged up, and, as they approached the morgue down a long, tiled corridor, a little fragrant.

'You done this before?' Triffler said to Keatley.

'Sure, sure.'

Triffler didn't believe him. He didn't want to make it a pissing contest – seeing which of them could take the sight of Cram's body more stoically – but he thought that Keatley might make it an occasion for machismo. 'I haven't,' Triffler said. In fact he had, but he thought that Cram was going to be really bad, and he didn't see any point in being brave here if he was going to go inside and lose his breakfast. Machismo be damned.

Al-Fawzi was holding one of a pair of metal double

doors for them. Beyond was fluorescent lighting, stone floors with rubber matting laid down the center, and sand-colored walls.

Cram was in a small examining room. There was no rolling out of a drawer, no sheet-draped gurney. No other bodies. He was on a waist-high tiled block, everything very clean, as if the surfaces had been wiped down for their visit. Triffler guessed that the body hadn't had much blood in it by the time the police had found it, anyway. Decapitation bled well.

'Lot of blood where he was found?' he said to al-Fawzi, trying to postpone the moment when he would have to look right at Cram. He was trying to acquaint himself by degrees, break himself in with peripheral peeks.

'Blood?'

'Was there a lot of blood where you found him?'

'Lot of blood. Much blood, yes.'

A bald geezer in a lab coat came in behind them and stared at Cram as if he was considering buying him if the price was right. Suddenly, he turned to them and said, 'Doctor Sharif.' They all shook hands – more time for Triffler to fill his peripheral vision. Then they all stood there. Triffler swallowed. He couldn't put it off any longer.

He looked.

It could have been worse.

But he didn't see how.

The autopsy had already been done, so the torso had been opened and the organs removed, and where the living Cram had had a fat gut, there was now a depression, two large flaps of skin flowing down from the ribs and hips but not meeting. The space between them was not something Triffler wanted either to look at or talk about. Cram's head had been put more or less where it belonged. Not something he wanted to dwell on, either.

Triffler made himself go closer. Doctor Sharif took this as a sign of eagerness and urged him closer still and began to point out interesting bits, keeping Triffler's right arm in an Ancient-Mariner grip. Doctor Sharif had Nutmeg-colored skin, with the top of his head – mostly what Triffler saw from his height – mottled with browner spots and shiny under the ceiling light. He gave Triffler a tour of Cram: burns, contusions, ligature marks. 'Penis removed, put in mouth – not found until we did postmortem –'

Triffler heard coughing behind him. Keatley was leaning over a sink, making unhappy noises. Mmm-hmm. Keatley was not setting him a good example.

'No drugs in system, somewhat alcohol. Food digested, perhaps five-six hours. Time of death difficult, but, putting together with police report, maybe early morning.'

Triffler took a deep breath and looked at al-Fawzi. 'What's the last he was seen? Last we know he was alive, I mean?'

'Half-eleven the night before the head was found, he was at police press conference. Many witnesses, no question of it.'

'So they may have had him for four, five hours.'

'Maybe less, no more.'

'And nobody saw anything.'

Al-Fawzi held up a finger. 'We have a snitch saw him leave the press conference room. With another man.' He smiled. Very good teeth. He was proud of 'snitch.'

'"Snitch"?'

Al-Fawzi looked panicked. 'Incorrect word? Meaning, man who saw it.'

'Well, "witness." "Snitch" is more, um, you pay him for information. On the street, you know?'

'Ah, "witness."' Clearly, al-Fawzi regretted losing 'snitch.'

'Any ID on this other man with him?'

'He says, only a man. This *witness* is a peasant, a workman; he was folding chairs so he could vacuum-sweep the carpet. He says, these were the last people in the room, except him. They leave together.'

'Force?'

'He says, he thinks they are friends. Smiling.' Al-Fawzi pushed the ends of his mouth up with thumb and index finger.

'Can I talk with this witness?'

'He waits for us at headquarters.' Al-Fawzi emphasized the second syllable, head-*quar*-ters. It sounded rather nice, Triffler thought.

'On to head*quar*ters.'

They found Keatley outside in the corridor practicing deep breathing. 'Kind of sucker-punched me,' he managed to say. His eyes were teary.

'Put head between knees,' al-Fawzi said.

'Hard to walk that way.' Keatley started up the corridor for the exit.

Over Mombasa.

'You catch that?' Soleck asked. 'I had a signal.'

'Roger, Jaeger Two.' Alan was still blinking. On their third image of the metal shed, something had flashed on the screen. The metal return from the center of the channel was different. Alan played back the computer's last hits on the passive electronic surveillance system.

There were two anomalous hits with vectors that could overlie the area they were targeting.

'Explosion?' Campbell asked from the front seat. They were all MARI veterans, and most of them had used the system while things were blowing up.

'That's what it looked like to me.' Alan ran his cursor over the center of the channel and hit IMAGE again. He ran back the vectors on the ESM and looked at the signals, logging them to the event. 'Everybody see that Charlie 1201 signal?' he called, reading off the alphanumeric ID code.

'Roger. That's nearly in the cell-phone range.' Soleck was puzzled.

'That's a long signal,' Campbell said. 'Did we get the whole thing?'

'We have it on tape and we've been airborne for three hours. I don't think we can claim we're checking hydraulics much longer.'

Opono moved around in his seat like a man trying to find a comfortable spot. 'I think we should go back on the ground,' he said.

Alan spent a moment taking that in. 'David, we have an order to these things. Right now, we take this data back and we scrub it. But off the record, yeah. Yeah, I want to go back. Okay?'

The plane turned hard, the pilot enjoying the excuse to pull a tight maneuver. Alan grimaced.

'Okay,' Opono said.

In ten minutes they were back in the stack over Daniel Arap Moi International Airport. Alan leaned out into the aisle and looked out over the nose as they started their descent. He could see their hangar, with the helicopter next to it. The big bird's rotor blades were turning. He looked at his watch. Time for the afternoon flight to the *Harker*. They had been in the air for four hours.

'You guys have a good story for Air Traffic Control?'

Soleck came up on the link. 'My daddy always says don't tell 'em unless they ask.'

'Roger that.'

Alan sat back and checked his harness for landing, his mind already going through the data and planning his next move. It was time to take the initiative.

Things happen in threes, he thought. *But not if we happen first.*

And he wondered what he had just watched exploding.

Utica, New York.

It was, in Houston, early in the morning for Colonel Brasher's voice to be loud in Rose's ear. He couldn't wait to start shouting, she decided.

'Commander Siciliano?'

'Yes, sir.'

'Well, well.'

She held the phone tight against her ear, as if she could hide the conversation from her parents that way. 'I'm at my parents' house in Utica, New York,' she said.

'I gave you an order to report here, Commander.'

'My orders were changed, sir.'

'Yeah, they were.' Sarcastic, not agreeing.

'I wondered when I should report back, sir.'

'Well, as I'm not writing your orders, I don't give a shit when you report back — how's that?'

Her temper stirred; she pushed it away. 'I don't want to be uncooperative, Colonel. I'm trying to do what's best for everybody.'

'Well, maybe that's your problem. Maybe you ought

to stop worrying about everybody and start worrying about the Johnson Space Center. You've made an enemy of Hansen and his department, I'll tell you that. You know what it's like to be an astronaut that the PR people don't like?' He waited. 'It's like death. But maybe you have pals who can pull strings for you on that, too.'

'I didn't pull strings, sir.'

'I don't like to have people go over my head, Commander. Let me tell you something – you Navy people think you're God's gift to command and control. Well, here we do what we're told and we get along by going along. We don't blue-sky and we don't grand-stand and we don't shoot up the landscape like a bunch of goddam cowboys.'

'I didn't ask to have somebody try to kill me.'

'What you didn't do was let Hansen settle it for you and get your ass back here where you belong and leave all that detective crap to somebody else! You looked like a valuable acquisition – on paper. Female, highly decorated, gunner. You get here and you turn out to be a fucking prima donna.'

She actually stammered. 'I didn't get into the program to be fodder for the PR department!'

'What the hell do you think makes this program run? Without PR, we're toast! If they were all like you, we wouldn't have the annual appropriation of the goddam Tea Tasting Board.'

She waited. He outwaited her. 'I – I don't know what you want me to do.' Again, she waited. After seconds of silence, she said, 'I'm missing training time.'

'Yeah, which reminds me. I looked over your latest test scores. You missed the VO2-Max standard by point-two.'

'That's not true.'

He laughed. 'Tell that to the physiologist. *You missed the VO2-Max standard by point-two.* Is that clear?'

'The technician told me I was good to go.'

'I don't take my authorization from the technician, okay?'

'I don't understand what you're telling me.'

'Two hundred people start this program for every one who makes it into space.'

She heard the flatness of the threat in his voice.

'You understand what I'm saying?' he said.

'Are you saying I'm out?'

'Lots of fine people never make it into space. We need people for lots of jobs here. Two years here can be spent very helpfully flying the weather plane.' Again he waited, and this time she outwaited him. 'You understand what I'm saying?'

'You're saying I'm out of the track for space flight?' She felt as if a hand had been put around her throat and was squeezing.

'All I'll say at this point in time is I wouldn't go out of my way to ask for a waiver on your VO2-Max. Which, without I do so, doesn't make the standard.'

She thought of two years of flying the weather plane. Seeing space flight *from the confines of mission control and our house in Houston.*

'I don't fit the profile,' she said.

'On paper, yeah – in person, you turn out to be a loose cannon.'

'"Too independent."'

'Too individualistic, too mouthy, too committed to some agenda has nothing to do with the NASA mission.'

She was trembling, but she didn't want him to hear

405

it in her voice. 'I need to think, sir. I'd like to end this call now.'

'My pleasure.'

She put the phone into its cradle without a sound. She leaned her forehead against her fist and her fist against the wall. An image of the mean streets through which she'd driven came into her mind. Was it to show them – the nuns, the neighbors, the guys who'd felt her up and told each other she was easy – that she'd wanted to become an astronaut? To get her picture on the cover of a magazine? Articles in the hometown newspaper, arranged by Houston PR? How much of her desire to be an astronaut had been vanity, how much a genuine drive to achieve?

She straightened and tossed her hair back, touched her eyes with a tissue. *He's handed me a lemon – how the fuck do I make the lemonade?*

Malindi.

Geraldine and Sandy learned many things in Malindi: that the woman who called herself Liese had been smuggled into a warehouse near the port to have sex with the watchmen, and the warehouse had been partly filled with zebra and impala hides and ivory and freezers full of some kind of wild meat; that a fisherman's boat went up the coast once a week with half a dozen of the whores on it to service 'soldiers' up there, the girls weren't sure just where – it was all tidal creeks and mangrove; that the 'soldiers' were Africans from many places, but there were also a few whites who bossed everybody.

Then they were talking to the woman who called herself Britney. It was afternoon, hot; they were sitting in the shadowy inside of a *hoteli*, a mud-brick tea shop

406

with rooms in the back. The road smell of tar and gasoline was strong, the tea weak and milky. Britney was skinny but had good breasts and long, oiled hair that she combed with her fingers as she talked. She had been up with the 'soldiers', too, she said. She didn't like them. 'We are not supposed to talk about it,' she said to Sandy in Swahili.

'Why not?' Geraldine said when Sandy had translated. Geraldine's pencil was poised over her yellow pad.

'Because –' Britney shook her head. She made a little gesture with her chin. '*Polisi.*' Then she was gone through the door the tea had come from. Seconds later, two Malindi policemen came in, slitting their eyes against the shadow after the bright sun. They were thin men, tall. It was clear that they didn't intend to be pleasant.

'What are you doing here?' the older one said. They had no guns but carried truncheons.

Sandy seemed unfazed. She didn't get up or even take her feet from the stool they were propped on. Her purse was on the tiny table; she reached in and got her passport and held it up, open. 'US embassy.'

'What are you doing?' He tapped his truncheon on the table. 'What is this woman writing down?' He took the yellow tablet and scowled at it and handed it back to his companion. 'Who is this woman?' he said to Sandy, exactly as if he already knew which of them spoke Swahili.

'She is doing research.' She translated for Geraldine, who got out her passport – the tourist one, not the diplomatic one she used when she was NCIS – and then produced the letters she'd forged the night before. They were colorful, with letter-heads pastiched from the Internet, rather grand in their academic prose, from the University of Southern Arkansas at Chicago, the University of Western California at Seattle, and Harvard Institute of Technology. 'This will introduce Professor Geraldine Pastner, whom we recommend for her on-going research toward a work titled, "The World Sex Industry and Images of Trans-Gender Liberation: Self-Esteem, Object Positioning, and Narrativity."'

The policeman scowled at the letters.

'Tell him it's about sex,' Geraldine said. 'Tell him I'm interviewing prostitutes.'

'I'd say he already knows that.'

The policeman passed the letters back and tapped his truncheon on the table some more. 'You must leave Malindi. You have no authorization.'

'Where do we get authorization?'

'Nairobi. All foreigners must get authorization from Nairobi.'

He kept tapping. Through the *hoteli*'s open front, Geraldine could see two more policemen hassling their driver. 'I think it's time to go,' she said.

Sandy stood. 'Just when I was going to wow him with my sheriff's badge.' She smiled at the two cops and retrieved the letters, but she had to give up the yellow pad, which was being held as 'evidence,' and led the way to the car.

'The fix was in, right?' Geraldine said. 'The cops are on the take, right?'

James said, 'Very bad – very bad men.' All the way back to the Nyali Beach hotels, he kept saying that it was very bad, very bad.

Finally, Geraldine said, 'You'd feel better if you'd taken one of those nice girls up on her offer.'

He shut up.

Cairo.

Al-Fawzi's snitch was a small man who looked rather like Sam Jaffe in *Gunga Din* and had the same puzzled expression. *What is a nice Jewish actor like me doing in a turban?* He came to Triffler's shoulder. He was wearing a white shirt buttoned to the neck but no tie, the trousers from a blue wool suit far too big for him, and Nikes with the counters smashed down so he could wear them as scuffs. No socks.

Al-Fawzi treated him with contempt. 'He has no English,' he said to Triffler. Since Keatley's moment of glory in the morgue, al-Fawzi had started acting as if he wasn't there. 'I speak to him in Arab, he answers, I translate.' He turned to the small man and shouted a single word. The man's eyes widened and his body sagged. Triffler thought, *I wish I could do that.* A rush of Arabic followed, then panicked responses from the witness.

'He says the man, this other man, was tall and European.'

Good, cuts the possibilities way down.

'Silver hair. Gray, anyway. Tall, he keeps saying tall. Not fat. No moustache or beard. Wearing coat, shirt, no tie.'

We got it knocked. The pool must be down to a hundred million or so.

'He thinks French.'

'This guy knows when English is spoken with a French accent?'

More abusive Arabic, more stammering, signs that the man might need air.

'He *heard* him speak French on his cell phone. He says he knows French when he hears it.'

'So where did they go?'

409

'Out. Out of the room.'

Triffler pushed his mouth out and wrinkled his nose as if there was a bad smell. 'And nobody else saw them.'

'Nobody.'

Keatley pushed a big hand between them. 'Ask him if this is the guy.' He was holding one of the photos that Alan Craik had had printed from the television tape.

Al-Fawzi held up the photo. The small man's face lit up. It was extravagantly clear that it was the man.

Triffler looked at Keatley. 'How did you do that?' he said.

'It came to me while you guys were ignoring me.'

'Don't be sensitive.' Triffler had al-Fawzi bully the little man through it once more. Nothing else emerged, except the insistence that the photo was the same man came out even more strongly.

Triffler looked at the back of the photo. 'Jean-Marc Balcon.' He looked up at al-Fawzi. 'Jean-Marc Balcon?' Al-Fawzi shook his head. Triffler looked at the witness. 'Jean-Marc Balcon?' The small man backed away.

'Who is he?' al-Fawzi said.

Triffler looked at Keatley, who said, 'French journalist. TV. Covered the bombing in Mombasa. How do we find out if he covered the bombing in Cairo?'

That was easy, or so al-Fawzi said. There was a government press office that granted credentials. When Triffler heard the word 'government,' he decided it wouldn't be easy.

Still, it was the necessary next step. 'Let's find him,' he ordered.

Near Mombasa.

There was a Kenyan Army checkpoint on the beach road in Nyali. There was another just before the traf-

410

fic circle where the main road turned for the bridge and the city. Geraldine was in front, trying to get their driver to laugh, and Sandy was in the back alone, which made her look like the important one to the soldiers. The soldiers scared Sandy, who had thought herself inured to them, adolescent thugs with guns. They shouted at the locals, and were quieter with tourists, more dangerous when they found the *wazungu* were police. They clearly had orders *not* to cooperate with Americans. The first checkpoint was rough, bad enough that Sandy thought they might beat her driver just to make a point. She got out of the car, afraid but angry, and used her passport and her big, fake badge to get her driver away from a crowd of adrenaline-pumped uniforms and back in the car.

'Needed the badge after all,' she muttered.

At the second checkpoint, she handed over her diplomatic passport with a hundred Kenyan shillings in the fold and they were waved through without any argument.

Geraldine was scandalized. 'Isn't there a State Department directive about engaging in bribery?'

Their driver just looked relieved. Sandy turned her head slightly and gave Geraldine a tight smile. 'Maybe they should send someone out here to remind me.'

The Nyali bridge was jammed, as usual. Somewhere ahead of them, a pushcart had overturned, its load of iron scrap filling the bridge. Young men in loose cotton moved along the lines of cars and *matatus*, and a very young man with a short beard leaned over and looked in at Sandy and then moved on.

A crowd of women in black veils suddenly appeared ahead of them, and then, without warning, there were young men all around the car, and Geraldine had her hand on her gun. Sandy reached out slowly and touched her shoulder.

'Too late for that, I think.'

There were AK-47s pointed at them and bearded faces behind them that meant business.

Geraldine sat frozen, her body fully charged to fight, her hand in her satchel on the grip of her Glock. Nothing moved except the heat off the pavement, and she had time to smell the patchouli on the young man at her door, look at his absurdly beautiful face marred by the passion of his stance, see the sweat on his brow and read his tension from the death grip he had on his weapon.

I'm going to be a fucking hostage, she thought. Her hand was still on the Glock, and her finger was through the trigger, and Sandy's hand was on her shoulder. She thought of shooting. Sandy seemed to have other ideas, and was speaking slowly in Swahili. The young men didn't move, and then there was motion, and a small man in a dark suit burrowed through the crowd of armed men.

'My apologies,' he said, as if the statement was a question. 'The soldiers and the police are working very hard to keep us away from the Americans at the airport and the port is closed and barred. You are with the embassy, yes?'

Sandy nodded. He had sweat stains right through his suit, and dark circles under his eyes. The man looked as if he had seen hell. She couldn't take her eyes off his face. It was like the face of a Byzantine saint. 'Yes, I'm with the embassy.' Geraldine made a grunt of protest, as this admission broke another State Department rule. Sandy had already decided that the little man was not a threat.

'Will you be going to the airport?'

'Yes.'

'Could you please give this envelope to Commander Craik, with my compliments? And tell him that the city will be quiet. Please tell him that we will keep the city quiet as long as we can, but there are others – my views are in the letter. There are those who wish to see a great deal of blood. Tell him that.'

'I will.' She wanted to help him. She believed him.

He called something, and the crowd dispersed almost as fast as it had appeared. James lit a cigarette with shaking fingers. Then he coughed. He had lit the filter.

Geraldine eased her fingers off the butt of her gun as the car moved forward. She had been so close to the edge – so close that it was with her still.

Utica, New York.

At one minute after nine in the morning, Rose was back on the phone. Her detailer was an A-6 pilot doing a shore tour, and a good guy. 'Hey,' he said when she gave her name, 'you're famous.'

'I need some advice,' she said.

'Shoot.' He'd heard *and no bullshit, please* in her voice.

'What have you got if I leave the astronaut program?'

He was silent. He knew, although he hadn't been in on much of it, that she'd been pointing her career for years toward space flight. And then he chuckled. 'Can you leave tonight?' he said.

She didn't get it. He said, 'I've got an urgent need for an O-5 helicopter pilot to take command of a squadron whose skipper fell and broke something. They're on the *Roosevelt* in the Med to replace the *Jefferson* in the Red Sea in five days, and they're hurting.

413

You know how hard it is to find an O-5 who's ready for chopper command? You'd have been my first choice if I'd thought for a second you were available.'

'I couldn't possibly do anything that fast. I haven't even made a decision yet.'

'New guy should have been there yesterday. You know what turnover of a BG is like. Actually, *we* thought we were going to sock the new skipper in while the boat was in the Suez Canal, but there was some glitch and they're still at Haifa. New skipper'll join at Alexandria – don't want him – *or her* – flying to Haifa and finding they just left.'

'I was only thinking.'

'Oh.' His disappointment was clear. 'So, what're you asking me? What are the prospects long-term if you leave Houston, is that it? And what's happened, anyway? You were hot to trot, last I heard.'

'It isn't working.'

'Hey, Rose, if I got the story right, somebody tried to kill you out there – that's bound to screw up your perceptions. You a little depressed, maybe?'

But she was hardly listening. She was thinking that the kids and her parents would be happy with each other. Alan and the *Jefferson* would be home in three weeks. That's all it would be, three weeks. And then – 'How long would the tour with the chopper squadron be?'

'This deployment and a couple months after flyoff. Next skipper is already scheduled in. Say nine, ten months.'

'My husband's tour ends in a month or so and then he goes to be intel to Admiral Pilchard at Bahrain. What would happen to me and the kids then?'

He chuckled again. 'You holding me up for a good

deal, Rose? Well, let me see if I can make you an offer you can't refuse. Just hold the line, okay? – let me check something on another phone and I'll get right back to you –'

She started to say she was only asking for information, but he was gone. She waited for six minutes, during which Reko walked through and they smiled automatically at each other, and her father poked his head into the entrance hall, where the phone was, and saw she was busy and vanished. And then the detailer came back.

'Would deputy naval attaché, Bahrain, tempt you?'

In other circumstances it would have taken her breath away. She said, 'Can you really do that?'

'Special circumstances demand special solutions. I went to the top and got the word: if you'll take the chopper squadron on the *Roosevelt* and save our asses in the BG turnover, I guarantee Bahrain after.'

'And –?' *And bye-bye to the confines of mission control and our house in Houston.*

'I can give you two hours to think it over. But there's a daily flight from Philly to Cairo that's servicing Operation Bright Star, leaving 1800 local. You'd have to be on it, meeting a chopper from the *FDR* in Alexandria, because the boat'll already be heading into the canal, and they can't launch or receive aircraft there. Two hours?'

Tears were in her eyes, but her voice was firm. 'Put me on the flight.'

'Rose –' She heard compassion in his voice and tensed herself against it. 'You sure? No matter what happened in Houston, Christ, you've moved mountains to get there! Even if you had some sort of personality conflict – I'll back you, I'll get other

415

people to back you – Rose, I need a helicopter skipper, but I don't want an officer to throw away something good because of, of – I don't know because of what. Should you see somebody, you know, somebody to talk to?'

'Put me on the flight.' Her voice softened. 'You're a good guy, Perk. But my mind's made up. Call it my moment of truth.' She sighed. *My second moment of truth.* She hung up and called a travel agent about the next plane to Philadelphia – from Utica, no easy matter, but there was one out of Syracuse, an hour away, at one. She went upstairs to pack.

Around midnight Mombasa time there was a flurry of phone calls. First, Rose called Alan from Philadelphia.

'I don't get it!' he shouted.

'I made a decision. I'll get Bahrain; *you'll* be in Bahrain. We'll be a family – two years –'

'You've wanted to be an astronaut all your life!'

'And it didn't work. Don't scold me, honey; I'm worn down as it is. I need you to say I did the right thing –'

The pain in her always husky voice turned him to mush. 'Anything you decide is the right thing.'

'That's what I wanted to hear.' She began to babble: the kids were with her dad; the dog was going to be picked up from the vet's by one of the *nice* people in Houston; she'd be on the *FDR* by the time he finished breakfast.

'God, I won't get to see you for five months,' he said.

Her voice broke. 'I'll wave when we pass the *Jefferson.*'

Langley, Virginia.

The analyst in the African Section who had first noted activity in Sierra Leone had accumulated five more bits of data. Her flag to the Brits had been noted with thanks and two reports from British agents on the ground had been sent. Over the same period, a second Tu-103 had flown into and out of Sierra Leone, filing flight plans to Mauritania for 'used agricultural material.' One of the British agents in Sierra Leone reported 'large groups' of men occupying a disused hangar on the freight side of the airport, with a few whites glimpsed among 'many' Africans. Satellite overflights showed eight pallet-loads of unspecified equipment and four vehicles identified from ground surveillance as Brazilian Jaguars.

The Langley analyst concluded from the continued presence of the Tupolevs that further onward flight was intended. She posted a brief report to Central Command and Sixth Fleet headed: 'Temporary Military Buildup Sierra Leone for Unidentified Onward Deployment.'

At seven that evening local time, LTjg Evan Soleck, avid reader of intelligence digests, read the report in the jury-rigged detachment office at Mombasa. He also read an analysis of residue from the bomb in Cairo, noting it as a match for the C-4 used in the Dhow attack in Mombasa and appending an Interpol report tieing it to more C-4 used in a bomb attack on an Italian federal prosecutor's motorcade. He put both reports in the skipper's read board and filed it all away in his cluttered magpie brain.

14

Mombasa.

It was the down time of night, the hangar quiet, snores rumbling, the African darkness like black velvet around them.

'I want you and your det out of there as soon as we clear this storm, Al.'

'Rafe –' Alan started quietly.

'Listen to me, Al. I'm telling you that I want your det back on this boat as soon as we have a working deck. Probably day after tomorrow. This storm probably won't close the local airport, and it sure as hell won't close Nairobi, and that means you'll have a new crew and salvage for the *Harker* and a special Marine force to cover it. The Kenyans are beginning to ask hard questions about your activity. We need to do our turnover with the *Roosevelt*, and you're a big part of that.'

Roosevelt. Alan had forgotten. End of cruise. Going home. The end of his command. And Rose would be on the *Roosevelt.* He frowned, bit down. This was *Rafe.*

'Aye, aye, sir.'

'Don't aye-aye me, Mister.'

'Sir, we've worked like dogs to get settled here, to stay connected with the *Harker*, and to support Mister Dukas's investigations, and it's like you're pulling us just when we're getting somewhere.'

'Tough, Al. Look, I can give you three days – did I tell you that the *Roosevelt* had an accident in Haifa? So they won't be in the ditch until tomorrow, anyway. Look, Al – I know you've played a big part in this thing. But the cavalry is coming and it's time to use it, okay?'

Alan looked at the cell-phone chart on the wall and nodded, although his mind was already moving to other things. 'Rafe, let me bring you up to speed on our overflight of this poachers' camp.'

'Sure,' Rafe said. 'Shoot.'

Bahrain.
Harry O'Neill called Dukas from Bahrain. Harry was in a room above the desert, looking out over the lights of the city. He had his own STU – in fact, he had his own everything.

'Drugs,' he said.

'No shit?'

'The guy in Lebanon coughed up everything. I believe him – Hizbollah don't fool around when they interrogate somebody. A big buyer – big, Mike, as in biggest – paid him to set up, he says, an Islamic terror group to do his dirty work. They think they're working for al-Qaida. Who they're really working for is a guy in Sicily named Santangelo-Fugosi. That's all I got. Hizbollah didn't want to give me even the name; they want the guy's balls, but I think they know already he's too big for them. *Big* balls. Brass, too.'

'Anything about Cairo?'

'Didn't know – he'd have given it up if he'd known. All he knew was Mombasa and the *Harker*. It's all compartmentalized.'

'What's the bottom line?'

'Drugs.'

420

'How?'

'He didn't get that far.'

'Somalia?'

'Wasn't mentioned. But I'd say, knowing some other stuff – the dhow –' Harry hesitated. 'But if you wanted to do something in Somalia, who'd you have to get past first?'

Dukas didn't even have to think. 'The US Navy, that's who. Jesus.' They were both silent, thinking about it. Finally, Dukas said, 'Need I ask what happened to the Lebanese who spilled his guts?'

'Nice turn of phrase, Mike. "The interrogation was taken to its logical conclusion."' Harry stared at the lights of the city, then at the velvet blackness of the desert. 'Say hello to Al for me,' he said.

Cairo.

Rose got off the plane at Cairo feeling rumpled and disoriented – too much, too fast. She wanted to be *there*, and as she walked out of the customs area and into the terminal, she realized that *there* was now here and she didn't have a next step. She just felt tired. She was certain she had made the wrong choice; long flights in cramped seats are no good for life planning. She was leaving her sons and her sick mother and she was sticky.

'Ma'am?' an American voice said at her elbow. She found herself looking at a gangly boy in a flight suit, with a shock of bright red hair and an enormous nose. 'Ma'am?' he asked again, hesitant. 'Are you Commander, um –?'

'I'm Rose Siciliano,' she barked. 'Commander Um, I'm not. Who are you?'

The boy (she could hardly think of him as anything

else, with his absurdly cherubic face and the nose) reached to take her bag, at the same time twitching in the direction of a salute. He couldn't seem to decide. 'I'm Cedric Llewellyn, ma'am.'

'Have a rank, Mister Llewellyn?' Rose was not giving up her luggage. They were standing in the middle of the terminal, with a thousand other air passengers making a swirl around them. It was hot, even through the air-conditioning. Rose wanted to move on. It had already occurred to her that this must be one of her officers. She shook her head, both inwardly and physically.

'Oh? Oh, sorry, uh, ma'am. I'm a lieutenant, junior grade, ma'am.'

'Mister Llewellyn, in the military we usually greet our superiors with the applicable courtesy and a firm announcement of our rank and purpose. I'll save you time and suggest that you are here to take me to the boat, right? And you have a helicopter?'

'Yes, ma'am.' Cedric shrank, although he still towered over her by a foot. She wondered what recruiting officer had decided Cedric could be a helicopter pilot. He probably had excellent grades. *Nerd*. She shook her head again.

'Where's our bird?'

'Sorry?' Cedric had paused to look at a sign, caught like a crow that has seen a bright object.

'Chopper. Boat. You here with me, Mister Llewellyn?'

'Yes, ma'am.'

'I'm going to use the facilities, and change into a flight suit. Don't wander off.'

'No, ma'am.'

While she changed, she fascinated three Arab

women who were changing from Western street clothes to head-to-toe black shrouding. Rose suspected they were going to Saudi, Yemen, or one of the other fundamentalist states. She wondered what they thought of her, changing into a onepiece with a zipper. Three minutes later, Rose was back in the main hall, dressed in her sage-green flight suit and with her helmet bag strapped to the top of her luggage. She stood at the door to the ladies' room and looked for Llewellyn. She found him at a fancy watch counter fifty yards away, staring blankly at the display.

'I'd leave you here, but I don't know where the plane is,' she said pleasantly. He jumped as if struck. 'Get me to the boat, Llewellyn.'

'Yes, ma'am.'

Mombasa.

Alan walked into the plywood shack that represented the intel area with his good hand full of images and found Dukas alone, reading from a stack of reports. Dukas looked up, flicked his report at Alan in mock salute, and told him what Harry O'Neill had said.

'Drugs.' He looked at Alan, eyes pouched with fatigue, but alert and skeptical. '*Drugs?* Harry thinks it's something about Somalia. Not too far from that cellphone hit and this poachers' camp you guys keep talking about.'

Alan poured some of the coffee. 'That's the camp,' he said. He tossed the MARI images in front of Dukas. 'I'm going to ask Rafe for permission to check it out on the ground.'

Dukas grunted. 'You mean, you're going to ask Rafe to let you hit it.'

'Yep.' Alan looked out the door, past the lounging

423

aircrew and into the evening light outside the hangar. The air was electric, with a taste of ozone and the promise of rain.

Dukas rubbed at the back of his head. 'Show me the connections. Rafe's going to ask, anyway.'

Petty Officer Menendez interrupted, pushing through the open door, his eagerness arriving a little ahead of him. 'Sir! We've been looking at the MARI and we're pretty sure your dead elephants are fuel bladders!' He hesitated then, seeing that the two senior men had been talking. 'Uh – sorry, sir –' But Alan nodded, and Menendez held up an enhancement of one of the MARI images, now pasted on plywood with colored-tape arrows and some inset photographs. 'We don't know much about elephants but, thankfully, Mister Campbell had imaged a whole pack of 'em on the same tape he got the camp. They have a lot more bone and they reflect radar real good.'

He handed Alan a single image printed on standard paper. The elephants were quite clear, especially their heads and tusks. Then, as Alan handed the photo to Dukas, he pointed at his enhancement of one of the 'dead elephants.'

'These things have almost no return at all. According to Mister Opono, the bones would be the last things left behind, not the skins, and they wouldn't ordinarily drag a corpse to the camp anyway, right? Okay. So we looked through some books and the best we can suggest is fuel bladders. Like they expect to refuel a big ship or some planes. And this big tent here? Under the canvas they got three, maybe even four vehicles. Like technicals from Somalia, right? Okay? See the tube? That's a rocket launcher, right? And that, that's some kinda vehicle-mounted gun.

Mister Opono says they wouldn't use these for poaching. Too messy.' He looked at Alan, then Dukas, his eagerness suddenly collapsing. 'That's all we got so far, but we're still working.'

Alan put his hand on Menendez's shoulder. 'You got something, Menendez. Good work.'

'Thanks, sir. Valvano has something for you, too.'

'Send him in.' Alan waved at the door. 'Mike, think of this as a flag brief. We're the flag.'

'Might as well ask for Sandy and Geraldine, then. They have something to say, too.'

Menendez called softly outside the door, then turned back. 'Remember the muezzin calls, sir?' he asked.

'Sure.'

'Remember that MP3 player loaded with the things? The one off the body? After the attack on the USAID office in Cairo, the NCIS guy – I don't remember his name –'

'Triffler,' Dukas growled.

'Him, yeah, he got us more muezzin calls in the data files of one of the guys there. We found they were the *same* muezzin calls again, with a few exceptions. Cryptologists on the boat and back home took those files to the Internet and did things to them, looking for embedded codes, and found nothing.'

Dukas leaned forward and interrupted. 'They did locate the website where the calls originated.'

'Sorry, sir. Sure. But Petty Officer Valvano, here, noted that there were two sets of anomalous muezzin calls. What both sets have in common is that they are posted repeatedly over the last five months, despite having the same digital content. We don't know what one set is, but thanks to Muzari and Valvano, we think we have the other.' Menendez was like an MC at a party, and he looked at Valvano like he was introducing his best act. 'Valvano?'

Petty Officer Valvano was clearly nervous about speaking in front of his skipper, so he stood beside Alan and spoke very softly. 'The one signal – the one I figured out, well, uh, I hope I – anyway, it's, uh, the time of the attacks. Well, minus twelve, I think. Except that once it didn't happen. That's, uh, all.' He gulped, and then breathed loudly, as if he had run a race.

'Thanks, guys,' Alan said. 'Get me Ms Cole and Ms Pastner.'

'Sure thing, skipper.'

Dukas was taking notes.

'Penny for your thoughts?' Alan asked.

'Time to write a threat assessment and put it out to the Nav,' Dukas said, never taking his eyes off the page. 'Cell phones, muezzin calls, fuel bladders, poachers, drugs.' He looked up and shrugged. 'I don't get it. I mean, I see the outline. The bastards hit the DEA clan-destine unit in Cairo. You can walk it back from that and maybe from the cellphone indications for Sicily.'

'What d'you think the camp is?'

'You tell me.' Dukas was writing again.

'I'd know more if I could go check it out. The wounded guy said they got the explosives on the coast, and the camp is on the coast.'

'He could have meant anywhere. Kismayu, even.'

'Like I said, I'd know more if I could look it over.'

'Knock it over, you mean.'

Sandy rapped at the door. Geraldine edged past her, sat on a chair with her legs either side of the back. Just the way Dukas was sitting. Sandy sat on the edge of the plywood table, barely resting her weight, as if afraid it would collapse.

426

Alan finished his thought. 'Yeah, Mike. I want to go in with the means to swing if I have to.'

Dukas waved at Sandy. 'You ready to talk about your interviews?'

Sandy squirmed. Geraldine looked deadpan.

'Sandy and I spent the day with prostitutes,' she said with a glint of humor. 'We interviewed twenty women in Malindi, got six hits on our target area, and took witness depositions from three. I've got to say that the Kenyan prostitute is a cut above her American counterpart in social status; it's a pleasure to interview a sex worker who will meet you in public and isn't afraid of the cops.' She glanced at Mike, who smiled back. 'The important data is that a few of these girls had been to the camp Opono described. They gave me a sketch map that matches our MARI imagery and they could describe the camp's garrison. According to Liese, a Luo girl from upcountry, there are ten or twenty soldiers in the camp, more than there used to be, and most of them are Hutus from Burundi. At least two are white, either South African or European. She also noted that there were three or four men who she thought were from India. Elizabeth, another witness, says the four are from Sri Lanka and won't have sex with African women because they are afraid of AIDS. They are short, have dark skin and very curly hair, and speak good English. They make jokes and flirt but won't have sex.'

When Geraldine mentioned Sri Lanka, Alan stood straighter and Dukas flushed.

'How reliable are these girls?' Dukas asked.

'As reliable as any prostitute. I think they've been there; their sketch map correlates really well to the imagery. Why lie about the rest?'

Dukas was shaking his head. 'What are frigging Tamils doing in Africa?' He looked around. 'Well, they sound like Tamils.' He stood and stretched.

Sandy spoke quietly. 'We were stopped on our way back.' She handed Alan a stained envelope. 'A little local man in a suit. He looked like Christ in an icon. You know?'

Alan nodded. 'Mister Nadek.'

'Maybe. He gave me that and said he'd keep the city quiet as long as he can, but that "there are those who want blood."'

'I'm sure that's true.'

Rain on the hangar roof made a gentle white noise. Alan opened the envelope and read the contents. Toward the end, his smile was wolfish. He looked at Dukas. 'They caught one of their own. He doesn't say much about it, except that the guy was paid a *lot* and it came from out of town.'

'If we had time, and manpower, we could run that down.' Dukas was leaning in the door. Sandy nodded. 'David's waiting to say something.'

Alan nodded, but he didn't move. Instead he thought of Mr Nadek, trying to keep civilization together. And being betrayed by one of his own. Dukas leaned out and yelled for Opono, who walked in and sat with dignity.

'Go ahead,' Sandy said. One of her hands trembled.

'These are poachers up there in that camp.' Opono said it with complete certainty. 'They are Europeans and they are Africans, and they are killers and exploiters and thieves. Evil must be destroyed.' He said that with utter certainty, too, and in the way you express beliefs you are sure everybody who can hear you shares. They didn't share, however; there was a

428

little flutter of looks and nervous movements, these people not accustomed to leaping from intelligence estimates to the idea of evil. Opono saw their reaction; he folded his hands and said by way of explanation, 'I am a Christian.' He said it in the way that an African would say it to Africans and be perfectly understood, but they weren't Africans and they didn't understand that he was telling them that he believed in good and evil and a Biblical idea of war.

Sandy Cole looked at him as if she was hearing him from hell; she twisted a pencil in her soft fingers. It broke with a snap.

Alan looked at Opono.

'Would you go on a reconnaissance with us to investigate that camp?'

Opono smiled. 'I would be happy to lead it myself.'

'Call Rafe now,' Dukas said.

USS *Thomas Jefferson*.

Rafe sipped cold coffee and thought of the old Navy saying, *Fair winds and following seas*.

'Sir, I have a call for you from Commander Craik on the radio.'

Captain Rafehausen turned in his chair and waved to the messenger. He was on the bridge of the USS *Thomas Jefferson*, watching rollers that had been born five thousand miles to the east roll at him like walls of water and then pass under the bow. *Jefferson* was steaming straight into the wind and waves, and spray was breaking over the flight deck from every wave. So far, she hadn't buried the bow. Putting the bow into a wave would wreak havoc with the deck and smash the two forward catapults, wrecking the *Jefferson* as a fighting ship for weeks.

Rafe knew that it was better to have a sea like this under his stern. A following sea. But that would bring the shore of Kenya, six hundred miles to the west, too close for the battle group commander's peace of mind.

In the big command chair above him, the captain of the ship conned her, trying to outguess the rollers and the wind, trying to ride the tops of the waves, keeping the great ship steady in thirty-foot-high waves.

And they hadn't even hit the *storm* yet.

'Got you, Al. Give it to me.'

'Sir, we think we've located a base from which the attack on the *Harker* was launched.'

Rafehausen smiled when Al Craik called him 'sir'. But he nodded when he heard the content. 'Where?'

'North coast of Kenya. It's a known poaching camp, a place the Kenyan government – well, part of the Kenyan government – has wanted to clean out for a couple of years.'

'What does poaching have to do with terrorism, Al?'

'Stick with me, Rafe, this ain't easy. One, we have a witness who can maybe put the dhow that made the attack at this camp on the day. Two, we have witnesses who have been in the camp and provided us with information about it. Three, I did a recce via MARI and got images of fuel bladders and other precursors for a follow-on attack. There's more, real nuts and bolts.'

'What's Mike Dukas say? And who did this, Al? Islamic fundamentalists, or other?'

'Other, Rafe.' Alan recapped the information for him, leaning hard on the MARI data, the fuel bladders, and the cell-phone connections. 'Mike says he wants evidence from this camp, Rafe. We think this whole thing is about drugs. It's all bought and paid for, Rafe: Kurds and Tamils and Pakistanis. At home they'd be terrorists. In this case, I think they're unwitting mercenaries.'

'You got a plan?' Rafe winced as he watched a fountain of spray leap ninety feet over the deck, but the carrier's knife-edge prow cut through the top of the great wave and the ship began to race down the far slope, gravity pushing her faster than her skipper wanted. Five feet from Rafe, he bellowed for the screws to reverse. Rafe had to put a hand over the earphones. 'Repeat your last? I'm losing you.'

'Two planes and a helicopter and some gas.'

'What?' Rafe was shouting. One of the bridge hatches had slammed open and four sailors were wrestling it back closed.

'No – draulics and –' Alan said. 'But I need the Marines. I'll have Kenyan rangers as scouts and their boss will be the –'

'Jesus!' the ship captain gasped.

Rafe turned and looked out. The next wave wasn't a wall. It was a mountain. He had heard the phrase 'mountain of water' before and had never seen such a thing in fifteen years at sea. Even two wave crests away, it towered over the other waves like a nightmare.

'Rafe?'

Rafe was silent. After his exclamation, the *Jefferson*'s captain was silent, too. Rafe had enough sea time to know he had nothing to contribute, but he didn't have the sangfroid to talk to Al Craik while the wave did its work. 'Wait one, Al. Mother Nature has done herself proud. We're about to climb a fifty-foot wave.'

'Jesus!'

'Been said,' Rafe snapped, reverting to aviator calm under pressure. Then he watched as the bow rose and

431

rose, until his weight seemed to be on his back and he wondered if the ship could fall off the wave. He wanted to look behind and see what the trough looked like, but there was no monitor for the stern. They continued to climb. Rafe watched the ship's angle on an analogue device installed above the captain's chair and wondered if there was some magic number at which the whole ship would flip or sink. Fifteen degrees? It didn't seem like much to an aviator.

And then he could see the sky over the top of the wave, and in a flash of lightning the tension on his back eased and they were over the crest, level for a moment, and then racing down the other side. A squall hit, blanking out vision, and the rain pounded at the bridge windows like bullets.

'Rafe?'

Rafehausen let go a deep breath he hadn't been aware of holding. 'Still here, Al. You want to take Marines in on the ground?'

'Roger that.'

'And you'll get evidence that might prevent another attack?'

'That's what I'm saying.'

'But this place is in Kenya. So you'll be launching an armed attack on Kenyan soil?'

'Yes, sir. But we'll have a Kenyan government officer with us, and his authority.'

'Can you make them shoot you first?'

'– again?' They were on their way down the slope again, less steep than the last one, but it still caused a loss in radio contact. Rafe waited until they were past the trough. 'I want them to shoot first. If there's shooting, make damn sure you can tell me they fired first.'

'Roger that. But I need some stuff. Big stuff.' He

heard Alan start to talk faster as he got to his requirements. 'I need an armed F-18. I need one of the smallboys. I might need medical and I might need a brig in US territory.'

Rafe watched the ocean roar by in awesome majesty and contemplated the order that would send one of his fragile escorts – a 'smallboy' – in a long turn across the front of these incredible seas, back toward a lee shore. It could be done, with consummate seamanship, luck, and more luck.

'Do you *want* a smallboy, or do you *need* one?'

'I *need* one, Rafe. If I capture anybody over the rank of peon, Mike Dukas doesn't want him going to Kenya. Can you hear me?'

'Roger, Al, I copy.' Rafe looked out at the water again and thought, *This is why I get the big bucks. 'Esek Hopkins* is northwest of me. I'll get her turned toward you. Why do you *need* an F-18?' He couldn't keep a hint of sarcasm out of his voice.

'Say again?'

'I would have to launch an F-18 in the next hour, before the deck closes. Even now, Al, I have intermittent forty-foot seas and freak waves. You copy that?'

'Roger.'

'You still want me to send a pilot off?'

Pause.

'Yes, sir.'

Rafe's voice was solemn. 'Okay, Al. I'm going on your judgment here.' Ten years of friendship in that sentence. And a warning: it could be both their careers. 'You go do what you have to do.' He paused. 'You remember what I told you this morning? It still stands. I want you out of there as soon as we have a working deck again. You got that? We're going to be late meeting the *Roosevelt* as it is. And this action of yours will have consequences with Kenya. No way it can't – right?'

'Roger that, Rafe.'

'And I promise you, I'm looking at the great-grandmother of all storms here. Due to hit me in four hours and your coast in sixteen. Get it done before then and get ready to move. God bless.'

'I copy on the storm. Thank you, sir. Craik out.'

Rafehausen held him with his voice. 'Al, I don't need to tell you we're putting lives on this and it's all down to you, right?'

Hundreds of miles over the stern behind him, Alan Craik was silent as the weight of the responsibility settled on his shoulders. 'Got it, Rafe.'

'Out here, Al.'

Rafe turned his back on the storm and waved to one of the bridge runners. 'Get me Chris Donitz from VFA-231,' he said. 'And get me some coffee.'

In the dimness of the det office, Alan left his hand on the phone and looked at Dukas. The light was pooled on the tables; where Dukas sat against a wall, it was more dark than light. 'We're a go,' Alan said.

Dukas nodded, frowned, nodded again. He stood, stretched. 'I'm done here, then. The job's in Cairo now.'

'You leaving?'

'Morning flight.'

'Better hit the rack.'

Dukas waved at his laptop. 'I want to get this threat out to the Nav. I want that done before I go to sleep.'

They looked at each other. Alan stood. 'I may not see you in the morning. I want to be up there at first light.'

Dukas nodded again and put a hand on Alan's shoulder. He seemed about to say something and then didn't. He patted the shoulder once. 'You be careful up there.' Their eyes met, and Dukas's hand tightened. He looked old in the poor light. 'You be very, *very* careful.'

Day Five

15

USS *Franklin D. Roosevelt*, **Suez Canal.**

Rose couldn't find Alan anywhere, and time was running out. Someone was going to do *something*. She looked again behind her seat, looked under the control pedals, looked out the big canopy into the swirling gray on the other side and then felt a growing panic as she realized that she was trapped in her seat and the chopper was sinking, was going to roll over any moment and pin her to drown.

She turned her head and saw her son in a small flight suit, belted into the copilot seat and pointing at something on his side of the canopy. She grabbed at him and something resisted her, and Mikey said, 'Ma'am! ma'am!' and she came awake at last, wrapped in her sheet and with her free arm grasping the flight suit of a small woman.

'Ma'am!' the woman said, backing away.

Tara something, Rose thought muzzily. A dim memory of meeting the woman in the ready room last night. She checked her watch. Three hours ago. The dream was still with her and her heart was going as if she had run a race.

The little woman's flight suit said 'Hunyadi.' *Tara Hunyadi*.

'There's an alert, ma'am. They want two birds in the air, two alert five's on deck, and door gunners. Ma'am.

XO said to wake you.' Tara pushed a stainless-steel mug of coffee at her. 'Sorry to wake you like that.'

'Not your fault. Bad dream.' Rose slugged down a third of the coffee, the dream receding as she drank. 'What kind of alert?'

'Terrorist threat warning from DNI. It's not very specific, but the message said it could be directed at this ship.'

Rose handed her the cup and pulled a flight suit off the back of the door. She stepped into her boots and pulled the Velcro tabs closed, wiped her face with astringent, and pulled her black hair back with a hair tie. 'You my copilot, Hunyadi?'

'Yes, ma'am.'

'Let's walk.'

USS *Thomas Jefferson.*

Chris Donitz looked like any aviator not on the flight schedule – rumpled. He was at the end of his second sea tour, enjoying his last months of freedom before he got his promotion to lieutenant-commander and had to do work besides flying. Rafe thought he'd probably been in his rack, asleep, and for a moment Rafe envied the shorter man.

'I need you to fly.'

Donitz's sleepy eyes focused. His spine straightened and he was four inches taller. He looked out of the bridge window and back, but all he said was, 'Okay.'

'Al Craik is going to launch some kind of strike against the guys who did the *Harker* attack. He's going in on the ground, but he wants an armed F-18 to fly cover. I want you to get a plane you like and take a full load of gas, two iron bombs, and maybe a HARM if you think you can get it off the deck in this shit.

Once you're airborne, you call an emergency. Up to you what you call; I'd stick with hydraulics, because the Kenyans must be used to that by now. Use the emergency to land at Mombasa. That way the Kenyans can't tell you *no*.'

'Roger that, sir.'

'Get it done, Chris.'

'Aye, aye, sir.' Donitz gave Rafe a smile that burst into a grin. Rafe thought, *I used to be the one they picked for these stunts. Now I get to send others.*

Three hundred miles north and west of the battle group, the skipper of the *Esek Hopkins* listened to his acting battle-group commander grimly. *Esek Hopkins* wasn't a three-hundred-yard-long supercarrier with built-in stability and deep draft to ride the rollers; she was a forty-one-hundred-ton frigate with a tendency to roll too far in heavy seas, and *Captain* Rafehausen had just ordered her to turn across the massive waves and head for the lee shore.

Tom Bento – captain by position on the ship, commander by rank – braced himself as the ship gave a buck like a horse and watched yet another cupful of coffee splash on the deck. The cup was still securely in his hand. He touched the rosary that hung from his command chair and started to give the orders that would turn the ship. He held up his hand to the helmsman and leaned out to watch the rollers, still only twenty feet high this far west.

'Stand by,' he called, waiting to cross the crest. Then they were over and into the full force of the wind, which he intended to use to get his stern around before the next roller came. The ship would ride better with the rollers under the stern, too; he had that in his favor.

On the other hand, in twelve hours, he'd have less than twenty miles between his keel and the coast.

He looked around the bridge, where every sailor was braced, some harnessed to their stations. He felt a subtle change in the motion of the ship, a feeling that told him he had reached the moment.

'Execute,' he ordered, and the ship began to turn.

Donitz had flown F-14s in the north Norwegian Sea and he had punched off a deck in high winds and heavy seas, but he had never worn a harness just to get to his plane. The wind over the deck was coming in excess of sixty knots. Donitz knew from experience what that would mean to his lift off the cat. To further complicate matters, he would have to time his launch with the height of the bow so that the catapult didn't shoot him into a wave front. In the dark.

All in a day's work.

He got soaked checking his plane and wished he had had the time to preflight in the comparative safety of the hangar deck. The plane looked good, although the constant stream of wind-whipped spray couldn't be good for anything. He got in and wrestled the canopy closed and enjoyed a moment of calm, then felt the action of the wind on the wings. He could almost take off without the cat. He got the engines started and raced through his checklist, eager to get the job done.

He was nervous.

He rolled on to the cat and felt the familiar vibration as the storm-harnessed sailor under the nose linked his nose gear to the catapult's shuttle. A burst of salt water marked their arrival at the bottom of the trough between two waves, and a net of spray leaped over the bow and fell on the plane and deck crew, obscuring Donitz's view of the launch officer. The catapult took the weight of the plane, and the nose came down like a feline ready to make a leap on its prey.

Tension.

The bow was rising. Chris scanned his instruments and took his engines to full power, his head moving and his eyes scanning steadily across the board and the heads-up display, noting again the presence of a 500lb bomb under each wing. He had a full bagload of fuel and he was heavy to launch, although the high wind whipping over the deck would aid him. He pushed and pulled the stick, driving all the control surfaces through full rotation and back to position for takeoff. They felt a little sticky, which was rare in a fly-by-wire airplane, but he took it as the result of an unexpected dose of seawater.

Bow rising faster. Touched the lock on his harness, eyes on the engine power one last time, a thought that he missed the old days in the F-14 when he had another guy to share the responsibility of a tough launch, and then an inconsequential thought that in the old days, sailors would wait for the top of the roll to get the most range out of a cannon. A little feeling of sag, or less acceleration up the wave.

Top of the roll. As he moved his eyes, he saw something he didn't like on the board in front of him, something that caught at his attention even as his hand went up to give his salute, snap –

Click, thud. And down the deck, zero to one hundred and twenty miles an hour in sixty feet. Left turn away off the cat, the water already far below. It was like launching out over a cliff, the ocean was so far down. The wind punched at him and he fought it, the back of his neck suddenly cold as he realized that he was fighting his controls; they were sluggish, and far below, the black water rolled on and the carrier started down the next slope toward the trough. His hydraulics were *really* bad.

He mentioned his control issue tersely while he brought the nose around. He continued to climb, already sure that he could not put the plane back on the carrier with controls like this and sure he wouldn't try. He could cross the distance to the beach in an hour. Unless the plane quit altogether, he'd get there. On the boat, the other guys usually called him 'Donuts,' but his other handle was 'the Dutchman.' They meant he was a stubborn bastard. He swept his eyes over the board again, thought about ditching the plane. Death sentence. No chopper could fly in this, and no one would be there to pick him up.

He got up on the guard frequency, calling Kenya Air Traffic Control and declaring a hydraulics emergency. He even got to laugh at the irony. Then he buckled down to the task at hand, six hundred miles out over a killing sea.

Rose kept the chopper level, so low that her down-draft flattened the water. The searchlight gave the water a transparency it lacked under normal conditions. She eased forward another few feet.

On either side of her two more helicopters swept the water, looking for mines, swimmers, anything that might be used to attack the ship. Behind them loomed the bulk of the *Roosevelt*. She was well into the entrance of the canal now, too late to turn around and go back. On her high flight deck, her Marine det were setting up a 30mm grenade launcher at a

444

forward mount, while lights on the bridge wings searched the shore.

'I wish we knew what we were looking for,' Hunyadi said.

Cairo.

In Cairo, Triffler was waked by his bedside telephone from a dream of basketball, a game he was playing with his son and several beautiful girls. It was a wonderful dream, like a TV sitcom, bright-colored and super-real and *happy*. He hated the telephone after it. He looked at his bedside clock, saw that it was one in the morning, hated the clock, as well.

'Triffler.'

'Here it is Sergeant al-Fawzi.'

'Yes, Sergeant.'

'We found the journalist, Mister Jean-Marc Balcon.'

Triffler woke up all the way. 'In Cairo?'

'He is in the city of Ismailia. He went to there day after death of the regrettable vic, Bob Cram.'

'Ismailia's on the canal.' Triffler's three weeks with Bright Star hadn't been wasted: he could see the Egyptian map, Ismailia halfway down to Suez from Port Said. 'How long to get there?'

'Two hours by car, drive very fast – straight road. But – I am Cairo cop, not national – jurisdiction is –'

'This is *my* jurisdiction, Sergeant. You come along as my guest, okay? And we'll take three hours to get there, because I'm driving.'

Two minutes later he was on the phone to Dukas, and then he was on the phone trying to rent a car, an impossible task in Cairo at nearly one in the morning, so he settled for waking Patemkin, the CIA man from Nairobi, and directing him to get them an unmarked car ASAP; and only then did he remember to wake Keatley and tell him that they were leaving town within the hour.

Off the Kenyan Coast.

Once Donitz had the plane straight and level, it was less of a fight to keep her in the air, and the flight passed in a tangle of control issues and vague prayers to the god of control surfaces to keep enough hydraulic fluid in the system to get him on the deck. He called ahead, savvy enough to keep the information about his armament to himself. He doubted that Kenya would check his plane at 0200L.

Then he was feet-dry over Nyali, the remembered pleasures of a beer at the Intercon a fleeting thought as he used his airspeed more than his control surfaces to descend. He made a clearing turn well out over the countryside, declined the tower's guidance for approach and asked instead for a straight-in, a simple approach that would keep him clear of traffic in the stack where he might have to make sudden maneuvers and equally clear of inhabited areas. He assumed from the feel of the controls (fly-by-wire, and thus not really telling the full story) that every motion pushed more of his precious hydraulic fluid out of the leak. His airplane was bleeding to death.

He started a long, slow turn to the north to get him to the end of the vector he had marked in his head for his approach. The plane shuddered and he corrected, twice, each time returning the controls to the same position. The second time, the surfaces played along and he was in the curve he wanted. Air Traffic Control tried to badger him and he gave them short answers. He hoped he sounded like a man flying a damaged airplane. Out east, over the ocean he had just traversed, there was a flash of distant lightning, but here it was calm. He traded a little more speed for altitude. His engines were fine.

Now turning again. This time he had next to no response from his portside control surfaces, and the plane shuddered again and Chris wondered if she would simply miss the envelope of aerodynamics and fall out of the sky. It was the principle danger with all fly-by-wire aircraft – without a computer and a constant guidance, the plane wouldn't really fly. He started to make corrections to end his turn and the shuddering got worse; the plane gave a buck in the air and he corrected and then he was good for lineup, his nose a little high but otherwise okay. He eased up more on the throttle.

Shudder. Buck. Twist.

Whatever it was, his plane was dying on him a mile short of the runway, and he *would not let it.* He had no intention of dropping a thousand-plus pounds of explosive and a burning jet on a friendly country. He corrected, then corrected again. The shuddering became constant and changed in pitch, so that Donitz wondered if he might have physical control-surface damage, as well. Now the whole plane was vibrating like a car with unbalanced tires.

Bam!

It was not his classic, top hook, three-point landing, and it sent a bolt of pain straight up through his spine. He started to slow the plane with engines and, later, brakes, no hint of flaps, still afraid even now that something could fail catastrophically before he had rolled out. He missed the sudden comfort of the three wire. On the boat, when you were down, you were *done.*

447

On the beach, you got to play one more inning. When the airspeed fell below twenty knots, he took a deep breath and relaxed his hands, flexing his fingers on the stick.

He taxied, called the tower, got permission to roll straight to Al Craik's det, and his ground speed fell below anything that his plane could use to generate further terrors.

He opened his canopy to a warm summer's night full of exotic smells and more than a hint of moisture and decay. It seemed like a reward.

Al Craik was standing beyond the ground crew, waiting. Donitz powered down the plane, waved the crew boss over, and took him, an S-3 guy, over the control-surface issue.

'I'm on it, sir. The skipper wants to see you.'

'I'll bet he does, Chief.' Donitz tossed his helmet to a guy on the ground, stuffed his kneeboard and some pens into his helmet bag, and reached behind him for his dop kit. Then he climbed out of the plane, retrieved his helmet, and went to Craik, who was looking at the F-18.

'You'd get an Academy Award for that performance,' Al said as Donitz approached. 'Chief Bakin is probably looking at your hydraulics right now!'

'Sir, I have some good news and some bad news.'

'Can I offer you an MRE? Okay, give it to me.'

'My plane is Tango Uniform. The hydraulics are totally fucked, and the fly-by-wire isn't so good, either.' Donitz suddenly sagged, his knees weak. A little *post-traumatic*, he thought wildly.

'There goes your Academy Award. Hey, you okay?'

'Sorry. Yeah. Tired, I guess, sir.'

'What's the good news?'

'I brought the bombs.'

'Yeah?' Craik stopped on the tarmac. 'And?'

'I'll bet your crew chief could rig a cradle and put them on the S-3s.'

Alan Craik was heading back toward Chief Bakin before Donitz finished his sentence.

USS *Franklin D. Roosevelt,* in the Canal.

Rose pulled her comm cord, tossed it in her helmet bag, and followed Hunyadi out of the chopper. The night was more gray than black as searchlights probed the banks on both sides of the canal and lights filled the sky in the towns on the Egyptian shore. It was like sailing through a city.

Rose walked across the crisp new nonskid to the side, down a ladder to the catwalk that ran around the flight deck, and a third of the way down the ship. In the north Norwegian Sea this walk could be dark and dangerous, with the sea rising forty feet below, but tonight it was like walking out on a balcony in a city. She got to the entrance to the O-3 level and went in, then followed Hunyadi down the passageway to their ready room. Hunyadi was a competent pilot, had a sense of humor, was still at the age where she ran on hormones, but Rose already liked her.

'I thought that plane was a little mushy, didn't you, skipper?' Hunyadi called over her shoulder.

Skipper. Rose glowed, even under jet lag and a two-hour nap-of-the-earth flight in alien waters.

'Mostly I thought I was mushy, Tara. The plane felt fine.'

'I can hear my rack calling already!'

They came to the cross-corridor: left to the ready room, right to the command spaces.

'Don't get your hopes up, Tara. Get me coffee and a slider, stop in CVIC and give a debrief.'

'We don't debrief. Who debriefs helo guys?'

'Stop in CVIC and give a debrief, then get back to the ready room. Unless that threat has been canceled, we'll be in the air again as soon as the plane is checked.'

'Sorry, ma'am, but no one ever asked me to do a debrief.'

'Just do it.' Rose smiled to take the bite out. 'Okay, Tara. In a terrorist-threat situation, when the helos are the only things flying and the ship is trapped in the canal with nowhere to run or hide, everyone wants information. Trust me. They'll want your debrief.'

'Okay. Sorry.' Tara smiled. 'I can be an airhead.'

Female insecurity. Not time for her lecture. 'Just do it.' She turned left for the ready room. Tara turned right.

Jack Rickets was waiting inside the door. He was part of her old life, pre-Alan, a guy she had flown with time out of mind, since they were both nuggets, and now her XO. He was the only guy in the whole squadron she knew from before, but if she had been allowed to pick one, it would have been Jack.

'Heya, skipper,' he said, and whacked her shoulder. *Skipper*. He said it in such an unaffected way, too. She gave him a quick hug. 'Good to see ya, Jack.'

'Sorry I was in my rack when you got here, but I was beat. Look, you okay to fly round the clock? Jet lag can be a killer.'

'I'm cool. When do you have me up again?'

'Next event. You cool with Hunyadi?'

'I like her. You?'

'Yeah.' A loaded *yeah*, like something he would tell her later. 'And I get to fly with Llewellyn. You guys have nine zero three for surface search. Nine zero three will have a big searchlight and a fifty cal.'

'Got any traffic for me to read?'

He handed her a flimsy. 'New message says Ismailia,' he said. Jack picked up his helmet, gave her arm a squeeze, and got his bag. 'Sorry to hear about the astronaut thing, but it sure is good to have you back in a real Nav, Rosie.'

'Thanks, Jack. Good to be here.' Then her eye went down the flimsy and ice touched her spine. 'Ismailia means it's us, Jack.' She meant the carrier.

'You been away too long, Rosie. These terrorist things never amount to anything.'

Rose wanted to agree, but at the bottom of the flimsy was a name, and the name was *Dukas*.

'Jack, this one's for real.'

16

Mombasa.

Alan had ordered that the hangar be kept dark so their preparations would be less visible to the Kenyan Air Force next door. He leaned against the bulkhead and watched the aircrews move quietly around their tarmac, the pilots using shipboard red flashlights to preflight their planes.

Once they were in the air, the decisions would come thick and fast, and he tried to anticipate them, to be familiar with the possible failures that would create conditions that would force decisions. Choppers could have mechanical failures. Men could be sick. Would he go without the S-3s? Would he go if the skipper of the *Esek Hopkins* couldn't make his rendezvous? Who were the critical personnel? He shook his head at his own nerves. Since his last conversation with Rafe, the whole weight had settled on his shoulders. For a moment, it all looked foolish; eighteen Marines and five Kenyan rangers, one SEAL and an intelligence officer against an unknown objective and a terrorist foe.

And my aircrews, exposed to God knows what. And Esek Hopkins *riding the storm.*

He began to pat his pockets, checking his gear for essential items, a ritual for him now. At his feet lay a Marine ruck-sack, still an alien piece of kit. He flipped through the few items in it, squatted down on his heels.

He smiled as his hand found the smooth plastic shape of his fishing kit, a rare survival item that had been issued to him as he prepped for his first combat mission, the night his father had died over Iran.

He had taken it on every deployment since. Now he pushed it deep in the pack as he felt somebody grab his elbow.

'Skipper?'

Alan raised his head to find Soleck standing at something like attention. Even in the near dark, his posture said he was nervous. Alan stood and dusted his hands.

'Evan?'

'Sorry, sir. I'm sure you have better things –'

'Spill it, Evan. What's eating you?'

'I want to have a really great wetting-down,' Soleck blurted.

Alan took a moment to understand what Soleck was saying. *Wetting down* was not a concept close to the surface of his thoughts. Then he got it – the wetting-down party to celebrate Soleck's making lieutenant. *Now?*

'We're about to drop bombs on terrorists and you're worried about your wetting-down party?'

'Yeah. See, I want it to be something great, sir. Something guys will talk about, remember, say to each other – *Hey, Spike! Remember when Soleck did that great party?*'

Alan thought back to his own party and a few others. The party he remembered best had been in Scotland, on Mull. Rafe had been there. He couldn't even remember if that had been a wetting-down. He started to say that now was not the time for this, and then he thought of being so young – and of being brilliant, bumbling Soleck. 'Nothing's coming to me, Evan. A really good party usually just happens. You can't make it. It's like – like an operation.'

Soleck moved in the dark. 'Like an operation?'

'You need luck. You plan, you prepare, and you train and get stuff together. The better you plan, the more likely you are to get the luck, but you still need it. I've heard guys say *You earn the luck with sweat*. See?'

'Sure,' Soleck said, his tone lacking conviction.

'So pretend it's a mission. Where do you start planning?'

'In CVIC? On a map?'

'Bingo. The first thing is where. Move on from there. Like you were in mission planning.'

Soleck brightened. 'Where are we taking our homebound liberty? Can you tell me?'

'I'll tell you when this is over. Okay?'

'Thanks, skipper. I don't want to let everyone down.'

Alan looked at the first ribbon of the dawn in the sky, and spoke softly into the last of the night. *'Neither do I.'*

He turned and lifted his rucksack, and Fidelio was there.

'You ready, skipper?' Fidelio was *on*. He had an edge to him, like a drug addict on a high.

'I'm still not sure why you're on this trip, Fidel.'

'You need a bodyguard. And I have more training than all of these gyrenes put together. They're nice boys, but –'

'I don't need a cowboy.' Alan watched him for a moment, the edge and the macho and the *desire*. 'But yeah. I'm glad to have you.'

'The muhreens are all ready to load. The gunny was just wondering if you wanted to say anything.'

Alan hadn't thought about it, but he could see that

both NCOs thought it was a good idea. 'Sure. Give me a minute.' He carried his kit over to the helicopter and handed it up to the AW. When he turned away from the plane, he found Sandy watching him from the edge of the light by the hangar. She walked towards him her posture slouched, her approach wary, as if she was scared of him.

'Can I have a minute, Commander?'

Over her shoulder, the whole force was waiting under the bright hangar lights, rucksacks up and on their shoulders, rifles slung. Every face was turned toward him, like a group shot for a cruise book.

'I need to talk to them, Sandy.'

She walked away quickly, her hands closed to fists at her sides.

Alan squared his shoulders unconsciously and walked into the hangar.

'Gentlemen.' His first skipper had always called everyone, sailors, women, officers, anyone he addressed as 'gentlemen.' Now it popped out. 'This is a reconnaissance in force. Our mission is to gather enough evidence to prove a link between a terrorist group and organized crime elements here in Kenya and abroad. We will accomplish that mission most directly by taking their camp and searching it at leisure.

'On no account will we fire first. If the camp turns out to be full of poachers with no ties to the attacks here, then we let the Kenyans under Mister Opono handle them. If these are our terrorists, they'll react with force. Once any element of the force has been fired at, the gloves are off. Any questions?'

They'd all been briefed, the leaders three times. None of them showed much in the way of a reaction. Alan smiled suddenly, and many of them smiled back.

'Let's go,' he said, without emphasis. It hadn't been much as a rousing speech, but Gunny Fife gave him a thumbs-up.

The gunny said something to his troops, and the Marines responded with a loud 'Hu-ah!' and began to file off toward the plane.

Alan had already turned away to find Sandy. She was right against the hangar doors, standing in the narrow space between a stack of MRE crates and the door tracks as if she was trying to hide.

'What can I do for you?' he asked. He could see as soon as the words left his mouth that this was going to be hard. Far harder than saying a few words to the troops.

'Please don't let David go,' Sandy begged. 'I don't want him to go.'

'I need him.'

'You don't need him! Take somebody else!'

'He's our authorization, Sandy. He makes it a KWS mission.'

She was weeping. 'Please – please don't take him –'

He stood and watched her weep. This was how he bought David Opono from her, by standing there mutely, taking her sobs like blows. He wanted to say, *I'll bring him back*, but he hadn't brought Craw back, and he wouldn't ever say that again.

When she had run down and the sobs were only small convulsions of her shoulders, he turned and walked toward the helicopter.

USS *Franklin D. Roosevelt*, Suez Canal.
Five minutes later and two thousand miles away, Rose worked the stick on her second bird in as many hours and pushed the throttle forward and then brought it back down. 'She looks good to me.'

Hunyadi gave her a thumbs-up.

'Everybody set back there?' She had a new door gunner and she didn't even know his name yet. And a rescue swimmer. She'd made the call; more eyes on the water was better in every way. All of them had night vision. The deck looked like a tangle of bouncing green blobs and she flipped hers up on her helmet.

'Ops says we're good to go. Search box three.'

Rose lifted the bird off the deck smoothly, a constant acceleration without any bumps, and flew over the bow, the huge shape of the carrier lit from below by the lights of the buildings along the canal. The carrier was crawling at less than five knots by canal regulation.

Her copilot glanced at her hands on the control, wondering when, if ever, she would be that good at a takeoff.

Rose felt the plane alive under her hand. Even with the fatigue and the mission and the threat, she felt her heart rise with her bird. She leaned into her turn and in a moment they were over lights and land, a situation disorienting to a naval pilot. She glanced at her kneeboard to confirm that box three was, indeed, off the bow.

Hunyadi hit the intercom button to keep her comment to the cockpit. 'Ma'am? Is this a drill? Or for real?'

Rose chuckled deep in her throat. 'This is for real, Tara.' She remembered the first time she had confronted the reality of what military service meant. She brought the plane level and said, 'Welcome to the real Navy, Tara.' She hit the intercom switch. 'Night vision off!' she ordered to the whole plane and thumbed the searchlight.

Somali-Kenyan Coast.

Up above a thousand feet, where the recon team had made the cold transit from Mombasa, the first light had been visible out to the east. It wasn't much light, because the typhoon was coming. Dawn was a hint at the edge of a sky devoid of stars.

The SH-60 helicopter went in with the last of the night, well inland from the poachers' camp and away from the nearest cluster of *bandas* that marked a Guryama tribal village. Out to sea, the two S-3s, loaded for bear, cruised above the storm-forced breakers, their MARI systems off, and the *Esek Hopkins* made its heavy way along a lee shore.

Alan was standing in the cockpit door with a borrowed flight helmet on his head and a borrowed comm cord plugged into the copilot's seat, listening to Soleck in Jaeger One. He touched the mike on his helmet.

'Ready, Jaeger One?'

'Roger.'

'Go active.'

'Going active and imaging. I have the target on image,' Soleck said, and then Alan heard something from the other plane that was too broken up to follow. His adrenaline began to rise. The helicopter was slowing, the sound of the great rotors changing to a lower note and the nose sinking so that Alan had to grab the doorframe. Both chopper pilots had their night-vision devices on and flipped down. Alan felt the press of a body behind him and looked back to see the bulk of the Marine lieutenant in the red light of the cargo bay.

'One minute,' one of the pilots shouted and Alan shouted it again for the lieutenant. He gave Alan a thumbs-up and disappeared into the cargo bay, where his men were sitting in rows against the fuselage. They started to stand, to check their equipment. The five Kenyans looked like boys in their thin khakis, without body armor or helmets or packs. They also looked cold.

'Target is green and clear.'

'Stay clear, Jaeger One. Puma is going in.'

'Roger.'

Alan nodded to the pilot, and the rotor sound changed again.

'Thirty seconds,' the pilot said. Alan turned and bellowed it back into the cargo bay. Everyone there was on his feet, weapons ready. Alan looked out the canopy, but without NVGs all he saw was a sea of grass rippling like dark water in the wash of the rotors. He pulled off the flight helmet and swapped it for a Kevlar and then they were down, a gentle touch rather than the expected jolt.

'Go!' the Marine officer yelled, over and over, and the plane emptied in seconds, the men moving like shadows. Alan followed the Kenyans, trying to watch the man ahead of him and gauge the progress of the Marines as they moved through the dark grass. They seemed to be going slowly. Alan found out why when he jumped down and landed in a foot of water. As soon as he was clear, the chopper lifted again, leaving him to slog along behind the party as they formed a perimeter.

Alan sloshed, bent under the throbbing rotors, trying to get forward to the lieutenant, whose voice had risen with the stress of command. His gunnery sergeant was a shape in the dark.

'I didn't expect us to be ankle-deep in fucking water,' the Marine shouted.

Alan grunted. There was a hand on his arm, and Opono was there.

'High ground off to the left. I've never seen the water come up this high. That must be a hell of a storm coming out there.'

The lieutenant started to move away toward one of his men and Alan grabbed his arm, towed him back to Opono.

'Mister Opono's men know the area. Let them find us some higher ground and then reset your perimeter.'

Alan waited, still holding them both, until the lieutenant said, 'Yes, sir,' and began to move.

High above, Cohen watched the screen in front of him. The motion of the airplane and the limitations of the big radar antenna in the nose meant that every so often the whole scene of the camp would blur and jump, then freeze, as the radar's tracking motion hit stops and lost contact. Then Cohen would ask Campbell to turn the plane.

'I have movement,' Soleck said in Jaeger One.

Cohen had no image at all. 'I just dropped track,' he said. 'Brian, get us to 040.'

'Roger, 040. Hang on.' Campbell turned the plane sharply toward the coast and Cohen re-imaged the target. One of the features Soleck had tentatively identified as a 'tent' was moving. It rocked back and forth and developed a streamer, as if it was leaking gas.

'What the fuck is that?' Soleck asked from Jaeger One.

Cohen shrugged, invisible in the back seat of another plane. 'Better tell the skipper.'

461

Ismailia, Egypt.

Triffler's convoy was half an hour late getting out of Cairo but made up for it on the arrow-straight road to Ismailia. Trapped between hell-for-leather oil trucks, Triffler gripped the wheel and kept his foot on the gas pedal; if he slowed down, he'd be run over from behind. Sergeant al-Fawzi sat white-knuckled in the back seat; Keatley, on the other hand, slept. Eighty miles an hour through the desert didn't seem any different to him from the morning drive time in DC – when his wife drove and he slept.

Behind them, Patemkin was in an unmarked car with two CIA people from the Cairo embassy; behind him, Geddes and another DEA agent were tearing up the road in their eagerness not to be left out. The oil tankers roared; the air stank; Triffler couldn't believe that he was in an automobile going this fast in the dark.

'Forsan Island,' al-Fawzi said for the third time as the lights of Ismailia winked ahead. Behind the lights and the jagged silhouette of the city, a knife-edge of sky was deep rose, then ochre. 'The perp's hotel is on Forsan Island.'

'Just tell me where to go.' Triffler didn't comment on 'perp.' He was sweating, even in the air-conditioned car. Outside, it was already pushing toward a hundred degrees Fahrenheit.

The sergeant had a hand-drawn map and some partly legible instructions. He didn't have a flashlight, however. The Arabic road signs left Triffler clueless, and he had a vision of driving straight into the canal behind the oil trucks, emerging on the other bank in Sinai, on and on.

'Get off,' al-Fawzi shouted. Triffler took this to mean

he could leave the highway. Relieved, he swung the wheel, and al-Fawzi directed him from there, holding his instruction sheet up to catch the light of the sodium-vapor lamps. Twenty minutes later, they pulled up on a residential block of dumpy apartment buildings where an Egyptian in a dark suit was standing with an opened umbrella in one hand.

Somali-Kenyan Coast.

The men were lying down in the cool grass on a knoll capped with a single knurled acacia tree that was swaying in the wind from the sea. Alan sat on a lower branch he had cleared of thorns and drank coffee from his thermos.

The Marine radioman knelt at his feet, smoking. The smoke smelled good. Alan had quit – again – only three weeks before, and the temptation seemed overwhelming, but he fought it. They were alone, the Kenyans gone into the night, headed to the village just to the south.

The radioman suddenly put a hand up against his headset and then pulled it off and handed it up to Alan. 'Something for you.'

Alan clipped the headset on and listened to Soleck. 'Keep an eye on it,' was all he said. He handed the headset back. He looked at his watch. Fifteen minutes until dawn. A few more minutes of dark after that, Alan figured, because the storm wasn't going to leave them much sunrise. It was still well out over the horizon, but it was coming.

Ismailia.

'Friend,' al-Fawzi said. 'Signal.' He meant the umbrella.

The friend was tall, thick, unshaven, smelling of

463

coffee and onions. This was the trustworthy pal, First Sergeant of Police Kassim. He looked at the three cars and pushed his lips out in disapproval. Sergeant al-Fawzi rolled his window down and they muttered in Arabic, and al-Fawzi said to Triffler, 'No parking.' Both sides of the street were lined with cars, also palm trees, and not enough trash containers.

'We have to worry about parking?' Keatley, now awake, moaned. 'This never happens to TV cops.'

'That's what "fiction" means.' Triffler waited while Kassim got in, the car listing to the left under his weight, and then drove under his direction six streets west to an abandoned shopping mall.

'His friend watching perp's lodging,' al-Fawzi said.

'How many "friends" did he bring?'

Sergeant al-Fawzi bridled. Any friend of his friend, he insisted, was trustworthy.

The Xerxes Palace Hotel, no matter how you cut it, was a two-storey motel with a four-star garden to hide behind. Lush flowers looked lurid in the early light – reds like splashes of blood, golds and yellows like egg yolk and butter. The grass – real grass, golf-course grass – was as green as Ireland.

'Irrigation,' al-Fawzi said. 'Egypt very wonderful country.'

The other local plainclothes cop – short, solid as a tree trunk, hairy hands – was waiting for them across the street. Nobody matching Balcon had gone either in or out since he had got there at five, he said; presumably, the French journalist had gone in last night and was still there.

Standing in the shadow of a wall, Triffler laid it out for all of them. They didn't know what sort of protection the French journalist might have. Only Triffler, al-

464

Fawzi, Keatley, and the two locals would go into the hotel; the rest would stay out of sight and be in touch by cell phone.

'How about I come along?' Geddes, the DEA man, said to Triffler.

'Nothing personal. Fewer is better. Next guy's yours.' Just in case he didn't get it, Triffler added, 'My show.'

He followed al-Fawzi, who followed the two local cops, into the lobby of the hotel, which had real marble floors and fluorescent lighting, too many gold-flecked mirrors and a bust of Nefertiti that looked as if she was recovering from a face-lift. Sergeant Kassim rousted the night manager, half-asleep and horrible under the fluorescents in a suit the color of an old bruise. But he was cooperative, once he'd seen the badges and heard something in Arabic that sounded remarkably like a threat.

'The other local guy stays with him,' Triffler said to al-Fawzi. 'Tell him he's got to be with him all the time – no phone calls, no chat with visitors. He could be a –' He searched for a word. 'Perp.' He didn't dare look at Keatley.

Somali-Kenyan Coast.
Before Alan finished the thermos, one of Opono's men was back. He sought Alan at the tree and pointed north, into the dark.

'No guards. Not so many men. People in town think maybe soldiers.' The man grinned, although Alan didn't know why, and opened his hand twice.

'Ten soldiers?'

'Sure, *bwana*.'

'Or more?'

'Might be more, *bwana*. Sure.'

465

'They awake?'

The man shrugged eloquently, a mime. *Who could know?*

Alan inhaled deeply, the smell of the cigarette and the leathery, woodsmoke smell of the Kenyan ranger all together. He thought of Rafe. *I want them to shoot first. If there's shooting, make damn sure you can tell me they fired first.* Right.

Alan motioned to the gunny and the Marine officer. They came over and he opened his vinyl map.

'Time for phase two.'

Ismailia.

Now there were four of them going up the stairs to the second storey of the motel. The rooms opened off a balcony that ran around a central courtyard; vines, their flowers Day-Glo orange in the early sun, gave some cover. Kassim looked at numbers, padded from door to door, quiet for a big man. He jerked his head. He held up the manager's keys in a large hand. Triffler nodded. Kassim inserted a key with the deftness of a burglar and turned it. Nothing budged. He inserted another key into another lock above the first and turned. The door opened two inches and stopped against a chain.

Kassim produced a short-handled bolt cutter from inside his suit coat and had them inside in seconds.

'Sweet,' al-Fawzi said.

Triffler wondered what the hell that meant, then saw that they were in a sitting room. *Suite.* Aha. The manager must have told him in Arabic that Balcon had a suite. Triffler pushed to the front and motioned the others back. Pulse up, leg muscles tight, Sigarms .380 in his right hand, stepping like a Tennessee Walking

Horse over a tray, a telephone book, two suitcases, a woman's dress – *hmmm* – and an empty (cheap) champagne bottle. At the far end of the room was a door on the right, closed. Triffler turned the handle and eased it open.

The owner of the dress was asleep on the left side of the bed, Jean-Marc Balcon on the right. She was Egyptian, long-haired, heavily scented even at this hour and from this distance.

Triffler pulled the door almost closed again and whispered to al-Fawzi, pointing at the man's chest, 'Bad cop.' He pointed at his own. 'Good cop. Okay?'

The sergeant showed signs of enthusiasm.

Triffler tiptoed in and took a step to his right, the gun ready. He nodded at al-Fawzi, who came through the door with a roar, something in Arabic probably contained in it, and threw himself at the bed, from which he snatched the sheet with one motion.

The woman woke, squawked, screamed, and bounced out with a flash of butt and pubic hair. Probably a working girl, Triffler thought, but very nicely put together, very jiggly, a bit fat – all this as he was moving toward Balcon, the gun preceding him. He resisted the temptation to watch her sprint to the bathroom, but she was interrupted by al-Fawzi, anyway, who scooped her up and wrapped the sheet around her like a tight gown. She began to scream.

Somali-Kenyan Coast.
Soleck turned the S-3 and burned out over the water, adjusting his trim every time a bigger gust moved the plane, fidgeting with his altitude to get the most out of his radar. He couldn't even daydream about his wetting-down party.

'Skipper's moving,' the chief called from the back end.

'Roger.' Just thinking about the next part caused his stomach to do a little flip.

Out to the east, the sky began to glow a baleful orange.

'"Red sky in the morning, sailor take warning." Ain't that what Master Chief Craw used to say, sir?'

Alan was already bone weary, and the light was growing all around them. The Marines never seemed to tire, but they were all fifteen years younger and did PT as a hobby. He crawled along behind the radioman, following a damp depression forward to a stand of brush. Somewhere ahead, one of the Kenyan rangers led their party. The other two fire teams were circling to the north, headed for the low ridge that would mask their movement toward the camp.

He was damp, and despite the warmth of the wind, it chilled him. He felt old. He kept moving forward, a few feet at a time, copying the elbow crawl used by the radioman, who, he realized, was carrying fifty pounds more weight than he. He was the last man into the relative cover of the brush.

Ahead, just visible because the tall grass was lying down in the wind, he could see the curved metal roof of the main building of the camp. He squatted down. They were three hundred meters away. Alan spared the energy to give the Kenyan ranger a big smile. 'Nice spot.'

Hakuna matata, bwana. No problem. Or, *Don't bother me, officer-man.* The man grinned, the smile like a light that flashed on – and off.

Alan looked at his watch. 'We're early,' he said quietly.

The Marine gunny was setting a watch while the other men lay flat. The veterans would sleep and the younger ones would worry or check their kit.

'Can we leave our rucksacks here, sir?' the gunny asked.

Alan shook his head, not understanding.

'I'd rather not have 'em carrying all that weight if we don't need to. Still got to cross the grass.' The gunny pointed in the direction of the hangar.

Alan nodded. 'Once we secure the camp, you can send somebody back for the gear.' He thought it odd, as the Marines had insisted on carrying the whole load to start with. The packs could have stayed in the chopper, or in Mombasa. *Marines*, Alan thought. He looked at his watch again. Then he dropped his own small civilian pack and felt ten years younger. He patted his gear one more time and looked at the unfamiliar M-16 that he had been issued. He'd never fired one and didn't trust it. He shouldered the pack and looked at his watch again, but, as far as he could see, the hands hadn't moved since the last time. Out over the ocean, the sky was lighter, although the early blush of red was gone. The sun was shining out there somewhere, beyond the wind.

Alan moved up cautiously through the thorn trees until only the high grass of the marsh separated him from the full view of the camp. He moved slowly, like a hunter in a blind, sitting well down before he pulled his Steiner binoculars from his pack and then rose cautiously to focus them on the camp.

The metal shed stood out immediately, even in the early light. There were men moving, but not in any kind of alarm. He saw a white man, his bald head reflecting a light inside the shed. The man was clearly giving orders. Two men in camouflage were carrying rifles. Otherwise there was very little movement.

Alan panned his binoculars to the left, inland, and found a line of tents alternating with the *ibandas* of marsh grass that Opono had predicted. Three of the tents were quite large, and between them was something – *elephant* was his first thought. Then he looked again. It was one of Menendez's fuel bladders, except now it was mostly full. Behind it was a fuel tanker, obscured by the tent.

'Got you,' Alan whispered.

The radioman behind him made a noise, and Alan froze, only to realize that the man was snoring. Alan touched his cheek and woke him. 'Get me the other team and Mister Soleck in the plane on one line.'

'Red Jacket and Jaeger One. Yes, sir.' The man pressed a few digits on his handset and gave it to Alan.

Alan knelt down. 'Red Jacket and Jaeger One, this is Big Blue, over?'

The Marine officer rogered up eagerly. 'Big Blue, this is Red Jacket! I have you clear and clear.'

'Roger, skipper, go ahead.' Soleck in Jaeger One was laconic by comparison.

'I can see and confirm that Menendez was right about the fuel bladders, and they are being filled right now. There is some kind of armored fighting vehicle parked under a tarp near the metal structure and there may be a second under a tent. Pass to the boat that they are in the process of filling the bladders and getting ready to move. Copy all that?'

'Loud and clear, skipper.'

Alan took a deep breath. This was it, the point of no return. 'Mister Soleck, I authorize you to take the detachment in as close as you can get. Get me photos and provoke a reaction. If they don't react, we'll go in on the ground anyway, but if they do, use the bomb. Red Jacket, that bomb is your signal to move and shoot. If the plane gets no response, we'll make a new plan.'

'Sir? That plane will cost us the element of surprise.'

'Roger, Red Jacket, but there's more to this than surprise, and I'm not sure that they'll assume we have people in the bush just because they see a US Navy plane. Okay, Soleck. Execute.'

'Roger. Estimate nine minutes out.'

Alan settled himself, a borrowed poncho liner under him, his back against a heavier twist of the thorny brush so that he could relax. He didn't want to sleep. He wanted to capture the rare moment on the edge of action to reflect. He sat and watched the grass move in the wind and thought about everything that might still go wrong. The next time he looked at his watch, it was time. And he could hear the distant noise of a jet.

Ismailia.

'Mister Balcon?' Triffler held up his badge and ID. 'Special Agent Triffler of the US Naval Criminal Investigative Service.' A scream and a slap from behind him. He didn't look. Balcon's eyes were large. 'This is my associate, Special Agent Keatley, and our colleague, Sergeant al-Fawzi of the Egyptian police.' The now-awake Balcon was naked and was trying to find some cover under his pillow, but Triffler grabbed it and dumped it on the floor. 'Get his clothes out of here.' He bobbed his head toward the other room. The woman, now a white lily with arms and head emerging olive-skinned from the top, had gone limp in the arms of Sergeant Kassim. 'Her, too.'

471

Clothes flew; the woman went swooning out; a minute later, Triffler was sitting on the bed next to the naked Balcon, Keatley and al-Fawzi standing at the foot.

'I demand to see the French consul,' Balcon said.

Sergeant al-Fawzi laughed and started around the other side of the bed. 'I teach you to demand!' he shouted.

'You don't frighten me!' Balcon shouted back. 'I am a man of note! I have rights –!'

Triffler waved al-Fawzi back and said to Balcon, 'No.'

'I know my rights. You!' Balcon pointed at al-Fawzi. 'Show me your badge! I will break you!' He looked down at himself, then said as an afterthought, 'I demand my clothes.'

Sergeant al-Fawzi launched himself across the bed again at Balcon, who pulled up his knees and protected his privates with both hands. Keatley caught al-Fawzi just as he was about to make contact and pulled him backward and upright. Sergeant al-Fawzi snarled in Arabic. He looked ferocious – one of the really bad guys from *Lawrence of Arabia*. 'I kill him!' he shouted. Sergeant al-Fawzi was a Method actor – really into it.

'Hold him, hold him, for God's sake!' Triffler said. He turned back to Balcon. He was still holding the gun. 'Do you know what these Egyptian cops *do* to terrorists? Don't get him stirred up!'

Balcon moved away, sliding his naked butt over the bed. 'I know no-thing about terrorists. I demand my clothes.'

'Yeah, well, they *hate* terrorists here. They shoot them.'

'I am saying nothing until the French consul is here!'

Triffler moved closer to him on the bed. 'Mister

472

Balcon, you have two choices. One is the Egyptian police – represented by Sergeant al-Fawzi there.'

'Give me five minutes alone with him!' al-Fawzi growled. 'Five minutes downtown and he'll puke up his guts.'

Triffler frowned a little at that, a bit over the top, but Balcon didn't seem to find it so. He was shivering and trying to hide by wrapping his arms around himself, his testicles and penis clamped tight between his thighs. He had pretty good legs, hairy, rather large feet.

'You got two choices,' Triffler said. He nodded at al-Fawzi. 'That's one choice – the Egyptian cops. That choice would also involve time in an Egyptian prison. I don't know if you've ever been in an Egyptian prison, Mister Balcon, but – well –' Triffler moved still closer; Balcon moved away. He'd about run out of bed.

'I don't know what you're talking about.'

'Your other choice is me. I'm the US Navy. We have clout.'

'The French government would laugh at you!' Balcon's eyes flicked to an alarm clock on the bedside table.

The sergeant pushed Keatley aside and came to the side of the bed again. 'Too much talk. He's mine – this is my country – I take him where I want, no more talk –!' He grabbed Balcon's shoulder and Balcon squealed; al-Fawzi swung backhanded and snapped Balcon's head around, the beautifully styled hair flying. The sergeant pushed his face down into Balcon's. 'Ever had your head held underwater, beautiful?' He grabbed Balcon's hair and pulled. Balcon squealed again, and Triffler started pulling on al-Fawzi's arm; Keatley grabbed the sergeant by the collar of his jacket and pulled him back and got him in a choke hold. The sergeant spat and said terrible things in Arabic, but Keatley seemed to choke him until he had to let go, and they backed out of the room that way, al-Fawzi gasping and cursing and looking as if he'd murder Balcon if he ever got free. Maybe he really meant it.

'You see,' Triffler said.

'You can't do this! It's against the law!'

'No, it isn't.' Triffler stood, put the gun into the belt-clip holster on his right hip. 'We're talking about terrorism. The law's different for terrorism. In Egypt, it means a secret trial and a firing squad. In my country, it means we go anywhere, do what we have to, to bring you back.'

'I am not a terrorist!'

'You conspired with the terrorists who blew up the USNS *Harker*. You conspired with the terrorists who blew up the AID building in Cairo. We don't discriminate too nicely between the people who placed the bomb and somebody who stood by and talked about it. For his own benefit.'

Balcon stared at him. For the first time, the rhythm of his replies was off. 'You don't know that,' he said. Again, his eyes went to the clock. Triffler checked his watch – six-twenty-two.

'I do know that. I know that you went to a Nyali Beach hotel and got the name of Lieutenant-Commander Alan Craik, following which there was an attempt on his wife's life. I know that you conspired in the murder of Special Agent Robert Cram. I have a witness who saw you with him just before you lured him away to his death.'

'I didn't.'

'Oh, yes, you did.'

474

Balcon opened his mouth. To his own slight surprise, Triffler shot out his left hand and caught Balcon's lower jaw.

'*Yes, you did!*' He stared into Balcon's frightened eyes. 'I'm a patient man, Mister Balcon – an honest man, a religious man – but *I won't stand for you telling me lies!* If you tell me lies, I'll throw you to the Egyptians – is that clear?' Triffler let go and sat on the bed again, his back to the room's door now, feet on the floor so that he was actually sideways to Balcon but able to turn his head to give him the full force of his eyes. 'You have no rights. You have no recourse. You are a conspirator with terrorists, and I am your only hope.'

Balcon tossed his hair, passed a hand over it, tried to wet his dry lips. When he spoke, his voice was thin. 'What do you want?'

'I want to know what you're doing for them next.' Balcon's eyes flicked to his left – the clock. 'And when.'

'What do I get?'

'What do you *get*? It isn't what you'll get, it's what you *won't* get! Don't you understand? You can be dead!'

'I have to get something.'

'You get not to die; you get not to have an electric prod shoved up your rectum; you get not to have twenty Egyptian hardcore prisoners make a toy out of you; you get not to be shot by three military marksman in some Egyptian prison you've never even heard of! You're in very, very deep shit, Mister Balcon. You're not Jean-Marc Balcon the three-day TV star anymore. You're a terrorist. You're a piece of shit. *You have no rights.*'

Balcon couldn't comprehend that. 'That cannot be!' he cried. He lived in a world of rights. Rights were inalienable, even if you'd conspired to kill people.

Somali-Kenyan Coast.

Soleck's first pass over the poachers' camp was high, well over fifteen hundred feet. He came in from the east, with the morning light at his back out of a shallow dive, and the S-3 made a valiant effort to reach three hundred knots as he passed over the hangar. Below him, he could see men spilling out of the tents (*they really are tents!*) and he could see where one had blown off its frame in the high wind. He couldn't see any vehicles, and the fuel bladders, if they weren't a figment of their collective imagination, were invisible in the pearly light. Before he was a mile past the camp, Soleck hauled at the yoke and pulled the plane around in a turn so tight that the wings protested and the SENSO made a noise, quickly hushed, and then he had the wings level on a new course. He had lost seven hundred feet of altitude and a good deal of his velocity in the turn and he had a lot longer to look at the camp this time. There were more men than he had expected, most of them with guns. Unconsciously, a wide smile pasted his lips against his teeth. His stomach turned over. Next to him, Donitz described the layout of the camp in detail. Soleck picked out the tent that Menendez said held vehicles.

'Check that out, Donuts!' Soleck pointed at the biggest tent, which two armed men were pulling down. Underneath the canvas was something metal with a mounted weapon, like a Somali technical, and then they were climbing and Donitz was describing the vehicle to the skipper, a mile away on the ground. 'Might have been two of them!' Soleck shouted, his voice too loud with fear and adrenaline.

Donuts waved at Soleck and tapped his comm cord and then switched the skipper to cockpit so that Soleck was also in the link.

'Any hostile acts, Mister Soleck?'

'Nothing, sir. They have some sort of armed vehicles –'

'But no fire.'

'No, sir. I'll just go around again. Maybe they were still asleep.' He suited the action to the words, pulling the plane out of a shallow climb and hard around to the north. The hi-bypass turbofans rose from a whine to a roar, like vacuum cleaners from hell, and the whole airframe shuddered.

'Belay that, Mister Soleck. I do *not* want you going around again. Do you hear me? If they have a Stinger –'

Soleck tapped his helmet at Donitz and shrugged, the universal aviator sign for lost comms.

Donitz laughed.

On the ground below, the Marine lieutenant had the fire-support team in place on the low ridge and an assault team ready at the base, with two hundred meters of open ground and windblown grass between him and the first outbuildings. Alan's team had farther to go, and he started to get his men up as he watched Soleck's plane.

Soleck pressed his intercom to switch to the back seat.

'Give us some chaff and flares.' He thought a trail of fire and silver chaff might provoke a response. He heard the chaff launcher start with a dull thud, and then they were over the camp. He pressed the nose down a fraction. This time he was going in at treetop level.

Directly ahead of him, the two vehicles were visible, and one of them had men on top. He saw the muzzle of their weapon sparkle.

'I'm taking fire,' he called, his communications miraculously restored.

Alan watched the plane dive for a third pass on the camp and cursed Soleck's bravado with the bitter knowledge that he'd have done the same and his subordinates all knew it. Three hundred meters away, the pounding noise of the auto cannon on the back of the hidden vehicle was clear even before Soleck's voice came through the headset.

'I'm taking fire,' Soleck said, his voice rising with excitement.

Donitz said, 'Bomb away.'

Alan looked at the Marines waiting at the edge of the brush. 'Let's rock,' he said, handing the headset to the radioman with a smile. He was happy. Worried about Soleck, worried about the mission, but happy. It was all beyond planning and worry now. They were committed.

The bomb exploded. A fountain of fire and dirt rose into the air over the camp, and the heat and shock wave knocked Alan flat where he was on the edge of the brush line and deafened him. He lay still a moment, stunned, the explosion beyond his limited experience of war, and then gathered his wits and rolled to his feet, looking around blearily like a fighter who has taken too many punches. Then he started to run forward, his intention of crouching in the long grass forgotten until Fidelio's hand pushed him down lower.

When he started, the Marines got to their feet, too, and a corporal shouted, 'Spread out; don't bunch up!' Those words were the first sign that Alan could still hear, and then he heard the sound of the S-3's engines laboring to climb out and knew that Soleck was okay.

Then all the sound came back to him in a rush, and he heard the rattle of automatic-weapons fire from the camp and a steady stream of fire from the ridge beyond, short bursts fired at intervals, *braat*, pause, *braat*, the Marines firing their squad weapon. Less than a hundred meters in front of him, Alan saw a small truck at the edge of the clearing. Even as he watched, the Marine fire-support team walked their fire across the vehicle and it burned, first a line of fire as the big bullets hit it, then a secondary explosion as the fuel went up with a hollow boom. It was gone in black smoke and fire in an instant, and the fire was moving on. Alan kept moving forward. He couldn't see the enemy or much else but the grass and the sheds and tents of the camp.

Ten steps and the ground began to rise and his boots no longer made squelching noises as he ducked his head and pushed on. Now there were low bushes in the grass as the ground rose, making the footing treacherous, and he got a long thorn in his leg when he decided to push through one. It burned there. He raised his head. He could hear the Marine fire to the north and, quite close, return fire from the camp. He had no idea where Opono's men had gone, but it seemed to him that the whole attention of the camp was on the lieutenant's men on the ridge. He didn't think anyone had noticed his party. He turned and saw the radioman just behind Fidelio, unheard in the wind and the chatter of the weapons. The radioman pointed off to their left and Alan saw the corporal. He pointed, and in a moment the gunny emerged from the waving grass.

'Gunny?' He had to shout.

'They don't even know we're here, sir.'

Alan nodded. The radioman held out the headset, but Alan shook his head. He signed to the gunny.

479

'Break the resistance any way you like, gunny. I'm not the tactician, here. I want this wrapped up.'

The gunny nodded, clearly pleased, and exchanged a glance with Fidelio. Fidelio touched Alan's arm, pointed, and moved off into the grass. Alan crouched and watched the gunny tap men he hadn't even seen in the grass, banging on their helmets and sending them off. He must have briefed them on their roles before the attack went in. In seconds, Alan was alone in the tall grass with the radioman. He checked his rifle and started forward. He heard four flat *cracks*, big rifles loud even over the wind, and then again, and then a burst of firing off to the west.

There was another rise, almost a berm, at the edge of the camp. Alan felt naked going over it and flung himself flat at the top, but all the firing was directed elsewhere, and he pulled himself up and forward into the shelter of a tent with an awning that seemed to function as a mess hall.

A Somali man in shorts and a T-shirt came out of the tent, saw Alan's radioman, and snapped off a shot with an assault rifle. Alan dropped to one knee and fired back, the rifle light and responsive. He didn't miss. The man fell in a heap and started to sob. Alan's radioman fired a long burst through the walls of the tent at waist height and then put in a new magazine and fired again, lower, ripping the side of the tent. Alan crawled forward a few yards. The man he had shot was close, rocking himself in a little ball and moaning. Alan fought the urge to shoot him in the head just to shut him up.

He saw several rifle pits and men in foreign camo shooting from any cover they could find, most of their fire directed off to the north. He heard someone just to his left fire a burst and turned his head in time to see one of the men in a rifle pit spasm in pain. He heard the S-3 engine noise again and didn't look up, instead rolling into the cover of a big oil drum. He almost had his muzzle on a target when a symphony of fire came from all around him. Two grenades sailed through the air and he ducked his head. *Wham, thump.* When he raised his head, the rifle pits were silent and Gunny Fife was leading his men forward cautiously. One enemy, a black man in ragged green shorts, apparently unwounded, had thrown his gun down and was trying to surrender. Gunny Fife waved one of his men to the job and Alan watched the man pushed to the ground, his hands behind his head. The Marine yelled '*Chini!*' as he had been taught, although Alan thought that all the enemies he had seen were Hutus, who wouldn't speak Swahili. To his left, Fidelio kept pace with the Marine advance, his rifle barking in short bursts. Alan didn't see him take any prisoners.

He caught up with Gunny Fife at the edge of the metal hangar. The radioman was still following Alan doggedly, and as soon as Alan knelt by the gunny he held out the headset. Alan took it this time while looking at the gunny.

'Skipper, this is Jaeger One, do you copy?'

'Wait one, Jaeger One. Red Jacket, this is Big Blue, over?'

Sounds of an AK-47 firing nearby.

'Big Blue, this is Red Jacket. Go ahead, sir.'

'Location?'

'Red Jacket is at the edge of the camp, sir. We have the berm as cover and we're clearing resistance on the north side. We're taking fire from the hangar.'

'They're taking fire from the hangar!' Alan shouted at the gunny.

The gunny nodded, rose to his feet, and went down. Just like that, and he was clutching his chest and men were taking cover –

'Move!' Alan bellowed. He ran to the corner of the building, suddenly at the point of the attack, aware that he was the least trained infantryman present, and then Fidelio pushed past him, a blur of motion that pinned him to the side of the hangar. Alan's radioman fired at something, and Alan leaned around the corner low and fired blindly, and then the second team went around the corner of the hangar. Fidelio had crossed the open ground to an abandoned vehicle and was covering them.

They took fire from somewhere; the shots threw puffs of dust off the concrete foundation by Alan's feet. He was slow to realize what they were, and when he did, he threw himself around the corner after the other fire team. The squad 30mm grenade launcher ripped a hole in the hangar. One of the Marines threw a grenade, and then another, and then they were at the side door and there was smoke all around them and Alan felt like a third wheel. The men hesitated at the closed door. Then one readied a grenade and another shot the center of the door in. The first man tossed the grenade and Alan followed the Marines as they threw themselves down. There was a burst of return fire from inside. No one moved.

'Follow me,' he yelled, rolled to his feet, and charged through the door.

Someone next to him said 'Jesus!' and he was thrown back against the doorframe.

They all seemed to go through the door in a clump,

and later Alan couldn't remember if he had been first or not, but the inside of the hangar was full of smoke. Something moved ahead of Alan and he fired, dropped his rifle and drew his pistol, and then he was out of the smoke and the Marines with him chopped down two white men in green fatigues with a heavy weapon. *Mercenaries*, Alan thought. One kept twitching and the other lay still. Alan found that his voice was raw from shouting and he looked down and saw that the slide of his pistol was open. He didn't remember shooting at all. Ahead of him a little clump of fighters in shorts and bush jackets seemed to melt as Marines ran at them from all directions.

'*Chini*, motherfucker!' yelled the Marine next to Alan. And Fidelio was there, grinning from ear to ear.

The fighters hesitated. The Marine at the berm with the squad weapon fired again; two of them threw their guns down, and then another, and then two more. Two of them ran for the bush, and a kneeling Marine began to lay down automatic-rifle fire as the man with the launcher dropped two grenades beyond them and the bush erupted. One fell; one turned and screamed at them and dropped his weapon.

'Get down, get down –!' The Marine lieutenant appeared behind them with the rest of the second squad and was screaming at them. '*Chini*, goddamit, get on your *chini*. *Chini* or you're dead meat –!' At the same time, he was running through and across his men, waving them into a wider front. Alan, winded, finally able to stop running, knelt and gasped for air. The mercenaries in their green fatigues were all on the ground on their faces.

'Get me the officer!' Alan panted. 'Cut out the officer –!'

A white face lifted. Alan saw the man as a big head, very black hair around baldness, high forehead. The man lifted a hand to identify himself. The Marine lieutenant screamed, '*Chini*, motherfucker!' and somebody fired a three-round burst at waist level above the prone men. Then the lieutenant was moving his men into a position on a mound above the lagoon, and two of them were cutting out the mercenaries one at a time, not letting them get close until they knew they were unarmed, shoving them down to the beach where they sat, exposed, at the water's edge. They had surprising numbers of hidden weapons. Fidelio joined the team searching them. He was ruthless and quick.

The officer was the fifth of the eight. They brought him to Alan.

Ismailia.
Triffler was hammering at the French journalist. 'Why are you in Ismailia, Mister Balcon?'

'There is gossip of new activity in Iraq; my agency told me to get footage of the canal, any US ships –'

'As God is my redeemer, Balcon, if you tell me another lie, I'll turn you right over to that cop who wants to pound you to pulp! *I want to know now!* Where are you going, and when?'

'If I tell you, you let me go?'

'If you tell me the truth, and it checks out, I'll help you.'

'No, no, oh no, you must –'

Triffler brought his right hand down on the bedside table so that the clock jumped and a pencil and pad tumbled to the floor. 'Don't tell me what I must!' He was looking at the clock, seeing for the first time that the alarm was set for six-thirty. Six minutes. Then what had Balcon planned? – a shower, shave, dress, get rid of the woman – half an hour? Something going down at seven? If so, time was running out. The thought that he'd have to turn Balcon over to the Egyptians made Triffler suddenly sick, because they would in fact do pretty much what he had threatened, what he could not, would not do – and they'd get answers. And he had to have answers. 'Tell me.' Triffler risked a leap. 'You're supposed to be ready for your friends soon.'

That hit home. Balcon chewed his lower lip once. He looked into Triffler's eyes. 'You're not going to call the French consul.'

'No.'

'You know this is a violation of international law.'

'I know that if I turn you over to the Egyptians, nobody will care about international law. What's the French consul going to do, cut off Cairo's supply of Beaujolais?'

'But I am – I am a person of some importance!'

Triffler stared at him. Triffler didn't need to act this part; his contempt for people with blow-dried hair who swanned about the small screen was profound. Balcon met the stare, tried to hold it, finally looked away. Triffler drew the .380 again. 'Mister Balcon, the bullet from this gun is nine millimeters across. *That* is how important you are. Nine millimeters' worth – one-third of an American inch.' He put the gun back, his eyes on Balcon's until Balcon again looked away. 'In your phoney little world, you may have some phoney importance, but here, now, you're nothing.'

Balcon swallowed, looked again at the clock. 'I, uh – I am supposed to get a call.'

'Yes?'

'From a, ah, guide?' His assurance had dissolved. 'To

485

tell me when he is coming to, ah, guide me? To the, mm, to a, so to speak – to film –?'

'To film what?'

'To film an event? That's all I know, I swear it – an event! They call me; somebody comes, takes me some-place – there is an event!'

Triffler thought of the Cairo AID building. Rubble, twisted steel, stink, a human arm hanging on a piece of stair rail. *An event.* 'Who goes with you?'

'Two guys. Film crew. They know nothing; they're nobodies – I pick them up as I go –'.

'Cameramen?'

'One for the camera, one to, mm, carry? – what you call a "grip" –?'

'Where are they?'

'Number four room – downstairs – all they know is to be ready –'

'When?'

The telephone rang. It was six-thirty. Triffler drew the .380 and motioned Balcon across the bed. When the journalist's hand was on the telephone, Triffler put the muzzle against his right temple. 'One wrong word, and you're dead.'

Somali-Kenyan Coast.

'Major Arnolt Vervoert,' the man said. Standing, he was big. He had a sneering smile and a confident voice and a South African accent that Alan hated.

Fidelio leaned around Alan. 'I could just waste him.'

'Sit,' Alan said.

Vervoert's smile got meaner. 'I am a major, mister –?'

'You're a fucking terrorist! Now sit, before I have somebody kick your feet out from under you!' Alan looked at Fidelio.

The South African stared at him, shrugged, sat with a slowness that was supposed to show that he was humoring Alan. 'Your Marines are good men,' he said. 'Better than my blecks. You –'

'Shut up.'

'I have a right to be treated as –!'

Alan put his face down close. 'You haven't got the right to piss standing up! You're a fucking civilian playing soldier! Shut up!'

'Twenty-one years in the South African Def –!'

Alan grabbed the man's hair with his good hand and twisted the head up and around, the pistol in his left with the muzzle just under the man's jaw. 'Shut the FUCK up!' They stared into each other's eyes. Vervoert didn't flinch – but he didn't fight, either. Alan dropped his voice almost to a whisper. 'It doesn't matter what you used to be. This is now, and now you're a piece of shit who's been poaching animals and killing civilians. Understand?' His fingers tightened. Vervoert grunted an assent. His face scowled with pain. Alan let go.

'All secure,' a panting voice said on his left. It was the Marine second-lieutenant. His absurdly young face was suddenly mature. And very dirty. 'My guys are in good shape, all accounted for. Two light wounds and Gunny Fife took a round in the body armor. Twenty-three prisoners in all, plus we count at least thirteen bodies. Nine of their wounded.'

Alan felt some of the postcombat rage drain away. Gunny Fife was okay.

'Where's the KWS guys?'

The Marine officer bobbed his head. 'Their head guy took off after a bunch of baddies; his guys followed. They did some fancy shooting and blew away all the weapons teams that this asshole tried to organize.'

487

Alan remembered hearing firing beyond the camp after they had moved in. Opono would have gone after them, of course. *Killing poachers was my business.*

'See if you can make contact with them. Then we need to get the hell out of here – call in the chopper. There's a landing area where we came out of the bush –'

'Already on it, sir. As for the Kenya Wildlife guys, they –' His eyes took in something beyond Alan's shoulder. Alan turned his head. He saw green shirts, black skin, four men trotting with their heads down and their bodies twisted because they were carrying weight among them. They didn't look up as they came into the open, but plodded on, small steps, rifles slung over their shoulders and the other hand grasping a leg or an armpit. David Opono was being carried in their midst. His head lolled back so that Alan couldn't see it, but he knew it was Opono from their faces, and he knew he was dead.

'We tried,' one of the rangers said when they had put him down. He had saluted the two Americans, his long fingers raised to touch his slender forehead, tears running down his cheeks. 'He died as we carried him. We tried –' His voice trailed off.

Fidelio looked at the mercenary. 'Fuck,' he said clearly. 'Opono was a right guy.' But his eyes said, *Let's waste him.*

Ismailia.
Triffler put his ear close to Balcon's, lover-like, their hair touching. He moved the gun to Balcon's throat.

'Answer it. Warning, Balcon – I understand French.'

In fact, his high-school French wasn't up to it, but Balcon didn't know that, and he did get the other man

488

saying something about *chevaux* – horses – to which Balcon said something in which Triffler recognized only the word for three. Mostly, after that, Balcon grunted. He said *oui* a couple of times. Triffler heard the word *sept* – seven – from the other.

Balcon put the phone down, his hands trembling. He didn't dare move because of the .380. Triffler took the gun away from his throat and stood, pushing the gun into the holster, and Balcon looked up as if for approval, as if needing Triffler to tell him that he'd done well. 'Seven o'clock,' he said. 'Outside in the parking lot.'

'What was that about horses?'

'A greeting, a, mm, recognition? He says he is looking for a man who wants horses, and I say I need three. Because we will be three – me, my crew. Okay?'

Triffler was already at the door.

Somali-Kenyan Coast.

Opono had taken a burst of fire in his chest, his green shirt black now. His face was untouched, made not peaceful but passionate by death. Alan closed the eyes, which were too staring, too hungry still for whatever dream he had pursued. 'Did you kill them?' Alan said to the ranger, voice husky.

'We killed them.'

'We'll take the body back,' Alan said to the Marine lieutenant. 'See if you can find something to cover him –'

The game rangers sat on the brown earth around Opono like guards, their weapons pointing at the sky. One of them began to speak in a language Alan didn't know, and he turned away; the words were not for him.

Vervoert had recovered his cockiness. He asked for a cigarette. Alan looked down at him, aware that he hated the man and blamed him for Opono's death and had to be very careful or he would kill him. 'I want to know what you were doing here, and I want to know what was going on in the lagoon.'

'My name is Vervoert. Major.' He smiled.

Alan kicked him in the crotch. The second-lieutenant recoiled a little and then set his face. Fidelio smiled at Alan as if he'd just displayed a virtue hitherto lacking. The Kenyan ranger spat.

Vervoert curled around his testicles, rolling on the ground. It was dusty at the edge of the beach, dry despite yesterday's rain.

Alan squatted in front of him. 'Tell me now, or –'

'I'm an officer.'

Alan smiled unconsciously, a little smile that his men would have recognized as trouble. His voice became very quiet.

'You are not a major. You are a criminal apprehended in the act of conducting a terrorist operation against the United States.' Alan looked over at the Marines, most of whom were busy. Two were behind him. 'Take off all your clothes.'

'Like fuck I will. Look, Yank –'

Alan tried to sound bored. He motioned to Fidelio, who raised one of the captured pistols so that Vervoert was staring down the barrel. 'Take off your clothes or I'll kill you and get another.'

The major started to strip. In Alan's experience, few men were brave when naked and helpless. He waved one of the Marines forward. 'Hog-tie him.'

The Marine obliged. Vervoert tried to stare at Alan but the Marine wouldn't let him, and kept moving him, rolling him on the hard earth until his body was coated in the fine grit. Fidelio laughed, a strange, high-pitched sound.

Alan knelt by him.

'You're a fucking terrorist, dickhead. You are already dead, and if I waste you, no one will ever care. See? Good. There is no fucking Geneva Convention for mercs, got me? You are just a fucking criminal, and this is Africa.'

The man rolled himself to face Alan, who got up and walked around until he was behind him. The man tried to roll again. 'You can't!' The strong voice had a touch of a whine in it. Alan thought the man might have been stronger if he believed in his cause, but as a mercenary, he would know that all heroic defense of his employers offered was a road to dusty death.

The man tried to roll up on his knees and fell over, banging his head on the ground, and Alan moved again, outside his vision.

'You fucking can't –'

Alan watched him thrash, panicked in his bonds, using his energy. Alan continued to move slowly around the bound man, careful to remain mostly invisible, using the time to master his rage at Opono's death. When Vervoert stopped thrashing, Alan went and knelt behind him again.

'A better man than you'll ever be just died because of your shit! Those four men sitting over there loved him.' Alan took the man's head and jerked it viciously, his pent-up aggression making him too violent. For a moment he feared he had broken the man's neck. 'See them? Now, you tell me what I want to know, or by God you're theirs.'

'You're crazy.'

'One chance. Tell me, or you're theirs. I'll give them ten minutes in the bush with you. Then I'm out of here *and you never will have existed*!'

Fidelio laughed again. It was a sound that Alan didn't like; as if by pleasing Fidelio, he was breaking a law.

Vervoert lay in the dirt and panted. He was hyperventilating. This was a big, dangerous man, and Alan was breaking him. He felt the press of time, but he also knew he was winning.

Alan hated it.

The man's eyes were starting to dilate, and he was ashamed of his filth and his nudity. It made Alan a little sick and giddy.

Vervoert's eyes slid over toward the four Kenyans. He was having difficulty speaking. 'I ha-ad a contract. Train those blecks and then –'

'Yes?' Alan laid his pistol gently against the man's head.

'Go into Somalia!' Vervoert could hardly speak. Alan let up on the pistol. 'To an airfield. Kusdasii.'

'To do what?'

'Take it, hold it – that's all! I swear. That's all I know. It was a job – train fifty blecks, go up there in the trucks, take it. That's all.'

'There's more.' He pushed the pistol, saw blood flow where the front sight was cutting the man's scalp. Vervoert's eyes searched for him, hated him. 'Tell me!'

'We would be relieved. By air.' He still tried to hold something back. Alan got up and walked away a few feet.

'All I have to do is leave you, you worthless piece of shit.'

Vervoert groaned and muttered something, and Alan went back, this time squatting down in front of the

492

man. Alan saw the sweat and dust crusting on his body. Alan leaned down close. 'You don't have to die here.' He wished he had time to coach Fidelio. It was less effective, acting as good cop and bad cop. 'Just stop lying. I'm in a hurry, and I don't really give a shit about you.'

'A force, okay? An occupying force! That's all I fucking know; they don't tell me more! I was to hold the fucking airfield until the planes arrive, the main force, armor. Big mortars, they said. A *force*.'

'To do what?'

'I don't know! What the fuck you think you do with a force in a shithole like Somalia?'

Alan thought he knew. *Drugs*, he thought. *They want to wall off southern Somalia and put the new poppy fields there*. He could see it, the quick grab, the local governments paid off, the US cut off from reprisal by selected terrorist acts. He was silent for a moment, and then he wrenched his attention back to interrogation. He lengthened his pause deliberately, like a man trying to think of something to ask. In fact, he had it: the real question, the pressing one. Hidden in the list, just like at school. 'And the lagoon? What were they doing in the lagoon?' He didn't even sound curious.

'They played with toy boats. Not my people; that wasn't my operation. Different people. They blew up little boats against that thing out there, that's all I know!'

'What thing?' Alan's eyes went to the lagoon. He remembered the odd radar return from out there, the brief flicker they had thought was an explosion. *Toy boats. Explosions*. He bent over Vervoerts. 'Who were they?'

'Just – guys. Little guys – Asians –'

'Not Africans?'

'Asians, man – Jesus, I'm telling the truth –'

Asians. The Sri Lankan Tamils had been known to use radio-guided boats to blow up ships in the narrow waterways of Sri Lanka.

'Where are they now?'

Vervoert's eyes went to the lagoon as if he was looking for the people with the toy boats. 'They left yesterday in the helicopter. I don't know where they went. I swear, I don't know. They weren't my people.'

Yesterday. Sri Lankans training to blow up ships in narrow waterways.

Alan ran for the radio.

Ismailia.

Triffler grabbed Keatley's shirtfront and told him what he had got from Balcon. 'It's got to be the canal!'

He indicated the newsman. 'Get him dressed.' He pushed al-Fawzi in front of him out the bedroom door and into the other room, glanced at Kassim and Balcon's woman in chairs, the woman recovered enough to be smoking a cigarette. She pouted at him. 'Tell Kassim there are two men in Room Four; they have to be neutralized. Also this woman. Maybe he has to arrest them – suspicion of conspiracy, or something. The men should have equipment – cameras, boxes – stuff like that. Leave the equipment but get rid of the men. Okay?'

'Okay!' The sergeant's look of enthusiasm was back. He spewed Arabic at Kassim.

Triffler strode back into the bedroom. 'You and I are going with this yo-yo,' he said to Keatley, pointing a thumb at Balcon. 'He's being picked up at seven by somebody who's going to take him to the action. He goes with a cameraman and a gopher. You cameraman, me gopher. You got any problem with that?'

Keatley spread his hands. 'Me, have problems? He-e-e-y –!'

He pulled Keatley away from Balcon and lowered his voice. 'The new BG started its transit yesterday – canal'll be full of US ships.' He plucked at the front of Keatley's shirt. '*Franklin D. Roosevelt* entered last night.'

'Oh, shit.'

Triffler tried to call Dukas's cell phone while putting on a pair of Balcon's blue jeans and a soiled T-shirt he found on the floor. No answer. He tried the det at Mombasa, got a duty EM; it was an open line, so little could be said, but he got through the idea that something was going to go down near the canal and he'd be there, and he asked to have Dukas call him back. But Dukas was on his way to Cairo, he was told, so he had to settle for an open-line promise from the duty EM to inform everybody he knew, starting with Rafehausen on the *Jefferson*, that something, something *big*, was going down near the canal. Only then did he call Geddes, still out where they had left him at the edge of the motel parking lot, and set up a two-car surveillance on whoever picked them and Balcon up at seven, al-Fawzi to go with Geddes.

Somali-Kenyan Coast.

Flying at thirteen hundred feet, Soleck listened to Commander Craik's tense voice. 'Soleck, pass this at once to the *Jefferson* as urgent priority, must be passed at once to Captain Rafehausen. The next terrorist target will be a ship in enclosed waters. The method's one used by the Tamil Tigers – two small powerboats joined by a line that gets trapped by the ship's bow; the small

495

boats are drawn against the hull by the line and explode. You understand me?'

'Yessir. What enclosed waters?'

'I don't know. It's within twenty-four hours' travel by a small chopper, because that's how they got out of here.'

'The Suez Canal.' Soleck said it without even thinking. It seemed obvious to him.

Craik was silent on the other end and then said, 'That's a good possibility, Evan. Pass it on to Captain Rafehausen.'

But Soleck's mind was leaping on. 'The *FDR*'s in the canal, sir. She's relieving the *Jeff* in the Red Sea; it was on the message traffic –'

'I know where the *Roosevelt* is, Evan. My wife's on board.' Then, astonishingly, Soleck heard Craik *laughing*, the laugh turning quickly to a groan. 'Jesus God, that's what all that cell-phone activity was about – the *Roosevelt*! That was the day the *Roosevelt* got delayed – they were scrambling to reschedule their attack!' He groaned again. 'Get on it, Soleck. Tell them there's something about attacking an airfield in Somalia, a place called Kusdasii – they're expecting more troops by air – get on it!'

Soleck tightened his grip on the yoke. 'Message will go out to the boat ASAP, sir.' But Soleck's brain was making a discovery, too – something he'd read in the last few days about aircraft and a troop buildup – where? And then he remembered: Sierra Leone, two ex-Soviet aircraft, a lot of ground troops.

He put the S-3 into a slow turn seaward and said to Campbell, 'Raise the *Jefferson* on guard.'

Ismailia.

With Keatley, Triffler raced down to Room Four and began to paw through the equipment there. They found

496

a television camera, shoulder-portable, and two aluminum suitcases, plus assorted and, to Triffler, mostly unrecognizable stuff. The suitcases were fitted inside with battleship-gray foam, into which wells had been cut for lenses, a meter, a still camera, and the gadgets of sound recording. An umbrella-shaped reflector had been tossed into a chair; an attaché case and a light bar were on one of the beds; the claptrap of a craft he didn't understand was spread over a cheap table and two chairs. The gopher carried a lot in this crew, he saw.

Triffler tore the foam away from the inside of one suitcase and cut a rough well on its underside and put his nine-millimeter in it. Replaced, with a lens on top, it would do. Maybe.

'Your cannon. It's got to be hidden, Keatley. They may search us.'

'Bull*shit*.' Keatley's .45 was part of his personality, a Detonics with a short barrel and no sights, made for what Keatley called 'close work.'

'You can't carry it. That's an order.'

Keatley began to take the camera apart.

The Egyptians had finished upstairs by then. Kassim was riding herd on Balcon, the woman, and the two technicians; al-Fawzi was in Room Four with Triffler and Keatley, looking out through the slats in the Venetian blind, very *film noir*. Triffler got him to hit up the hotel manager for a roll of duct tape – nine minutes to go – and Triffler taped his .380 between two plastic boxes that had started life as sealed videotapes, which he ripped apart with a Spyderco knife, flinging videotape on the beds and letting it billow around the room, the hell with it. Then the gun fit. Five minutes to go.

Keatley showed off the reconstituted camera. It

wouldn't hold tape anymore, and it wouldn't take video pictures, but it had a place inside via the loading door that would hold his .45. He hefted the camera. 'This sucker doesn't leave my hand.' He looked through the finder.

'What about your nine?'

'Never use it, hate it – forget it.'

'You may be sorry.'

'Well, I won't live to know, right? Shitty gun, fuck it.' He tossed the nine-millimeter on the bed. Al-Fawzi grabbed it and held it in his hand while he looked through the opening in the blind. Keatley put the camera over his shoulder and sighted down at Triffler. 'How do I look?'

'Like somebody who doesn't know thing one about television cameras. You got two minutes to learn.'

He ran upstairs and into Balcon's suite and grabbed the startled journalist by the front of his safari jacket. 'We're on.' He pulled the journalist close. 'One wrong word, and you're the first one dead.'

Balcon pulled his head back. 'You assure me you will get me safely out of Egypt?'

'I will get you safely out of Egypt.'

One minute later, they were out in the parking lot.

Out on the storm-swept *Jefferson*, intel was processing Soleck's read on the buildup in Sierra Leone and Alan Craik's information from the South African officer at the poachers' camp. Seventeen minutes later, an urgent message went to LantFleet and DNI. Fourteen minutes after that, Sierra Leone closed the Freetown airport, and a British SAS special-forces team was diverted from the Liberian border to the task of securing the two Tu-103s.

17

Along the Suez Canal.

The Suez Canal looked to Triffler like a streak of brown paint laid down a green gutter; beyond the gutter's edges was red desert. The colors were stark in their separateness. This was almost the canal's narrowest section – a couple of hundred meters wide, actually too narrow now for the world's biggest ships, although it must have seemed generous in 1869 when this long, straight ditch cut travel from Britain to India by weeks. Now, the canal was wide enough to take an aircraft carrier – but not wide enough to allow the carrier to turn around. Once in, ships had to go through.

Triffler stared out at the too-bright landscape. The sun hurt his eyes. The temperature in the car was already above a hundred. Balcon was in front with the driver, Keatley and Triffler in back. He could smell the dirty T-shirt he had snatched from Balcon's floor; it was the thing that most distressed him about the moment, worse than the heat, worse than the harsh light, worse than the sweat-cigarette stink of the driver.

Balcon still seemed to be looking to Triffler for approval. Now and then on the ride, he glanced back and tried to smile.

A beat-up Fiat was following them, two men in headscarves in it. They hadn't appeared in the parking lot, only the driver of Balcon's car, who hadn't patted them down or shown the least interest in the suitcases or the camera. Then, on the road, Triffler had seen the Fiat behind them; so had Keatley, who had fired a meaningful look at Triffler. Guards, or enforcers? Both, probably.

One surveillance car was somewhere back there, too, one somewhere in front. Too obviously Americans, Triffler thought, and too early in the morning for tourists to be out looking at de Lesseps's ditch, but there wasn't a parallel road, and the only way they could stay out of sight was to get way ahead or way behind. They'd apparently decided on both; at the moment, he couldn't see either car.

The road ran along the canal for miles. You could pull off and watch one of the world's great ships seem to slide along between the green banks; if you aimed your tourist's camera just right, no water would be visible, and the ship would seem to be sailing through the red desert beyond. Triffler didn't care about any of that, but he took it in. No tourists would come out here today, however, he thought; they had already gone through two roadblocks, and three times he had seen light aircraft flying low over the canal. The alert was on. But the roadblocks weren't serious – Balcon's press credentials were enough to get them through. The trailing car somehow came under his umbrella, too. Maybe it was an umbrella of money. Or maybe the roadblocks were simply a way to show willing on the part of the police, and they were really going to let through anybody who wasn't hauling a mobile rocket, because tourism was big business.

Their driver watched the road behind him in his mirror; sometimes, his eyes met Triffler's there. The man looked worried, had looked worried when he had picked them up – a fusser, a fidgeter. Had he seen Geddes's car back there? Probably not, Triffler decided; he was simply being overcautious. Then, however, he increased speed for several minutes, glancing back, speeding up, glancing back, then abruptly turned off toward the canal, the trailing car wheeling into his dust cloud as they barreled down an unpaved lane that took them past a stand of low, spiky palms. Down along the canal now were small houses, each one with a dock, a boat, an Egyptian flag. Just like any lake in the States, except that a hundred feet off the end of the dock, an oil tanker was passing. They headed down toward the houses and then turned to their left, north, sandy little pairs of ruts heading away to their right toward the houses. The driver, Triffler decided, had wanted to make sure nobody was in sight behind him when he made his turn. Very nervous guy.

The car stopped. The trailing car stopped. The driver turned and looked at them. '*Nous voici,*' he said.

Triffler got out and the sun hit him like a club. The two men in the trailing car were already out. They had AK-47s and they were pointing them at him.

The pat-down in the blazing sun by the men with the AKs had been cursory, but enough to cause Keatley to cock an appreciative eye at Triffler. When they were done, Keatley hefted his camera and then put it to his eye and panned around and stared at each of the gun-toting guards with it. One of them gave an embarrassed little smile, then did a vaguely Chaplinesque parody of a soldier with a gun, and, laughing, withdrew into the shade of the Fiat with his buddy. They weren't Egyptians, Triffler thought – from farther west, maybe Algerians.

Balcon was standing out in the harsh, hot light, hands on hips, staring down at the canal. He and Triffler exchanged looks, Triffler giving a little nod to say that, so far, Balcon was doing all right. Earning brownie points, in fact. Balcon gave a small, sad smile.

Triffler set up the reflector umbrella and put himself and his suitcases and boxes under it, just on the canal side of the dusty road. The cars were on the other side, trying to get some shade from the tall grasses that grew rankly there. Balcon's 'guide' was sitting on the driver-side doorframe of his car, the door open, his back against the side of the driver's seat. He looked despondent but was probably simply bored.

Triffler pretended to take a reading with what he hoped was a light meter. He trotted over to Keatley and showed it to him, and Keatley muttered something about goddam play-acting and when were they going to get serious?

Triffler lowered his head. 'When we know it's going down.'

He puttered under his umbrella. Keatley pretended to pan over the canal, first north, then south. An Indian freighter moved past them, and he pretended to video-tape that. On its deck, men burned almost black with sun wielded big paint rollers and spread glistening white over the bulkheads. The ship glared with it. Brown bow waves spread and lapped against the green bank, and all the little boats by all the little docks bobbed up and down. The Egyptian flags lay limp in the oven-like air.

Balcon chewed his fingernails and paced and looked north, where the ships would come from. He was wearing a softsided safari hat that was meant to look dashing and that at least kept the sun off him and hid the anguish on his face. Partly because of that unhappy face, Triffler kept the hollowed-out tape boxes with the .380 close, in case Balcon couldn't stand the strain and decided that, after all, he'd be better off with the guys with the AK-47s.

Then Balcon was standing out in the sun, hands on hips, looking north through the haze, standing there so long that Triffler put his head around the dazzling umbrella and looked north, too, and saw, as if it floated on the haze itself, the incredible mass of the carrier up there where the brown, red, and green of the landscape merged in muted grays.

Somali-Kenyan Coast.

Alan was on his satphone with Dukas, who was waiting to get on an airplane from Nairobi to Cairo, running through what Vervoert had told him and watching Fidelio, who was planting a jury-rigged charge to blow up the rest of the weapons and ammo. 'There's a force of men and material, some of it pretty big stuff,' he said, 'waiting someplace to fly into southern Somalia. Have Campbell check an airstrip at this place called Kusdasii, see what sort of planes it'll take. I think they'll be pretty big – Yeah. Right. Exactly my thinking – we guess at the range and go looking for a bunch of military waiting to fly – Exactly.' He listened to Dukas speculating about where the force was and how far they'd fly, and then he was talking about the operation in the lagoon. Alan had already explained to him the Tamil use of toy boats to trap explosives against a hull. 'Yeah, this shithead said that it wasn't part of his operation, but it's got to be part of *the* operation. That's the ping we got on MARI – they'd dummied up a prow for practice. They're going to blow up another ship, and it may be another Navy ship – Yeah, I'm guessing. But, Mike, they flew out yesterday, so they're in place by now. Yeah, even in a little helicopter; if they refueled, they can be in the Med by now. Or Yemen. Or the canal. Yeah, where Rose is. Oh, shit, I don't know –'

He listened to Dukas's demands for more information – Dukas acting like the head of the investigation now, not his old friend Mike. Dukas wanted prisoners interrogated, the site searched with a fine-tooth comb, documents –

'I haven't got the personnel, Mike! Neither have you. No, you listen to me for a second – I don't have interrogators who speak the languages; we've captured Somalis and Rwandan Hutus and Nigerians, at least; we don't have those languages! Plus I haven't got time to dick around up here, the goddam – I know that. Please, Mike – Jesus, will you listen? – I'll put Hahn and Mink on the interviews, they can go out to the *Esek Hopkins* with the prisoners and the wounded. We'll do what we can on the weapons, but I'm not going to leave any up here. No, they have to be destroyed. Yes, that's a military decision, not an NCIS decision. Okay? Documents, records, whatever, we'll do a quick search and I'll bring back what I can. Malindi? Jesus Christ, there are more important things than – Okay, I'll ask him about Malindi. Okay. Okay, okay.'

Along the Canal.

Triffler carried the hollowed-out videotape boxes in his hand to Keatley, who was now wearing his blue button-down shirt as a hood over his head against the sun. Triffler said, putting his left hand on the duct tape where the .45 was hidden in the camera, 'See the carrier?'

'See it? I'm filming it.'

'I've got to get on my cell phone to Geddes and Patemkin. It's going down.' He stripped off some of the tape. 'Take out the two guys with the guns, okay?'

'About time.'

Keatley worked his fingers under the tape, the camera pointed more or less at the rank grass between the cars so that it hid what his hand was doing. 'I want to get closer,' he said.

Triffler lifted the piece of duct tape that held the two hollowed-out video boxes together. He stripped it down and rolled up the tape and pushed it into his borrowed blue jeans. Neatness is all. 'I'll take care of the driver and Balcon,' he said.

'We move together?'

'We move together. We're pretending to talk about the carrier – got your piece? – point the camera as we walk – good –' They reached the edge of the dirt road, halfway between the two cars. Triffler moved them two steps closer to the guards. 'Now,' he said.

Triffler pulled the .380 from the tape boxes and turned toward the driver, who was asleep now under the car. He would wake soon enough. Triffler allowed himself a glance at Balcon, who was shading his eyes with his hand and looking toward the carrier. Two shots roared at Triffler's right, then a third; Triffler stepped forward and knelt and pointed the .380 at the driver's left eye, which was about eight inches from the muzzle.

'That wasn't so hard,' Keatley said. His shadow fell over Triffler's hand. A helicopter chuffed overhead.

Two hundred yards away in one of the little houses, one of the Sri Lankans raised his head and said, 'Gunshots.'

'The journalists?'

The older one shrugged. The noise of a passing helicopter shook the walls. 'The carrier has been warned,' the youngest one said. He pointed upward at the noise with his thumb.

'That changes nothing.'

Two of the Algerians were in the house with them, two outside. One of them went to a window and looked out. The house was hardly bigger than a garage, everything small, so he had to stoop to look out a window that was the size of a large book.

'They're planning to kill us when we've done the job,' the youngest of the Sri Lankans said.

'I think so. But not yet.' The older one, Karun, was squatting, a cigarette between his brown fingers. He thought that the Algerians were amateurs and he had contempt for them. 'Where is the carrier now?'

'Maybe four hundred meters.'

Karun inhaled deeply and tucked the cigarette into his palm so the glowing end was hidden, then stood and went down the stair to the boathouse that was the house's canal-level storey. The boats floated there next to a duckboard walkway, two twelve-foot fiberglass dinghies whose tops a local *fundi* had covered with steel plate, tent-like, protecting the outboard motors and the two hundred kilos of C4 that each carried in its bottom. The weight put them so low in the water that their gunwales were almost awash.

'Very sluggish,' the young one said for the tenth time. They hadn't seen the boats until they had arrived yesterday. They had always used this technique before with off-the-shelf model boats that were big enough to carry only the explosive needed to knock down a coastal freighter.

'When I have started both motors,' the older one said, 'you and Tarim go up and shoot the Algerians. You have to get their automatic weapons quickly and kill the other two as they come in.'

'Then?'

'Then come down and guide the boats, fool, what do you think? When the job is done, we go up and kill the journalists and take their car, as planned.' He tossed his cigarette into the brown water and bent forward to open a crudely acetylene-cut hatch in the steel plate. 'Ready?'

The other men nodded. He pulled the starter cord of the outboard.

Standing in the ruins of the military camp, waiting for the chopper to lift him off, Alan had time to think about the complexity of the operation he had just wrecked, tried to see the toy boats and the attack. Soleck was right – the target had to be the *Roosevelt* in the canal. He trotted back to his Marine radioman, heard the helicopter returning from the *Hopkins*, where it had taken the wounded. The toy boats – if they were the mechanism used to deliver the C4, then they were radio-controlled. And that meant the signal –

'Get Jaeger One on guard,' he snapped to the radioman. 'Tell him to get me a patch through to the *Roosevelt*.'

Along the Canal.

'It's going down *now*,' Triffler shouted into the cell phone. 'I can see the carrier; we're on the bank where we're supposed to be able to shoot TV footage, so it's got to happen soon – it's going to be close to where we are!' Geddes was on the other end, shouting back at him. 'Where *are* you guys?' Triffler shouted. They didn't know. They'd been stopped at a checkpoint, and Geddes had got lippy with an Egyptian soldier, and there'd been a bad scene. They'd lost Triffler's car then and had gone on and on; Patemkin, in the lead car, hadn't seen Triffler's car turn off, and finally Patemkin had pulled off and waited and seen Geddes. By then, they were out of it.

'I'm back down the canal!' Triffler shouted at the phone. 'Come back down – we pulled off on a dirt road. There's cottages here on the water – docks, small boats – dammit, if I knew what they were going to pull –' He looked for a landmark, finally realized that the biggest landmark in the canal was moving down toward him. 'Oh, Lordy, drive south and look for the goddam carrier! We're at most a quarter-mile south of it! I don't *know* what you're going to do when you get here! Just *get here*!'

He could see the helicopters now flying ahead of the boat, outboard of it so that they were almost over the banks of the canal itself. Their heavy chuffing came on the warm air like drums. Triffler looked helplessly to left and right, searching for anything – a missile, a suicide boat, a mine –

He tried to call Mombasa, but the signal was bad, and he stood helplessly, not looking at the bodies by the farther car, the cell phone useless in his right hand.

Until he thought of the NCIS office on the carrier itself.

'*Toy* boats?'

Triffler was connected with one of the NCIS agents on the *FDR*. Everybody on the big ship, it appeared,

508

was looking for two toy boats that were going to blow off the carrier's bow.

'Tamil Tigers? What have the Tamil Tigers got to do with –?' A Navy helicopter passed almost directly overhead and he couldn't hear. He looked up, down, then at the canal – and thought he heard shots. The helicopter moved south and he waited, and then it came clearly – a short burst of automatic fire.

'Something's going down!' he screamed. 'We've got automatic fire – it's between us and the carrier –' He looked around for Keatley. The big man was using the last of the duct tape on Balcon. 'Let's go!' he shouted.

'Go the fuck where?'

'Like the man said, toward the sound of the guns!' He turned and began to run.

In the boathouse, only the older man and the younger one were able to work with the boats; the third Tamil was lying on the floor upstairs, gutshot. The Algerians had not been quite such amateurs as they had thought.

Both motors were running, filling the boathouse with blue-gray smoke and the smell of burned fuel. The line that connected the boats was coiled on top of the forward steel plate of the boat on the men's right, so that it would pay out smoothly as the boat pulled out into the canal.

'Can you see, Nala?'

'Yes, yes –' The younger man was down in the corner closest to the canal, looking out the opened doors. Each man had a plastic box with a joystick – the technology they were familiar with. 'Thirty seconds,' the boy said.

The older man took out a packet of Kenyan-made cigarettes and pulled one free with his lips and lit it with a yellow plastic lighter. He drew deeply on it, coughed. He watched Nala, who was tensed up but still. A trustworthy boy, a little high on amphetamines, but not too much so. He was glad it was the other man who had been shot and not Nala.

'Now,' the boy said.

Karun whipped the cigarette from his lips into the water. He bent, revved the engine, and slammed the steel plate shut as Nala let go the bow end of the spring line that held it to the walkway. The boat moved forward, banged against the other one, and Karun took control of it with the joystick.

The boat moved into the canal. Nala watched it with a look like greed, his hands on his own joystick, waiting to steer his own boat out just before the line between them went tight.

'This canal is a goddam city!' Hunyadi said into her helmet mike. 'There's another goddam marina ahead.'

Rose gave the plane more throttle and a little more angle of attack; the rotors got more vertical bite into the air and the helicopter gathered speed. Rose used the speed to get altitude and turn. She wasn't watching her direction. Her attention was fixed on something just below them, less than one hundred meters away.

'Did you see that, Tara?'

'Wazzat, ma'am?' Hunyadi was tired. Rose felt fresh. She knew she'd pay tomorrow, but she had the energy *now*.

'Powerboat, just pulling out of some covered dock like a boathouse. There! See it?'

'Big Eagle, this is Argive One, over? I have a contact report.' Hunyadi had her kneeboard card out. 'Bogie is a brown fiberglass boat, length five meters, bearing 010 relative from Big Eagle, do you copy?'

She hauled the stick harder, pulling the nose around and struggling to get the door gunner facing the boat. But she couldn't see the boat anymore – it was somewhere under her.

'Where the fuck is it?'

Hunyadi looked at her, wide-eyed.

Rose let the hull rotate under the blade, leaning well out. Something struck her cockpit window and it starred. She opened the window and leaned out, heedless of consequence. *There* was the boat.

'Fire when you see the brown hull. It has some sort of deck over it.'

'Got it.'

She felt the plane rock as the big gun amidships began to fire. *Wham wham wham. Wham wham wham.* The old fifty cals fired bug bullets and you could hear each one go off, like a slow jackhammer. She could see the rounds ricocheting with little sparks off the decks. *Steel plates.* Her door gunner put a whole burst into the boat and it sailed on, low in the water.

Rose cursed, took the chopper lower to get the gunner a different shot, went down and down until her skids were near the canal and her own updraft was jolting the plane under her hands. The door gun continued to fire in steady, disciplined bursts – *wham wham wham.* The damn boat was like a monitor. It had no freeboard showing and the top was armor plate.

Wham wham wham. The cockpit stank of cordite. Hunyadi flicked a glance at her, her knuckles white on the stick and her eyes huge. Rose willed her to relax, gave the plane a few meters of altitude to get out of the danger zone, and started for the bow of the boat. It began to move faster.

Somali-Kenyan Coast.

'Soleck, get me the goddam radio signal from yesterday! The explosion – in the lagoon, we saw it on MARI – Jesus –! You know what I mean! The explosion here. Yesterday.'

'Roger, yessir, I understand – stand by –'

Alan walked in small circles, jerky steps that showed his impatience, his fear that the minutes were draining away. It could be any second, this one, the next, now –

'I have the *Roosevelt*. You're in the link, skipper. Go ahead.'

'*Roosevelt*, this is Commander Craik of Det 424.'

'Roger, Commander. Go ahead.'

'Give me the TAO! This is priority – now!'

'Wait one.'

Soleck's voice broke in. 'There's firing on a boat in the canal, skipper. I got it on Guard.'

'Get ready to pass that radio frequency to the *Roosevelt* for immediate transmission to every ship in the canal. Am I right, that's a possible R/C transmission signal?'

'Well, it –'

Another voice broke in. 'TAO. Make it fast, Commander.' *Roosevelt* sounded far away.

'The weapons being used against your ship in the Canal are radio-controlled. Do you read?'

'– body already passed that –' the TAO almost shouted at him.

'Signal to follow. I think you can disable their weapon by jamming it! Do you read?'

512

'Didn't copy your last.' And then, in the background but clear, 'Another one? Jesus, engage it with the deck 30 mil. Engage!' And then static.

'He cut you off,' Soleck groaned.

Along the Canal.

Triffler ran toward the canal at an angle that would take him, he hoped, to the place the shots had come from. Ahead, looming above the houses, the carrier looked as if it was going to plow right through them; the farther he went down the bank, the more the carrier seemed to rise, to take over the landscape, to be a thing separate from the scene and from the water, a monster coasting over the green and red land.

Triffler had an AK-47 in his left hand, his cell phone in his right. He hoped that he still had contact with the NCIS office on the boat, because it had occurred to him that two men running along the bank with automatic weapons might not look like loyal Americans to somebody in a helicopter or an Egyptian police car. Navy choppers seemed to be all around them now; the sound made it impossible to hear the voice on the cell phone. All Triffler could do was repeat, 'Tell the choppers – it's us – blue shirt, khaki pants, white T-shirt and blue jeans – we're running on the bank – tell them it's us – two guys –'

He was panting and he thought the heat was going to kill him, even if friendly fire didn't. Keatley's face was purple. When had they last had water?

Triffler saw a helicopter lurch and turn so suddenly it seemed to spin on its nose. He looked where the nose pointed and saw a thin, chocolate-colored wake, hardly visible, something moving slowly into the canal, something weirdly shaped – a floating tent?

Keatley shouted something he couldn't hear. He had seen it, too.

Alan was still pacing, the little circles tighter now. 'Get me one of their helos!' he shouted into the link with Soleck. 'Get me any plane that's airborne up there. Get me Alpha Whiskey, Soleck!' He stamped his foot, looking at the coming storm, and wanted to shake his foot. He had never felt so useless. 'Get me the senior officer in the air. Do it!'

'Roger. Wait one.' Soleck sounded calm.

Alan's hands were shaking. He sat down in the long grass, his back against the radio. Above him, Soleck's S-3 turned again, high above the heat and the smell of blood, trying to hold his contact with the *Roosevelt*, way off over the edge of the world. And still climbing. Alan had time to think – to wish that he had shot Vervoert. To wish he had more time.

'Go!' Soleck said.

'What!' Rose shouted, her husky voice familiar over two thousand miles.

The lead boat was past the bow of the carrier and the trailing boat was well out in the canal. Both had been hammered by the choppers and the lead boat had taken two hits from the 30mm grenade launcher on the deck and neither seemed damaged.

Rose was steeling herself for the next move, where she dropped the plane in the water in front of one of the boats. It was all she could think of. She gave the plane some power and flew so close to the bulk of the carrier that the projection of the flight deck was over her for a moment. The lead boat was starting to turn.

'Ma'am? Rose? Commander Craik wants to talk to

you *now*!' Vaguely, she thought the shouting guy on her link must be Evan Soleck.

'What!' she shouted, her rotor blades skimming past the knife-edge of the bow.

Her husband's voice hammered in her ear. 'Boats are radio-controlled. This is the freq, Rose. Jam it! Jam it!'

A set of numbers scrolled by on the digital link. She turned, giving the door gunner another chance at the bow of the lead boat, and she squashed the intercom button.

'Hunyadi! Get this freq jammed. Do it!' She hit the button again. 'Big Eagle! Get the freq in the link jammed. I don't know! Maybe an EA-6B on the deck. Get it now!'

Hunyadi's hands were flying around the cockpit and she heard the winch going in the back. *Wham wham wham*. Her door gunner was still using the old solution. *Wham wham wham*.

She could see the cable between the boats now, just starting to stretch, the bow of the far boat turning in toward the carrier. *Maybe twenty seconds*, Rose thought. *If I can't jam it in one go, I have to use the plane*. Next to her, Hunyadi toggled a switch and gave her a thumbs-up. Nothing changed.

Wham wham wham.

Karun moved the joystick, and his boat, well out in the waterway now and turning back to run parallel with Nala's, did not respond. He pushed the joystick farther, then pulled it to the right, back left – anything to make it respond.

Nothing.

He looked at the boy. He was doing the same thing,

but he was frantic. He used the joystick the way a child did now, ramming it back and forth from one extreme to the other.

'Nala!'

Nala's boat was also in the waterway, but still heading straight out, not quite ready to make the turn toward the carrier. If they went on in the same way, one turning, one crossing the channel, the two boats would cross paths but would not collide; then the line would come taut between them, and –? Karun was not sure.

He tried his own joystick again. His boat continued its turn. Overhead, a helicopter was so loud it seemed to be landing on the house roof.

'They have a jamming device.' He put the joystick down on the walkway with care, as if he were leaving it for somebody else to use. 'It is over.' He jerked his head at the stairs. Nala threw his joystick against the wall. Karun made a face, shook his head. He went up.

The house was too small for so many bodies. Flies were already gathering, and there was the disgusting smell of death – blood and shit. Tarim was lying to the left of the stairs near the far wall, his hands folded over his abdomen as if he were holding something in. Karun bent over him. Tarim's eyes were alive but dying.

'I will see to your family,' Karun said. He shot Tarim in the forehead with his pistol, the sound sharp and quick over the roar of the helicopter.

Nala was bending by the little window near the door through which they would have to leave, the AK-47 ready to shoot. He had been just about to speak when Karun's pistol had gone off, and he jumped and then crouched down. 'Two men,' he shouted, 'one European, one African. With rifles.' He pointed out toward where he had seen them; now there was nobody. Maybe they had heard the shot. 'In the grass.'

Karun went to the window on the other side, stepping over Tarim's body to get to it. He looked out. Four white men and an Egyptian were coming down the slope in the funny half-trot that such a descent imposes on men not quite young. They had handguns. He went back to the first window and looked over Nala's shoulder toward the journalist's cars, whose roofs he could just see over the slope. Two hundred meters, he thought. Uphill.

He went back to the window through which he had seen the men. They were still coming. He pointed the automatic rifle and fired three short bursts, taking out the closest one, putting the others down on their faces. Behind him, Nala smashed the glass of his window with the butt of his rifle and Karun winced, knowing it was a mistake, wanting to tell him to shoot through the glass and not wait, but it was too late. The air seemed to pulse with the noise of helicopters and heavy machine guns now, and he never heard the rifles firing from outside but saw Nala's back burst open, blood spraying the room with red mist and the boy's mouth wide to scream, no sound because all the sound in the world was taken by the helicopters and the machine guns.

Karun crawled below the windows to Nala, saw the sucking wounds in his chest. He dropped his Kalashnikov and put one mercy shot from his pistol in the boy's temple and went back down the stairs to the boathouse. The gray wall of the aircraft carrier was sliding by the open doors, seeming close enough to touch, seeming to fill all space as the guns and the machines filled all sound. It was over.

Karun slipped into the water.

Three hundred yards north of the boathouse, the larger of the two out-of-control boats struck the concrete at the edge of the canal. It was a glancing blow, and the boat scraped along the concrete for twenty yards before the second boat, the one locked in a circle, struck the first amidships and they vanished in a roar. The blast wave tore the nets off the bow of the carrier and destroyed two F-18s parked on the forward catapults, and the flight deck deformed by almost two inches. The fireball reached out toward the choppers, trying to pluck them down, and Rose fought it, flying on instinct as the dust and then the vaporized water obscured her vision. And then she was level, fifty feet above the deck and suddenly *behind* the ship, which was already plowing forward across the wreckage and the mud. The side of the canal had collapsed, and the whole deck of the ship had a coating of something dark, but Rose didn't have time to worry about that because her bird was a cripple; something was seriously broken in the handling and she had to get down.

Rose took her plane down the side, decided she would never get it back to the altitude she needed to put down on the deck, and headed for the sand of the Sinai seventy yards to the east. The rotors were complaining because something was seriously wrong, and she tried to get a little glide out of their continued rotation. She slammed her airplane down on the sand before the engine started to take itself apart. Hunyadi was right on with the numbers, her fingers sure on the switches, shutting down the damaged engine and getting the aircrew out of the damaged bird.

The rotor stopped turning. The plane was silent. It wasn't going to blow.

Hunyadi was smiling. Rose smiled back, and thought, *You'll do.*

Triffler had sprinted back up the rise to the cars, Keatley gasping behind him and losing ground, and now Triffler was kneeling over Balcon, tearing the duct tape from the journalist's legs and ankles with one hand. 'A chopper, for God's sake, give me a chopper!' Triffler was screaming into his cell phone. 'Yes, *another* chopper – goddamit, don't question me –! I know there's a crisis, what the fucking hell do you think I'm doing out here?' The obscenity wasn't like him, and later he'd regret it, tell his wife and his minister about it, but now he felt urgency like a hand at his throat. He had no time, zero time; the Egyptian cops were pouring down the green slope toward the little house now, and in no more than a minute they'd head up here, and then it would all belong to them. 'Yes, we need a chopper for a wounded man, yes – a CIA guy, yes, I gave you that message, he's down and he's bad, but they're trying to save him until a – yes! Yes, and now I need another! No, not a goddam medevac, I need anything that flies and can pick me up within the next forty-five seconds! What can be so fucking difficult – the fucking air is filled with fucking helicopters!'

Keatley, gasping, threw himself down in the shade of the car.

'Wave your shirt,' Triffler said.

Keatley stared at him.

'Wave your goddam shirt! So they'll know it's us!'

Keatley crawled out of the shade and stood with the help of the car and pulled his blue shirt off. He was ten pounds overweight and pale, his chest blotchy with heat, sweating. Leaning on the car with one hand, hyperventilating, he waved the shirt.

'Harder!'

Triffler looked down toward the house. Somebody was pointing toward them. He and Keatley had needed only one look inside that abattoir before he'd known it was time to go. Five bodies, one just outside, blood everywhere. Then al-Fawzi and Geddes had come around the corner of the house, and Triffler had almost shot them with the AK because he was jazzed by then, not knowing that his eyes were wide, his speech too fast. He had never been in a firefight before. Never killed anybody before. If in fact he had killed anybody in that carnage. Geddes had shouted that Patemkin was hit; al-Fawzi had looked into the house and started screaming into his own cell phone, and Triffler had spun around and sprinted up the slope, knowing that he had only minutes to collar Balcon before the Egyptians got to him.

'How long do I got to keep waving this thing?' Keatley moaned. His face was purple. Triffler heard a change in the discordant throbbings that filled the air over the canal and saw a chopper turn away from the carrier, now a magnificent bulk sliding away from them to their right, the stern just changing from profile to an end view.

'You're doing great.' Triffler got the last of the tape off Balcon's legs and then ripped the piece from his mouth. He stood, grabbing Balcon's shirt and pulling him up. 'On your feet.'

The journalist's eyes were dilated with fear and

shock, and he, too, was red-faced and gasping. 'You told me – you said –'

'Shut up.'

'You promised you'd get me out of Egypt!'

Triffler didn't say that he hadn't promised anything; he didn't say that a promise to a piece of contemptible shit like Balcon wasn't a promise at all. He kept his fist balled in the sweat-stained fabric of Balcon's shirt and watched the helicopter swing toward them, slanting a few degrees so the pilot could check them out, then start a descent into the flat green grass a hundred feet from them.

'Come on.' Triffler began to drag Balcon toward the landing zone. Keatley followed, sagging, head down, his shirt flung over his shoulders.

Balcon tried to resist. 'Where?'

Triffler waved his free hand at two Egyptian cops who were walking up from the charnel house. 'Away from them.'

The three of them stood together in the wind of the chopper's descent, grass swaying back from the rotors as if a big hand were sweeping it flat. When it was down, Triffler crouched and began to drag Balcon along.

He didn't tell him that in twelve hours he'd be in the naval brig at Guantanamo Bay.

Somali-Kenyan Coast.

Near the Somali border, Alan was back on the radio, hearing what was going on in the canal and watching Fidelio walk toward him. When Fidelio got close, he stood with his hands on his hips, waiting. Alan nodded and held up a hand. 'Yeah,' he said with a catch in his voice. 'Yeah, that's just like her.' He looked over at Fidelio

521

and the radioman. 'Rose got the boats. They're safe.'
Fidelio was bold enough to slap his skipper on the arm.
'Where's Triffler now? Shit.' Triffler was out of contact,
somewhere down near the canal. He handed the radio
back to the operator. He looked at Fidelio, who said,
'Ready to blow.' Alan nodded and walked down to the
beach and told the lieutenant to get his men aboard the
helo. The prisoners, all but the white officer, were sitting
on the sand with their knees raised and their thin arms
resting on them, models of patience. Vervoert and two
black noncoms, hands cuffed behind them with plastic
restrainers, were standing between two Marines.

'Let's go,' Alan said.

'The other prisoners?'

Alan shook his head. 'Leave them.'

Alan was the last one aboard. From three hundred feet,
he looked down at the beach, where the black mercenaries were trying to get two rowboats into the huge
waves from the storm surge. Out to sea, the sky had
been replaced with a line of purple-black. The wind
was rising to a scream against the sound of the rotor
blades. At the fringes, down where they had left the
bush to begin the attack, other people were gathering.
The Guryama, looking for justice.

The storm was about to break.

Mombasa.

Alan was the first out of the chopper, the blades still
turning, red dust churning with the rain into the glare
of the lights. He ran for the hangar. People straggled
out, roused from sleep, yawning. The Marines came
behind him and headed for the mortar strongpoint.
Geelin was already there.

Alan was almost at the hangar when he saw Sandy Cole. She was standing in the shadows in front of the hangar, her dress limp on her body. She didn't notice him; her attention was fixed on the chopper. He turned and looked at it. One of the crewmen was out looking at the underbelly. The rotors were taking their last slow turn. Four of the Kenyan game rangers were out, clustered by the door. They waited. They watched something inside. Then two of them reached in and began to pull.

She recognized it when the two inside and the four on the ground had his weight among them. Even wrapped in a blue plastic tarpaulin. She knew.

She made a sound that a dying, angry animal might have made, the sound rising and growing in her throat and becoming a scream that tore the hot night apart. Alan saw a young sailor flinch away and cover his face. The sound went on and on, fell, and then started again. On and on, the scream beyond language that is disbelief and loss and utter despair. He would have to hear it for the rest of his life.

Coda

Eleven officers from Detachment 424 and the carrier's air wing were relaxing in the warmth of a Sicilian outdoor café. The Mediterranean, under the hazy sun, lay blue-green and slack, its sparkle dulled by a thickening of the air that may have been dust blown over from North Africa. In the late-afternoon near-silence, the laughter was muted, but the men smiled a lot. They were headed home.

'Great party, Soleck,' Captain Rafehausen said. No longer the acting BG commander – a vice admiral had been flown out from the States six days before – he was the one-hatted CAG again, and a happier man for it. Rafe put his hand on the young man's shoulder. 'Saw you got two more okays on the landings since you were on the beach. Great – great –'

'There's going to be dinner later!' Soleck said, as if he knew that this gathering at the trattoria wasn't memorable, but maybe the dinner would be. It was his wetting-down party. It was what Lieutenant-Commander Craik had told him to do.

But so far, it wasn't *memorable*.

At another table, Alan watched Soleck with a smile. 'Were you ever that young?' he said to Mike Dukas.

Dukas, who had a laptop open before him and a Peroni beer bottle in his right hand, squinted at Soleck and shook his head. 'I was born older than that.'

Alan laughed. 'How's your teenaged girlfriend, by the way?'

'She's not a teenager and she's not my girlfriend!' Dukas had been shying away from the subject of Leslie Kultzke since he had arrived that morning. 'She's my office assistant – period.' He was wearing reading glasses and he really did look old, maybe deliberately so – slumped in his seat, glasses on his nose, deep frown. He typed something into the laptop and waited and reacted with a grunt to what came up.

'She invited you to dinner yet?' Alan said.

'How'd you know?'

'Women do that sort of thing. Did you go?'

Dukas squirmed in his plastic chair. 'Only once.' He gave Alan a hard look. 'Nothing happened!'

'Did I ask a question? Funny how sometimes you get answers without even asking questions. Little sensitive, are we?'

Dukas punched a key as if he was putting out an eye and muttered, 'Some people know when to find a new subject, or else.' He looked over the glasses. 'I've been here two hours, you haven't asked about the case.'

'I figured you'd tell me when you were ready.' He looked at Soleck, who was moving from table to table like a nervous maitre d'. Alan waved. 'Soleck's party isn't very jazzy, is it? I feel responsible.'

Dukas peered over the tops of the glasses again at the relaxed figures. 'What you need is some Greeks in this Navy.' He went back to the laptop. 'Yeah, I'll tell you when I'm ready. Now I'm ready.

'What's happened is, the French guy opened up like a clam in a steam bath when they got him to Gitmo. Turns out the French already had a sheet on him –

funny how they didn't make a diplomatic stink; in fact, they asked quite nicely if they could have a round with him. Guy turned out to have connections with the Marseilles mafia; they were clapping their hands that we'd grabbed him. So he gave us a little stuff, played some footsie, I offered him immunity if he'd puke it all up, and he did. Some names, some dates, some places. Yes, he got instructions to ID you at your hotel; yes, he walked Cram into the elevator and got out on the first floor, leaving Cram with two heavies who were headed for the basement – end of Bob Cram. Yes, he gave us the guy in Sicily, whose name is Carmine Santangelo-Fugosi and who lives in the fancy palazzo you can see over your left shoulder if you turn your head about ten degrees.'

Alan turned his head. 'Holy shit –' The laughter went on around them; something was going on with a pretty woman who worked in the trattoria. 'The cell-phone calls came *here*?'

'Why d'you think I told you to hold this love feast *here*? Santangelo-Fugosi's a player. Friend of a lot of biggies, right up to maybe the president, also the Vatican; owns a bank that the EU keeps trying to bring down and can't. This is crime big-time – not breaking guys' knees and running a little dope, but scamming corporations and rigging markets and busting economies. Interpol thinks he's made a connection with the Russian mafias. In fact, some of the money that funded the hit on the Cairo AID building came, we think, from Moscow. Big player.'

'This didn't all come from the French guy, Mike.'

'No, no, he didn't know any of this shit. All he knew was his good friend Signor Santangelo-Fugosi was going to make him rich and famous by putting him on-site at some big events before they happened, and ask him to help out in the occasional murder. But he didn't see the big picture at all – didn't want to see it, in fact. No, we put the big picture together from little pieces – from Harry, from Russia, from DEA, from the guys you captured in that camp, from Hizbollah, who're mad as hell and willing to share information with me if it'll get them some revenge.'

'And the big picture was?'

'And the picture was –' Dukas keyed the laptop and waited and then smiled at what he'd brought to the screen. 'It was creating a new source for opium, with the labs right in the fields. In Somalia. A dope combine that would have their own country: Somalia from the border to the Juba River. Fuck the Taliban, who were unreliable; fuck the Lebanese and Hizbollah, who were demanding and expensive; fuck Colombia, and maybe pull the rug out from under their economy, and then go in and buy for ten cents on the buck. Do it all yourself – grow, harvest, extract, distribute – what you call your vertically organized industry.'

'And the Navy was in the way.'

Dukas nodded. 'Twelve hundred Marines and a carrier air group could screw them good. But, if the hit on the *FDR* had worked – and you were right, the first hit was supposed to be the gator freighter and not the *Harker* – they'd have moved in and got a crop in the ground before the canal was cleared. Remember, when the Egyptians scuttled ships in the canal in "fifty-six, it took *three years* to clear. These guys needed one year. And all the time we'd be trying to come back at them, they'd be paying off people like Balcon to bullshit about American aggression in the Horn, and Carmine's fucking bank would be buying politicians, and the media would be getting press releases about the glory days of Italian Somaliland. Every year they could make it work was worth billions to them. Three years would have been worth a life-time of smaller stuff. And would we really go back into Somalia because of *drugs* – especially drugs that were probably going to wind up in Europe and not the US?' Dukas looked straight at him. 'You know how many people in the Congress would like to say, "Fuck Europe"?'

'So what're you doing to Signore what's-his-name?'

'Nothing. Zip, zero, nada. Santangelo-Fugosi's the Teflon scumbag. We don't prosecute; the Italians don't arrest. That's the news from Foggy Bottom – he's too close to too many people.'

'He almost killed my wife!'

'That's right. And he really did kill Bob Cram, and seven DEA guys, and a bunch of people on the *Harker*, and some Egyptian and Kenyan civilians.'

'And Martin Craw. Goddamit, Mike –!'

Dukas took several folded sheets from an inner pocket of his wrinkled jacket. 'Can you translate into Italian on sight?'

Alan's angry face clouded, uncertain where they were going now. 'If it isn't technical shit, sure.' Alan had spent part of his childhood in Naples.

Dukas put a cell phone on the table. 'When I tell you, read what's there – but in Italian.' He looked around. 'Okay, tell your birthday boy it's showtime.'

'I don't get it.'

'You will.' Dukas pointed a thumb over his shoulder up the hill. 'We're going to have a little *conversazione* with the pride of Sicily.'

Alan studied Dukas's face. 'You're serious.'

'Dead serious. This is the Dukas-Craik response. It's all we're going to get.'

'And Soleck?'

'He wanted memorable, he gets memorable. Plus, he's young – this'll be something that's going to last the rest of his career.'

Alan waved Soleck over, and the young officer came too fast, a glass of red wine slopping in his left hand. Alan sat him down, rode over his questions and his nervousness and told him to listen. Dukas pulled the laptop around where all three could see it. The screen was filled with a photograph of the *Harker* as Alan had seen it that first morning: tilted, burning, wrecked.

Dukas explained it to Soleck. 'The guy who caused this is in a room in that big house above us on the hill. Right now, he's behind the third window on the right. He's looking at the same picture on a computer up there as I am on this one down here. He doesn't know it, but there's a laser eaves-dropper pointed at the window so we can hear everything that goes on in the room.' Dukas fitted a headset over his hair. 'Satchmo, you there? This is Dizzy. Got it? Okay?' He waited, drummed his fingers, smiled. 'We're a go.' He turned back to the two officers. 'Our scumbag's got two other people in the room with him.' He hit a key, and a picture of Bob Cram's severed head came up. 'That's why they're in the room. All three of them got this picture and a message to be up there at this hour.' He hit another key and a picture of a Tomahawk cruise missile, nose-on, appeared. 'They also got that.'

Dukas hit a number on the cell phone, pressed his head-set against his right ear. 'Ringing – ringing – got it.' He winked at Soleck. 'Their private cell-phone network, courtesy of NSA.' He waited, then pointed at Alan. 'You're on.'

Alan put the phone to his ear. A male voice was saying *'Pronto!'* in the angry tone that tells you he had said the same thing several times already.

'Give me Signore Santangelo-Fugosi, and don't give me any shit,' Alan said in Italian. The man did start to give him shit but was cut off; the cell-phone sound was hushed as, Alan thought, somebody put a hand over it.

Dukas smiled. 'Carmine's reaming the guy's ass. I don't speak much Italian, but I know reaming when I hear it.' He pointed at Alan. 'He's back. Now it starts.'

'What?' a different voice said in Alan's ear. Alan looked down at the script Dukas had given him, and, translating as he went, he started through it. 'Signore Santangelo-Fugosi, this is Lieutenant-Commander Craik of the United States Navy. You tried to kill me, and you tried to kill my wife. You failed.'

A new picture came on the screen.

'This is a photograph of the room in which you are at this moment.' The laptop showed a large room, gloomy, overdecorated.

A new picture appeared – an old man sitting by a flower garden. 'This is your father, on the private terrace of the house you bought him in Taormina.' The picture changed again: a small boy sitting at a desk, photographed through a window. 'This is your grandson Giancarlo in his bedroom at his school in Switzerland.' And changed again – a handsome man in his thirties, just coming out of a Baroque doorway. 'Your son Emilio, leaving his mistress's apartment, where he spends each Tuesday and Thursday night.'

And then to a clinical atmosphere, a medical table, a man lying on it, naked from the waist up. 'You, signore, visiting your doctor in his office last Wednesday.'

The Tomahawk missile reappeared.

'If you ever make any move against the Navy or any of its people again, these photographs and the details of where and how they were taken will be passed at once to the command directorate of Hizbollah.

'And what they do not finish, we will.

'If you understand and agree, come to the terrace and wave. If you do not, these pictures and the information will be e-mailed to Hizbollah at once. They have a team standing by. It takes only the pressure of a finger on a key.'

Soleck, who spoke no Italian, was looking from Alan to Dukas and back. Dukas put a finger to his lips and pointed up the hill. 'Watch.'

They waited. And waited.

Dukas pressed the earpiece into his ear and listened. 'They're arguing. Somebody's bullshitting about *omerta*.' He held up a hand. 'Footsteps – he's walking –'

A figure appeared on the terrace. Dukas whipped a pair of compact binoculars from a pocket and jammed them against his eyes. 'It's him. The big prick.'

The figure – white shirt, dark trousers, hair almost white in the thin sun – looked out, down, away. He must have seen people in the café below him every day. Then his gaze returned to the café and he leaned forward over the balustrade.

He waved.

'Wave,' Dukas said.

He waved. Alan waved. He nudged Soleck. Soleck turned all the way around and studied the small figure and, not knowing why, waved. Alan jumped to his feet. 'Hey, guys – everybody – wave! Wave!'

The small figure waved. And stopped. He looked down at them – a dozen unknown people waving at him. *He could bomb the shit out of us*, Alan thought. He leaned close to Dukas. 'How many people have you got around us right now?'

Dukas was watching the figure back away, then turn and disappear. 'About thirty.' He grinned. 'And Harry standing by to contact Hizbollah if Asshole does something really stupid.'

'Yeah, but Mike, we'd be dead.'

'The kid wanted memorable, right?' Dukas grinned and walked into the center of the party. 'Next round's on me! Everybody drink up! Hey, there any Greeks here? We need some Greek music – hey, signorina, any *musica greca* – huh. *Balare?* – huh, dance – dance? – *Noi, um, voramo balare greco, okay? Ce ouzo, signorina? Ouzo –?*'

The café was in a port, so of course they had some Greek music, at least such Greek music as had made it into a movie's album. Dukas helped carry glasses and bottles; he got people on their feet; he shouted, 'Louder – turn the music louder – *piu forte, piu forte!* – I want them to hear it up the hill –!' Tables seemed to push themselves out of the way; plates of antipasto appeared; the music blared; and American officers and locals put their arms around each other's shoulders under Dukas's direction and formed a circle, moving clockwise, Dukas counting tempo and giving directions, singing, 'LA-LA, la-la-la-LA-la, LA-la-la –'

Soleck was watching, eyes shining. 'It's getting good – now it's getting really good – but –' His face clouded. 'But why is it *memorable*?'

Alan grinned. He had to shout over the music. 'For one thing, Mister Soleck, Mike Dukas is *enjoying* himself! As for the other –' He couldn't shout it. 'I'll tell you over dinner. Shall we dance?'

Swansea Libraries

#		#		#		#	
1		25		49		73	
2		26		50		74	
3		27		51		75	
4		28		52		76	
5		29		53		77	
6		30	10/15	54		78	
7		31		55		79	
8		32		56		80	
9		33	10/18	57	1/15	81	
10		34	9/6	58		82	
11		35		59		83	
12		36		60		84	
13		37		61		85	
14		38		62		86	
15		39		63		87	
16		40	3/18	64		88	
17		41		65		89	
18		42	6/14	66		90	
19		43		67		91	
20		44		68		92	
21		45	7/19	69		Community Services	
22		46		70			
23		47		71			
24		48	10/17	72			